A World Divided: Blazing City

Jesse Roman

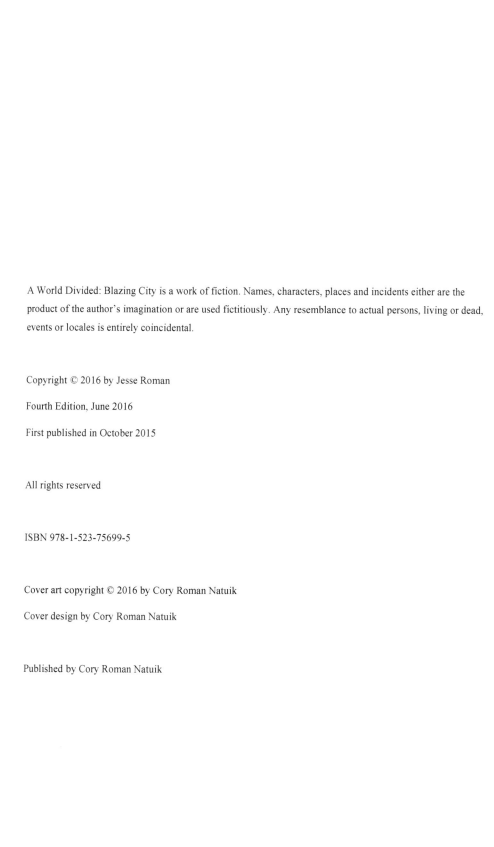

A World Divided: Blazing City is a work of fiction. Names, characters, places and incidents either are the product of the author's imagination or are used fictitiously. Any resemblance to actual persons, living or dead, events or locales is entirely coincidental.

A World Divided: Blazing City

Jesse Roman

The lamps now glitter down the street;
Faintly sound the falling feet;
And the blue even slowly falls
About the garden trees and walls.

Now in the falling of the gloom
The red fire paints the empty room:
And warmly on the roof it looks,
And flickers on the back of books.

Armies march by tower and spire
Of cities blazing, in the fire;---
Till as I gaze with staring eyes,
The armies fall, the luster dies.

Then once again the glow returns;
Again the phantom city burns;
And down the red-hot valley, lo!
The phantom armies marching go!

Blinking embers, tell me true
Where are those armies marching to,
And what the burning city is
That crumbles in your furnaces!

- Armies in the Fire,
Robert Louis Stevenson

ONE.

RECORD BREAKING PARANOIA

IT WAS LIKE THE WHOLE OF A CIVILIZATION WAS BURNING right there in front of you. It was the life that trapped Sortonia City in a sudden rise of unimaginable humidity within its industrial core. The heat was a plague and would not go away; it was a festering pot of desolation. It came in and made itself known by settling over the city like an eclipsed shadow, bringing with it the surge of dread that lead to the start of a downward spiral of record breaking paranoia.

Within just a few short weeks, all four corners of the planet would sporadically learn of the contained and soon to be dangerous epidemic. It would appear that one of the greatest tourist capitals of the world was going up in flames. It wasn't literally going up in flames though, but it was a fine line between the literal and figurative. Headlines all over the world warned of what to expect when traveling to the blazing city, stating that the newly nicknamed "City of Hell" was nowhere to be during one of the biggest heat waves of the century. But let's reverse back a bit to a few weeks prior to when the heat first struck the city. The first sense of a major decline was when the tourists stopped visiting… and then the rumors began…

"Did you watch the news about that deadly heat wave across the pond? Everyone is talking about it. That beautiful Sortonia City is so warm that flowers are melting! That's right, flowers are melting! People are also dying, but the flowers are melting! Could you imagine such a thing?"

"What? That's absurd! Absolute nonsense if you ask me. You can't be talking about *the* Sortonia City, built on the largest island in the world. My husband and I were supposed to take the kids down there this summer for vacation but thanks to all this freak show business we aren't anymore!"

"It's a death pit where civilians are dying on sidewalks. You heard me correct there! Dying on sidewalks, and face first! I heard that a woman stepped onto the street with her bare foot and it burned so badly they had to cut it off! You're right, it's such a freak show."

"My friend told me that he heard from his sister that she heard from her hairdresser that several cars lit up in flames from how hot the rays of the sun were. It was like an action movie from how my friend described it. The hairdresser was there and saw it with her own two eyes! The car blew up and formed a crater in the ground the size of a house! Poor girl was stuck on a bus and had to worry about getting blown up by the sun before it was even lunchtime."

"Heat stroke can get very bad when the weather gets out of control like this. I've heard from my gardener that the illness it brings is contagious and will spread to the rest of the world and kill us all! That's what a news reporter said as well, she sure did. I already informed all my family and friends to take caution."

Those were just some of the more, let us say, creative stories being discussed. For the past several weeks, the raging sun created sweltering temperatures above one hundred and twenty, sometimes reaching as high as one hundred and thirty. Not a single raindrop or thunderclap had been felt or seen since the beginning of June, and everyone who was living in the city was in an extreme uproar. There was only so much that one would take before a major breakdown would occur. It would create a chain reaction of anxiety and hatred that would eventually effect every other person in the city. There was no stopping it.

Environmentalists were regarding this summer of '07 as a bad case of heat wave paranoia, which would soon die off and fade away. Reports were issued that this abnormal weather hadn't been encountered in the city or country for several decades and that it could potentially cause severe physical and stress with high risk suicides. For those who lived in the city, many decided to take a leave of absence and others permanently moved within days, quitting their jobs, uprooting their families and not looking back. The airport was a constant fill up with people leaving and aero planes were departing faster than anyone would expect them to on a normal day. No one was coming. Everyone was leaving.

Since the year of its founding in the late 1800's, the island that Sortonia City was built upon was always considered the "standout" piece amongst everything else. As the decades went on, the city flourished and grew grander in scale; reaching the heights no other city had ever reached before. Fast forward to today, and the city was constantly being modernly updated into a sprawling scenic tribute to the fantasies of what a dream world should be. You would never see the roads or parks dirty and unkempt, as everything needed to always be in tip top shape for its citizens and tourists. Littering was considered illegal and included a hefty charge if anyone was found doing so. To describe all the beautiful features that the city had to offer would be virtually impossible. It was a place where there was always something to do, and rarely would someone feel bored or out of place from all the attractions and sights. The ocean surrounding the city was a pure turquoise blue, almost unnatural, as if it were dyed. Millions were spent each month to keep it clean and refreshed and to insure the marine life were healthy and well cared for.

Conversely, the city's true beauty was not showing through at present and it was drastically turning disastrous. It was overwhelming actually. Grass turned a sickly brown color and gardens withered and died. Garbage had been piling up behind stores and side streets for several weeks now, creating foul smells that were attracting unwanted pests and vermin. The garbage collectors just weren't able to attend to them fast enough. Paint peeled from walls and cement absorbed heat that was hot as lava making it impossible to stand on, even with shoes, for longer than a minute. It was pointless to describe how many people were sent to the hospital daily from heat strokes and severe sunburns, but even more pointless trying to estimate how many of those people would end up dead, succumb to their sun inflicted injuries. Every nurse and doctor were kept up around the clock from sunrise until sunset. Some even had to be flown in from other cities to help with the demand. But enough just wasn't enough.

Everyday during the usual rush hour from four to six o'clock, car accidents were a common regularity and traffic jams were a must.

Whoever was trapped in a traffic would have to be warned, as police frequently patrolled the streets at all hours of the day. People would get out of their cars to yell at each other, fight one another, to slash tires and smash windows. People often passed out while in their cars, stuck in traffic and getting their car violated with weapons from others who were equally angry and exhausted with their children crying and arguing in the backseats. Arrests were made every ten minutes and jails were quickly being filled up. This was now considered very common, amongst other deadly occurrences. The city had turned from a peaceful getaway into a criminal distortion within weeks and it was starting to look like there would be no end in sight.

Not too far from the havoc of the city was a small island that wasn't feeling the effects of the heat wave and catastrophe. It was called Sortonia Crest. This miniature island was connected to Sortonia City by means of a long white bridge called Mergers Bridge. It was the biggest bridge in the entire world and was the only way to get back and forth between the two islands. Sortonia Crest was populated within a suburban and occasionally gated neighborhood home to families that had money. It was not considered a place for the financially low. The houses, of course, were something to marvel at and many visitors would drive up and down the streets just to stare at all the beautiful and expensive homes such as the Anderson Manor. Many times a tour bus would drive through, filled with tourists whipping out their cameras and remaining speechless at such splendor. The pristine lawns and emerald grass, palm trees and smooth roads were major jealousy factors of several passersby. Could it even be possible that Sortonia Crest was home to its very own breed of flower?

How could you not notice those blue petals and red stems lining the sides of the white sandy beaches?

The Crest's tiny community was mostly peaceful, but interesting things did happen. There were disappearances from local students that were never explained, nor were they ever found. Robberies and floods were, of course, very common, as well as nosy neighbors. Yes, it was your typical suburban town. But something different was about to happen. It wasn't the fact that Sortonia Crest was living in normality and wasn't feeling the effects of the heat wave like the city was; something that boggled meteorologists. It was the subtle and whispering fact that a shadow had turned its gaze from the City of Hell and towards the Crest itself.

Inside a sleepy bedroom where our story begins, a simple alarm clock went off.

PART I

LIGHTING THE MATCH

TWO.

HANGOVERS AND WHISPERS

THE SMALL AND FAINT ELECTRIC FAN WAS BEATING ITS propellers furiously against the constant updraft from the warm and humid air that was blowing in through the open window. It was quiet and peaceful without any disturbing noises… until the alarm clock started buzzing. The silence was broken, then traffic, lawnmowers and the yelling of children could be heard outside in the distance. An irregular breeze seeped into the room, making the bedroom door vibrate slightly as if it wanted to release itself. It finally swayed fully open.

It was past three in the afternoon, on the first Sunday of July, and he was not ready to get up. When seventeen-year-old Ryan Davidson opened his eyes, the first thing he noticed, besides the buzzing of his alarm clock, was the incredible pain that was pounding away inside his head—it was attacking his brain like a tumor. He reached over and shut off the alarm then fell back down onto his back. He closed his eyes and tried to remember what happened, slapping the side of his head as if that would stop the throbbing. He knew what occurred the night before, he just didn't know why he couldn't remember anything specifically. He sat back up and looked down at his clothes that were lying beside his bed, then at his cell phone that was perched on top of his wallet on the side table.

He leisurely got out of bed in nothing but his boxer briefs and wobbled over to the window as if he had been sleeping for eighty years inside a coffin, pulling the blinds up and feeling a gusty warm breeze and bright sunlight hit his face. He squinted out at the houses across the street from him. They were all large and modernly well built with gorgeous lawns and sleek driveways that had the occasional sports equipment scattered around on it. The cars that were parked in the driveways glistened and shined from recent carwashes. Numerous homeowners were mowing their lawns and the sprinklers were watering the emerald green grass as children ran about. There were palm trees in all the front yards, creating a small shade where one could read beneath. The greenery and plant life blossomed and grew like the untamed wildlife it was, feeding the tropical scenery into the unbelievable. For Ryan, who lived on the island for the majority of his life, this *was* paradise. Birds flew blissfully in a V-shape formation across the cloudless blue sky, the wind sliding through their feathers.

He raised his hand to feel the rushing air of the fan as he picked up the television remote that was lying on the floor and turned on the plasma mounted on the navy blue wall. He flicked to the weather channel and saw that the current temperature on Sortonia Crest was in the high seventies, but in the city it was one hundred and thirteen degrees and rising. The reporter was stressing that there would be no precipitation for another week and that everyone should prepare themselves for the continuing humidity.

Ryan turned towards his side table and picked up his cell phone, browsing through his various text messages and missed calls. Switching over to voice mail, he had only one message. He smiled as he listened to the message and shut off the television, throwing the remote on his bed.

After quickly texting a brief message in reply, he went over to his closet and grabbed some clothes from the top shelve where all his shirts were stacked and folded perfectly with his hoodies and dress shirts hung exactly two inches apart from one another. As he slid a hanger back into position, he caught a glimpse of himself in the small mirror hanging on the wall. He always did think of himself as a handsome and attractive guy but he didn't feel like he had an ego about it, but others begged to differ. For the longest time his classmates had often thought he was a jock by nature. Okay, so he loved to play a sport here and there; basketball and baseball (his chosen favorites) but that didn't mean he was a douchebag or anything like so many people had lead him to believe. His scruffy brown hair, dark tanned skin and pretty brown eyes where attributes that people did compliment him about, and perhaps it did make him a little conceited, but not nearly as conceited as others he knew of. He was just your average grade twelve guy. Was it so wrong to be happy with yourself and to exude confidence? Apparently it was. He didn't care what others thought though. He was just being himself.

He rubbed the brown peach fuzz that started growing along his chin and up his jawline. What would he look like with a full beard, he wondered every time he looked in a mirror. He never actually let it grow out before, usually having to shave every couple weeks or so because it'd bother him if he didn't. It was also embarrassing. It was just showcasing to the world that he couldn't even grow a proper beard yet. He considered just letting it grow though. He wanted to feel more mature. He wanted people to see him as an adult, which he almost was. His friend Bobby Blair could grow a full beard and he was the same age as him, but looked older than he really was. He secretly hated him for that. Girls loved facial hair, and girls always went to Bobby. But Bobby was a rocker in his own band. Of course girls ate that shit up. But of course, he was just being a hypocrite now. He himself was an athlete, and girls ate that shit up too. We all had our own strengths, and Ryan's was a ball.

It just so happed that today marked the start of the summer carnival. It was the annual carnival that took place over a span of eleven days. Why it even took place at the High School was Ryan's guess. Probably because of the wide open field, for no other reason could rationalize placing such an entertaining amusement in an area of great boredom other than that.

He walked out of the room with a red t-shirt and pair of shorts in his arms and made his way down the hallway and into the bathroom to get ready and shower. Before he entered the bathroom, he stopped on the threshold and turned around. He stood there for a couple seconds then walked back into his room and examined his alarm clock, checking to see if it was set for tomorrow morning as he had to be up early for his summer job which was working at one of the games at the carnival. He would turn the dial to set the time and stare at it for a few seconds. Then he'd turn the dial off and on again to make completely sure that the time was correctly set to wake him up at eight. He was never truly convinced that his alarm was set after leaving his room, even when he checked it a few seconds before and made sure it was. The feeling became worse when he would close the lock on his locker at school. He'd walk away, thinking that it somehow wasn't locked and that someone would steal something. So he'd have to go back and check again.

O.C.D was the least of his worries though. Ryan was more concerned with his memory loss. He had the worst short-term memory and occasionally would forget the simplest of tasks or ideas. The worry enhanced when he learned Alzheimer's ran in his family. His grandfather struggled with it tragically even to this day and would soon die with it. He just hoped that that would not be him. When Ryan did die, he wanted to die with memories, fulfilled. He wanted to die knowing that he did something in this world so that when faced with death, he would be accepting of it. Not in darkness. He wanted to remember, not forget. Why worry about something that was going to be a part of you for the rest of your life anyway? *It was all bullshit,* he thought.

He stared at the time on the clock. "Okay, it's set," he reassured himself. He turned away, but had the urge to check one last time. Maybe he set it wrong. What if he woke up at the wrong time?

"It's set," he said again, leaving the room for good. He closed the door to the bathroom and, at the same moment, a sudden gust of wind slammed his bedroom door shut.

Later, he still felt the pulsing headache in his skull. This was ridiculous. He opened his hand and popped the pain relieving pills into his mouth and swallowed them, washing them down with a cup of water. In his other hand he held three beer bottles that were left in the bathroom, still full as if someone forgot them. Of all the things he didn't remember from last night, he knew that one of these bottles was his. He walked through the joined dining room and kitchen, placed the bottles on the table, then entered the main entrance to put on his sneakers. He looked around and noticed dozens of plastic bowls and brightly colored cups all over the place as well as random objects that didn't belong to him and a large cardboard box on the counter. The living room table was turned upside down and hoisted on top of chairs as it was converted into a beer pong table. Why it had to be flipped upside down was Ryan's guess. There was dirt all over the carpet and ruminants of what could have been vomit. He wouldn't dare look in the main floor or basement bathroom. Instead, he decided to block out the rest of the visually unpleasant. When he sat down to lace up his sneakers he could hear the soft melody of music playing on low. When he was ready to close the door to leave, Charlie, his beagle, went zooming past him like he would if he were chasing a squirrel.

"Hey buddy. I'm not taking you for a walk right now." Ryan grabbed him and led him back into the house, petting his head. "I'll take you later though. You're so good." Charlie looked at him with his dark eyes and made another attempt for the door and started scratching at it repeatedly.

Ryan sighed and smiled down at him. "Do you want to stay outside today?"

Charlie's tail started wagging back and forth as if he had just been offered fifty treats. Ryan grabbed the leash from the closet then took Charlie to the fenced off area in the backyard. He gave him a large bowl of food and water and tied the leash to the gate.

"Don't bark!" he yelled back as he cut through the front lawn (while tripping over a loose water hose) and down the sidewalk.

The walk to school was very unusual and at times amusing. You never knew what you would see, and the situation would always be new and suspenseful. For instance, last week there was an argument between Mr. and Mrs. Deming. Mrs. Deming came out of her house late one night and threw a suitcase out onto the front yard with Mr. Deming's belongings. She yelled and screamed that he had to sleep in an apartment for the week because he ruined her dinner party that she had planned for months by getting drunk and setting the couch on fire (as well as the many fire trucks and sirens that kept everyone up the whole night was another reason). There were always those neighbors from block to block who wanted to know the new daily dish on everyone. Who's dating who? Who married who? Who murdered who? Who cheated on who? Who went to prison and why did they go? Were drugs involved? Who got fired? Who got suspended? Who stole the garden gnome from Mrs. Sushi's Japanese garden collection? Who's pregnant? Who's gay? Who's moving out? Who's moving in? Which student got a new Ferrari for their birthday? Who smashed the windshield and slashed the tires of their neighbor? Who robbed the local mini mart and made off with a jug of milk and two packages of cigarettes? And the question of Mr. Dreamy, and if he proposed to Ms. Brunette last month then why was he seen a week later taking Ms. Blonde out to dinner?

He passed through the parking lot and onto the field in front of OceanView High School minutes later. The whole field was filled with hundreds of people and dozens of game stands, rides, food stands, animal petting centers, video game rooms, pools and skateboarding parks, platforms for singing and entertaining, and lounging areas. Not to mention the lion tamers, sword swallowers, magicians and fortune tellers were a constant buzz. The sign over the entrance was very generic, with just the word *Carni-Val* printed onto a bright banner with flames lit around the border. He looked at the sign and noticed that sometimes a small flicker of flame would be pulled by the wind and get pushed towards the greenery that was sprawled around the entrance.

Not very safe, he thought, looking around. What a stupid looking sign. And how original was the name, not. He secretly wanted to see it set on fire and burn, just so it would teach a lesson on how unsafe it was.

The school itself was on the very edge of the island on a short overhanging cliff. The cliff was only a few stories above the beach, and beside it was a short steep trail so anyone could walk back and forth between the school and beach. There were people playing on the sand courts and swimming in the ocean, laughing and having a splendid time. The soccer field was occupied on part of the field beside the school. There was a clump of trees to the side of the football field, and during the school year, if you took drama courses, the school's English and drama teacher, Mrs. Faria, would take the class out to the trees and act out Shakespeare plays while reading them out loud. Ryan remembered two years ago when his drama class acted out A Midsummer Night's Dream and he was chosen to play Puck, which Ashlee Anderson later said fit his "mischievous and backstabbing self." He was neither of course. She was just a bitch.

As a whole, OceanView was a large two story High School. It was recently renovated inside and out to look modern and brand new, such as an extension for the new auditorium. A brilliant scenery was one of the best features for the school. The overhanging cliff was on the edge of Sortonia Crest; therefore it had an incredible view of Mergers Bridge that connected the two islands together and expanded out far into the distance. The scenery of the city across the water was extremely spectacular, especially during sunset and at night when the whole city was lit and the lights were reflected and sparkling in the clear ocean. Right now, however, it wasn't a very pleasant sight—smoke rising from the towers and helicopters flying all around the skyscrapers because of the unbearable heat. It was all a little dramatic he thought.

Ryan made his way through the masses and tried to find somebody that he knew. One of the bumper cars had crashed through a wall and landed inside the craft shop nearby and had to close. There appeared to be an angry woman yelling at the manager for having yellow glue spilled all over her floral shorts. Children were running around everywhere with water guns and water balloons, attempting to throw them at random people then quickly running away.

Ryan hurriedly walked in the opposite direction and stopped beside a cotton candy booth where a boy was yelling and crying because he only received one cotton candy and not two. He resorted to kicking his mother in the leg until she gave in and bought him three more chocolate bars and a bag of doughnuts for his piggy mouth. He stuffed them into his food dispenser so fast that Ryan thought he would choke. Another lesson would be learned.

Behind him, and coming out of a nearby tent that had a banner across the top that read *World CARE, We CARE* were two of his best friends; Tommy Blair and Janelle Sanchez.

"That was really sad," said Janelle sympathetically. "I want to donate money to them now. Tommy, you donate too. We will help the world become a better place."

"Sure," he said, but didn't sound reassuring.

"Oh, there's Ryan!" yelled Janelle, pointing. "How random. It's like seeing a tomato in a vegetable factory."

"What?" said Tommy. "That doesn't make sense. Are you still drunk?"

"Of course it makes perfect sense. A tomato is a fruit now. They changed it because they just realized that tomatoes have seeds, which vegetables do not. It's like how Pluto isn't a real planet anymore because they just found out that it's a dwarf and it's too small."

Tommy raised an eyebrow. "Who is this they you keep talking about? And vegetables don't come from a factory you know."

"I'm talking about where they make the juice. You know, the tomato juices."

Tommy rolled his eyes and laughed. "Whatever. You lost me at vegetable."

Janelle Sanchez was a vibrant girl with blonde hair, almond shaped blue eyes (from the help of blue contacts which she constantly denied using) and a natural glow to her face that needed very little makeup. She tended to wear her hair up in various different styles and rarely completely down. Her outfit was often a reflection of how she was feeling that day which were often light pastel colors. Tommy Blair was Ryan's best friend since grade one, and was good friends with a lot of people with the simple fact that he was a nice guy. He had cute boyish features and shaggy, dirty blonde hair. He often looked like he lived in a fraternity with his choice of clothing, and almost always had green incorporated into his clothes because it was his favorite color. It was well known that Tommy had a thing for Janelle ever since Junior High, and vice versa with her for him. It was always hard to tell if they were dating or not, since they never officially declared that they ever were.

They were bickering behind him, but Ryan wasn't paying attention. There was a large metal pail filled with water in front of him that had numbered rubber turtles swaying on the top as participants tried throwing a hoop over the correct numbered animal to win a prize. All other sounds seemed to dim and soften as his eyes were gazing into the blue, his sight piercing into the depths below. He wasn't blinking. This water in front of him was demanding. Was it best to kill himself now? Right here? Yes, that would be best. No one would care. He felt his throat closing as if someone was choking him.

"Come to me."

Ryan looked ahead. *That's not my voice.*

"I found you. Come to me."

The whispering voice seemed to be coming from all around him, like he was inside a cave.

Who are you? asked Ryan subconsciously.

A low growl and hiss answered him.

"RYAN!"

His eyes flashed open and he was staring at the bottom of what felt like an ocean, water all around him. His brain felt like it was going to explode when he opened his mouth, water seeping into his lungs. He couldn't pull his head from out of the tub. It was as if a magnet was pulling him down. Once he couldn't hold his breath any longer, an arm reached in and pulled him out. A world went from dark to light as a warm sun sprayed onto his face and he stumbled to the ground, coughing. A massive surge of water poured onto him and a soft clunk hit the grass.

"That's not how you play the game!"

There were a bunch of laughs that caused him to look around then up towards the young game manager. The pail was now on the ground, empty, and the water and rubber turtles were spread out over the soaked grass. He himself was wet down to his waist, his nipples poking out through his wet shirt. Tommy was standing beside him when he reached down to lift him up.

"He's right," said Tommy who looked like he was just laughing moments ago. "It's not bobbing for apples, buddy."

Ryan rubbed his face and looked at Tommy then to Janelle whose expression revealed that she wanted to say something humorous about his predicament. He quickly walked ahead with Tommy and Janelle as more people where staring mockingly and pointing at him.

"Please, let's not talk about what just happened," said Ryan as if it was an order. "I feel like such a moron. I don't even know why I did that. I think I'm still drunk."

Janelle smiled at Tommy sarcastically. "What a coincidence. Tommy thinks I am too." She rolled her eyes.

"Don't worry about it buddy," said Tommy, patting him on the back. "We all do weird stuff. It happens to all of us."

"No it doesn't," said Janelle.

"I was trying to make him feel better."

"Oh," she said. "Yes, in that case, something unfortunate happened to me last week. Don't feel embarrassed. I accidentally locked my cat in the kitchen cabinet once. Sugar Roger was not happy at all."

"Guys, I'm fine. I'm just a little tired." Ryan tried to change the subject.

"Ryan," cut in Janelle, budging in between him and Tommy. "Let's change the subject. Did you have fun last night?"

Ryan's mood lightened up a bit. "Last night? Oh yeah, I totally forgot about that. How did it go?"

"It was epic man," said Tommy enthusiastically, seeming interested in the topic. "You were out after the first two hours, totally wasted. It was ridiculous. You basically slept through the whole thing. Blame it on Kameron. He was the one who kept giving you shot after shot of nonstop tequila."

"Ugh," snarled Janelle in a disgusted voice. "You guys sicken me. There's a reason I don't do shots. They give you a total lack of judgment!"

"And fun," said Ryan, grinning at her.

"You didn't even drink anything," blurted Tommy. "You had half a beer then switched to water for the rest of the night. It wasn't even real beer either. It was light beer. Like, one percent alcohol."

"I was pacing myself," she shot back. "And stop being so dramatic it was like four percent."

Tommy put his hands to his mouth and bent down as if he was super surprised. "Oh wow! Really?! You're such a rebel darling!"

Janelle flipped him the middle finger.

Ryan laughed. "I don't remember any of that. I didn't do anything stupid, did I?"

"No," said Tommy.

"Actually, yes," said Janelle. "The goat…"

"What goat?" asked Tommy stupidly. "Stop bringing up this goat because there was no goat! Jesus."

Janelle responded by flipping her hair in his face. "But it was so funny," she said, speaking to Ryan now. "Kameron suggested that you go to bed, because you couldn't even stand up, and you said yes. So he lifted you up the stairs and put you in your room. It was so nice. How he made it up the stairs, I have no clue. I took a picture though. I laughed."

"So I missed everything?" asked Ryan, as if it was the saddest thing that could have ever happened. "Passed out after the first two hours? Wow. Just partying like a rock star I guess."

"Don't worry," she said. "You didn't miss anything exciting. I think there were max thirty people there."

Tommy cleared his throat and glanced at Janelle, who looked back at him, shaking her head slightly. Ryan darted his eyes back and forth between the two. Someone didn't want to tell him something.

"What is it?"

"Don't tell him!" shrieked Janelle.

"Kameron broke one of your dad's table lamps by accident!" said Tommy quickly. "Sorry man."

"You guys were in my dad's studio?! What the hell!"

"I cleaned it up," said Janelle. "He might not notice. It's an illusion." She waved her hands in front of his face like a mime.

"Okay, I get it." He smiled, pushing her hands out of the way. "And why were my clothes on the ground anyway? I mean, that's weird to begin with. How was I able to take them off if I was unconscious? Did I strip for y'all?"

Janelle burst out laughing like it was the funniest thing she had heard. "Well you must have taken them off before you went to sleep. You don't remember that?"

"Janelle," said Tommy. "He was unconscious."

"No, I don't remember much," mumbled Ryan. "I'm starting to question things that have happened because I feel like people aren't telling me everything. For example, did I puke?"

Tommy smiled and patted him on the back. "Oh yeah. I think twice actually."

Janelle gagged. "The reason your clothes were on the ground was probably because you had a great time with someone in your bed."

"Jennifer," said Tommy automatically.

Ryan smiled. "You think?"

"Has she exceeded your limit yet?"

Ryan shook his head. "No way. We're tight right now. What about you two?" He pointed to him and Janelle.

Janelle looked at him with a confused face. "Us two what?"

"Dating."

Janelle burst out laughing again, obviously fake this time.

"What?" asked Tommy, seeming offended by it. "Am I not good enough for you?"

Janelle smiled and looked away.

"Jennifer left me a voice mail," cut in Ryan. "The fifteenth one in two days."

"Bro, are you actually committed to her?"

"I think so. She loves me."

"Do you love her?"

Janelle's eyes widened. "You guys are ridiculous I laugh every time. He's seventeen. What does he know about love? You two have only been dating for three weeks!"

"You're jealous," said Ryan matter of factly. "And you're a girl. Didn't you grown up with the whole meeting a prince and marrying him the next day?"

"And you're a boy," she said. "Didn't you grow up with the whole meeting a princess, rescuing her, then marrying her the next day?"

"No. I watched superheroes," said Ryan.

"You watched Bambi and you loved it!" yelled Janelle.

"Bambi wasn't a princess!" shouted back Ryan.

"He was prince of the forest!" she retaliated. They both looked at Tommy.

"Um, yeah. Bambi was... so cool guys." There was an awkward silence as Janelle glared at Tommy, squinting her eyes at him.

"I think you have something on your face," he said. "Here, let me get it for you."

"Rape!"

"Oh my God, really? Where's your whistle?"

"So," interrupted Ryan, "back to the party."

"Nothing interesting happened," said Janelle in a final sort of way.

"Except I left my cups at your house by accident. I need them back for my cousin's wedding social next Saturday, which I am also planning by the way. Decorating the whole event. I'm so excited! When they said—"

"Anyway," said Tommy, coughing slightly. "I would like to agree with her and tell you nothing interesting happened, but I think a couple things are worth mentioning. So first—"

"Seriously?" blurted Janelle. "If you're talking about Mickey trying to chase invisible goats in the front yard, then it wasn't that interesting. He didn't even make it to the fence before he tripped over a garden hose and tumbled onto the street, almost getting run over by a truck. Everyone ended up cheering for him and he felt like a celebrity for the rest of the night."

"The goat thing again," said Tommy under his breath.

"They were invisible," clarified Janelle. "You see, there were goats at the party but they were invisible because only Mickey could see them."

"So there were no goats," said Tommy.

"They were invisible goats," clarified Janelle.

"Same thing! God!"

Ryan laughed. "You guys are so messed up. I'm just glad everything went fine with the amount of people that were there. And no police either."

"No police," repeated Tommy. "We kept it quiet though. You know, with the neighbors and all." His eyes drifted to looking behind Ryan, and he grinned. "Ashlee was there though, wasn't she?"

"I don't know," said Ryan. "Who cares."

"I so was there," said a demanding voice behind him. As if on cue, Ashlee Anderson jumped in front of them and stood there with a yellow stuffed animal in her arms. Janelle screamed in surprise.

Tommy looked seriously disturbed. "How do you do that all the time? You always appear out of nowhere when someone mentions your name."

"She's a witch," said Ryan.

"Shut-up. I'm a will-o'-wisp," said Ashlee. "I left at one because I wanted fast food." She looked at Ryan, almost disgusted, as if his skin was melting off. "Why are you here? Were you just having a bath in a pool of beer or something? Why are you so wet and disturbing to look at?"

"Because I want a hug," he demanded with a fake smile, reaching forward to embrace her.

She quickly whacked him with her animal several times in the head. "Stay away from me!" she yelled, making a few people look in her direction. "Well, anyway, I'm here to play games of course. And look, I won!" She caressed her yellow bunny tightly. Ashlee Anderson was defiantly a breed of a different kind of something special. Though she was considered quite popular, the only reason she hung out with Ryan in the first place was because they both had the same friends and hung with the same crowds. She had bleached blonde hair and green piercing eyes, which looked quite fierce with her dark eye liner and eye shadow, giving them a smoky look (very unnatural for a summer afternoon). She wore a lace crop top with a large bow in the center and a flowing pink skirt. The main reason for Ashlee and Ryan's hateful relationship could be tracked down to middle school, when Ryan did something so embarrassing to Ashlee that it created such a rage in her that it lead her to hating him for four years and counting. They rarely discussed the incident. It was the giant pink elephant in the room, and everyone knew it. You could be the most awkward person known to exist, but that title would be stripped away the moment those two were left alone together.

"Cute!" said Janelle. "You actually won a prize? Can I have it?"

Ashlee pulled her plush bunny away as if Janelle was trying to grab it. "No, it's mine. It was so hard to get. I had to throw bean bags into this basket thing. So stupid. It's going into my collection. I'm trying to break Debbie's record from last year, and because she isn't here I might actually do it! So I need to beat her—literally. Are you ready to go then?"

"Where are you guys going?" asked Tommy.

"We are going to her house for a bit then coming back here later tonight," said Janelle. "Wanna come? We're walking."

Ryan glanced at Ashlee who was busy texting in her pink flip phone. "Are we allowed?"

Ashlee didn't look up as she spoke. "I suppose."

All four of them went back through the crowd and out of the carnival, passing beneath the flame-bordered *Carni-Val* sign.

Ashlee pointed up towards it. "That doesn't look very safe," she said. "It could catch something on fire."

THREE.

THE ANDERSON MANOR

THE ANDERSON HOUSEHOLD WAS IN COMPLETE CHAOS FOR the upcoming anniversary party celebration for Mr. and Mrs. Anderson. Walking through the wide open gate and up towards the house was a task in its self. The road curved in large loops up and down several stubby hills along the open front lawn (it literally could have been transformed into a full golf course if Mr. Anderson wanted it so). The luxurious Anderson manor was the biggest building on Sortonia Crest. It was constructed out of beautiful white and grey stone and had powder blue roofs along the tops. There were many windows and balconies accompanied with intricately constructed iron rails lining the walls.

The manor itself was almost fifty years old and was built by Ashlee's grandfather, Wes Steven Anderson, in his early twenties. There were countless theories from relatives and people from around the community about who stayed inside the bedrooms and who died within its many rooms (for a short time the house was a bed and breakfast).

Debbie Mullusk, one of Ashlee's friends, stated that there was a family of five that all murdered each other for sacrificial purposes. Another theory was that a prince married his long time sweetheart on the lawn outside the house so that he could inherit his family's fortune in a far off country. The most outlandish theory was from Mr. Sushi. Mr. Sushi was an Astrologer who lived in a rundown house with his wife next to the lighthouse and worked full time at the city's planetarium. He believed the Anderson house was cursed and that it had the ability to destroy people's lives, convince them of evil thoughts and ruin their lives from the inside out. It was well known that part of the house was built on top of a grave site that once belonged to a small village that had existed for hundreds of years before it was demolished by Wes Steven Anderson so he could use the land for his manor. This lead to other myths that if you walked backwards around the house three times during the midnight hour on any given night, you would slowly begin to disappear and only your bones would be left behind as your soul was dragged into the graves beneath the house. Over the decades after the house was built there were cases of people feeling suicidal after staying inside, and this was the proof that convinced Mr. Sushi that he was correct, as well as information that he received from the stars. "The galaxy is a time machine and a keep sake box of our world's history," he would say. "We should no longer be fools and no longer ignore the stories and secrets they tell us when we sleep, because they know." Ashlee also bragged about the fact that when she was ten she found a hidden room behind a bookcase in the living room, and inside were journals and books concealing the answers to the purpose of life and immortality and youth. When asked by her friends if she could bring them to the room, she would say that the room was set on fire and destroyed by people who did not want the world to know the secrets and all the secrets were then forever lost.

Today, the front yard was being set up for a party; Ashlee's parents twentieth anniversary celebration. Cousins, aunts, uncles and distant relatives would be attending this celebration from all over the world.

"I'm so excited," said Ashlee. "I can't wait. I've been waiting for this for months. Party time!"

"Is that what I think it is?" asked Janelle as she pointed to one of the trucks. "Are those ponies?!"

Ashlee began jumping up and down in excitement. "Yes! There are also parrots, giraffes, deer, coyotes and baby elephants!" Ashlee went dashing for one of the trucks when she heard a voice call out her name.

"Oh, sweet Ashlee!" The voice came from Mr. Anderson who was sitting on a lawn chair beside a mobile trailer. He was talking into his phone and scribbling notes down onto a pad of paper. He looked incredibly busy and every few minutes a person would run up to him to get his approval on a certain party decision. Mrs. Anderson was away at the store with a professional party planner to pick out napkins, straws and confetti.

"What?" she wailed as she walked up to him, but not easing down her excitement.

Mr. Anderson put down his phone and looked at her through his sunglasses. "I need your help putting up some signs around the yard. You know, directing people were to go so they don't get lost. Remember last time? We don't want that to happen again."

"I can't do that right now!" she shouted as a lawnmower was turned on, drowning her out.

Her father got up and walked into the trailer to help someone carry out a wide abstract painting. "You can do it whenever you want, but just make sure to have them done by tonight. Decorate them and make them look pretty. You're in art; you should be good at that. Get your friends to help, okay?" Mr. Anderson put down the painting and rushed past her, patting her on the shoulder.

Wow, he's actually acknowledging my existence, she thought.

"Hi, Mr. Anderson!" hollered Janelle, waving her hands ecstatically.

"Dad, it would have been easier if you just got some sign making place to do them," she said. "What do I look like?"

"Hm," mumbled a party planner as he passed Ashlee and looked her up and down. "Well, that isn't hard to answer."

She smirked at him icily from behind. *I'll get you fired bitch.*

Her mood suddenly changed when she saw a random pair of expensive sunglasses lying on a table beside her. She threw her stuffed bunny to the ground and put the sunglasses on without anyone noticing. She looked around and spotted her first victim.

Ryan was busy petting one of the few dozen parrots and trying to teach it to say, "Ryan's a king," but instead it kept squawking, "move it to the left, Garry. Okay, put it down. Now to the right—watch it, will ya!"

"Ryan," Ashlee demanded, "I need you to make me signs. You're in art; you should be good at that. Do you concur?"

The parrot jumped onto his shoulder. "You're in art too. You do it," he said, petting his new friend.

"Just because I'm in art doesn't mean I can draw," she snarled. She rolled her eyes and turned on her heel, whipping her hair at the parrot. "Whatever. I'm going inside."

"There goes the bitch. There goes the bitch," gawked the parrot.

Janelle came strolling over with a fudge sundae in her hand. "This is just so good I have to have another one. I'm gonna have a caramel apple then a cotton candy next."

Ashlee looked at her with wide eyes as if she was going to yell and choke her at the same time. "Are you done? Those are for the guests."

"Aren't I guest?" asked Janelle. "You should try one; the kitchen just finished making them."

"I don't want food, I want to tan," she said, stretching out her arms. "I look like shit. Do I look pleasant to you?"

"You look fine to me," said Janelle, not even looking at her but focusing on her cotton candy instead.

Ryan put the parrot back into its cage, giving up on teaching it his awesome phrase. He glanced behind him to see Tommy talking on his cell phone and covering his ear from the distracting sounds.

"What is it?" asked Ryan.

Tommy closed his phone and put it into his pocket. "My brother just called me. Wants to know when we're heading back down to the carnival. He wants to hang out because he's not performing tonight. I said we'd be there tonight sometime."

"Cool," said Ryan. "Let's go inside though. It's too hot out here."

They managed to slip into the air conditioned sanctuary of the grand entryway where caterers and volunteers were dashing in and out of the house.

"So," said Ashlee, fixing her hair in a nearby oval mirror as she caught a glance of Ryan and Tommy coming in, "someone just told me that Janice Murphy from TH3 News is going to be interviewing my father for some kind of special. He never does these things, so it's kind of a big deal." She turned around, grinning from ear to ear. "Isn't that exciting y'all?"

"Totally," said Tommy.

"Amazing," said Ryan.

"Do you think they'll serve Crème Brulee at dinner?" asked Janelle.

Ashlee rolled her eyes. Ashlee's grandfather was the founder of Coulter Hotels and Resorts, named after his future wife's last name. From an early age of only twenty-one, Wes Steven Anderson built his first hotel in Sortonia City. The business skyrocketed a decade later in the seventies, and Coulter hotels got on the map all across the country as one of the most luxurious and wealthiest hotel chains in the world. In the following decades, the business spread to all corners of the planet. Now that Wes was in his sixties, his son Richard was now taking care of the business. His daughter, Ashlee, was the current heir, a fortune that was estimated to be several billions of dollars. Ashlee's enthusiasm about the prospect of being the sole inheritor of the business was never very high. Deep down, she just didn't want it.

"Anyway," she said, "let's go to the kitchen. I need refreshments." Before leaving, she glanced at herself one last time in the mirror. Her reflection lingered a few seconds longer after she left then it vanished.

They all walked out of the main lobby that was made of white marble and went into a sub-lobby where there was a two-way spiraling staircase with a crystal chandelier hanging gracefully in the middle and being wiped down by a butler. They passed caterers and maids that were running around making last minute preparations for tomorrow. As they made a sharp turn to the left and down a brightly lit hallway with abstract paintings on the walls (which Ashlee stated were done by her), their footsteps ricocheted off the marble floor and walls. At the end of the hall was an arched, cherry wood door. She swung open the doors to a magnificent room—which couldn't really be called a room. It was a family room fit for royalty; a ballroom. The caramel colored marble flooring was reflecting the afternoon light from the stained glass windows that were all lined around the circular wall. There was a domed glass ceiling, with marvelous colors and symbols crafted into the glass. It all looked quite medieval, with many parts of the room, including the dome, said to have come from ancient countries that had them preserved for hundreds, if not thousands, of years. Dozens of individual tables were being brought in as well as chairs and trays for dessert. A large and round royal blue carpet that looked like it had been there for decades was laid out on the floor in the very center of the floor.

"I really like that dome," said Tommy, "I always just want to stare at it whenever I come here. Kinda freaky if you ask me."

"I know, so does every other person that comes through here," said Ashlee, her voice echoing throughout the room as if they were inside a coliseum. An assistant holding a basket full of table cloths came up to her and muttered something into her ear, and she responded with a head nod.

Ryan walked beneath the dome with his head up, staring at the afternoon light filtering through the colored glass with particles of dust floating past. "The zodiac symbols look really cool—same with the flower in the center."

Ashlee was already at the other side of the room. "My grandfather was obsessed with astrology and all that stuff. That's all I know. Why, what's your sign? You better not say Sagittarius, because every Sagittarius that I have ever met was a total bitch."

"Aries," said Ryan. "I'm a ram."

"I wish I was an Aries," said Janelle as they both left the room, her voice trailing away. It was sometimes common for Janelle to always mention all the information that she knew about whatever topic was being discussed at present, most of it being about her and not about any accurate information that would benefit one's knowledge.

Ryan was about to pass the threshold when he turned around and saw Tommy touching some old and tattered pictures on a nearby table. "Tommy! Don't touch those!"

Tommy looked up at Ryan and put the collection of pictures back down onto the antique table. "Sorry, I'm just fascinated with pictures from older times. The people in them always look scary."

Ryan grabbed Tommy's back and pushed him towards the door. "Yes, I know you are. But the last time I touched something valuable in here, I broke it. I was never yelled at so loudly in my life."

"What about the time you were caught watching porn in the library?"

"Hey," said Ryan as a smile broke in. "It was a music video."

"Yeah, well, you had your hand down your—"

"Tommy! Why are you even bringing this up? It was a year ago."

Tommy laughed. "Ryan, it was last month. And regardless, it's true."

"Yeah?" asked Ryan. He looked around before quickly smacking Tommy aside the head then running out of the room.

"Hell!" said Tommy, going after him. "Did you see that?" A nearby party assistant looked at him with a confused face, but was holding back a smile. "I'm afraid not young man."

Ryan ran out of the living room and was now in another hallway. Straight ahead of him was a set of double doors leading into a kitchen. Chefs and waiters were preparing platters and creating new menus. In the middle of the kitchen was a bloated island filled with fudge sundaes, cotton candy, caramel apples, salads, chicken, beef, gravy, cakes, drinks, sandwiches, dips, lobster, steak and other tasty assortments. Across the room was a patio door.

Tommy finally appeared behind Ryan and pushed him forward, making him run for the door. He slid it open and found Ashlee and Janelle sun bathing on beach chairs beside a pool while drinking frozen margaritas.

"What is wrong with you two?" said Ashlee loudly as Tommy ran out behind Ryan and pushed him into a chair, sending him sprawling onto the grass. Both were laughing.

"Why do guys always push and touch each other for no apparent reason. It's so sexual and suggestive. Do you agree, Janelle?"

"Agree with what?" she asked, looking up from her phone.

Ashlee rolled her eyes. "Just say yes. It's too difficult explaining. My jaw hurts."

Throughout the backyard, there were party assistants decorating the tables and trees and greenery. None of them seemed to notice the four of them, clearly too busy. The backyard was a very Zen and colorful jungle, with various exotic flowers and plants growing along paths leading to greenhouses and the pool. Everything just seemed so overly saturated with color.

"You guys came here to tan? Didn't you do that yesterday?" asked Tommy.

"Yeah, but I didn't get to finish," said Janelle. "She wanted to eat at that crap restaurant before it closed."

"No, no, no," snapped back Ashlee, sipping on her pink margarita, "Firstly, it's not crap at all. You just have a shit palette. And two, I was hungry and wanted to eat there, and so did you. You were just too day drunk to remember."

"It's still your fault," said Janelle accusingly.

Tommy got up and sat down on a beach chair and debated in his head if he would take his shirt off, and decided against it. "I'm not really pale, so there's really no point for me."

"Who cares, do it anyway," said Ashlee.

"I don't think my skin will even tan anymore," said Ryan. "It's pretty dark."

"Do you ever use spray tan or lotion?" asked Janelle.

Ryan shook his head. "I mean, I have once. Didn't really work for me though. I turned orange and all my clothes got screwed up."

"I like the coconut scented ones," she said.

"They're all coconut," added Ashlee.

Janelle furiously put her drink down for the now crucial debate that was now occurring. "Bitch, don't go there. I know my tanners and I know they are not all coconut scented. I remember using a lemon one last year."

Ashlee laughed. "So did I bitch. Lemon's boring though. I just used a pomegranate and strawberry shortcake infused periwinkle orange muffin scented one yesterday—this morning actually."

Janelle's mouth fell open. "Where did you get it?"

"From across the sea at that place you visit every winter."

"Can I use some?"

"Sorry, it's all gone. Oh, and there's a spider on your pasty leg."

Janelle almost choked on her brownie as she screamed and suddenly sprung up. "Ewe! Oh my God! It's going to kill me!" She ran around the backyard as if she was on fire, attempting to flick off the spider before it would kill her.

"Go Janelle! You can do it!" shouted Ashlee, cheering her on and clapping her hands. A bright yellow butterfly fluttered past her, but she barely noticed it as its wings caressed her ear and flew away.

"Anyway," she moaned. "I'm so miserable right now. I don't know if I should just talk, go swimming or just crawl onto my bed and do nothing. Life is so hard for me. Janelle, make a decision for me before I die from boredom."

"Don't you have to make those signs by tonight?" asked Janelle as she sat back down on her chair, still eyeing her blanket as if another spider was lurking beneath it.

"Damn it, I forgot about that. Apparently I have to slave today via crayons and markers." Ashlee continued slurping her margarita in annoyance. "I'll get someone else to do it." She looked at Ryan, who suddenly had a slight terror in his eyes.

"Excuse me, Ms. Anderson."

All four of them looked towards the patio door and saw Theodore, the family butler, standing outside with a cordless phone on a silver platter.

Ashlee smiled kindly. "Yes, Theodore?"

"Yes. Sorry for interrupting your important conversation, but there is a call for you on line eight Ms. Anderson."

"Who is it? Don't they know I have my cell phone? God."

"I believe it is Ms. Juno," replied Theodore, handing her the phone.

"That is the ugliest phone I have ever seen. I refuse to touch it."

"Yes, well, it was given to your parents three years ago as a Christmas present. I discovered it in the basement and decided to start it up. Put it to use."

"Who gives a house phone as a present?" she asked, grabbing the phone and running into the house. "That is basically saying, here, we don't care about you, so have this hideous gift! Trash."

Theodore sighed and trailed behind her.

Minutes passed as the shadows on the lawn spread out, the sun looking down with extreme heat. Something smashed on the concrete as a caterer accidentally dropped a few plates, trying to hold ten in one hand. The patio door slid back open again and Ashlee came walking out with a towel wrapped around her head and a bowl of pineapple in her hand. She chucked the cordless phone into the pool.

"Rebecca told me that she is at the carnival and that I should come on down now. Are you losers coming?"

"Oh, I am," said Janelle who jumped up as if there was another spider on her.

"You guys are here for less than half an hour and now you're leaving?" asked Tommy.

"That's our life. It is always on the move and never stopping. I wonder how we even sleep, go figure."

"Yea, I wonder that too," added Ryan. "You know, from the time you both wake up at one o'clock in the afternoon to the time it takes you to shower, then eat, then tan, then talk on the phone, then lay on the floor for three hours while laughing for no reason. I always wondered how you did it. Guess I'll never know."

"That's right," said Ashlee, apparently not listening to what Ryan was just saying. "That is a lot of work. Tight schedule washing those dishes and breathing in air, it is." She turned to Janelle. "What time is it? I somehow lost the cordless phone. My cell is in my hand, but I'm too tired to lift up my arm and read the screen."

Janelle grabbed Ashlee's cell and read the time. "Almost four-thirty. And you just threw the phone into the pool, you didn't lose it."

"What was that? I couldn't hear you," she said, screwing up her face. She looked at Ryan and Tommy. "Are you leaving? Or are you going to stay here and tan in sunlight that is now impossible to gain any possible rays from, hence not giving you a tan since it's already passed four and the shadows are now blocking the rays to your skin."

"No, we're leaving," replied Tommy, looking at Ryan who nodded his head in desperation.

"THEODORE!" screamed Ashlee. Ryan flinched a bit, as did the people around the jungle, making them drop more things.

Theodore came running out with a panicked look on his face. "What is it, Ms. Anderson?"

"Can you clean this up for me? Thank you," she said, pointing to the blankets and chairs on the grass. "We have to leave now. I love you—you deserve a medal."

"Of course, Ms. Anderson. I will have it done in a jiffy."

She handed Ryan the bowl of pineapple and all four of them walked into the kitchen, which was still very hot from the continuing cooking, and left Theodore to his cleaning. They barely made it into the living room when Ashlee stopped them at the door.

"Wait. I have to make a detour to my room. I really need to change."

"Personalities," muttered Tommy under his breath.

"What about those signs you have to make?" asked Janelle, munching on a caramel apple.

"Crap. Whatever, I'll do that later." She ripped the caramel apple out of her hand. "Stop eating those. You'll gain ten pounds."

"I don't gain weight because my doctor says that I have low metabolism," said Janelle, following Ashlee down the hallway and up the stairs to her room.

"You guys can leave," yelled back Ashlee.

Ryan smiled. "Finally, some good news."

"Just get me out of here before I kill myself," joked Tommy.

Ashlee burst through her bedroom door and threw her new sunglasses onto the bed. Janelle walked in with her with a chocolate muffin in her hand and went straight for one of Ashlee's closets that was filled with hundreds of clothes and shoes. Ashlee's room was quite majestic; the style most exotic with colors of rich golds, purples and silvers. One of the walls was almost completely taken up by a large window; a window that Ashlee hated because she always feared that she would sleepwalk into it, or someone would push her through it. She always made it known that she wanted a bigger bedroom with a balcony, the bedroom her parents had. But her mother didn't like the fact that she would be able to look down and see people she didn't appreciate and throw things at them, like the time she threw apples at a girl she detested named Chelsia Bitz.

"Oh my God," droned Ashlee, fanning her face with a piece of paper. "Why is my room so warm? Hasn't anyone heard of air conditioning? God, it's July." She looked over at her window. "Why isn't my window open? Why aren't my sheets changed? Why are my flowers dried and dead? Where are my new fresh flowers? Who was on my computer? Why am I still breathing the same air in my room that I breathed in yesterday?" She ran over to a part of the window and started tugging at the lock, but it remained shut.

"It's not opening! Janelle, make this ghetto window open before I stab it!" She started banging on the glass and made a crack appear. She slammed her cell phone against it and, when it still didn't open, she hurled the phone across the room. It smashed into the wall and broke into several pieces.

"Maybe the heat made it stick to the frame," said Janelle from inside Ashlee's closet.

"That's the stupidest thing I've ever heard! Whatever, I won't be here long." Ashlee left the window and went into her closet. She picked out some articles of clothing and a pair of black stilettos.

"I love this skirt. It's so funky purple and fresh." She winced at what Janelle was holding. "Ewe you are not wearing that ratchet thing Janelle."

"I found it in your closet though," she said.

"I don't ever remember owning that disgusting thing. Must be my moms."

Janelle tossed the shirt into the hall. She looked towards Ashlee's bed and noticed a cute stuffed bear placed on the pillow.

"Cool bear."

"I know," said Ashlee as she strolled into her bathroom. "I stole it from Father Michael when he was giving them out to all the kids at church. I just had to have it."

Janelle walked out of the closet with her chosen outfit and stared at the window. "As if she couldn't open it." She went over to it and began pushing the lock down, and in a matter of seconds managed to get it open. She bent over the edge to look below and saw the remaining trucks and people running around. "They are going to be here all night." She looked over at the gate and spotted Ryan and Tommy walking out.

"HEY! HEY! HELLO!" she shouted, waving her hands.

Down below, Tommy stopped and Ryan walked into him.

"Why did you stop?" asked Ryan.

"Did you hear that?"

Ryan looked back at the house. "No."

"Whatever. Now I know I'm hearing things in my head. Seriously, that house does things to you."

"Do you blame it on the house, or do you blame it on the person living in it?"

"Both," said Tommy. "Anyway, I need to get home to grab my brother. I'll meet up with you later tonight, okay buddy?"

"Yea, sure. See you later man."

Tommy patted him on the back and left. Ryan turned around a second time to look back at the house, thinking he heard someone yelling to him as well, but went on towards his own home to chill for a couple hours.

The sun slowly spilled into a deep red, then within seconds faded back into a ball of raging yellow light.

FOUR.

THE BLACK DOOR

THE REPETITIVE TAPPING OF REBECCA JUNO'S FLIP FLOP WAS the only thing distracting a young boy from throwing a ball into the correct basket. He threw the ball one last time but it missed the net and hit a stuffed tiger hanging on the wall instead.

"That's it buddy," said the game manager. "Better luck next time. Have a balloon for trying." The boy took the red balloon and groaned as the manager called up the next person to play.

"Thanks a lot." He stuck his tongue out at Rebecca and slugged away in despair. Rebecca stepped forward and took one of the orange balls from the bin. She closed her eyes and began to move her arms in fast circular motions as if she was trying to get rid of a fly. The game manger eyed her strangely, thinking that she might tip over.

"Please let me win that big orange lion," she whispered to herself. "One... two... OUCH!" She felt a light kick at her leg, making her drop the ball. She looked behind her and saw the boy running away through the crowd. He sought his revenge.

"That's it. Better luck next time."

Rebecca looked up at the manager and reached for another ball from the bin as if establishing her own rules for the game. "No, that wasn't fair. Didn't you see him?" She pointed behind her, but the manager didn't seem to care one bit.

"Sorry, better luck next time," he said in a boring tone. "Here, have a balloon for trying."

Rebecca rolled her eyes and walked away. She continued her journey passed the soccer field, and doubled back when she spotted Mickey Morgan sitting in a lawn chair on the sidelines. Rebecca walked up and sat down next to him on the grass, picking up an empty soda bottle that someone had thrown on the ground and putting it in the recycling bin. The mere sight of it angered her.

"Enjoying the game?" she asked.

Mickey continued to stare at the field. "It's junior high kids; how good could it be?" He glanced at her for a quick second. "You look mad. What's wrong? But most importantly, why would you sit on the grass while wearing that new white skirt you told me so much about. Grass stain?"

Rebecca jumped up as if she were electrocuted and looked over her shoulder to see the back of the skirt. "When is anything *not* wrong Mickey? I don't even want to talk about it," she said, completely disgusted. "It's not worth the time to explain. Please tell me my ass is fine."

Mickey slapped her ass and squeezed it a bit. "Still perky as ever and the envy of housewives everywhere. No stuffed animal yet?"

"No," she sighed. "The games are too hard. It's all about luck most of them. And we both know I have the worst."

"Like your Biology exam," he offered. "That one long answer question that you got a zero on and brought your grade down to what? An A? What was the question about again?"

"Mendelian and Molecular Genetics," she mumbled. "I just a drew a blank. Then time was running and I panicked. Total bullshit."

Mickey nodded his head in agreement. "This is a tragedy that we're in now. Even I got a two out of five on that one."

Rebecca pursed her lips. With her long, wavy brown hair and black rimmed glasses, Rebecca Juno prided herself in her known intelligence (particularly gifted in the art of chemistry and science). She was most defiantly high fashion as well, as her need to wear the most beautiful outfits never went a day unnoticed. She always said that her love for science came before her love for clothes. Mickey Morgan on the other hand had a great air of humor about him. His hair color was unknown to most because he always wore a different hat every day ranging in every style and color available, even at school where hats are banned. The teachers seemed to have given up on telling him no. Everyone who wasn't his friend or family could only guess the color of his hair from the shade of his eyebrows, sideburns or stubble, which was either dark blonde or light brown (it was hard to guess). His clothes were always very sporty, which complemented his love for sports and working out. He was your boy next door with an ambition to go professional and join a professional soccer team. What was there not to love, honestly?

"GO JIMMY BOY! MOMMY LOVES IT WHEN YOU KNOCK

DOWN DEM LOSERS!"

Standing behind Mickey was a sun burned woman yelling towards the field with a cinnamon stick in her hand and a fry in her mouth. Others quickly chimed in with shouts supporting their children and cruel insults for the others.

"Look at that slow child trying to run!"

"Hey, that is my child!"

"Okay, enough of this," muttered Mickey as he got up and stretched. Rebecca smiled and shook her head at him, as she was aware of his current showing off by casually flexing his arms. He grabbed Rebecca's shoulder and stepped over her so he could get into the open. Rebecca got up and dusted off her flowing brown hair and white skirt from saliva and bits of food she suspected might be present from the woman behind her.

"My feet hurt so much," complained Rebecca as she followed Mickey away from the soccer game. "Why didn't I wear better shoes today? These flip flops are for shit. They're literally falling apart. I hope I don't get my orange blouse uglied up."

"I think you already got it uglied up," he said. "I mean, you were sitting behind that ugly chick."

Rebecca gave him a half-hearted laugh. "Or it could have been from you sitting beside me."

Mickey looked horrified at what she said.

"I'm just kidding. That pretty face of yours could never ugly up anything. By the way, I like your new earring. Makes you look so suave."

"Hey there, wasn't I already?" He slid to the side and bumped into her.

"What's new in life?" she asked him.

"You just mentioned it. And it's too damn hot to think anymore."

"At least it's not as bad as it is in the city. I had to go there yesterday, and it was boiling—ten times worse than here. I must have seen four ambulances."

Mickey put his sunglasses on. "Please keep talking as I die. I'm going to need an ambulance soon from heat stroke." He stumbled to the side and purposely knocked into her again.

"Don't," she said, pushing him back a little.

"Awe," he said in a baby voice. "I thought you were my friend."

"You are," she said. "But come on. You look drunk and rapisty."

"Rapisty isn't a word."

"Thanks Webster."

"Well, you know there are people looking at us right now and they're thinking, wow, what an unsteady relationship those two have. And I would have to agree with them."

"And this is the part where the annoyed girlfriend walks away," she said and wondered off, abandoning Mickey.

"Who are you looking for?" he asked, trying to keep up with her. "And now I guess this is the part where the ill fated boyfriend is now running after his love to beg for forgiveness for the embarrassment he just selfishly spilled upon his girl. Please baby. Come on baby. I need you baby…"

"Ashlee. I called her thirty minutes ago. And no! You know what you did to me. You know how awful you made me feel. Go away!"

"How's Debbie enjoying the lake house with her parents? Has she talked to you since she got there? Oh please baby, I'm sorry. I'm such an asshole. I'll never do it again. I swear."

Rebecca looked around and turned to her left. "Yeah, she arrived yesterday but she's been too busy to get back to me. She's been fishing and hiking and whatever the hell someone does at the lake. She said she'd be back in Sortonia next week. How do you expect me to believe you? You've hurt my feelings so many times already!"

Mickey grabbed her from behind and came face to face with her. "Because I'm nothing without you. And when I see you in pain, it breaks my heart and makes me strive to be better than I am. I can be better, I know that. And I will be better, for you. I just want to see you smile. Just smiles."

They both looked longly into each other's eyes for several seconds with stern faces, holding onto each other's hands. After a moment, Mickey's face was the first to break into a grin then into a full smile, omitting a burst of laughter.

"I win... again!" cheered Rebecca, jumping up in triumph. "But you were good. You should really be an actor."

"I have prospects," he said. "But I get to pick the one for next time. Boy sees ex girlfriend with another guy and tries to win her back?"

Rebecca nodded her head, accepting the challenge. "Done."

Later in the evening, a black GMC pulled up to the school parking lot. It was honking its horn for people to get out of the way.

"Crap," said Janelle. "We should have come earlier. Rebecca is probably gone now."

Ashlee looked through her tinted window. "I'm sure she will understand. Benjamin? Can you drive us a little further up to the gate? I don't feel like walking all the way up there."

"Of course," said Benjamin, her driver. He drove up to the very front entrance, accidentally knocking over a garbage bin and blinding a clown with the car's headlights.

"My my," said the clown. "Someone had a little drinky drinky before driving. Naughty naughty.

"Shut-up shut-up," said Benjamin mockingly. In reality, this was Benjamin's first week as the Anderson's new driver. He was in his early thirties and came across this job as a weird coincidence. The previous driver had a heart attack because of the heat, and died while sleeping. Therefore, the poor man was taken out of the house on a stretcher. Ashlee needed to go to the mall and she spotted Benjamin walking past the gate to her house. Benjamin used to be a city bus driver for three years with horrible pay, so he took the position as the family driver and the rest was history.

"Thank you Benjamin," said Ashlee and Janelle together as they got out.

"Will you need me to pick you back up later tonight?"

"No, I'll walk back Benjamin. Thank you and good night Benjamin. Drive home safely Benjamin. Beware of ducks crossing the road Benjamin." She shut the door and followed Janelle into the carnival. In the far corners of the parking lot, groups of people were yelling and breaking bottles onto the cement, revving up their engines and racing.

"So where are we going?" asked Janelle.

Ashlee twisted her mouth. "I have no clue. Here, give me your phone for a second. I lost mine."

Janelle sighed and handed Ashlee her cell. "Lost it? I thought you threw it against the wall and broke it?"

"Lost it," she confirmed. Seconds later, she screamed in fury. "Ugh, why the fuck is no one answering their phones?! Your screen is all messed up too."

"No it's not!" exclaimed Janelle, looking at it for herself. "What the hell! It wasn't like that ten seconds ago!" Her eyes drifted ahead. "Hey, there's Kameron. Wonder what he's doing."

Ashlee glanced at him for a second then turned away. "Have you seen Ashton Richards? If you see him, tell me. I need to tell him something."

"Let's go say hi," said Janelle, running over to hug Kameron.

Let us not, thought Ashlee.

"Janelle!" yelled Kameron. "What's up?"

"I'm positively splendid and wonderful!" she said excitedly. What are you doing?"

"I'm just waiting for Tommy and Bobby to get here. This place is crazy tonight."

"I know, right? I was—"

"JANELLE!" Ashlee came jogging up to her. "Just don't wonder off and leave me there you selfish bitch!"

Kameron opened his mouth in shock. "What the hell. You didn't say hi to me." You could never tell with Kameron Ferrari if he would come up to you and start a playful fight with you or give you a warming hug. These were just a couple of his unique attributes along with his caramel colored skin, buzzed haircut and exotic appearance.

Ashlee gave him an exasperated look and hugged him. "I'm not in the greatest mood right now. I lost my phone and I can't get a new one until tomorrow. I'm sorry that I'm so evil right now."

"Awe," he said in a childish voice, embracing her warmly. "Don't worry. Want a joint? It'll make it all better."

"No," she said. "We're at a carnival with pure and innocent children. Don't be such a bad role model."

"Hello pot," said Kameron. "It's kettle. Just calling to ask why you're always calling me black. And believe me, a lot of these kids aren't so innocent. A lot of them are brats actually." He glanced at her up and down for a second then looked away, grinning.

"Excuse me," said Ashlee, putting her hands on her hips. "Was that comment smoothly and subtly indirectly directed at me?"

"Of course not!" yelled Kameron happily, putting his arm around her shoulder and squeezing it. "I would never say that about you. You're too special for that."

Ashlee smiled at him.

"Oh, I didn't mean to make you blush," he said quietly, wiping his hand against her cheek. Ashlee glanced at Janelle, as if trying to communicate with her, but she seemed to be transfixed with something in the distance.

"And if anyone did say that to you," said Kameron, leaning in closer to her, "they'd be eating through a tube for the next six months. You like that?"

Ashlee laughed slightly. "No, honestly. That wouldn't be necessary."

"Why not?" said Kameron, looking at her seriously. His hand was squeezing her shoulder more tightly now. Ashlee smiled at him again, but this time awkwardly, and coughed a couple times.

Janelle looked at her suddenly. "What?" she said. Kameron looked at Ashlee as if he was extremely pissed off.

"Um," said Ashlee, sliding away from Kameron. "Um, well, where's Rebecca? Why are you just standing there doing nothing?"

"Oh I'm sorry. My name isn't Theodore," said Janelle. "Why don't you go find her?"

Ashlee smiled at her slightly. "Fine then." She looked back at Kameron. "Have fun." Kameron raised his eyebrows half heartedly to acknowledge her.

"I'll just stay here with Kameron and keep him company till Tommy and Bobby come!" yelled Janelle.

Be my fucking guest.

Tommy followed his brother Bobby into the carnival behind the other carnival goers who were geared up to take on the several rides. Tommy was Bobby's adoptive brother from the age of one and they were very close. One would think that they were real genetic brothers from the way they interacted, but they couldn't be more different in their appearance or style. Though Tommy had more of a casual style, Bobby was more rock and punk oriented and often had his hair constructed into a faux hawk tipped with red and a black t-shirt with some kind of graphic on the front as part of his attire. Heavy black stubble often lined his jawline. Since an early age, Bobby always wanted to be a rock star in his own band. So he decided to form one back when he was fourteen called *Torch Down.*

A person dressed as a clown was greeting people into the carnival with a big smile (though the smile started to falter several hours ago). "Have an excellent time and may the time you share at *Carni-Val* be the best experience you experience for the rest of your life's experience!" The clown started dancing around as another person, this time dressed as a tiger, started handing out wristbands and cotton candy. Tommy walked past the tiger, but it jumped out in front of him.

"You forgot your treat, young man!" The tiger handed Tommy a stick of green cotton candy.

"Thanks man," he said as nicely as he could. "You freaked me out there."

The tiger chuckled. "Tidbit the Tiger does not freak. He only brings fun and excitement!"

"MOVE IT YOU FREAKISH BOZO!" A young girl who looked ten pushed the tiger to the side and dragged her dad through the gates. "You're just a man in a suit!"

"What a bitch," said Bobby in shock.

They both hurriedly ran away before the tiger tried giving them a hug. They went through the gate and stopped in front of a pin ball machine that an annoying child was screaming at to give him more points. The boy grabbed a plastic sword and started slaying the machine with it until a small screw fell off. The girl with her father started crying because her dad only gave her ten dollars instead of fifty.

"What a freak show," said Bobby. "That tiger was psychotic. Now I know why I'm scared of them—it literally tried to rape me."

Someone suddenly lunged at Bobby from behind. "I'll rape you you little bitch!" Bobby was pulled to the ground by Kameron and pinned down hard so he couldn't move.

"Hey, what's up man?" said Tommy, looking down casually as if his behavior was nothing strange.

Kameron looked down at Bobby who was pinned beneath him. "What's up Bob? How ya doing down there?" He laughed and got up, pulling Bobby up with him.

"I found that strangely arousing," said Bobby, adjusting his pants.

"Haha I'd be offended if it wasn't. Where's Ryan?"

Tommy shrugged his shoulders. "Dunno. He said he would meet up with me later. So that means soon I think."

"I can't get a hold of Mickey," said Kameron, glancing at his phone. "Janelle was with me, but she said she had to go to the washroom and never came back." He quickly slapped Bobby across his back. "Whatever, they're loss. I guess we'll have to start the party without them, boys. On to the beer gardens!"

"Did you get Ashton's ID?" asked Bobby.

Kameron whipped out the driver's license. "I swear this dude could be my brother."

Ashlee was sitting at a table beside the stage in the beer gardens, drinking out of a plastic cup with her hand on Janelle's flip phone, waiting for Rebecca to text or call her back. Why was she even sitting here? There were dozens of other things she could be doing right now. Instead she was waiting for friends that wouldn't even call her back.

The phone vibrated and she grabbed it. "Hello? Finally, where are you? I'm getting so bored. I'm resorting to alcoholism." She opened her mouth in shock and laughed. "You shouldn't feed your cat, it's so fat. Ten minutes? I'll go now, so like fifteen maybe? Don't start it before I get there. Okay, bye." She closed the phone and put it back on the table, accidentally feeling the edge of the table. "Ewe, why is there gum under here? Disgusting."

"Oh, Ashlee?! Can you come here please?!" Ashlee looked behind her and saw Lunch Lady Margaret waving her hand frantically from behind a hamburger stand as if she had heat stroke and needed desperate help. Ashlee waved back, but turned back around and her head suddenly exploded with excitement. There he was. Ashton was only a few feet away, talking to a group of sluts three years younger than him. One of the girls noticed her and waved to her, smiling. Ashlee hesitantly smiled back and returned the wave. Ashton turned around and glanced at her as if he was surprised and happy to see her.

"Hey there!" he shouted.

Ashlee grinned from ear to ear. "How are you?!"

He shrugged his shoulders and grinned, taking a sip of his beer. "Better now I think."

"Oh Ashlee honey, can you come here please? Oh Ashlee! Ashlee, can you hear me? Ashlee dear! This is important!"

This bitch.

Ashton was waving his hand for her to come over, but Ashlee put her hand up to signal "just one minute" to him and got up. She dragged herself over to the hamburger stand and waited for a customer to move.

"You can come around here, dear. Ashlee, around here. Can you hear me? Are you deaf, child?"

Ashlee walked around the booth and went through the curtain to the front. "Yes?" she asked.

"Dear, I'm sorry. I'm frightfully busy right now and I would appreciate it if you would take these bags of frozen hamburger patties to the cafeteria freezer for me. These ones are just not selling and they need to go back because they are taking up too much room around here!" She handed the two plastic bags to Ashlee and she took them grudgingly along with a small rusted key. She stared at them as if they were going to explode.

"I thought students weren't allowed in the kitchens behind the cafeteria," she said suspiciously.

"Yes, I know. But I'm giving you permission. I can't leave my post, and you're the only person I've seen for a while who is capable of doing this. You better hurry though. I don't want them to thaw. Look, they're already dripping!"

Ashlee watched as she flipped over several patties for a family of three. Margaret was pudgy with straw like hair and terrible sunken in skin. A career in working in a High School cafeteria had added at least ten years to her appearance. Rumor of her retirement was floating around for some time, ever since her daughter ran away a few years ago. Ever since, the poor woman was never really the same.

"I'm the only one capable of carrying plastic bags and walking to a freezer?" asked Ashlee stubbornly.

"Oh, can't you?" replied Margaret in a babyish tone that annoyed Ashlee, as if she was mocking her. "Is it too difficult for you to handle? Too much work?"

Ashlee threw the bags back at her. "I have an idea. Why don't *you* do it yourself? Or is that too much work for *you* to handle?"

Margaret's smile faded and she continued on with her cooking seamlessly, chatting back up with customers and burying her obvious resentment.

Ashlee walked away as a father of three, who overheard what had happened, shook his head at his wife and said: "spoiled brats are being bred by the thousands now apparently. Who raises these kids?"

She stopped in her tracks as if she was suddenly kicked from behind. She had no courage to turn around. She continued onward in a brisk pace towards Ashton, but then detoured away and ran in the opposite direction.

No, she thought, thinking about what the man said. *It wasn't like that. It wasn't like that at all.*

Ryan entered the carnival gates with a red cotton candy stick in one hand and his cell in the other. He went past the lion tamers and Ferris wheel and stood beside a long line waiting to go on a ride called *The Plunging Firebomb.* He sat down on a bench before finding his friends. He threw the rest of his cotton candy into a garbage bin and leaned back against the back of the bench, staring at the screen on his phone. Maybe he had better just go into the school to look for someone. Apparently no one was answering their phones. His own phone seemed to have stopped working.

He got up and twisted his way up towards the school, hoping to come across someone that he knew. He bumped into a familiar face who appeared flustered.

"Oh hi," he said awkwardly to Ashlee, who looked like she didn't want to talk to anyone, let alone him, as her eyes were red and her makeup a mess. She sighed and whipped away her bangs for no apparent reason.

"I have to be somewhere," she said calmly.

So let me go with you, said a voice somewhere close to Ryan. He looked up abruptly and realized the voice was inside his head. It felt like someone just spoke for him... again... but it was a different voice than last time. It wasn't telling him die, it was the opposite. It sounded right.

"I don't want to go with her though," he said out loud, his eyes still looking up. He looked back at her. This was the most embarrassing thing ever. He just wanted to disappear. Run.

Ashlee's mouth opened slightly as if in disbelief.

What the hell is her problem, he thought. *So she finally realized I'm a crazy freak who hears voices in his head and talks to himself out loud.* "Uhhh..." he trailed off. "I have to be somewhere actually. Bye."

"Wait!" said Ashlee fiercely, as if her life depended on it. Ryan stopped and turned back around. She looked nervous for some reason. "I need to talk to you about... something."

"Talk to me about it later, okay? Like when school starts. Or never."

"It's important."

"Not that important," he said half heartily, his back still turned to her and walking in the opposite direction. He had barely made it a safe distance away when he heard his name called out again. He really needed to change his name or something.

"Ryan dear!"

He turned to his left and saw Lunch Lady Margaret running up to him with two dripping bags of hamburger patties. She had to catch her breath for a moment when she reached him, as if she just ran a mile. "Please do me a favor young man and take these to the cafeteria freezer for me. I'm just too busy to do it myself."

Ryan was a little stunned as she put the bags into his hands. The strangest thing he was ever asked. He obviously didn't want to do it but he kinda had no choice now.

"Of course," he said. "I'll get it done."

Margaret smiled from ear to ear. "Oh, you are an angel. Not like that beastly girl. Thank you dear." She hurried back to her workplace.

Ryan looked down at the bags and sighed. "Whatever," he said and made his way towards the school.

The school was still dark inside from its recent power outage that happened half an hour ago. The only light to guide Ryan were the lights from outside—if only he had a flashlight. The hallways were empty as expected and Ryan's footsteps echoed off the lockers and walls as if he was in a crypt (which technically, he thought, made sense since this was a school). He looked down at the wet plastic bags and saw that he was leaving a trail of dripping water down the hall. He wiped the bottom of the bags with his hands and (very tempted to through them into a garbage bin) turned down the hallway that lead into the cafeteria. This hallway was where Ryan's locker was. It was somewhat of a pain because the smells from the kitchens always made him hungry (because, surprise surprise ladies and gents, the food from the cafeteria was actually decent).

Oddly enough, he saw a few young children running around playing games such as hide and seek. One girl was hiding inside a locker.

"Please don't tell Luke I'm in here," whispered the girl as Ryan walked past.

"I won't," he whispered back, putting a finger to his lips.

"Cross your heart and hope to die?" she asked, giggling a bit.

Ryan took a second to reply back. "Cross my heart... and hope to die."

There were faint footsteps coming from down the hallway and Mickey came around the corner, his hat turned to the side. He seemed to be a bit out of breath from the way his chest was heaving up and down. He gave Ryan a deer in headlights look when they made eye contact.

"Mickey, is that you? What are you doing here all alone man? Why is no one answering their phones?"

Mickey smiled in a sheepish sort of way, as if he wasn't expecting him. "I guess everyone is having too much fun to answer their phones dude. And I don't have a cell anymore, remember? I can't afford one right now because I don't have a job. The lights have gone out too. Kinda spooky."

"I know," said Ryan. "Blackout."

Mickey smiled. "You're familiar with those, aren't you?"

"Wonder if we'll see those ghosts," said Ryan, avoiding the jab.

"Ghosts of classmates past? No thank you." He looked down and saw the glimmer of the two plastic bags that Ryan was holding and heard the soft trickle of water dripping off the bags and onto the floor. Ryan noticed him looking down at the bags.

"Oh, these? Just doing a favor for someone. Have to get these to the cafeteria."

Mickey nodded his head unconvincingly as if he didn't believe him. "That's odd. Students aren't allowed inside the kitchens of the cafeteria."

"Just being nice," said Ryan. "And I was bored. It's okay though. Lunch Lady Margaret said I could."

"So don't do it," suggested Mickey.

Ryan gave him a dumb look. "Well, I'm practically there already. I might as well just... finish it. It's not like anything bad will happen if I do it."

Mickey stared at him in amusement. "Nothing bad is going to happen if you don't do it. But alright. I guess you're the good guy out of the rest of us villains." He put his hand up for Ryan to high five him.

"I'll get back to you in like three minutes," said Ryan. "It won't take long."

Mickey took a second to respond. "Yea, cool. Just don't take forever. I need to tell you something when you get back. I just... I just need to tell someone, and with you, I feel like I can. I don't want you to think I'm crazy though. It's just been bugging me."

Ryan was caught off guard, but he reached over and patted him on the shoulder. "Don't worry. I'd never think you were crazy." *A night of secrets. A night of confessions and people wanting to spill their secrets to me*, he thought. Of all nights, what was so special about this one? He blew off one person already, and he wasn't going to go there with this one.

He turned the corner of the hall and walked up to the cafeteria door and opened it. He tried flicking on the lights, but remembered that they weren't working. He knew the cafeteria good enough to be able to find his way around. There must have been thirty circular tables lined up in rows. The room was divided into the sitting area and a lounging area where students could play pool, video games or watch television during their free time. Ryan walked over to the counter where the food was prepared. It had its blinds drawn and the door was locked shut—the only way into the kitchen.

For a mere second, it was dead quiet, the dark encasing him like a fog. There was a small and distinct noise coming from behind the store counter, like a mouse biting at wood inside a wall. He got a tingly feeling on the back of his neck, the sensation you get when you feel like someone is watching you from behind. Then, there it was again, that noise. His ears perked up and he heard a squeaking sound, followed by a *clunk* on the tile and finally a long *creak*. Then silence.

Ryan saw that the black door beside the store was now wide open, almost like it was welcoming him with open arms. He curiously stepped forward, but accidentally hit his funny bone on one of the legs of a table, making him swear loudly and swing the bags around. Pushing the table to the side, he went towards the threshold and closed the door behind him, except it wouldn't close. There wasn't a doorknob for him to grab—it was on the floor. He reached down and grabbed the knob, which was slightly warm. He put it on the counter, along with the key that Lunch Lady Margaret gave him, and let the door swing back open on its own accord.

"Place is falling apart," he said, laughing to himself.

He was now behind the counter where the food was sold. There was a hallway to the right of him with an archway at the very end to where the kitchen was. When he reached the kitchen, he tried switching on the lights, but rolled his eyes in embarrassment when realizing the power was still out. With what little light that was available through the windows, he felt for a nearby cabinet and opened it, searching for something that would produce light—matches or a flashlight. Fumbling around, he touched water bottles, aprons, bags full of seeds, a broken knife, matches and two small flashlights. The flashlights were broken so Ryan put both of the hamburger bags into one hand and lit a long match with the other.

Once he could properly see, he expected to see a dilapidated, old and disgusting kitchen but instead saw exquisite, stainless steel appliances and all the high quality equipment that any professional kitchen would have.

"And we aren't allowed behind here because? Looks better than my kitchen."

He looked around for something that resembled a freezer, and saw a metal door built into the wall with the word FREEZER on it in bold red letters. He opened the door and felt a cold breeze that could have given him frostbite if he lingered too long. He threw the bags to the ground and quickly shut the door and locked the door shut. Lunch lady Margaret wasn't the only cook in this school. There were four others that took different shifts during the year and they were all rarely seen.

When he was about to leave, he caught sight of a door at the other end of the kitchen that was hidden behind a metal baking rack on wheels. It wasn't the door that he noticed first, it's what was above it. There was a rustic sign bolted to the wall that said DETENTION ROOM. He smiled and went towards the door, looking over his shoulder to make sure no one was coming in to check up on him. He raised the flame a bit higher and could see that the door beside the front counter was still wide open.

Ryan pushed the rack out of the way and opened the wooden door, which didn't have a lock on it. The door creaked open and a burst of warm air gusted out like a vent and a few spiders scurried out. It was a tiny room, no bigger than a small bathroom. The whole room was made out of old paneled wood that was falling off with hundreds of rusted nails sticking out. There were dozens of shelves on the walls, all of which were empty. Cobwebs draped along the ceiling and an inch of black soot covered the ground. It still felt like someone was watching him. He stared into the dark, damp room and snickered. "I feel sorry for the kids that had to stay in this room. Detention room? Okay then."

The back wall of the tiny room was made of brick and in the middle of it was a type of framework to a door. Where the actual door should have been was a thin plastered wall. The plaster, however, was ripped apart and there was a gaping hole in the middle to what looked like another room on the other side. Ryan stared into the hole, mesmerized and curious about what was on the other side. He stepped inside the paneled room and heard a crackling beneath his shoe as he stepped onto the ash. He extended the match through the hole in the plaster but couldn't make out anything, except blackness. It was like it was a black hole that sucked up all the light and wouldn't let him see what was inside.

"Come on," he muttered as he looked at his watch and was curious as to whether Mickey left or not.

"Sorry, buddy. Gotta check this out." He would never have a chance like this again. Whatever Mickey wanted to tell him, it would have to wait for now. He'd understand. He would have done the same. Ryan ducked through the hole and stepped into the other side.

The ceiling was unnaturally low and all four walls were black from ash. Ryan moved the match around everywhere he could while hunched over because the ceiling was so low that it slanted downward the further into the room he went. There was nothing in this room. Not a single object, just soot on the floor and darkness all around.

Ryan began to sweat from the creeping warmness of his environment. It could possibly be a type of boiler room, but there was no boiler to be seen. As he stepped further inside, he could make out two red orbs in the distance that were the size of golf balls, just floating in one spot. Ryan tilted his head, as if he was drawn to the lights. They were like two small stop signs telling him to turn around. But the further he stepped, the more curious he became. He looked behind for no apparent reason, feeling paranoid as if there were people behind him. The flame from the match kept flickering as it was getting fainter. *Of course it was,* he thought. Everything in his conscious was telling him to turn around. *Don't be an idiot, Ryan. Turn around!* But he wouldn't listen to it. It was all too captivating.

"I can't believe I'm doing this," he muttered, his voice ricocheting around the room and causing even more ash to fall from the ceiling and into his hair. Something was pulling him forward, and it reeked of death. The two red lights ahead grew bigger and brighter. Ryan's eyes widened as he lowered the flame's fading aura onto the two red dots. The dots vanished, and then the unthinkable happened.

The match's flame suddenly erupted into a furious fireball and shot itself against the wall. Like a spider-web, thin strands of bright red started to spread across the wall, lighting the room with crimson. There was a ringing in his ears like nails on a chalkboard and scratching and slicing like tires screeching to a halt. He had to close his eyes tight, putting his hands to his ears to close out the noise, but it wouldn't go away.

He turned around and attempted to get away, but he tripped over onto the floor—more like pushed unwillingly. Ryan tried getting back up as the atmosphere around him rose one degree every second, as if someone turned on a furnace. Flames burst out of nowhere and they spread across the floor then up around him like a wall of flame. The ringing turned into waves of fire, as if he was in the middle of a house fire, but worse. Sounds of splitting wood escaped into his mind's eye. Sounds of cracking cement pierced his brain and he heard a tremendous and evil demonic roar of terror that made him what to cry, and he did, like a three-year-old. There was laughing somewhere close by, and it was disturbing to hear, as if someone was taking delight in his fright. Then came the drums, the sounds of iron bars rattling, of chains shaking and glass breaking—was he all of a sudden thrown into an insane asylum, a room designed to scare him straight with sounds and noises of terror?

Ryan remained spread on the floor as the fire grew around him, his hands held firmly around his ears, tears burning the back of his eyes. The floor beneath him cracked and split. An earth-shattering smashing sound engulfing the air as the floor fell apart and he crashed down through it, dying in fright almost, unable to get away or comprehend what was happening. He was suddenly knocked out and his world went dark.

It was a blood-red dark.

PART II

FEELING THE BURN

FIVE.

TWO GATES

HIS MIND FELT DIFFERENT. HIS BODY FELT DIFFERENT. HIS soul felt different.

Ryan rolled over onto a hard stone surface and dragged his eyes open to the horror that were his thoughts. The comprehension was unsustainable. He flipped sideways onto his back and saw the canvas of a dark, blood-red sky spread out above him with particles of ash slowly drifting through the air like fresh snow on a December's night. For a moment he thought his eyes were full of blood and torn apart. He quickly felt his eyes with anxious breaths, his heart beating a mile a minute. He examined his entire body for any signs of injuries, burns, broken bones… anything that seemed wrong. Who was he kidding. Everything was wrong. *I messed up*, he thought to himself. *I did something wrong. This wasn't supposed to happen.*

The air was thick and dry and he sneezed and coughed like he was dying from a poisonous fume that was clogging up his throat and distorting his breathing patterns, making his eyes water and preventing him to stand up. He forced himself onto all fours like a weakened dog, gagging salvia and spurts of blood onto the ground. The smell in the air indicated that he was somewhere that was unfamiliar; a pungent aroma that was equivalent to a recent forest fire or volcanic ash. When Ryan gained control of his senses after several minutes he finally looked around.

"Hello?!" he half-shouted. That's what people said in movies all the time when they were lost. It seemed like a good idea.

Nothing responded back to him, not even the snap of a branch or the rustle of leaves. There was no greenery or any indication of nature around him. Just stone and brick on all sides except the sky where no heaven was sure to exist. He coughed again, tears spreading down his eyes from doing so numerous times already or from fear of his horrific situation—he could not tell.

Beneath his body, he was crawling on top of a cracked stone pathway that went further on into the distance, incased within a light red fog. The path was crudely constructed and looked quite old. Its surface was faded and chipped with dirt in between its crevices and soot getting blown over the top by faint winds. A brick wall was erected on both sides of the pathway, making the path the only option for going anywhere. The wall on his left went mountainously high up and seemed to vanish up into the sky itself, almost inhumanly built. The wall on his right was around forty feet tall and had dark vines growing and spreading over the several cracks in the ashen brick.

He tried getting back up onto his feet but instead fell back down again, frustrated and agitated. His body was aching intensely and it was hard to move his joints.

"HELLO?!"

It was useless. He turned his head around, suddenly noticing what was behind him all along.

It was a portal. It was about ten feet tall and the whole frame was made from great craftsmanship; jet black with engraved red etchings like veins that seemed to throb with light like a beating heart. The wide oval opening in the center looked like silver waves hitting against the surface of water and wasn't making a sound, just moving slowly, in a hypnotic motion.

Ryan painfully rose up and walked the short couple steps up to a stone platform where the portal was perched. At closer examination, it almost looked like it was an entrance into the depths of the bottom of the ocean. The portal was flat with two large horns growing out of from the top, stabbing up into the sky like razors. Right in between them was a glowing red number.

It read: 64,680,607.

The number kept going up and down; never remaining still for more than one second.

Ryan stared into the entryway. Dare he touch it? He put his hand forward until it was inches away. He stepped forward and pushed his hand until it hit an invisible barrier, his hand making a *clunk* sound against it. His one and only hopeful thought was now tarnished. He was blocked from entering.

He turned away from the portal and looked at the path in front of him. The two brick walls on either side kept on going. It reminded him of being in an alley, except instead of buildings on either side there was a wall. The one on his right was possible to get over if he had a ladder or rope, but the one on his left… impossible.

He descended down the stone steps and made his way down the path, since there was nowhere else to go. He kept looking behind him, expecting for something to change or happen. As he limped down the path full of ash and fog, he glimpsed up at the red sky and saw a white full moon—the only thing that looked familiar to him.

He couldn't stop coughing and hacking, his body being internally invaded with foreign plagues. His head was throbbing as the headache returned. It was like the worst hangover ever, times infinity.

"Anyone there?" he mumbled, not having the energy to yell nor wanting to if he could. It was silent around him but there was a certain uneasiness in the air. He could feel the air making a soft beating sound; like that of a beating heart. Except the sound was very low and slow like a dying heart. Ryan felt his own heart as it started slowing down a bit. His whole body was shaking out of fear. Where the hell was he? What happened? He felt tired and exhausted, like he wanted to collapse onto the ground and sleep forever. He was still in a dream—like a trace of some kind. He didn't feel like he was still in reality.

As Ryan went further down the pathway he came to a black gate that was embedded into each of the walls. Ryan walked up to the one on his left and noticed that the closer he got to it, the more chilled he felt his body become. His breath was visible and he stopped a couple feet from the gate, looking through the bars. He saw a white landscape full of snow and the tallest trees he had ever seen—they must have been as tall as skyscrapers.

He didn't dare touch the bars, for they appeared to be frozen solid. He remembered when he was seven and purposely stuck his tongue to a frozen fence at an outdoor hockey rink—a dare from Tommy, which to this day he never let Ryan forget.

He again tried walking closer, but his nose began to freeze and his ears started to sting from the proceeding frostbite that was occurring on the tips. Cautiously, he backed off and turned around to face the other gate that was open ajar. This one had an excess of rust on it, and when he touched the bars they burned his hands. He limped his way through and went behind a pile of broken bricks that were bunched together on the ground close by. He leaned his back gently against the rubble and tried to ease the aching pain he felt throughout his body. He was less conscious of his actions and more into taking risks. He just couldn't think right now. The pain wouldn't let him.

It took him some time to actually contemplate what recently happened. It all still seemed a blur in his mind. Though he knew for sure that he was now dead and in hell. He slowly crept over to the side of the brick pile and looked around at his surroundings.

He was looking at an extensive and destroyed courtyard with burned shrubs, smashed statues and pedestals, burned weeds and a large stone fountain in the middle that held no water in its basin. It must have been beautiful at one point. There was steam rising loosely from the ground, and Ryan didn't dare touch the ground with his bare hands, fearing that he might get burnt. It was hard enough to touch it with his clothes on. He could feel its stinging pain and had to get up before it singed through his shorts and flesh. He saw another brick wall encasing the courtyard, making him feel even more trapped. The place did feel haunted, like an underworld graveyard. The courtyard was shrouded in darkness—a kind of red ghostly mist. When he reached for his cell phone inside his pocket, he didn't feel anything. It was gone. It wouldn't do him any good anyway. He was dead and in hell… nothing could save him.

He achingly got up from behind the rubble and attempted to walk back out through the gate. He poked his head out and looked down the left and right of the path. There was nothing. He went back into the courtyard and tried to think, staring into the blackness ahead. He needed to know what had happened and where he actually was. He just couldn't wait here and hope for the best to happen (which from the looks of his surroundings, wouldn't happen anytime soon). The courtyard continued on ahead into the nothingness. Anything could be out there, anything… waiting.

A second choice, he could continue following the path and hope to find someone or something that would help him. But, for some reason, he felt safer here in the courtyard. There were more places to hide if he needed to. Expect the unexpected.

Ryan decided to walk the courtyard, to examine it and find an answer to something while telling himself mentally to be careful and to stay alert. If it was a dream (which he already ruled out too many times already) then he couldn't die… right? The image of a serial killer shot into his mind; the horrors from childhood that were created from evil babysitters that let him watch such movies.

He limped his way across the courtyard until he reached the dry water fountain, having to sit on the edge to catch his breath. He glanced into the basin and saw nothing except ash and rocks. There were dead vines over the stone and thorns were penetrating its surface. He lay down on the rim and stretched out his back muscles, looking up at the center statue. The statue, which at one point must have produced the water, was wrecked upon recognition with the exception of the shape of a wing that was still partially visible.

His brain wasn't working properly and he was becoming more tired with each passing moment as if he'd been awake for several days. The ash particles kept drifting into his eyes and making them sting. He was so thirsty and his throat was dry and parched. He would kill for a beer right now. He grinned at the thought. He thought about when he dunked his head in that pail full of water at the carnival. Ashlee was right. It should have been beer. Oh how lovely that would feel right now.

Still lying down, he was able to make out something in the distance. With the lack of light that was available it was hard for him to make it out, but with enough concentration he discovered that it was a building.

He pulled himself up and walked towards it as if it was lion that he needed to be cautious of. As he got closer he saw that it was a spectacular structure. It was made of white stone with tall columns that were unstained from the ash and were supporting each of the three levels. There was a wide triangular roof, one hundred windows in various rows and a single door for the entrance. It felt very government. It was built on top of a wide platform made of hardened earth that rose dozens of stories above ground level. A thin and slanted stairway escalated from the ground and up to the platform, almost like a slide.

Ryan let out a deep breath. How the heck is someone supposed to walk up that thing? He would literally need suction cups glued to his feet.

He was so baffled at the construction and design of it all that it gave him even more of a headache just looking at it… but it was what was beside this building that shocked him even more. He walked back a bit in astonishment to marvel at the two black gates on either side of the building. There were no words to describe how big these gates were because it was as if a giant had built them—the size was indescribable. They were hidden behind the darkness of the atmosphere, but Ryan's eyes had started to adjust so he was able to see them more clearly. Both were made in the same tradition as the gate coming into the courtyard. They both appeared locked and he could barely make out what was on the other side because the bars were so thick with not enough empty space in between to see beyond. They were terribly scary, as if a monster was staring down at him. A big triangular black metal sign was posted above the gate on his right. In red electric letters it read:

YOU HAVE ARRIVED AT BLAZING CITY
!CAUTION!

Entry is prohibited by persons without LEGAL consent. Failure to comply will result in LETHAL punishment. Please be CAUTIOUS. Seek APPLICATION and APPROVAL from Mainbreak Hall to GAIN Access.

B.C.S.S: The Blazing City Secret Service

Ryan's eyes drifted down and saw a few small booths in front of the gate, like houses in front of a mountain in stature. Groups of white lights like tiny pin pricks bordered all along the ground and booths like surveillance. One could see the shadows of personal moving in and out of the booths against the lights, patrolling the gate.

There were other people here. That was a relief to him. Ryan was far enough back to not be noticed and he could easily hide in the shadows of the night without suspicion if need be. The sign wasn't lying, that was for sure. He was not going to get through there without getting caught. Another dead end. But the hairs on the back of his neck suddenly went up.

Walking up the slanted stairs and up to the front door was a figure dressed in an orange cloak covering their entire body and head. Ryan stood still, watching as it slowly slouched its way towards the entrance in a slow pace so as not to tumble down. They were doing it with such ease that it almost looked unnatural. Once they reached the top, the person slowly turned around and stood in front of the door, their hands placed in front of them. The figure looked down at him and remained in the same spot for a couple seconds. Then, slowly again, the figure spun around as if on a wheel and opened the front door. They entered and closed the door behind them.

It was a lure. Or was it help?

Ryan was being pulled in several different directions. He didn't know if he should go back to the pathway where the portal was or enter the mysterious building in front of him. Someone was trying to lead him inside, and part of his confused brain was telling him that it didn't feel right at all. Ryan stood in the warm night air and stared at the moon above him. He wanted answers to what was happening, but they weren't coming to him. He looked back at the gate where security was patrolling. Maybe they could help him. Maybe if he explained what happened...

He was strange boy in a strange world. At least to them he was the strange boy and to him this was the strange world. In this moment he could make the right decision or the wrong decision. He had no chance of sneaking past the gate without them noticing. The other gate on his left was another option. It had no security at all guarding it like the other one. It was free for him... but where would it lead to? This was stupid. Ryan sighed angrily and put his hands through his scruffy brown hair in frustration. He can't just stand here. Someone might already be looking at him, spying on him.

The conclusion was made up after minutes of mental torment, and he made his first few steps towards the building. What was the worst that could happen? He could die? All in all, he just didn't care anymore. He was already dead, in his eyes... but the pair of large eyes that where watching him from up in the sky knew different. If only he had the thought to look up and see them...

The walk up the stairs was treacherous as the steps were small and slanted, forcing Ryan to bend over and walk up on all fours. *How the hell did that person do this?* he thought angrily. He must look ridiculous. Eventually he reached the top of the flight and saw the large white door with the letters MM engraved on it in fancy script. He was debating if he should knock, just enter, or if it was even possible to enter without anyone noticing. Ryan just grabbed the door and pushed it open with all his energy. Light flooded out onto the threshold and the brightness blinded him for several seconds—he wasn't used to light for the past couple hours. He stepped in and shut the door quietly behind him.

The room was an elegant library and waiting room. The light, once he got used to it, came from candles in their wall sconces and the strong fires in their hearths. There was a wide parquet maroon rug with wooden circular tables and comfortable red velvet chairs all around. Against the walls were shelves filled with scrolls, maps, books and bizarre objects and trinkets.

Ryan walked curiously throughout the room. It reminded him of a library you would see in a professor's house or that of a scholar. At the far end was a long wooden counter with two door frames behind it with white curtains covering them. His journey to that end of the room was slow. He kept stopping to see the many artifacts or to read some random papers that made no sense to him. He now knew why Tommy was so interested with pictures and literature from older generations and places. He personally couldn't care for literature or history. He hated taking them in school. He was an athlete, wanting to be a professional one day. Why should he have to waste his time learning things he wouldn't remember in a year? Now if the history was about sports and the literature focused on famous athletes and their accomplishments and lives, then he was all for it. In the end though, he didn't want to read about history, he wanted to be history. He wanted to be remembered for what he did and what he could achieve. He wanted his name in a book, a book about him. A book about a hero.

He stepped up to the counter and stood behind a chair. A *ticking* sound was making the only noise in the room and he didn't know where it was coming from. He was expecting to see at least someone he could speak to though. Where was that person in the orange cloak? He wanted to yell out something but he was scared of the possible response he would get. He was feeling like he was in another state of mind, that the pain he felt before was gradually going away. He was slowly getting his wits back. If he had to play a game, he was ready.

He was looking across the surface of the messy counter when he noticed a tiny silver bell. Beside it was a sign:

PLEASE DING FOR PERSONAL ASSISTANCE. THIS MAY TAKE A WHILE, SO PLEASE BE PATIENT. IF YOU AREN'T PATIENT, YOU MAY LEAVE. GOODBYE.

Ryan shrugged his shoulders and *dinged* the bell, wondering where this would take him next. A minute went by and he sat down on one of the chairs. His eyes drifted to the filing cabinet behind the counter and wondered what contents it held. In between the door frames was a portrait of a youthful looking man with the most conceited smirk. His hair was black and slicked back and he had stubble around his cheeks and chin with slightly squinted eyes that suggested an ego. Below the picture was a plague stating:

Carson Jenkins
DEAD Mayor of Blazing City

Ryan noticed that the word *DEAD* was scribbled over the word *Current* hastily with think red ink. The ink still shined from its recent exposure. Or was it even ink? Ryan fidgeted a bit. Well this was a lovely idea.

Once the five-minute mark came around, he became restless from nerves. He looked down at the counter and noticed the many pens and pencils scattered across its surface. Ryan eyed them and put them into perfectly straight lines. Those loose pieces of paper were a mess too. He couldn't stand it. As time went on, he was tempted to press the bell again but the sign made him question to do so. In an attempt to ease his nerves, he got up and roamed around.

The room was extremely quiet and you could have heard a feather drop, except for the distinct sound of flickering flames from the fireplace. He walked up to the nearest bookshelf and started reading the titles on the book spines. There were a couple of empty slots in the rows where books used to be, probably because they were signed out or possibly stolen. He slid his finger against the several spines that were titled: *The Great Imperial City and Its Lies Discovered, The Island in the Sky, The Contract's Origin, Orbs: Necessary or Flawed? The Hateful Goddess, The Path to Our Lord* and *The Lord and His People: A Children's Story.* He pulled out all of these books and sat down on the nearest chair at one of the circular tables. Maybe these books would help give him some information that he needed.

Ryan placed them all on a table and picked up the orange covered book entitled *The Hateful Goddess* and flipped it open to the very front page. It was a rather thick book (as they all were) and was easily falling apart (as they all were). Ryan glanced over towards the counter to make sure no one was there then started to read.

But he didn't get past the first sentence when he looked up and saw a woman staring at him from behind the counter. She was standing still like a statue with the orange cloak over her body. Though this time her hood was down, letting her long black hair fall down to her waist. Her bangs covered her forehead and eyes and her expression was nonexistent against her pale skin. She smiled suddenly.

Ryan didn't say anything, for he too froze in place as if he were a five-year-old just caught stealing cookies. *Why is she looking at me like that?* he thought. He was going to die, he knew it.

He was ready to bolt at any second, raising himself a bit from off his seat. He had a terrible gut wrenching feeling in his stomach, wanting to run back out of the building and escape. Or should he run over and attack her? Better her than me. As if reading his mind, the woman slowly spun around and stepped through one of the curtained doorways and disappeared out of sight.

Before he was able to turn his gaze away, a different woman appeared from behind the other doorway. It was like a game of magical doors.

"Why, hello," said the short, plump woman.

Ryan cleared his throat. "Hi," he said boldly, still alert.

"Sorry about that terrible wait. But I don't care. You should not be here this late. We are about to close." She spoke awkward, Ryan thought. Somewhat different than what he was used to. He got up and approached her steadily, but keeping the right amount of distance.

"I didn't know you were closing… I'll just leave then." Ryan turned around but the woman sighed and called him back, smiling cheerfully.

"No, it's okay. May I help you, homeless child?"

Ryan just stared at her awkwardly, forgetting that he must look very rugged from the smeared ash that was all over him. "No… um… I just wanted to see if you could help me… um… help me?"

"Of course dear. What did you need?" The woman looked as though she could have been in her mid-thirties. She had short auburn hair underneath a sophisticated little purple hat with a peacock feather sticking out. She wore a purple jacket and pants to match. She appeared nice but a little stern, her eyes unusually wide and alert with a bold selection of make-up and tanned skin. She was pretty.

"Excuse me?" asked the woman, putting her hands on her hips. "What are you smirking at? Are you smirking at me? You must because there is nothing else to be smirking at unless you're insane... are you insane?"

Ryan stopped smirking. "Yes?"

"Good," said the woman. "So your purpose of wanting to talk to me? You need help? Why?" She seemed very impatient.

"I just need to... find out... how to get past those gates outside. How do I get into the city?"

She gave him a suspicious look then pulled out a piece of paper and started writing on it. Ryan noticed a nameplate on the counter that said *Renny Kendall.*

"So you would like approval into entering Blazing City? Ha."

Ryan went along with this interview, but didn't like how she laughed at him. "Yes."

"It will take several weeks to know if you're approved," she said in a voice that suggested she had said this many times before, her lips pursed. "I will need to ask you various questions, and you will have to fill out these sheets." She whipped the bangs from out of her eyes and fluttered her long eyelashes as if annoyed. She continued to scribble on the various pieces of paperwork then handed them to him. "Please fill these out with your information. Come on, come on, while we don't have wrinkles, sir. I'd like to leave here in the next five minutes."

Ryan looked at the documents and his heart sank. He would have to make up everything and lie.

The front door suddenly flew open and two men stepped inside. It was like a cloud just covered up the sun on a summer afternoon. The two men held various gadgets and controllers in their hands and around their waist. They wore dark sunglasses and professional dark navy blue suits with polished shoes and hats that resembled police visors. Along their waists were a dozen round objects the size of marbles attached to their belts. Stitched into each of their suits right beneath the collar was a number and beside it the initials B.C.S.S.

"Sorry, this is not valid," said the woman, snatching the papers from Ryan, her eyes wide and darting around.

"But I didn't write anything," Ryan declared.

Both men stepped towards the counter, placing themselves beside Ryan on either side. He felt instantly uncomfortable.

"Who is this?" asked the first man, motioning his head towards Ryan.

"Just a someone wanting access into the city, Number Sixteen," said the woman irritably. "I get dozens of them a day you know."

The men looked at each other, then to Ryan.

The woman cleared her throat. "What can I help you with?" she asked with a smile.

"We need to close down the hall for the rest of the night," said the second man. They both talked in calm, quiet voices but were still stern and powerful.

"What for?" asked the woman.

"There has been suspicious behavior that we have tabulated and sensed during the last hour here." The man named Number Sixteen looked at Ryan again. "We would like to investigate. As the B.C.S.S., we pardon you for the rest of the night."

The woman rolled her eyes. "Sure, I'll just pack up everything and be gone in one minute," she said sarcastically. "It takes thirty minutes to close this building. Unless you two want to do it, then by all means be my guest."

So much for saying she would be gone in five minutes, thought Ryan.

"We will do the necessary closing procedures," muttered the second man, Number Seventeen. "Both of you must leave. If there are any others inside, then we will dismiss them." He looked at Ryan, and in return Ryan looked at him, but not into his sunglasses because it felt like he could mentally dig into his brain and gather information.

"Does Otis know about this 'suspicion'?" she asked.

"He is the one who told us to carry out this procedure," muttered Number Sixteen. "He wishes for you to go home."

"Does he now?" she said, half laughing. She looked at Ryan. "Come on then. You had better come with me. We two are the only ones in here."

"We will check for ourselves, thank you," said Number Seventeen. "You may be deceiving us."

The woman rolled her eyes again. "Whatever," she said.

Ryan was about to say something, but remained quiet. The woman in the orange cloak must still be in here.

"Who did that?" asked Number Seventeen abruptly, pointing towards the portrait of Carson Jenkins, Mayor of Blazing City, and the word *DEAD* written over the word *Current* in red ink. Ryan realized that is was actually blood.

"What?" asked the woman, turning her head and looking taken aback. "Oh dear. What happened there?"

"It's a threat. Warn Number Two," said Number Sixteen urgently, lifting up a slim object and muttering into it. "Both of you are now suspects. You may have to be retained."

The woman turned around, her eyes wide in anger. "Excuse me?! Me?! Absurd! Why would I do such a thing?!"

"I have no idea. But it's sick," said Number Sixteen. "But command says that you both can leave. If we need you, we will find you. Leave now please. No one shall enter this premise." He moved the object he talked into back over his mouth. "Code Three and Two please. Thank you."

"Nonsense," spat the woman. "Me do such a thing? Ha!"

"It's just some light vandalism," said Ryan.

All three looked directly at him and this made Ryan shut his mouth.

The woman sighed. "That will do," she said, motioning her head forward, signaling for him to leave.

"He should actually stay here," said Number Seventeen. "You think?"

Number Sixteen looked at Ryan too, his hand around his belt as if about to withdraw something. "I do think."

"He will leave with me," said the woman matter of factly. "If you need him I assume you will be able to find him." With a flustered face, she stepped around the counter and marched towards the door with an armful of paperwork. Ryan followed in her wake and exited the building. Before he shut the door, he saw the two men staring at him at the other end, not taking their hidden stares behind their sunglasses off him.

"What is your name?" asked Number Sixteen, smiling.

The woman shut the door before Ryan could respond and he was swallowed in darkness once more. His eyes were just growing used to the dimness inside and now all he could see was black.

"Don't worry," said the woman confidently. "They do this once in a while. Secret Service think they can do anything. I will have to have a talk with my husband when I get home. Nonsense. Half the time it's for nothing..." She smiled at him. "Well, I guess you're off to your street where you sleep? Or do you have a home?"

Ryan had to think quickly. "Um, actually, I just moved here. I don't really have a place to stay yet, so..."

"No worries," said the woman, waving a hand and making papers fly out which she didn't seem to mind. "You can stay with me and my husband for the night if you wish. You shouldn't have to sleep outside. Don't worry. We're not that bad." She laughed. "What is your name? Mine is Renny." She fumbled around inside her pocket for something and when she withdrew her hand she slammed her hands together. A white light appeared out from her hand like a powerful flashlight... like magic.

"Ryan," he said, automatically hating himself for giving his real name but forgetting about it after seeing the light from her hand. "How did you do that?"

Renny looked at him as if he was deranged. "What? Don't be silly Ryan. You must have done it hundreds of times yourself."

Ryan quickly nodded his head, never seeing anything like this before in his life. "Oh yeah. I've shone a light out of my hand loads of times.

Totally forgot."

"Of course you have. Well, come along. Surely you can tell us all about your adventures from where you come from. The kids would love to hear that. You do like children, don't you? Our two little ones are always anxious for adventure and stories, but what child isn't?"

Ryan nodded. "Yup. Love children," he lied.

"Wonderful." She looked back to the door and her face hardened. "Probably laughing about nothing right now while eating my supplies of cakes," she mumbled disapprovingly, descending down the steps. "They just do this to make themselves look busy. Rubbish this is. They did seem interested in you however..." she suddenly stopped and examined him. "You're not a criminal... are you? Is there a warrant for you? I hope there is because then that would mean that I'm rich!"

Ryan looked offended. "Of course not! I didn't do anything. I don't even know who that Carson Jenkins is other than he's mayor... or was... or I don't know!"

"You didn't vandalize the mayor's portrait, did you?"

"No! Listen, I'm not that kind of person. I'm not a criminal, vandal, murderer... whatever. Let's get that straight. I'm not a bad guy!"

Renny smiled and continued on. "I hope not. You don't want to go around getting yourself into trouble like that. It's not hard to do in this city, let me tell you now. There are criminals running amuck in there every night. Disgusting beings. Awful city."

Ryan sighed loudly. "I know," he mumbled. "Disgusting." He was glad he didn't find a way into the city before. Criminals everywhere? Probably murderers too. He could have been dead now for all he knew, if he wasn't already.

With her handy help (pun intended), they both carefully walked down the flight of slanted stairs and made a turn to the right once at the bottom. A few meters more and they were standing in front of one of the large iron gates that were on either side of Mainbreak Hall. This one had no security patrolling it.

"I should probably tell you," said Renny, "that this gate is the entrance into Copper Town." She pointed towards the other gate on the other side. "That one leads into the actual city. That's the one that you wanted entrance into. The only way into the city is through that gate unfortunately. I guess I'll have to approve your forms tomorrow so that you can start moving in. You are moving into the city, correct? A young man like yourself looking for business in the big city? I know, I get them all the time."

Ryan grinned nervously. "Yup," was all he said and followed Renny through the gate and into Copper Town. The gate was open all along, he realized.

Once inside, it was possible to make out his surroundings thanks to the help of Renny's light and the few street lamps along the dirt road. Along the road there were row houses, all designed so that their appearances on the outside resembled something that would have appeared in a third world country; dirty, weathered stone that were in the shapes of tall, square boxes that were chipped and cracked on the sides. The occasional small cart or merchant's booth would grace the side of the one road, and they were often used for selling fruits and vegetables or trinkets of some kind. There were very few people on the street, but noises could be heard from inside buildings and inside wooden carriages that were being pulled by horses and coachmen. Ryan felt like he was in the eighteenth century and started to wonder if he went back in time. Meanwhile, Renny was explaining a few details about the town to him. It didn't really seem like a town at all though, but more like a single street. His eyes were trailing all around, only paying attention to half of what she was saying.

"People here are nice and friendly... *if* you are nice and friendly to them. So don't be shy about making new friends for the short time that you are here. Copper Town does have its questionable residents but we are much safer here than inside the city. Once you know what parts to stay away from and who to avoid it's all quite nice... kind of. Copper Courtyard on the other hand is terribly distracting. Nothing interesting or exciting ever happens in there."

Moments later they stopped in front of a row home identical to the others. They walked up a short flight of stone steps to a tall and crooked door with a window to its right and curtains covering the view of the inside with light spilling through.

"This is my house," said Renny as she pulled out a single key and unlocked the door.

The house was bigger than he expected it to be and was made mostly out of wood paneling. It practically resembled a cottage. The joined kitchen and dining room was curved and homey with three fridges and dozens of cabinets. There were three other archways leading into rooms out of the kitchen and dining room, which were all dark from the result of no lights on. The ceiling on the other hand was quite tall and went high up like a short tower. Ryan could see a long staircase spiraling up two floors. Almost immediately, two young children ran down the stairs from the upper floors and started to cheer and laugh, their arms flailing in the air.

"Goodness!" said Renny angrily. "Demi! Jacob! Get to bed!"

"Who is this dirty person?" asked Demi, staring at Ryan.

"I don't know," said Jacob. "But let's push him and find out!"

Both Demi and Jacob had their mother's facial features, deep brown eyes and full faces. Demi had short brown hair which appeared it had been recently cut to give a resemblance to her mother. Jacob was the same age as his sister but slightly shorter, with thin streaks of silver hair against the brown. Both could have been twins, but Ryan wasn't certain. He backed away and was ready to whack them with his watch if need be. He wasn't really a fan of children under the age of fifteen, let alone two six-year-olds.

"No, no, no. Where is Denise? Did she go home?"

"No! Dad is home!" shouted Demi. Ryan never understood why children, or Ashlee, always shouted.

A tall and slender man stepped out from the darkened living room and stood in his tracks at what was standing beside Renny. You would think Ryan was holding a knife about to stab her at any second.

"Hi," said the father curiously. "Who are you?"

Renny laughed. "Oh dear. Otis, you must be wondering who this is. His name is Ryan and he just needed approval to get into the city... but as you were apparently informed, we were dismissed."

"Which is perfectly okay," said Otis. "I felt it was for the best. They told me that someone went into your building at this late hour and they felt it was necessary to investigate."

Renny took off her peacock hat and placed it on the table along with her paperwork. "Well they are stubborn cows. Rude too."

"Now, now," he responded. "I told them to dismiss you and to return home after what they told me about the portrait."

Renny stood still. "Which I did not do," she said.

"Of course you didn't," he said. "It was just a safety precaution." He looked at Ryan and smiled. "Anyway, sorry for being rude like that." He went up to Ryan and shook his hand, giving him a firm grip. "And sorry for asking, but why are you here?"

Otis looked around the same age as his wife, mid thirties. He was handsome with a tall, slim build and a healthy, generous complexion. He wore suspenders with a white button up shirt that was half undone and his suit jacket was draped over a kitchen chair. His hair was chocolate brown and slightly messy with some greying streaks in the mix like his son. His skin was tanned, as was everyone else's Ryan realized.

"Renny asked me to stay the night. I mean, I only came here because I didn't really have anywhere else to go…"

Otis surveyed him and smiled again. He seemed like a friendly person. "No problem. Any homeless child can stay here for the night, but I have to kick you out tomorrow." He laughed, as did Ryan, but then Otis stopped, his face suddenly stern. "I'm serious," he said, patting his shoulder and turning around. He reached for his suit jacket on the chair and put it on, buttoning up his shirt.

"Off again?" asked Renny as she went into the kitchen and turned the faucet on, putting a pile of dirty dishes into the sink.

Otis nodded. "No sleep for the wicked. I would like to have a look at that portrait as soon as possible. I will be back later tonight." He nodded to Ryan then left the house in haste.

Jacob and Demi were still standing beside Ryan. They looked up at him with their curious bulging eyes.

"Adventure time!" yelled Jacob.

Demi grabbed Renny's purple peacock hat and tossed it into the air like a baton.

"Children, this man's name is Ryan. He will be staying with us for the night. Please have respect for our guest." Renny grabbed both children with her hands that were filled with soap suds and attempted to drag them upstairs. The kids just thought it was a grand ol' game. "And it's time for you two to go to bed. Up you go now."

"Not at all!" yelled Demi and she broke free. She ran towards one of the fridges and grabbed a cup of milk then threw it onto the ground and danced around it. Ryan chuckled and smiled. It was beyond hilarious. She saw Renny look at him and he suddenly stopped smiling.

Renny put her hands on her hips and shook her head. "This will not work at all. Ryan, it may be best if you go to bed before them. You appear very tired." She put her hand to her mouth and whispered to him from across the room: "It should give them the illusion that you are gone and they'll get bored and go to bed. It's not often we have visitors."

He nodded. As he went past her she whispered: "Go up to the first floor and the first room on your right. There is a washroom if you need to clean up. You can come back down tonight and get something to eat if you get hungry. Nobody will mind in the least." She looked at him and gave him a nervous smile, putting her hand on his shoulder. "It will be okay,

Ryan. It really will. No need to worry, dear."

He smiled back and continued up the stairs. He did feel somewhat alright, until she said that. If you needed to tell someone it was going to be okay, it wasn't going to be okay.

The yelling was continuing downstairs as Ryan slugged his way up the creaky wooden steps. He turned to the first floor hallway where there was a small loft where he could look over the railing and down to the kitchen and dining room where the kids were still running around. He felt his way against the wall and found his room. He pushed the door open and a light instantly came on. Ryan pushed the door shut behind him, but the light cut off the moment it closed. He opened the door again very slightly and the light came back on. The room was bare with only a bed, side table, a few clean blankets in the corner and random objects lying on shelves over a window. There was a door to his right that went into a washroom. Ryan rubbed his eyes and shut the door behind him, completely shutting off the automatic light. He walked over to the bed and threw himself onto it. The bed was flat but comfortable, and it helped his aching back. He could tell he was filthy because of the smoky aroma his clothes gave off as well as the stains that had already been made on the sheets.

He got up and opened the window beside him, feeling the rush of the warm breeze. He looked outside and saw nothing but an empty street and row homes across from him. Above was the bright moon against the darkened red sky. Ryan kept staring at the houses across from him, and behind the line of houses was a brick wall that expanded in both directions. The wall was white lit from the moon and shaded red from the sky. It was gigantic compared to the houses—the two brick walls along the path didn't even compare to this beast. From behind the wall, the black sharp tops of buildings peaked out above. It was the city, sealed off from Copper Town.

"Where am I?" he asked himself in disbelief. He felt his eyes growing heavy and more tired. His mental capability wasn't very good and he seemed to have been going with the flow of things the whole night. Renny could have been taking him to a death chamber and he still would have gone along.

His head started to bop up and down and he felt his body tilting to one side. He turned his head away, collapsing onto his bed and finally closing his eyes. It only took a couple of seconds before he was off in a dream world where he would be for the only the next couple hours.

However, it only felt like a couple of seconds when he was awakened by a desperate face and a tugging pull. Ryan opened his eyes and saw someone looking down at him in the dark room.

"What is it?" he asked suddenly.

"You must get up," she said quickly, but quietly. "Come with me. You must hide... they are here."

SIX.

INVASION

RYAN WAS YANKED FROM HIS BED SO QUICKLY THAT ONE moment he was laying down for a good night's rest, and the next he was grabbed by a hand and thrown onto the bathroom floor. He looked up in pitch darkness at the figure standing over him.

"What is it?!" he yelled. "Who are you?!"

"Don't yell," whispered the woman in the orange cloak. It was her. "This is urgent my friend."

"I'm not your friend if I don't know who you are," he said, then abruptly stopped when he heard commotion from downstairs. "What is that?"

"Evil people are here to capture you," she said. "Now be quiet."

Ryan heard her rummaging around on the ground then a sharp *creak* cut the air inside the tiny bathroom.

"Get in," she said hurriedly, pushing him forward.

Ryan grabbed onto the floor, but instead of grabbing wood or marble, he felt an empty space.

"Wait! Don't just push me into some random hole in the ground!"

"I couldn't care less," said the woman. She pushed Ryan forward with the ball of her foot and shoved him down through the hole. "It's an emergency."

Ryan felt nothing but air for two seconds, then a *flump* and curse word shook the soft ground that cushioned his fall.

"No talking, yelling, screaming or shouting. I suggest you stay quiet if you want to keep that precious possession of yours."

Ryan looked up. "And what is that?" he asked furiously.

"Your life. You will thank me one day. And what a day that will be."

The door was fastened shut and Ryan was left in pure darkness and stillness. He was somewhere that was small and damp. The sand that comforted his fall was cold and claylike. He crawled around the small quarters and felt a wooden ladder against the wall below the trapdoor. He carefully got on it and began crawling up the short distance. Within seconds he reached the top and felt the trapdoor. Sure enough, it was locked. Ryan slammed the door with his fist and jumped back down onto the wet sand.

He rolled onto his back and stared up at the blank nothingness above and all around him. The occasional water drop would hit Ryan's face, and it felt refreshing. The thought of thirst crawled back into his mind.

With each minute that passed, Ryan grew increasingly antsy and started to bunch the sand together to create a type of pillow for his head. At this point he wasn't particularly nervous, only because he didn't know what was happening. He wasn't sure for the entire night. The longer he waited, the more paranoid he became and started moving around just for the sake of doing something. He desperately wanted to bash the door open and escape.

"What am I doing here? I'm going to die."

Out of frustration, he started kicking sand around. Once the sand settled, he spotted a small sliver of light out of the corner of his eye. He turned around and saw a stream of light coming from out of the ground. The faint aura was escaping out of a small hole that was beneath the sand where he had been kicking around. Not only was there light, but there was also sound. Ryan crawled towards it and pressed his eye against the small hole (which was slightly bigger than his own eye). The room that was beneath him appeared to be the kitchen, but Ryan wasn't able to make it out clearly enough because the staircase was in the way. There was something moving around down there, and whoever it was, their footsteps where the only sounds being made. He barely heard them talk, and when they did, it was quiet and barely noticeable.

Ryan listened to the heavy crashes and bangs from things being thrown around. He backed off from the hole and had a look of complete horror on his face. Were they the men from Mainbreak Hall?

Footsteps emerged above him and whoever was up there began throwing things on the ground once more. They were coming from his bedroom. He quietly slid his body to the far corner of the dark pit and made himself as small as possible.

The ones who were above did some talking, but only in one word responses. Both were male.

"No?"

"No."

One of them snapped their fingers.

"Next."

Ryan dug his hands into the sand and felt the hardwood below its surface, hearing the slumping of footsteps entering the bathroom.

Everything was quiet, until...

Something slammed against the trapdoor and started banging against it repeatedly. All Ryan could do was hold his breath and pray that they didn't manage to pry the door open. He didn't even know if it was hidden under anything.

After a few seconds, the hitting gradually became slower then stopped all together.

"Anything?"

"No."

"Are we done?"

"Not yet. Next."

Their footsteps faded down the hallway and into the next room. Even though they went to search the rest of the house, Ryan still didn't want to move. At this point, he was just too scared to do anything. The most scared he'd ever been in his life. Even more scared than the time he forgot to buy something for Ashlee's sixteenth birthday party.

Hours passed and yet still nothing felt normal. It could have been morning, or at least on the verge of daybreak. Ryan was slumped down on the freezing sand, which was now completely soaked. There must have been water leaking somewhere, but Ryan was too shaken up to worry about such a thing. He had no clue what to think and didn't even know if the two intruders were gone or not. He felt like a bat or some type of cave creature of the deep. He considered yelling something out through the small hole, but he knew it would be stupid of him to do so. Was there anybody even in the house? Where were Renny and the kids? Perhaps he made the wrong decision by coming here. But it felt like no matter what direction he took out there in the courtyard, the outcome would have been bad regardless. Maybe this was the least dangerous of his other choices. He would never know now.

For the last hour, the sound of water trickling down the wall enraged his dry mouth that was aching of thirst. As time passed, this sound only increased. Once the sound increased, so did the dampness of the sand. Ryan was sitting on the bottom step of the ladder when he felt water begin to circle around his shoes. He looked to his right and could feel the strands of water pouring down the wall from the room above. A *creaking* sound tore the silence and Ryan looked up, figuring that the trapdoor was opening. The water around his shoes started to rise to his knee and slip against his exposed legs. He soon found out that the creaking wasn't from the trapdoor itself, but from the floor of the bathroom. The plumbing above him must have been leaking for hours, ever since those intruders entered. They must have done something to it by accident or on purpose, making a pipe break or puncture. He looked down and the water was climbing up his legs, past his shorts and closer to his waist.

"Crap!" he yelled, forgetting about being quiet. He climbed up the short ladder and started pushing at the door, trying to budge it open. The water was slapping at Ryan's waist as if it wanted to drag him down into it. He tried pushing his whole upper body weight against the door, but it just wouldn't budge. He heard wood cracking and splitting as the door weakened but it still wasn't enough. *So much for my upper body strength,* he thought miserably.

"Open up you piece of crap!"

The noise all around intensified. Ryan was hoping that someone would hear him, good or bad. The water was now over his shoulders and the ladder was beginning to break from the pressure of his weight. He took one last breath and banged against the door with all his force, not caring if he was bleeding or getting bruised.

The door opened just as the water started to spill into his mouth. An arm reached in and pulled Ryan out and helped him up onto the floor. He coughed several times and lay flat, breathing like he had just ran a marathon.

He opened his eyes and saw the familiar face of a six-year-old. "Jacob?"

"Wow, so you were down there! I'm a hero again!" Jacob got up and started jumping up and down.

"Where did you think I was?" asked Ryan, coughing into his t-shirt.

"I don't know. I saw water leaking from the ceiling when I was downstairs. Out of a tiny hole. I was only looking for my parents."

Ryan looked up in shock. "Your mom isn't here?"

"No," said Jacob, his brown eyes worried. "Neither is my sister. But I don't care for her."

"You mean to tell me," began Ryan, "that if it weren't for you, I would have drowned?"

"I guess so," said Jacob.

Ryan smiled. "Well, thanks buddy."

The water was now spreading across the bathroom floor and into the next room.

"Oh no," blurted Jacob, shutting the trapdoor quickly.

"Aren't you going to fix that?" asked Ryan "You can't just leave it running."

Jacob looked at him. "Mother usually fixes problems like this with an Orb of some kind. She had better come home soon."

Ryan walked out of the bathroom and into the corrupted bedroom, grabbing the soot stained bed sheets from off the floor and wrapping them around himself to dry off. He looked out the window and saw that the moon was still aglow in its red sky. Ryan still wasn't used to the red…

"What time is it?" he yelled out.

Jacob ran into the bedroom. "I think it's almost dawn. But wait! You can't leave me without my parents!"

"I know," said Ryan. "But that isn't my problem. I don't live here." He moved Jacob aside and left the bedroom, making his way down the hallway and down the stairs. He stopped halfway and turned around to face Jacob who was close behind him, following him like a shadow. "Why are you the only one here?"

Jacob shrugged his shoulders. "I don't know."

Ryan signed and continued on. He entered the kitchen and saw that the entire place was a mess.

"I think they were looking for you," said Jacob.

"You think?" Ryan picked up a chair and collapsed into it.

Jacob looked around cautiously. "I think they're from the city… I'm scared." Ryan could tell that he was on the verge of tears. "Where is mother?"

"Jacob, I just want to ask you something. Those people. They aren't… you know… half wolf or have fangs… or breath fire, do they? They are people… right?"

"Haha, yes," said Jacob, smiling. "That would be so cool though!" He opened and closed his mouth as if invisible fire was flaring out.

Ryan was thinking of the men from Mainbreak Hall. "Did they wear sunglasses?"

Jacob thought for a moment. "They did."

Ryan knew it. He had the suspicion all along. They asked for his name before he left the hall. They were after him. He *was* the suspicious activity. "Did you see anyone wearing an orange cloak?"

Jacob was still busy running around, slicing the air with invisible claws. "Nope!"

Ryan sighed. He honestly didn't know what to say. The front door was still open, and it kept shutting and closing as a breeze blew through the kitchen. The sight of this door, the disastrous house, him almost drowning and the disappearance of Renny and Demi made Ryan look around himself nervously, as if the men were hiding behind a chair. He wanted to know who the woman was who aided him, the same one who lured him into Mainbreak Hall. She obviously wanted to help him, and Ryan needed her again. But right now, he just wanted to leave.

"I'm going now," said Ryan, standing up.

Jacob suddenly jumped up and looked straight past Ryan, his face turning stone cold. He started breathing heavily.

"What is it?" asked Ryan. "Jacob, are you okay?"

Jacob walked back slowly, continuing to stare past Ryan, his eyes showing terror. He ran out of the room in a flash.

Ryan felt a shiver down his spine from the sensation of something walking towards him from behind, a creaking sound from the floor inching closer towards him. He slowly turned his head but couldn't even yell as a small, hideous creature jumped onto him and started hitting him rapidly. Ryan was pushed to the ground and the creature's red eyes were glaring into his. It started to laugh like a psychopath and resorted to beating him furiously.

"You must die! You will die! Die, die, die!"

Ryan attempted to get up and run away, but the creature ripped the bed sheets off of him. Jacob was nowhere to be seen. The creature continued slapping Ryan, then the hitting became slower and less forceful. Ryan lay still and frozen. The creature's face wasn't moving as it started to laugh a high pitched giggle.

"Do you know who I am?" asked the creature.

"No," said Ryan with a scared look. He looked closer at the face and soon realized that it wasn't a real face, but a mask.

"It's me!" The creature ripped off its mask to reveal a face that Ryan was embarrassed to see.

"Are you serious?" moaned Ryan. The face under the mask was Demi, all smiles and giggles.

"Haha, I scared you! Don't lie. I can see it on your face."

"You're right," said Ryan, sliding Demi off of him. "But come on, that wasn't very nice.

Demi threw her mask to the ground and started jumping up and down. Jacob came bouncing into the room with a soaked face cloth and hurled it at Demi's face, who in return threw a broken candle at him. "Jacob and I only wanted to prank you. We *are* bored. Duh."

"Don't you realize that your house was just raided and that your mother is missing?"

"Help us look for her!" cried Demi, now wearing a towel around her head. "It will be such fun. What an adventurous night this is!"

Ryan looked at the front door as the wind kept pushing it open and closed. "It's not for me," he said.

"I saved you!" yelled Jacob. "Demi, I saved him from dying."

Demi stuck her tongue out at her brother. "So!"

Ryan smiled and patted Jacob's head. He walked around the kitchen, scratching his head and picking up broken objects. Jacob and Demi stood huddled behind a chair and were whispering to each other. Ryan eyed them suspiciously.

"No, you tell him…"

"Why me? You go ask him…"

Demi stepped forward. "Can you stay until our mom and dad come back?" She looked back at Jacob. "We don't like being alone at night by ourselves. There, happy?"

"I could've said that," said Jacob.

"NO!" yelled Demi.

Ryan thought for a second. He really wanted to leave. "I should really go," he said.

"Please no!" pleaded Jacob, running around the table and grabbing his shirt. "What if they come back?!"

"Well, what am I supposed to do? They came here for me. Since you two were here when they came, and clearly are not hurt, then you should be okay if they come back."

Demi pouted. "What about the banned stuff?"

Jacob's eyes lit up. "Oh yeah... we don't need you now Ryan. You can go."

"What's the banned stuff?" asked Ryan curiously.

"Do you know where they are?" whispered Jacob to Demi.

She shook her head. "Dad hid them again."

"Hey, what are they?" asked Ryan desperately. "You gotta keep me in the loop."

"Orbs!" yelled Jacob. "Dad banned them from us. We would use those to protect ourselves, but we don't know where he hid them. Can you stay now?"

Ryan wanted to ask what Orbs were, but decided against it so he could hold his identity as someone from their world. Asking would just increase the suspicion that he was foreign. At the same time, he wasn't at all inclined to be their babysitter. He sat on top of the counter and leaned up against the cabinet, closing his eyes in grief. "Of all things," he muttered. "Fine... I'm going to sleep though. Wake me up when something bad happens." Ryan smirked and closed his eyes, pretending to be sleeping.

Half an hour had passed when Renny came running through the open front door in a frantic state, her voice cutting the silence.

"You're still awake?!" she said. "How dare you two run away from me like that! Never again! Do you know how worried I was?!"

"I saved him from our secret hideout," mumbled Jacob from the table, his head buried in his arms and appearing to have just woken up. "You will need to fix it. It's broken."

Renny smiled at her children with a relieved expression. "Good job my brave knight. I thank you for that. But neither of you are to run away from me again. Is that understood? Now please, go to bed. It's very late."

Jacob and Demi lifted their heads from the table and ran up to hug her. Renny looked around and saw Ryan dosed off on the counter.

"Oh, Ryan dear…"

Ryan opened his eyes. "Oh, hi. Where were you?"

She let out a long sigh. "Well, to start from the beginning, I was outside sitting on the steps reading a book as I do every night. I like to read in the fresh evening air when it's peaceful. But that was short lived when I saw those two men coming. They were walking straight towards the house and I knew what they were doing." She picked up some chairs and Demi's mask from off the ground as Demi and Jacob made their way up the stairs.

"Goodnight Ryan," said Jacob, then Demi afterward.

"Goodnight guys. And you knew who they were coming for… me?"

She nodded. "I was so frantic and scared that I grabbed the children and slid away. And I left you behind. I feel so ashamed of myself. But what was I going to do? They wanted you, and nothing would stop them. Not even me. Please don't think ill of me. I would have had no power against those two. I'm so glad you found our hideout though. I did think of that, but I just knew it was too late to run upstairs. Quick thinking dear."

Ryan nodded his head and looked away as if he wasn't impressed, trying to ignore the fact that she basically threw him to the wolves. *You could have done something*, he thought. "Why do they want me though? Who are they?"

"They are members of the Secret Service of Blazing City. They were the two who us leave the hall earlier tonight. It was no surprise when I saw them coming towards the house. I knew it had to do with you."

"Your husband knew," said Ryan automatically. "What if he tipped them off? He's the head of the Secret Service, isn't he?"

Renny sat down and looked at him, now agitated. "This is not because of him, Ryan. And he is not the head of the Secret Service, he is only Number Two. He is like the supervisor, only second to the head of the Secret Service."

"Then why did he leave then? He was looking at me weird. He knew who I was!"

"Who are you then? Are you a criminal?"

"No! Those guys in the hall saw me and knew that I came out of the portal!" There. He said it. He said it all.

Renny closed her eyes and smiled. "Of course. I'm glad you finally told me."

"When did you figure it out?" he asked, embarrassed that she knew all along.

"The first time I looked at you. You are different, Ryan. Your clothes, the way you talk. It was very easy for me to belief that you are not from here, or anywhere in Pheonexia."

"Then Otis would notice that I was different too," he said in a panicked voice. "He ordered them to come here! I have to leave."

"He wouldn't do that," she said quietly, shaking her head.

"Then who else would? Not many people have seen me. He's the head of the Secret Service. That is what he's supposed to do! I'm like a plague or something foreign that needs to be exterminated it seems."

Renny put her hands up to calm him down. "I told you Ryan, he is not head of the Secret Service. He's Number Two. The mayor is Number One. The Secret Service are the protectors of the city. They keep this place as best in order as they can. I feel a bit foolish myself for overreacting earlier. They are only trying to keep things safe around here. Lord knows we need more of that more than ever."

"Whatever! What if they come back?! I need to do something here! My life is on the line Renny! Help me!"

"Calm down!" she blurted intensely. "I understand your panic and worry, but you won't speak to me in that tone. Now, they didn't find you by some miracle and you're safe. They won't come back. At least, not until later. I will talk it over with Otis when he returns. It's all just a little mix up. They will see reason. But until then it would be dangerous for you to wonder around out there with no sense of direction. At least here you have a place to stay. Where you came from and what you did has nothing to do with me and I shall not question it. But you will be protected to the best of my ability until they know you're not a threat and there is nothing to be worried about."

How am I a threat? "But when can I go home?"

Renny smiled at him sadly. "I don't know, dear. Otis would know about the portal and how it works. He's quite well read in those types of areas, apparently."

He turned away and looked down, upset.

"You should go back to bed now, dear. Don't worry. You'll be safe. It's morning now. They won't do anything rash in daylight and Otis will get it all sorted out. It was just a miscommunication. You are a sweet young man Ryan, hardly dangerous. But a little hot under the collar at times I might add."

Ryan smiled. "I get it from my dad. But why did you help me then? Why would you bring me here?"

Renny looked down, her lips pursing. "You are near a man Ryan. I can see that no doubt. But you are still a child as well. I couldn't just leave you behind. I knew you weren't dangerous so that wasn't a problem. And Otis didn't think so either if he felt it was okay to leave me and the children alone with you."

Ryan smiled sincerely at her. "I don't know what I could do to repay you."

She returned the smile. "You can repay me by getting back to your home and being safe again. I don't know why you ended up here but that doesn't matter to me. I'd think something terrible of myself if anything was to happen to you. You are a nice boy—man." She got up from the chair and took his arm, walking him towards the stairs. "Now you go back to bed. When you awake in the morning… well, we will start the process of getting that portal open again for you. There must be a way."

"Thanks," he said. He had never met someone who was this kind to him before. Let alone risk their life for him. "Have a good night Renny."

Ryan tiredly jumped his way up the stairs and back into his bedroom. He shut the door and collapsed onto the bare bed, purely exhausted. He flipped onto his back and noticed the faint glistening of water on the floor. The water must have stopped leaking.

Too tired to worry about it, Ryan shut his eyes and went into a dozing trance. Coming up the stairs, he told himself he wasn't going to sleep tonight. But once he hit that bed his body wouldn't let him stay awake. He didn't know why those men were after him. He didn't do anything wrong. All he wanted was to go home. Was that innocent enough? Why did they want him? Why were they looking for him? Of course the suspicious thing that they were talking about in Mainbreak Hall *was* him. And they told Otis… or the other way around. Something wasn't adding up.

Ryan fell asleep and didn't dream that night. Dawn was approaching, as well as an angry wrath of fury from inside the city's walls.

SEVEN.

THE HIDDEN ROUTE

THERE WERE NO BLUE BIRDS SINGING. NO LAWN MOWERS cutting freshly watered grass. No children were laughing and no planes were flying overhead. No horns honking or hockey sticks gliding across pavements. It was just quiet. It was like a dead silence you found in an abandoned house. It was as if it knew.

Ryan watched the red morning light spread into the bedroom to signal the start of the day. It wasn't comforting to know that he'd have to get up and begin the process of finding a way out of here because he knew it would be an incredible feat. It was a daunting obstacle. The sky itself was still red but somehow seemed brighter than that of night. The orange sun was a full blaze above the row houses across the street from him; an orange disc of melted lava purging the sky into blood shades of crimson. It was time to face the world and the people that he didn't know... and to try and find a way back home as soon as possible, starting today. The thought of having to stay longer than a day here made him want to throw the towel in and surrender, but he was not a weakling. If they wanted to take him down, then he wasn't going to let them do it without a fight. From what he witnessed last night, no one was going to play safe. It was bad, and he could only imagine what would happen if they finally got what they wanted. Renny was just trying to calm him down by saying it would all get sorted out, that is was all a misunderstanding. Like hell it was.

He gathered his thoughts for a few moments in his room then went downstairs into the kitchen for something to eat and perhaps speak with Renny again. However, no one appeared to be home. The silence all around suggested the absence of human life except himself. He was familiar with the feeling of being the only one waking up to an empty house. It happened most of his life. His parents were busy entrepreneurs. His dad was a prominent figure in the recording industry and his mom a housewife. Her entrepreneurial skills were starting up afternoon luncheons with the neighbors and creating her own travelling parties to different exotic locations without her family. She may or may not have tried starting her own bakery at one point, he wasn't sure. She recently took up event planning though, so that was a nice change. There wasn't much he knew about her come to think of it. Ryan wondered how his mother would react if she traveled to this place. She no doubt would have thought of it as… unique.

He passed the kitchen table and saw a note placed beside a handful of polished gold and silver coins along with a folded pile of clothing that looked grotesque and faded. Was he supposed to wear that?

Ryan picked up the note and read Renny's neat handwriting.

Dear Ryan,

I have left you some gold and silver for you to spend on whatever you wish to in the marketplace. I'm not expecting you to leave us so blindly, so please stay with us longer. Otis won't mind. Though please know that he is trying everything he can to find you a way back home. In the meantime, get out of the house and look around. Familiarize yourself with the town. On that note, you can only do this if you wear these clothes. You must not let your identity be noticed for what it is, so therefore I have provided you with the necessary garments. Please use them. I should be back home early in the evening. The children are at school and will be home in the afternoon. At which time our babysitter, Denise, will be here preparing supper and keeping the children in order. I must stress that you don't stray far from the house. Don't wonder into suspicious areas and don't speak to anyone that gives you a wrong impression. Anyone could be watching the town, the house even. If I had it my way, I would keep you inside at all times, but I know that that wouldn't be possible. Please be wary of your surroundings. There is also food and milk in the fridge for you to help yourself to.

Best regards,

Renny.

What happy instructions, thought Ryan displeasingly. He tugged at the clothes that she had left for him. There was a bulky brown top, grey pants, tweet jacket and a patched brown hat placed on top of the bundle. They weren't even slim fit. He looked down at his own clothes and figured that his red t-shirt, shorts, leather strapped watch and sneakers would make him stand out from everyone else in the obvious sense. One of the dead giveaways. He was different, and he needed to change that. He needed to become like everyone else. But by concealing his identity, Renny must have translated that as dressing him up as ugly as possible. Surely not everyone in Copper Town dressed like this. Renny had nice decent clothes, as did Otis and the kids, so as to why he was given these was annoying to him. He grabbed the clothes, as well as the pile of coins, and went back upstairs to get ready.

Once he was dressed and grabbed a bite to eat, he was second guessing if he should actually go outside. He was thinking that there might be someone waiting to kill him or take him away the moment he stepped outside. He glanced out the window beside the front door and saw that everyone walking around looked just like him in terms of clothing. Apparently everyone in this town dressed like beggars, so he would blend in perfectly he realized. The sense of worry started to leave him.

Before leaving the house he went back into the kitchen and dug through the many drawers and utensils. It wasn't hard to find a knife. There were several, each sharper than the next. He picked one out and slid it into the inside pocket of his brown tweed jacket. He had never stabbed anyone in his life before. The thought made his body shudder. He tried to envision himself doing it; where he would puncture the skin and draw blood, but he couldn't. If anyone was thinking of bringing harm to him though… then it would be messy indeed.

Neurotically, he stepped out of the house and into the new world. He looked at the other row houses beside him, all cracked and weathered from the heat. Across the dirt street were similar buildings, with the gargantuan brick wall behind them. He could see the tops of a few spire-tipped towers and skyscrapers poking out from the top. The cityscape was showing presence from behind the wall like fingers rising up into sky, as if they wanted to escape. Inside the row homes themselves were people in the windows shaking out their laundry and sitting on the windowsills reading. Hundreds were walking up and down the street, and the occasional horse drawn wooden carriage would grace Ryan's eyes. This all looked like nothing he was used to. It still felt like he went back in time to the eighteen hundreds or some other time period.

Stepping into the one and only street, he looked up and saw the horribly red afternoon sky with the vile sun staring down at him. He made his way down the road with little confidence in his walking, constantly bumping into people and making them drop things. He wasn't usually clumsy. He was usually well-coordinated and balanced from years of playing sports.

When he made it a bit further down the road, the houses on each side were accompanied with dozens of small booths where townsfolk were selling food, clothes, animals, random trinkets and home supplies. He must now be coming into the marketplace. The cramped and smelly area was crowded, and if anyone was indeed spying on him or trying to scout him out then they would be in for a challenge. It was like trying to find a needle in a haystack.

The merchants were yelling out to him and every other person that walked by to come and purchase something from their store. Ryan felt the few coins that were inside his pocket and decided to buy some fruit because he was hungry again (he had high metabolism, and had to eat almost every hour it seemed).

"What would you like? What would you like?" asked a big sunburnt man with a long and black braided beard. There was a goat beside him who kept going up to people and nosing around in their bags so the man yanked the rope and pulled it away. "You buy this goat here," said the man, his face grinning in an overly friendly manner that freaked Ryan out. "Just three silver. Three silver, ya hear boy? Milk it or feast on a week's worth of good meat. Make a good pelt coat for yur mama as well, yes?"

Ryan grimaced. "I think I'll pass," he said warily, waving his hand away. He looked around at the booth and saw clumps of berries and fruits placed in wooden bowls.

"I'll take this," said Ryan, picking out a bowl of pears and peaches. His mouth started to water just at the sight of them. Every morning he'd make himself a smoothie before school, and the craving for anything fruit related made him crazy, especially peaches.

"One silver!" shouted the man, snapping his fingers for Ryan to hand over the coins, thinking that he would maybe run off without paying. It was probably something that occurred often.

"One silver?" asked Ryan, holding up the coin.

"Yes, yes!" shouted the man, snatching it from Ryan then leaving him to tend to another customer but still keeping one eye on him.

Ryan walked away and bit into the fuzzy skin of the peach, the savoy juice squirting down his chin. Ryan rolled his eyes to the back of his head. It was ridiculous how good he felt right now, and all because of this peach. All the other fruits in the bowl were bright and shiny, as if they were recently harvested.

His nerves and anxiety began to falter as he became more confident in his disguise and that no one was noticing him or looking at him awkwardly. He would occasionally step up to a booth and look at the types of things that they were selling. There was one in particular that had a little girl selling fresh orange juice in wooden cups. The girl looked up at him as he approached her, a shy smile on her plump tanned face.

"How much is your orange juice?" he asked.

"Three coppers," replied the girl meekly.

Renny didn't give him any coppers, Ryan realized. He dug into the coin pouch and pulled out two silver and placed them into the girl's dirt stained hand. She looked down at the coins, her eyes growing big and her mouth opening in surprise as if she couldn't believe it. She turned around to look at her mother and the mother smiled and nodded her head politely. The girl handed Ryan the cup of orange juice then reached behind the counter and pulled out a flower that looked oddly familiar to him, but different at the same time. It had blue petals and a red stem with the thorns cut off. He took it in between two fingers of the hand that was holding the bowl of fruit.

"It's for luck," the girl said.

Ryan's smiled back at her. "Thank you. I think I might need it."

When he got further down through the marketplace, he noticed that there were fewer people. As he kept walking, the light became fainter and the booths less cluttered. He looked behind him and saw that everyone was all the way back in the light. Then he looked ahead and saw only a couple dozen people. The booths in this area had hooded individuals behind counters, showing bizarre and strange objects to other darkly looking customers. There was very little talking.

He stopped moving and felt suddenly afraid. Maybe he shouldn't have come all the way down here. There was hardly any light except for an occasional candle that was lit on top of a counter or a small flickering fire in a random fire pit. A woman with a missing eye and bright red lipstick stared at him blankly as she bought a carved box from a hooded man. A ragged black dog appeared at his foot and started growling at him and sniffing at his clothes. Ryan responded by throwing the bowl and cup at it in hopes that it would run off. The dog bolted away and a man with a hunchback hissed at him as he walked by, glass eyes glaring at him.

Ryan was about to turn back when his eyes caught sight of a something different beside him. Unlike the other booths, this one had cement walls and a door, which made it look more like a small, square building instead of just a counter and drapery. There was a purple rug hanging over the entrance and a light was sliding out from the bottom. The shop was right in front of the wall that divided the town from the city. He looked further ahead into the dark and saw a few other small shops like this one scattered in various places. Ryan slid his way towards the entrance, lifted up the rug and slowly walked into the miniature store. He would run out if he felt uncomfortable.

The space inside was no bigger than a basic bedroom. The room was lit with a few candles all along the shelves and on the counter towards the back. The space was awfully cramped. The most random things that you could imagine were here. Broken plates, old birdcages, ripped books, bed sheets, bowls, pipes, chairs and various other odd items stacked from floor to ceiling. *It was all just junk*, Ryan thought. It was just like a second hand store of some kind. The back wall of the store was actually the brick wall that separated the town from the city. You would think it would be safer for him in the city since no one would think he would be able to get inside unnoticed. Ryan suddenly had an idea, and all within seconds of entering the shop. He had to find a way into the city.

There was no one else in the shop, so Ryan gave himself free range to walk around. He didn't even notice the hooded someone behind the counter who looked up the second he entered, grinning. It took Ryan minutes to realize they were staring at him. When he looked towards the counter again, he flinched in surprise. Definitely a freaky situation to be in. Someone who is watching you without you knowing, and they don't even say anything until you notice them. He could have sworn he was alone…

"I see you," said the man in a raspy voice. "Can I help you with something?" He was slightly shorter than Ryan, but bulkier. A black hood was covering most of his face and a robe covered the majority of his body. All Ryan could see was the man's mouth and nose and his tanned skin. He didn't sound or appear to be over fifty years old.

"I'm fine," said Ryan casually. "I was just browsing a bit. I'm leaving though."

"Wait," said the man quietly. He smiled. "Come here boy."

Ryan looked at him nervously. "I'd rather not." It wasn't a good idea to come in here. What if it was trap to lure him in? *Lures,* he thought. *It was all he was good for.*

The man chuckled disturbingly. "I don't bite," he said. "And I also know things that you don't." He tilted his head downwards. "Nice shoes you have there. Get them from around here, did you? I think not."

Ryan followed his gaze and looked down at his black and white sneakers. He looked back up at him. "What do you know? You don't know me."

The man frowned. "From the moment you walked into my shop I knew that you were different. So different and weird to look at. From the way you moved and your body language. Your hideous clothes don't do you much justice either."

Ryan stepped slowly backwards towards the doorway.

"Most people who live around here stay away from this part of town. Apparently we have a bad reputation for selling to the black market and this causes people to look down upon us. Therefore, they don't just stumble into a place like this unless they were new here and weren't made aware of this before."

Ryan stopped and fought the urge to run out as quickly as possible. "But I am new here. I just moved here from…"

"From where? If you must lie, you must be quicker than that my lad." The man reached behind the counter for a white candle in a cardboard box and broke it in half. He threw it into another box filled with other broken candles. "Mystery one who no one knows. Mystery one who lies in his responses, therefore is hiding something." He snapped another candle. "Mystery one who comes out of the portal."

Ryan shook his head. "I don't know what you're talking about. You're crazy. I moved here to look for work in the city. Stop assuming things about me."

The man was still frowning. "So tell me your name. Surely if you

have nothing to hide then you can tell me something as simple as that. I'll
you mine in return. Deal?"

What are we, in grade two?

"Alnardo," said Ryan. He tried not to swear at the pathetic name he
just came up with from the top of his head. *Alnardo? Alfuckingnardo?!*

"Bad, bad liar," said the man, snapping another candle and smashing
it into the box. "You are a liar! I'll tell the Secret Service where you are
and they'll be here within minutes!"

"It's Ryan!" he blurted.

The man smiled, showcasing his surprisingly white teeth. "Good. My
name is Brazz. I can always tell when someone is lying… it shows in their
eyes. In your case, it showed in your stupidity. Anyway, what kind can I
do for you?" He cleared his throat. "Or can you help me?"

"No, I'll leave," said Ryan quickly, and was past the threshold before
he turned back around. "What are you talking about, me help you? Why
would I help you?"

"Have you ever wondered what the city beyond Dunger Wall looks
like?" asked Brazz, still in his raspy voice.

"Not really," lied Ryan.

"Are you sure? Would you like to see? If you moved here and are
looking for work in the city, this is the quickest and most convenient way."
Brazz got up and pulled away a dark purple rug that was hanging on the
wall behind the counter. It was the first time that Ryan noticed it, what
with the boxes and everything distracting him. Behind the rug was a dark
and hollow tunnel.

"You think I want to go in there?" he asked. "You're mental." Ryan rubbed his jacket above the part where the knife was concealed.

"Am I really?" asked Brazz, dropping the rug and giving him a smug look, as if mocking him. "I have already gathered enough information about you. You are a selfish and vile child who goes to school, am I correct? A conceited and nasty child who thinks he is better than everyone else and happened to stumble upon a world where he is scared and alone. No mommy and daddy to save you. Am I correct there too? Oh, I am so good. A complete and utter moron to say the least. Looking for work in the big city are you? That's a lie right off the bat. Did I mention the part where you came out of the portal that so few know about?" He glanced down at the flower in Ryan's hand for a brief moment then back up at him.

Ryan was angrier than ever, causing him to confess the secret that Brazz already knew. "How do you know about the portal?"

"Because I do," said Brazz simply. He pushed his head forward and leaned over the counter. "And am I also correct in saying that you are very curious about doing something you know is very illegal. But knowing perfectly well that you won't get caught or hurt in the process?"

Ryan laughed. "I guess you know everything about me then, huh? If you say anything about me to anyone, I'll take this knife and stab it right into your skull." He pulled out the knife and let the blade glisten in the candlelight.

"Oh, I won't tell," said Brazz, grinning, staring at the kitchen knife. "I like you. I think we could make a good team. With your hormonal teenage anger and threats and my sly wit and great knowledge, we could take over the world you and I."

Ryan gave him a humorous expression and placed the blue flower onto a nearby shelve. "Fuck you."

"I was serious about that last part," said Brazz, but Ryan had already left the shop, heading back to Renny's house, quick on his heels. The idea of going back into that shop or any other shop down here didn't even cross his mind. The fact that Brazz was insulting him was enough for him to leave, and to prevent himself from doing any physical harm to him as well. He wasn't ready to cross that line. Yet.

He arrived back at Renny's house a few minutes before Demi and Jacob got back from school, and their behavior was worse than yesterday. Luckily Denise, the babysitter, was there so the house wouldn't burn to the ground. She was probably around his age and had great control over the kids, more so than Renny or Otis.

Ryan immediately went up to his bedroom. He was hungry, but food would have to wait. He was still thinking about Brazz and his willingness to let him into the city. He was also angry with he said about him. Ryan was always ready to admit that he wasn't the nicest guy in the world, but he wasn't half the things that freak said. What a creep. What makes him think he can talk to him like that? But for what Brazz was, he didn't come across as someone who would betray him. Was he just a Secret Service agent that was bluffing him? Ryan didn't think so, but heck, what did he know. He was just an idiot to so many people.

As he sat on his ash-smeared bed, he was second guessing himself like he always was. Brazz said that he wouldn't get caught, but Ryan wasn't sure about that. There were so many things to consider, and all of them dangerous. Brazz knew who he was right away even with his new attire, so why wouldn't the people in the city know as well? He shut his eyes and felt the warm breeze come sweeping in through the open window. He *did* want to see the city though, even for a second... just a quick minute... one short hour... for eternity.

The door was suddenly flung open, making Ryan jump up. Demi came strolling in with a cup of water in her hand. "It's Ryan! Are you sleeping? You are not!" She ran out of the room and started making bizarre sounds for no reason as so many children, and Ashlee, often did.

Ryan went down to the kitchen and smelt the delicious dinner being prepared by Denise. He grabbed a chair and sat down beside Jacob, who was peeling carrots while Demi set the table.

"Hey," said Ryan.

"Hello, hello," said Jacob.

"Not you," he hissed.

Denise turned her head and smiled, her face beaming as if he was a friend she had known for years. "Hello. You are Ryan? What a pleasure it is to meet you." She continued stirring the gravy and attempted to reach for a plate that was almost out of reach. Denise was quite average. She had long brown hair that was done up in a ponytail and hung down to her waist. A type of red bandana was wrapped around the top of her head and her skin had a glowing tan. Her clothes were bland and peasant looking, like mostly everyone else. He came to realize that the townspeople of Copper Town were poor folk who had very little money, except, it appeared, for Renny and Otis.

"Do you need help?" offered Ryan, but didn't feel like getting up if she said yes, but would if she did. He kind of just wanted to look at her. You didn't see many girls like her at his school, in a good way. She was a natural beauty, not caked with makeup and layered with glitzy clothing and jewelry.

"It's quite alright. I've got my little helpers. You are a guest."

"That's right," said Demi as she wiped Jacob's carrot peelings onto the floor and placed forks beside the plates, humming a tune to herself.

Ryan looked around the kitchen as he tried thinking of what to say next, but Denise quickly stepped in.

"Did you do anything exciting today? Probably not. There isn't much to do here."

"Actually," said Ryan, "I bought a bowl of fruit. Quite fun... I guess."

"Yummy. What kind? Sounds like fun to me."

"Pears and peaches. I love peaches."

"Peaches are my favorite too. I do like to garden for fun, but it doesn't go over too well because of the weather we have here. Whenever I visit my grandparents in the valley, I do a great deal of gardening under the blue. Do you garden? I guess not. You're a boy and boys don't find much pleasure in such things." She turned around and smiled at him with her unusually large teeth. "Um... do you fish? Of course you do! Where is your favorite fishing spot?"

Ryan laughed. "I actually don't really fish... but I do love to swim and play basketball."

"Swimming is such great fun," she exclaimed excitedly. "I have never heard of, what did you call it, basketball?" She opened the fridge and pulled out a bowl of milk as Demi started washing the vegetables under the sink, while arguing with Jacob about how to fold napkins properly.

"It's all quite fun," she continued. "Back to fishing, I do enjoy it. But I prefer scouting for rare and beautiful flowers that grow in the water instead of sitting in a tiny boat. My little sister joins in sometimes."

"Flowers grow in the water?" asked Ryan.

She nodded. "Of course. Only one though. It's called the Danity flower. It's quite rare to come by. I've never actually found one before. Great luck is said to come to those who find one. Do you enjoy flowers?"

Ryan put his hand on the table, drumming his fingers. "Roses are nice."

"Roses are red," sang Demi, "and violets are blue."

"And you always smell like poo!" ended Jacob.

"THAT IS NOT HOW IT GOES!" shouted Demi, who resorted to chasing him into the living room.

"Tell me what your world is like," said Denise with wonder, ignoring the children's fighting.

Ryan sighed. *I guess she knows too*, he thought. He wasn't expecting this. "Alright... um... we have computers."

"Gosh," she said. "What are those? A type of mechanical robot that does house cleaning?"

Ryan laughed. "Not quite. It's like a television. You can even listen to music and watch movies with it."

"Really? I love music," she said, completely amused. "I play music with my sister during the summer. She likes the violin... not a fan of movies though. I hate moving. So many boxes."

Ryan sighed again and smiled. This was going to take a long time.

At seven o'clock, the sun began its decent behind the houses and people were beginning to go home for the day. For the longest time, Ryan always wondered if time was passing at the same pace as his own world. He hoped that time wouldn't be passing in years, or decades. He'd go back home and Sortonia would be nothing more than a hole in the ground, washed up by the sea and forgotten forever.

Once Denise finished preparing the food, all four sat down at the table for a delicious meal. Denise appeared to be an excellent cook. There were mashed potatoes with garlic and rich gravy, stuffing, salad greens with plums, broccoli and cheddar soup and roasted chicken and leeks.

"Do you make this every night?" asked Ryan, looking over all the food. "It's like Thanksgiving."

"I try and do a different theme every night. The children enjoy it, and that's what makes me happy. I love to cook. It's my passion."

"Nice. I wish I could cook. It's so hard though." Ryan put some salad onto his plate. "What about Renny and Otis?"

"They eat the leftovers most of the nights. They don't mind. It still tastes the same." She giggled. "And back to what you just said. Cooking isn't the hardest thing to learn. You get the hang of it over time."

Ryan laughed. "Not if you've cooked in my Home Economics class."

The whole dinner was very talkative and nice, something that Ryan hadn't had for several months. His parents were always away and Ryan often had to order in or make his own meals, which sometimes turned disastrous. He often ate at Tommy and Bobby's home. Their parents were more than gracious enough to have him at their table when his parents weren't around. Denise on the other hand never seemed to run out of topics to discuss.

"Your world truly does sound amazing," she said as she poured more gravy onto Demi's mashed potatoes. Demi, however, picked up a handful and threw them at Jacob's face, in which he retaliated with chucking pieces of chicken at her.

"It's nothing special, to me anyway." Ryan had never met someone who didn't know half the things that he did. It was kind of exciting to speak of all the knowledge that he knew of.

"You see, we have ships too," said Denise, chewing on some tough chicken. "But they are made of wood. Some of them are used by criminals, too."

"Like pirates?" asked Ryan excitedly.

"Sort of. Some of the ships sail around the ocean seeking valuable trasure or try to import people into their crew. So yes, I suppose they could be called pirates. Most are controlled by the king in that fortress thing out in the ocean."

"Wow," he said. Ryan was fascinated with her world just as she was with his. It was long after they had finished eating did they stop their conversation, the candles so low that they were melting wax onto the tablecloth.

"That was beyond great," said Ryan, pushing his plate to the side.

Demi and Jacob seemed to be quiet towards the end of dinner, probably because they were too busy shoving food into their mouths every other second.

"Dessert!" shouted Demi and Jacob together as they started banging their forks on the table. Nope, scratch the quiet part.

"Aren't you full?" asked Denise in an amused tone. "You had two plates full."

Demi and Jacob looked at each other.

"Yes," said Demi. "We want it later then. In one hour, please." Both jumped from their chairs and ran into the living room to build forts out of the couch cushions.

Denise leaned over to Ryan. "I didn't make dessert tonight," she whispered, giggling.

"That's alright. They're so random though." Ryan got up and started clearing the table with her. He never did this when his parent's made him dinner. For the first time, it made him feel bad thinking about it.

"Yes, they are children after all. I suppose we were like that at one time. Always doing idiotic things, yelling for no reason and making fun of one another." Denise got up and stacked the plates. "Please Ryan. I will clean up. You are a guest. Go and relax. I think there are some books in the living room if you don't feel like playing with those two." She bit her lip. "I do hope I'm not talking too much, because I can sometimes. My grandmother notices it too. I always distract her and she ends up burning the fish."

"Of course not," said Ryan reassuringly. "I always love a good conversation." He looked at her and smiled, but turned away and ruffled his hair up for no reason.

She grinned and flung her arm to the side, accidentally knocking over a cup to the floor. "Oh! How clumsy I am."

Ryan bent down and quickly picked it up for her.

"Thank you," she said, not looking at him as he handed it back to her.

She stared at him for a couple seconds then quickly went over to the sink to wash the dishes.

His smile lingered for a moment then he left the kitchen and jumped up the steps to the bathroom. Once in, he stared at himself in the mirror. His face was slightly dirty and his hair a sty. He was embarrassed that he actually ate at the dinner table like that. He washed his face and hair in the sink then went back into the bedroom to look out the window. It was nightfall. The moon was bright and shined ghostly light on a few people having a stroll down the street with their children. He was going to do it tonight. For the last few hours, it was in the back of his head. Why was he doing it, he didn't know anymore. Was it a trap? Probably. But it didn't seem like one. Brazz seemed sincere, in a black trickster sort of way. It would only be a few minutes, that's it, and at night. No one would see him. Brazz was right, he was curious. His plan was to do it once everyone was sleeping. He could sneak out easy enough; it was something that he was good at and rarely got caught doing. He would just have to wait.

Ryan went back downstairs for the remainder of the evening. Half an hour later, Denise finished cleaning the kitchen and came into the living room to play with Demi and Jacob. Ryan was sitting on one of the couches, watching Jacob tackle Demi.

"Ryan!" shouted Jacob. "You play the monster that I must slay!"

Ryan cautiously got on the floor. "Um, okay. Garr…"

"No!" yelled Jacob again. "Not a goat. A monster! I have to kill you!"

"Jacob," said Denise softly. "He doesn't want to play right now. I'll be a monster."

Demi pulled out the mask that she tackled Ryan with last night and put it on. Ryan glared at it and wanted to rip it to shreds.

Breaking the play time fun was a knock on the front door. Demi and Jacob ran from the living room and into the kitchen to greet their mother.

"Hello!" said Renny happily as she hugged both children. Ryan and Denise looked at each other then went into the kitchen as well.

"Hello you two," said Renny to Ryan and Denise. "I see you two have met. Did you have a good day, Ryan?"

"Yes," he said. "And you?"

Renny nodded. "Everything has calmed down now." She put her yellow hat on the table and sat down, running her fingers through her auburn hair and tidying it up a bit. The color of choice for her attire today was lemon.

"Where's daddy?" asked Demi. "Is he still at work?"

Renny took a few seconds to respond. "Of course he is. He's been very busy lately. He should be home later." She looked at Ryan and he looked back at her. She was lying.

There was an awkward silence.

Denise ran over to the fridge and pulled out a plate of food. "Here, have some of the supper I made Renny. It was a hit tonight."

"I most definitely will dear," she said. "Thank you. You're too sweet. I think, however, your meals are a hit every night. Aren't I right children?"

Jacob and Demi looked at each other. "The vegetable soup is gross," they said together.

Ryan looked at the food that Denise pulled out then back to Renny. "I think I'll go to bed now," he said, walking towards the staircase. "I'm really tired."

"Goodnight Ryan!" yelled Denise.

Demi sat down beside Renny and placed her head on her shoulder. "Ryan, I..." began Renny.

Ryan turned around. "Yes, sorry?"

It looked like she wanted to say something, but couldn't with the other three in the room. "It's alright, dear. I will tell you tomorrow. Have a good sleep. All will be fine."

Ryan smiled and nodded his head. He went into his bedroom and shut the door, making the automatic light turn off. He looked back at the door.

"It's shut," he said to himself, having to count to three before going getting into bed.

Now he waited. Hopefully he wasn't about to do something that he would regret. Renny indicated he would be safe... at least for tonight. All was good.

He had only dosed off for a couple of hours when he woke up, afraid he might have over slept. He looked around the room then got up and went over to the window. No one in sight. Would it look suspicious if he was the only one on the road? What if Brazz wasn't there? Or perhaps Brazz wouldn't even let him go after his rude departure. Ryan was living up to his reputation of a stupid boy. But as long as he had his knife secured in his pocket, he felt fine.

It was like an adrenaline rush. Sneaking out and doing this; it was pumping him up, having done it enough times back home to go to parties. He opened the door to the bedroom and looked around, listening intently for any noises. There wasn't any. He slowly crept out and tip-toed towards the staircase, like a cat. He walked down into the dark kitchen and made for the front door. He opened it and stepped out.

Ryan was bewildered on how easy his escape was. He jumped down the few stone steps and quietly jogged down the dirt path; keeping to the shadows. At least he knew that no one would see him if they looked out their windows, but his greatest concern was that someone would jump out and attack him.

Not before long, he was in the black market. He was horrified to learn that there were even more people than before. He knew that it was a black market, so of course it would be more popular at night. He felt a little better knowing that he wasn't the only one lurking around, and no one seemed to care about his presence.

He quickly found the shop that he needed; the one that had the same faint light seeping out from beneath the dark purple rug hanging over the entrance. Did Brazz ever sleep?

Ryan poked his head inside first to make sure that whatever was supposed to be inside was still there and that nothing was out of the ordinary. He pushed the rug to the side and stepped in, seeing Brazz behind the counter wearing his dark cloak with almost all of his face hidden. He was busy tearing wooden bars off of broken birdcages. The useless junk all around seemed more overwhelming than last time. Honestly, who would buy this stuff?

"Well, who do we have here?" said Brazz in a scratchy chuckle. "I always thought one got more flies with sugar than vinegar. But it seems to be the opposite."

"I want to see the city now," said Ryan, which sounded more like a demand. "Just for a second. Or a minute."

"Or for sixty-four million years?" asked Brazz in what sounded like a serious voice. "It will not be a minute or a second. It may at first, but then you will want to come back to see more and more until you want to stay for good. It's an interesting dynamic."

"No, just one look for me thanks," said Ryan. "Have you seen it?" It was hard to talk to Brazz because you could never see his eyes, only his mouth and nose. His teeth were beautifully white, with light stubble forming around his mouth.

"Of course I have seen it, boy. Hundreds of times." He motioned his head towards the rug covering the hidden route. "I have a great luxury to go whenever I please. As does my gang."

"Gang?" asked Ryan.

"I thought you wanted to go," said Brazz. He threw the rest of the wooden birdcage into a cardboard box. "You don't seem that eager to see the city so I suggest you leave now and save us both the disappointment."

Ryan sighed loudly. "Yes, I want to see it. Will you let me?"

"Absolutely," said Brazz confidently. "But first…" He reached under the counter and retrieved a square metal box with a lock. He opened the lid and pulled out a tiny object that looked like a black marble with a small tag attached to it. "You will need this," he said, handing it to Ryan.

Ryan looked at it in amusement. "A marble? Am I supposed to protect myself with this?"

Brazz gave him a weird look. "Marble? No such thing. Have you any idea what Orbs are?"

"Have no clue," answered Ryan, but then thought for a moment. Of course he did. He heard Demi and Jacob talking about them the previous night.

"Orbs," said Brazz, "are tiny capsules that hold amazing powers that no normal human can posses. They are mostly used by people who are normal and aren't special in any sort way such as yourself. There are hundreds and hundreds of different kinds and most are manmade. Most are made here in the city of fire."

Ryan rolled the capsule in his palm. "And the other ones that aren't made here?"

"They are made... by other means," he said. "Those, most believe, are the most powerful of all Orbs. The ones not made in Blazing City but by people like you and me in their homes or out in secret. All illegal however. They produce actual magic... dark incantations of the darkest nature. Or, perhaps... even white magic. The one you are holding was created by myself from years and years of research and development. No other like it exists. Instant death would fall upon me if I was to be found out."

Ryan looked down at the black Orb rolling in his palm. "What does it do?"

"Read the tag," he said.

Ryan held the tiny tag up to his eyes and tried reading the writing. "The prints too small."

"It takes a few seconds for your eyes to adjust," said Brazz. "Just wait a moment."

A couple seconds later, Ryan saw the letters increase in size until he could read the black ink perfectly.

The Veil Orb

May you use this to become invisible only under the black of night.
T.U.D: 15 Minutes.

"What does T.U.D stand for?"

"Time Until Diminished," answered Brazz. "That is how long it will last until the power wears off. I tried making one that would last longer, but I wasn't successful. Creating Orbs is a dangerous business."

"Explain," said Ryan.

"City."

"I know, soon. I want to hear this first. Please? I'm interested."

Brazz rolled his head as if annoyed. "Fine, but you need to go soon before the sun rises. They only work at night. So like I said, making Orbs is a mad business. You can't create one that has already been made by someone else, or you will die for attempting a forgery. It takes years of patience and desire... and blood."

Ryan nodded. He shouldn't have asked. "Alrighty then. Don't think I'll be doing that anytime soon. How do I use this thing anyway?"

"Simple. You are an Orb virgin. All you do is drop it on the ground, against a wall, slap your hands together, whatever, and the shell will break and the power will be unleashed. If it's an attack Orb, you must be sure to throw it at your enemy and not accidentally use it on yourself. That would be disastrous. For certain Orbs, the power only goes to the individual that activated it—like this Veil Orb here. It is always best to break it in your hand. The power will work faster that way."

Ryan put the black capsule between his fingers and closed his eyes. He slapped his hands together and broke the Orb in his palm.

He opened his eyes. "Did anything happen?"

"Yes," said Brazz. "See? It happens just like that."

"How do I know you're telling the truth?".

"I never lie," mocked Brazz, reaching under the counter and pulling out a silver hand mirror that had little blue crystals embedded along the sides.

Ryan grabbed the mirror and looked at himself. He couldn't see his reflection through the cracked glass.

Brazz turned around and reached for the purple rug covering the tunnel. He lifted it up and revealed what looked the inside of a demon's mouth. It was so dark.

This was all happening so fast. "Should I know anything else?" asked Ryan as he walked into the tunnel.

"Just be back before the invisibility wears off. Security is very good at spotting unauthorized people at all hours of the day. Don't get caught… or die."

Brazz dropped the rug and Ryan was left in darkness as he walked through the tunnel. He felt blind, he also felt like he was back under the trapdoor beneath the washroom. He couldn't believe that no one would be able to see him. He wondered if Brazz would let him take some back with him. Could you imagine what he'd be able to do? He'd torture Ashlee for months.

It must have taken thirty seconds to pass through the wall. The exit was smaller than the entrance so when Ryan reached the end he had to bend over in order to pass under it. He stepped out from the tunnel and stood in an alley behind a group of buildings. The alley was dark, damp and secluded—so secluded that it seemed as though no one ever came down here. Running towards him from down the alley were two masses wearing hooded cloaks. They ran passed him carrying two black sacs over their broad shoulders. Both were taller than him, as he himself was only five foot ten where they must have been six four. They stopped beside him and laughed.

"Are you new guy?" asked one of the hooded figures.

"He is," said the other. "He just came through Hoarder's Tunnel."

"I did," replied Ryan. They must have been invisible as well. People who were using the Veil Orb could probably see others who were using it as well.

"Brazz is hiring again after all these years," mumbled one of the cloaked men. "You shall have fun newbie. We will see each other again."

They both chuckled and went into the tunnel, which you could barely notice because it blended into Dunger Wall and the darkness of the alley so well.

Ryan took a deep breath and went on going down the alley until it opened up to a street where the light was more apparent. Everywhere he seemed to go, whether it was Copper Town or the city itself, the light always had a slight red tinge to it.

Ryan steeped onto the street and saw the vast scale of Blazing City all around him. Most of the buildings along the street were solid black and incredibly tall, the tops ending in sharps tips or spires. They seemed to be rough in texture like rock. The street lamps lit up the wide concrete roads as people in red carriages rode passed him and others walked up and down the sidewalks with no sense of purpose in their destination. It all looked so vile, like a strange city from a gothic comic book. All the skyscrapers were magnificent creations. Apartments and hotels littered the side streets, towering above him like mighty ghoulish fingers. Great business towers overpowered the others and various other shops accompanied the scene. The towers that rose above him were all equally threatening, like he was entering a dark lair that was forbidden to all. It was also quiet, very quiet. He could hear faint noises in the distance, like hammers being hit against metal and strange spurts of anonymous sounds. It wasn't what Ryan expected. The black marketplace seemed like a fun amusement park compared to this.

He continued walking down the sidewalk and noticed that whenever he passed someone, they would look at him and scratch their heads in confusement, thinking that a wind blew passed. There was no wind blowing however. No wildlife or vegetation to be seen or heard of. There were pubs with flashing neon lights over the entrances and groups were seen walking in and out, laughing drunkly. There also seemed to be brothels across from it, with women in loose clothing standing by the entrance as they smiled and held the hands of men. Further ahead, smoke was billowing into the sky from the tops of factories. He might have been in a part of the city that was very shady, like a bad neighborhood. Hopefully the rest wasn't like this.

He saw a security personal walking along the streets, the same ones who were patrolling the gate beside Mainbreak Hall. Their black sunglasses made them almost anonymous and their navy blue suits were pressed neatly against their bodies while they walked around with their heads up. Beams of light shone from their hands, the same light that Renny used before when she brought Ryan into Copper Town. The Secret Service was no doubt the police of the city.

Light particles of ash was blowing in the air as Ryan stopped and squinted ahead of him, not wanting to go any further because of distance. It was like he was attached to a leash and had reached the end of it. He couldn't risk going any further… he only had fifteen minutes.

Ahead of him, the road seemed to curve downward like a steep hill and he was able to see the whole of Blazing City stretched out below him. If the devil had ever built a city, this would have been it. Of all the buildings, there was one tower in particular that attracted Ryan. The hundreds of windows were specs of pale grey against the black, smooth texture of the glass sides. The top was also flat, the only one of its kind. It was the biggest building in the city. There was something important about that tower though, he knew. It was the focal point, as if all the other buildings were secretly guarding it. It felt dangerous, but he was drawn to it at the same time. It was like he needed to be there, like it would have the answers to his questions.

He pulled his mind out of the gutter. He just gave himself some food for thought. It was time to go back. He wasn't saying goodbye though.

Ryan turned around and made for the tunnel. As he ran back, a man was looking down at his vast city from within that far away tower.

EIGHT.

TO TRICK A MONKEY

IT WAS HARD FOR RYAN TO SLEEP THAT MORNING BECAUSE he kept tossing and turning constantly. He would sometimes wake up involuntarily and be yanked from a dream that felt like a fifty-hour film. It was probably one of the worst sleeps in his life, and his dreams were just as unnerving and kept getting more violent with each passing day. He only had three hours of sleep, and once the screams from Demi and Jacob signaled the start of a new day, Ryan rose up agitated and threw on his own clothes instead of the grey and grotesque ones that Renny gave him. He just felt more comfortable in his own. He figured that he was safe now, and that his clothes weren't that obvious to the people of Copper Town. All he had to do was throw on the tweed jacket and hat and he would be fine.

The instinct to go back into the city pounced into his mind almost immediately after getting out of bed, for that was all he was dreaming about. That city and its dark and haunting appearance. The beautiful lights and bustling factories with spire tipped skyscrapers. The gorgeous blood-red sky plagued with awful smells of decaying matter of all sorts. Yet, he only saw a small part of it, and in the distance he knew that there was more to witness and be a part of.

Another issue that had been biting away at his brain for the past couple days was Otis and why he hadn't been around. Renny was always reminding Ryan that he was one of the heads of the Secret Service and that he was very busy. It could even be possible that the reason those men didn't come back again was because of Otis. Was all of this commotion happening because he came from another world? There was no other reason as to why they wanted to capture him. He was obviously seen as some kind of threat. Overall, Ryan didn't like Otis. He didn't know what to make of the guy. It's not like he was here, in this house helping him like Renny was. But maybe he was helping him in other ways. Renny kept saying that if the city wanted to capture him then they would have done so by now. She knew that he was getting paranoid, but he felt like he had to be. It would have been naive of him to think he was safe in a corrupt world like this one.

As always, Renny wasn't home when Ryan went down the spiraling stairs and neither were Demi and Jacob. He felt guilty that they had to go to school (but not too guilty). Ryan didn't even notice a school around here when he was roaming around the town, but it could have just been in a house somewhere.

After eating leftovers from last night, he rushed out the door and made the short distance to Brazz's shop. This time he knew where he was going, but he still had the habit of bumping into people and making them drop their belongings. They were reasonably nice about it though.

Another thing that Ryan noticed over time was that there wasn't any wildlife. He saw horses pulling the wooden carriages, but no birds were flying in the afternoon sky and no squirrels were scurrying around on the few burned and naked trees. To be truthful, Ryan was a little anxious about seeing possible wildlife, thinking that the birds might breathe fire or the squirrels would have massive claws to rip through flesh—basically a reincarnation of Ashlee, which would be equally terrifying.

As he entered the darkened portion of the marketplace, nobody seemed to look at him strangely or awkwardly like last time. It would be silly to say that Ryan wasn't nervous about venturing back into the city, especially when it was light out. But he'd be invisible, and you just couldn't see the same things at night as you could during the daylight hours. It would be like a whole other experience.

He walked into Brazz's stone shop and there he was again, sitting behind the counter and polishing silver spoons and forks. *Most likely stolen,* he thought. He knew he was a part of a gang. He said so himself last night but Ryan blew it off before he could further question him about it. Those two men he met in the city worked for him, obviously. He was getting deeper into a world he never wanted to be a part of in the first place. But the scariest part of it all was that he secretly liked it. He wanted more.

Brazz's head was down; the material of his hood made of silk with gold embroidery along the edges. "You know, these aren't even real silver," he said, throwing a fork onto the counter. "I can't sell these. Nobody wants fake. They want the real deal. My team has been doing very poorly lately. Probably because of tighter security. I guess we'll just have to become even smarter than them."

"Well, you are stealing," replied Ryan as he stepped forward.

Brazz grunted. "What I think is that the city is becoming more aware of spotting the regulars now. I've been using the same men for a while. Countless years. I guess it's time for a recruitment of sorts."

"How can the city spot them if they're invisible?" asked Ryan.

"They can't see them. But the fools are slacking off and are staying longer than the Orb's T.U.D and people start seeing them. Some were even caught by Secret Service and taken away a couple weeks back. Very nasty business. Never saw them again." He examined Ryan.

"Can I go back then?"

"Back where?" asked Brazz.

"Into the city." He wanted to go back, but didn't at the same time.

Brazz laughed. "Don't you remember? The Veil Orb can only be used at night. Come back later."

"But I want to go now. Is there not a way?"

Brazz reached for the purple rug over Hoarder's Tunnel and lifted it up. "Go," he said.

"I can't. People will see me."

"I'm sure you'll be fine. Just stick to the side streets and hide your face. It's quite easy. I do it all the time." He grinned and flashed his straight, white teeth.

Ryan looked down the dark tunnel but didn't move. *Wow, he clearly thinks you're an idiot,* said a voice inside his head.

"What was that?" asked Ryan, looking around.

Brazz tilted his head. "Did I say something?"

"Yes, you… never mind." Ryan pursed his lips. Great. Now he was hearing things again.

"But before you go," continued Brazz. "I must ask a favor from you."

Ryan gulped hard. He didn't like where this was going.

Brazz coughed, and it sounded suffocating, like a chain smoker. "You see, none of this stuff in sellable. Complete garbage." He pointed to the clutter around his shop. "And I need something shiny and expensive to sell pronto… that is where you come in. Not many people have been visiting my shop lately, and I need more traffic."

Ryan looked around the shop. "There are tons of stuff in here. Look, there's mops, plates… um… bottles."

"That's all junk. Just stuff to dress the store up with. Nobody actually buys those things." Brazz tossed the box of silverware into the garbage. "It's an illusion, see."

"I would buy something," replied Ryan.

"You would do no such thing."

Ryan went around the counter and lifted up the rug. "If you're asking me to steal something for you, I'm not going to do it. I'm not a thief."

"I believe you," said Brazz. "But with great risk comes great reward."

Ryan looked at Brazz. "What reward?"

"Would you like to spend a night in the city of fire? It may come in handy later on."

Ryan shook his head. "Can you please start making sense? Why would I want to stay in *that* city? There are people who want to capture me. I'm not going to make it easier for them by being a sitting duck. Do you think I'm stupid?"

Yes, said the voice in his head.

Brazz thought for a second. "If they wanted to capture you, they would have done so by now. All I'm saying is that the irritating mayor is the one who ultimately wishes you captured. The longer you aren't, the brattier he'll become. I believe this is the calm before the storm for you, young man. I'm just giving you the chance to have a safety net in case anything was to happen. If I were you, I would want something to protect myself with."

Ryan sighed, rubbing the jacket above the part where he hid the knife. "What do you want?"

"For your own safety, I think you should stay in the city of fire. Carson doesn't know about my hidden route through Dunger Wall. He still suspects that you're still here in Copper Town. He knows you can't get through the city gate because it's always monitored by his Secret Service. He will send them to look for you here, not in the city. They could already be here, waiting for their move. I'll give you gold and silver to purchase a room inside a hotel if you were to get something valuable for me to sell."

"But what about Renny and Otis?" he asked. He didn't like how Brazz used the word "get."

Brazz frowned. "Forget them. What a horrible idea it is to care about those two. You talked about being a sitting duck in the city, what do you think you will be in that house? A sitting goat, perhaps. The Secret Service will come back to that house when you least suspect it, mark my words. They could be following you right now, listening to our conversation as we speak. You think that woman and her poorly behaved trolls will keep you save once the time comes?"

Ryan knew that he was right. How stupid he had been—or will be.

"Anyway, are you excepting of my offer? I'm only trying to help a fellow minority out. The only reason I'm even suggesting this is because my men are pure useless now. It's like they don't care anymore. So drown them I say."

Ryan looked down at the dirty floor, kicking a small pebble of rock to the side. "I can't steal something from inside the city. I won't feel safe if I'm not invisible."

"Then get something here," offered Brazz. "Renny's house, perhaps. Who knows what she has stashed in there." He looked at Ryan's clothes. "What happened to those rags that that silly woman gave you?"

"I decided not to wear them anymore," he replied proudly. "I think this jacket and hat do just fine."

Brazz surveyed him up and down. "I suppose," he said. "But you aren't confident enough in them yet to venture into the city wearing them?"

Ryan shook his head. "Just safe around here."

"I must tell you then," said Brazz. "That you must not tell anyone about Hoarder's Tunnel. If you do, I will have to kill you. Or…" at this he gave a big and terrible smile, "…you will have to join my gang of thieves—the Thefty Thieves of Thirty—and once you join, you can never leave, or you yourself will be hunted down and killed. Agreed?"

Ryan looked horrified. "Yes," he said quietly. What had he gotten himself into? But he knew for a fact he would never reveal Brazz's secret.

"Don't look so scared my wee boy. But if you're going, go now." Brazz lifted up a small black pouch. "You may put whatever you find in here once you have retrieved it. It's all quite simple. I'm not asking for anything big, just big enough to fit in here." He dangled the little pouch in front of his face like someone would dangle a toy in front of a cat.

Ryan snatched the pouch and put it into his jacket pocket. Without another word, and the look of extreme seriousness on his face as if he was going to war, he left the shop to set his task in motion. *Let's just get this over with*, he thought. Every little thing will help him get closer to home. He'd try and find something that he knew would not be missed by its owner.

He went back up to Renny's house and dreaded the hateful task he was about to do. He felt like he was betraying Renny's trust. He went inside and looked around the kitchen, knowing that what he needed wouldn't be here, but upstairs. He jumped up the stairs until he reached the loft and turned towards the hallway where Denise suddenly emerged. Ryan was startled at the sight of her.

"Hi Ryan," she said enthusiastically, reaching behind her back for her long ponytail and adjusting it for no reason. "How are you today?"

He smiled awkwardly. "I'm really good. How about you?"

"I'm actually in a tight pickle. You are just the person I need."

"What can I do for you?"

She brought out a small red bag and quickly went to the railing of the loft and looked down to make sure no one else was home. "I have a birthday present for Demi. She is turning seven in two days and I got this for her." She opened the bag and withdrew a dark blue pendant in the shape of a flower.

Ryan looked down at it and gulped. "It's beautiful." He couldn't believe the freak coincidence that was happening at this very moment.

"It's the Danity flower. Could you hold on to this for me until tomorrow when I find good wrapping for it? I was going to hide it somewhere here, but I just know she will find it. Her and Jacob, that's all they do is snoop around. I have a bad tendency of miss placing things and never being able to find them." She placed the pendant back into the bag and handed it to him.

Ryan shook his head, not taking it. "I really shouldn't. I lose things all the time too. You'd be better off holding on to it." He couldn't take his eyes off of it… it was so pretty, like her.

"Oh please? Maybe you can put it in your pocket." She held it out to him again and when he still didn't take it she shoved the bag into his hand. He slipped it into his jacket pocket unwillingly.

She smiled and hugged him. "Wonderful! You are a great friend to me. Thank you. But look at the time. I must prepare lunch for the little ones. Do you want to help?"

"I thought I would maybe go outside and play in the street first." Ryan tried not to laugh at his response.

She smiled. "Of course! Have fun and try not to get dirty. Lunch will be ready in about an hour. Trout sandwiches. Yummy in my tummy!"

When she left down the stairs, he removed the pendant and slipped it into the pouch that Brazz gave him and put it back into his jacket. He didn't care anymore. He needed it more than Demi.

Ryan left the house and walked back to Brazz's shop with a heavy heart that started to emerge from within him. What was he doing? This was not him. He fought the urge to run back and give it back to her, to tell her of what he doing and to tell her all about Hoarder's Tunnel and Brazz. But then he would think about the city… and that all disappeared. This was about his safety. Hopefully she would understand.

He went into Brazz's shop feeling like crap, but relieved that he didn't have to go to extreme lengths to take something that wasn't his. And really, what would Demi do with the pendant besides throw it at the wall? Stupid gift for a young child.

"Oh my," said Brazz shockingly. "That was a mere half hour. I must say you are quite good at this. Do you have the treasure that I seek?"

"Yes I do," said Ryan, placing the bag with the pendant inside onto the counter.

Brazz opened the pouch and his mouth dropped in awe. "This," he said slowly, "is a great find." He removed the pendant and held it between his fingers, examining it. A sapphire ring was gleaming on his index finger. "This is very expensive and rare. Are you sure this belongs to that woman?"

Ryan shook his head. "No. It was… someone else's."

"I figured," he said. "This is worth hundreds and hundreds of gold if not more. If it was hers, then someone must have given it to her, or she herself stole it. I have never seen one like it before; blue gold I presume."

Ryan stared at the pendant and couldn't help but be transfixed by it; the blue stone seeming to glow and shine… he wanted to rip it from Brazz's hands and run off. Brazz looked at him then quickly shoved it under the counter as if he could read his mind.

"I'll now give you the coins necessary to stay in one of the pleasant hotels within our great city. And for doing such a fierce job, I'll give you triple."

"The city isn't that great," replied Ryan.

"No…" said Brazz quietly, "… no, it's not. You're right. It's a terrible place." He fumbled around in a drawer and retrieved a sack of silver and gold coins, then handed them to Ryan inside a pouch.

"What is your money called here?"

"Dressels are gold," replied Brazz. "Comets are silver and flaks are coppers. Flaks are basically worth nothing, comets are worth fifty coppers, and one dressel is worth ten comets. As you can see I gave you a fair mix of gold and silver. It should keep you happy."

"I have no doubt," said Ryan with a grin. He took the bulking pouch and shoved it into his pocket. His eyes glanced around the store at a wooden birdcage hanging from the ceiling and bronze candlesticks grouped on shelves, then back at Brazz, pondering a question that had suddenly risen. "What I don't understand," he said, "is if you sell stuff like crystals and jewelry, why do you have so many pointless and random things in this store? How do you… sell your… valuable items, may I ask? How do you have all this money?"

Brazz closed a drawer and nodded his head, appreciating Ryan's question. "It's all an illusion," was all he said, saying nothing else. Ryan left it at that even though it didn't really answer his question.

"So are you going tonight?" asked Brazz.

"I don't know."

"Well," he said. "You'll have to figure it out on your own. You must leave me now. I'm busy and need to concentrate. Have fun with whatever you're going to do."

Ryan looked at the purple rug then slowly turned on his heel and departed out of the shop.

"I think though," said Brazz casually. "That if you really wanted to go home, you would be trying all you could to do so, even pushing me for more answers."

Ryan stopped but refused to turn around. He was going to say something back, but didn't and continued out of the shop.

It was midafternoon when Ryan made it back to Renny's house. He wasn't sure if he was going to use the hotel that evening. Would he be safe enough for another night here, or would tonight be the night the Secret Service came back to seize him?

He lazily opened the large refrigerator door and looked around, completely disgusted at its contents and wrinkled his nose. There was milk that had spilled everywhere, moldy bread and countless leftovers that Denise had cooked and had gone bad. He slammed the fridge and sat down at the table with a bowl of raw carrots. He really did hate this house. The wood paneling and mismatched furniture gave it a terrible cottage feeling. If Renny and Otis had money, why were they living in a place like this? Why not in the city?

As usual, Demi and Jacob were running around as Denise was working on the trout sandwiches. He wasn't that hungry, probably because he lost his appetite from the smell that was coming from the burned trout that Denise was cooking.

"Oh no..." she moaned. "I guess I'll have to start over again. Looks like a late lunch today."

Ryan yawned. "That's too bad."

Out of nowhere, Jacob came running towards Ryan with a wet bar of soap and threw it at his face. This was the last straw.

"Stop it!" he shouted, pushing Jacob down. "You're such a stupid little troll!"

Denise turned around in shock as Ryan ran up the stairs and into his bedroom. Jacob immediately started crying his eyes out and Demi pointed and laughed at her brother's misery. Denise picked up Jacob and propped him onto a chair. "He probably just had a bad day," she assured him. "I know! I will whip up an extra special dessert to make him feel better. No boy can resist the taste of one my delicious pies."

Ryan stormed into his room and slammed the door behind. This was just getting silly now. He hated being here. He just wanted to go home, back to his portal, but he couldn't. It was too risky to go out there in the open. He just didn't want to stay in some random hotel and he definitely didn't want to stay in this house any longer. He slipped into his bed and tried falling asleep. One good thing that had come out of this place was that the environment let him fall asleep quickly, even if he wasn't tired at all. But the sleep itself was often times very short lived and full of nightly terrors. But if he was sleeping, then the day would go by faster and he would then decide what to do in the evening when he could freely move around. He did want to go home, regardless of what Brazz said. Just not yet. There was something inside of him telling him that he needed to stay a bit longer. Just a bit. It was like a game of tug of war. Did he want go home, or did he not? Of course he did… or did he?

Within the very center of the city, inside a grand and powerful tower, there was a large room that was drenched in fine dark wood and soft red lighting. Maroon curtains were drawn across half a window that took up an entire wall, a glass balcony protruding out from the middle. Everyone else was gone, but he needed to think during these late hours. As he leaned back in his chair at his oak desk with a glass of wine in his hand, he pondered. Surely that little brat couldn't get into the city without his knowledge. The Secret Service wouldn't allow it. And surely he wouldn't have left all together... possibly into Frostbite Village, or maybe back through the portal? Impossible. He still had to be here. The Lord would have told him otherwise.

The mayor drained the rest of his wine then got up and paced around his elegant office room that was as large as a gymnasium and as tall as a cathedral. There were dozens of paintings hanging on the brown washed walls as well as beautiful bookcases and posh furniture littered along the maroon carpet. He stepped out onto the glass balcony that expanded out from the middle of the window and looked down hundreds of feet; his glossy slicked back hair glowing red in the night. The full city spanned out in front of him, and he hated it all. The red city of fire. He needed to act, and now.

There was a knock on the door that echoed off the walls.

"Come in," he said, still looking over the balcony. His guest had arrived.

The door opened and two large men in tuxedos entered. No human could be built as muscular as these two were. They were Durt and Koi; the mayor's bodyguards who lived up to the definition of men of steel. Durt was dark skinned with a clean shaven bald head that was recently waxed, his face firm and assured. With flaming orange hair and a busy red moustache to match, Koi was surprisingly the more intimating one of the two. He also made up one of the very few in the city that had pale skin which accompanied his sly beady eyes and permanent smirk, freckles engulfing his nose. Following behind them was another man who was one third their size. Wearing sunglasses, a visor and a navy suit with a belt equipped with Orbs and various other gadgets, he strode in with unreal confidence. The two bodyguards left the room and shut the door behind them, leaving Otis to walk up to the desk in front of the window. Carson turned around and walked back inside.

"I'm very disappointed with you Mr. Kendall," said Carson, flattening the front of his black suit with his ring filled fingers.

Otis was stern and serious, his sunglasses covering his own annoyance. "I can see that. And since when did you call me Mr. Kendall, Mr. Jenkins?"

"Because you're a bitch. So why haven't you done it yet? I'm waiting and waiting. The rat is still alive, sir."

"There have been a few drawbacks and—"

"Oh what are you talking about?" drawled Carson. "How hard is it to bring me someone who I command to see?"

Otis looked up, his face readjusting. *This twenty-one-year-old kid was not going to talk to him like this*, he thought. "We are working on it your honor."

Carson's eyes flashed towards him. "Clearly not hard enough. You work for me, and they work for you. There is no other way around it. Are you guys not taking this seriously? I know what they do when I'm not watching. Slacking off, getting drunk at the pubs, doing nothing. You tell them what to do either because of something you need done, or for something that I need done, and they do what you ask like their life depended on it. That is how it has always been up until a few days ago. Now all of a sudden there are 'drawbacks' and 'working on it' excuses. Can you explain this to me? There are forty-eight of you, and as stupid and brainless as the last. I guess that isn't enough, now is it? Do I need to hire one hundred? Tell me."

Otis rearranged his tie and took off his shades. "The person you want captured, I feel, is not necessary. There are other things we could be doing other than trying to fetch some boy who doesn't even know where he is, let alone a danger to society as you say he is. There are robberies happening every hour, innocent people being beaten and homes invaded and sacked. Our attention should be on those issues, not all on one harmless boy."

Carson looked at Otis like a hawk with his brown eyes. "I do not ask this of you, Otis. You and I are under command from the Lord to have him captured and exterminated before he destroys the world in which we live. He is only looking out for us, and He knows what is right for us all. He knows the future. He sees it. He tells me what is to come. So we must obey. But, because I'm not getting what I want, I have to make the difficult decision of relieving all of the Secret Service from duty. They are banned and will be ordered to go home until further notice. Some major reconstructing will be taking place around here."

"The city will have zero protection," said Otis as if he couldn't believe what he was hearing. "You think bad things are happening now. What until people hear that there are no Secret Service monitoring the streets. It will get bad. Really bad, Carson. What's wrong with you?"

"Lots of things," replied Carson, saddened. "But it's just temporarily. For a day or two. So once they realize their jobs are at risk, they'll smarten up. They'll do their jobs right. They'll learn their lesson. We need the upmost seriousness if we plan on defending our city, our world, from destruction and chaos. A chaos our Lord has foreseen."

Otis chuckled. "You think this kid will destroy the world? He emerged from the portal a couple days ago and that's it. He just wants to go home Carson. To use the Lord as an excuse for what you want done is highly unnecessary." He raised his hands as if he gave up. "Both of you are delusional. Think about what you were going through when you were in Ryan's shoes. It wasn't that long ago. Or is *that* Carson gone now? Is Mr. Jenkins, mayor of Blazing City, all that's left now?"

Carson sprang up from his seat. "Who are you talking to?!" he demanded. "Your wife or your superior?! You do not tell me what to do. I tell you what to do! Got that?!" He walked around the desk and stood in front of him, his height a couple feet shorter but his shadow arching over him. "If you don't bring him to me, then there will be a great deal to pay for in the end. The Lord is watching everything that we do and say and He wants the boy dead before he can blow up the city."

Otis couldn't believe what he was hearing and had to laugh. "Blow up the city, eh? Better run and hide."

Carson's eyes widened, as if he was about to go mad. "He has foreseen it. He has foreseen the fire and the smoke. The Lord is our creator. He is a great and knowing mind who has foreseen it all. That's who I take orders from. And you, Number Two, are taking orders from someone more grand and powerful than yourself. Me." Carson lifted his hand into the air and with a wave of his hand a small flicker of flame ignited from his palm.

"Fire is the destroyer of everything."

Otis looked at the flame in his palm, unable to take his eyes off it. "I would not disagree with that. But if you want to get technical, water is a force much more powerful than anything fire could do."

The mayor rolled his eyes. "If you won't do it... then..." He snapped his fingers, signaling Durt and Koi to enter the office. "I might as well fire all of you dim wads. Literally." He smiled and let the fire in his hand curl around his fingers. He motioned to Durt and Koi. "Take him to the dungeons."

Otis laughed quietly as the two bodyguards grabbed hold of him and drew his hands behind his back.

"I relieve you of your post as Number Two," said Carson calmly. "You refuse to protect me and the city, so therefore you are no longer needed."

Otis kept smiling. "I'm fine with that. Just watch your back, kid. You don't know what lurks just to the right and left of your own shadow... *dead* mayor of Blazing City."

Carson got a glint in his eyes. "I don't take kindly to vandalism either."

"It wasn't me." Otis laughed. "But I have a pretty good idea of who did."

"Threatening me, withholding knowledge," mused Carson. "How typical of a lesser human being. I have no clue why I kept you for so long. Zephyrus was a fool."

Otis was pushed towards the door but put his foot against the frame so he could respond. "Zephyrus was a great mayor who trusted his people and took care of this forsaken city. You are just his sad replacement who has corrupted it in every way. If you think this will have a happy ending, then you are wrong. So very wrong Carson."

The two men dragged him out and shut the door behind them, leaving the mayor to stand frozen on the spot. He closed his eyes tightly.

"Okay, my Lord. What do we do?"

NINE.

NO TURNING BACK

DENISE DIDN'T BOTHER WAKING UP RYAN FOR SUPPER THAT evening. She felt he was either too tired or he was coming down with something, so she preferred to just give him some private time. It wouldn't be surprising if he was going insane. He didn't live here, after all. She remembered the first time she came to this city years ago to find work as a house cleaner when she was thirteen. Her first few families were in the upper class and stayed in exquisite penthouses and apartments. She took pride in what she was doing. She was earning this money not just for herself but for her family back home who were struggling as most families were in the Hustel Lands; the great stretch of plains, hills and forests that took up a great chunk within the heart of Pheonexia.

All good things would have to come to an end though. One mistake, and it was almost the end of her life. She wasn't proud of stealing from them. She did what she had to do to survive. The rich take from the poor and the poor take from the rich. It was all a game, and a well known one if you weren't caught. Many made a living off it. Many gangs. She hated herself for doing it. She cried herself to sleep so many nights for the disgrace she brought herself and her family. When she finally was caught and charged, the family she stole from threatened to burn her family's farm down and take everything they had which wasn't much, but enough for them to suffer. The son was so furious he threatened to abuse her in horrifying ways that weren't just physical. So she ran. She ran all the way home and vowed never to come back. That vow was broken when she returned instead to Copper Town. She knew she would make a great deal less here, but she would be more safe with the lessons she had learned. She still had a few pieces of fine jewelry she could sell if she needed to. But the gift for Demi was the last she had. This piece wasn't going to be sold. It was going to be a gift for someone, to make them happy. It was the least she could do for herself. She dearly loved those children.

"I am almost a woman now," she would tell herself when she had doubts. "No more childish mistakes." The red bandana she wore to work everyday wasn't just a fashion statement either. It had belonged to her mother, the hardest working farmer she knew. It was her mother's ambition and strength that made her want to strive. When her father died when she was ten, her mother was left a farm and two daughters to raise. "It is my duty to keep the family going," her mother would say. Denise had to take care of her during her last years, like she took care of her when she was a child. She had to grow up a long time ago.

Once she started serving the cherry pie she had made for Jacob and Demi, she knew that Ryan wouldn't turn down a slice that was fresh and hot out of the oven. As Jacob and Demi began savagely eating away,

Denise carefully walked up the stairs with Ryan's slice and knocked quietly on his bedroom door. There was no response.

"I guess you're sleeping. I'll come back later." He was sure odd that one. Strange, even. It was in her best interest to keep her eyes open and ears alert with him around. Even Renny was acting strange and nervous around him. One thing she did know for sure without a shadow of a doubt was that she was never going to see her flower pendant ever again. It would seem her childish mistakes were still being made. Her trust in people was just too high.

The following morning was cloudy. The ominous black blankets rolled in against the red sky and made it almost appear like night time. Rain was falling; barely enough to actually call it rain but light spitting. It rarely rained here. But today was different.

Again, Ryan didn't want to wake up. But he did so much earlier than usual. After checking his appearance in the bathroom mirror to see that he wasn't completely filthy, he caught a glimpse of the clothing that Renny had given him laying on a heap on the floor. He put them on and discovered that they were even more grungy and worn out, still with the small holes torn in the sides of his shorts, shirt and tweed jacket. He felt like he had been homeless for weeks, and his joints and muscles were making his body feel three times older than he actually was. Ryan hated it here. He just wanted to leave and get back into the city and find the hotel he was planning on staying in for the remainder of his stay here. He couldn't tell Renny about where he was going, because he dared not break his promise to Brazz about speaking of the hidden route. Ryan came to the conclusion that he would just leave, and not come back here. He didn't care. He would never see Renny or her annoying children ever again.

He had awoken before Jacob and Demi left for school. They were running around in a frenzy, throwing things at each other like usual. Ryan's headache was growing, and he had no pills or medicine to get to rid of it.

"Stop doing that!" shouted Renny. "You two are animals. Eat your crackers. We have to leave soon."

Ryan walked into the kitchen and slumped down onto one of the chairs.

"Hello, Ryan dear," she said kindly as she picked up crumbs from off the floor. "Would you like a bite to eat? How about some crackers with cheese?"

"I would like some of that pie that Denise made last night," he said.

Renny laughed slightly. "Pie doesn't last long in this house. Unfortunately, there was a pie throwing contest and a big mess to clean up."

"Yes!" said Demi with bits of cracker in her mouth. "And I won!"

"Cheater!" mocked Jacob.

Ryan looked around to find something else to say. "Is Otis back yet?"

Renny's face turned from happy to upset. "No… no news of him. It isn't like him, you know. He's probably just very busy." She smiled to hide her worried thoughts.

"Pity," mumbled Ryan.

"Or maybe he got kidnapped by pirates!" yelled Jacob. "Ooh, let us go rescue him and find treasure!"

"No treasure," said Renny. "Have you any idea of when you might be leaving Ryan? I don't exactly know how your portal works... I guess you would have been gone by now if you could."

Ryan shrugged his shoulders. He hadn't checked in on his portal since he first came here because he didn't have the right opportunity to do so yet. And it was dangerous. There were more important things to focus on at the moment. He couldn't go home just yet even though he wanted to so badly. His portal was blocked anyway. It wouldn't let him through when he tried before, so he needed to find a way to get through it. If Otis was the only one who knew, then he was doomed because at this point in time no one knew of his whereabouts. *How convenient,* he thought.

"Well, we had better be off now," said Renny, placing a pink hat over her short auburn hair. Demi and Jacob jumped up from their chairs and ran for the door immediately. "Have a good day Ryan. I hope it won't get too boring for you."

"No, it won't," said Ryan with a smile and a wave as she shut the door behind her. "Goodbye."

The rain was coming down harder now, which was a huge surprise to many of the residents of Copper Town since it only rained once every few years or so. Ryan took it as a blessing and a bad omen at the same time. Was he doing the wrong thing? Was he doing the right thing? He didn't know anymore.

The last few people ducked for cover as if acid rain or toxic chemicals were dropping from the sky. Some of them had probably never seen rain before. They were all looking at Ryan as he passed the marketplace booths and he was getting uncomfortable to have eyes following him everywhere he went. He jogged off the dirt road and continued walking beneath the wide ledges of the windowsills that had large sheets spread out in between them. They kept going *thud*, *thud*, *thud* as rain dribbled on top of the fabric. He wondered if these people knew where he was going and what he had done. He wondered if they knew who he was and where he had come from. Had someone sent out spies to scout out the place? Were *they* here? It was quite unsettling, like walking past a group of people that were most likely talking about you a few seconds before, which if you went to a high school, happened all the time.

Lost in thought, Ryan accidentally tripped over a pile of books that were stacked behind a booth. He fell forward and banged his head against the wood of a counter, uttering a swear loudly.

A brown skinned man with a long black beard and dingy robe covering his large gut rushed over to the books as if his own daughter was just injured.

Ryan looked up, holding his head where it was sore. The man grabbed the books from off the ground and started whacking him with them repeatedly.

"What is wrong with you?!" said Ryan defensively, pushing the man back, defending his face with his arms.

"HOW DARE YOU!" roared the man. He grabbed Ryan tightly around the arm with one hand and slapped him in the chest with the other, hard, almost like a punch. The force made Ryan stumble back, his eyes watering from the strong pain. He never had someone physically attack him outside of sport before. The stinging in his chest was like a burn. It wasn't until Ryan attempted to escape did a crazed looking woman come running up to him and start throwing stones at him from a pouch she was carrying.

"These were pre—pre—precious. Now they are cu—cu—cursed," stuttered the man as he shredded the books. The woman was jumping up and down in excitement as if this was all good fun. She wretched a loose wooden plank from off one of the booths and started thrashing it at Ryan. He looked around trying to find something to defend himself with, but everything was a blur, the rain coming down harder and mixing with the panic in his heart and in his soul. He couldn't think. He was lost. He tried grabbing the knife that was supposed to be in his jacket, but it wasn't there. He was defenseless.

"You terrible monster!" she howled. "You do not belong here! Curse is the curse that you bring! Look at the rain that is staining the red earth! Soon comes fire, next comes thunder! Then comes the lightning, screaming and killing! Lastly comes the sorrow, pain and sin!"

She cried hysterically then ran into the open dirt street and kneeled down, her sleeves rolling down and revealing her bony arms when she raised them above her head, muttering nonsense. The man continued ripping the books and throwing the pages at Ryan. The man's hands were bleeding from the paper cuts that were slitting his skin as he tore the pages out.

"Go now!" he yelled, spit flying from his mouth and hitting Ryan's soaking face. "Go now! Ethklemena is where your life will lead. It is where you will cry and sorrow and weep!"

Ryan glanced around him as more civilians examined the commotion that was taking place. Most were confused as others nodded or shook their heads. Ryan was terrified and he could feel moisture swelling up in his eyes, and it wasn't from the rain. He swiftly made another attempt to run, but the man grabbed him. The rain seemed to gradually increase in volume and sound with each passing moment.

"You must leave now! LEAVE NOW! Or die, die, die!"

"Die, die, die!" screamed the woman in the street as she continued raising her arms up and down. "Such beautiful words to cleanse the soul!" Ryan cornered himself against a wall as more people came forward and attempted to hit and attack him. He was going to pummel them if they wouldn't let him leave... or worse.

"He must die!" demanded the large man, reaching over and slapping Ryan across the face with a large hand and sending him sprawling onto the ground. "It would be better now than later! Yes, this filth that walks our world will be punished his vile ways! He must be destroyed! May our powerful Lord, the Lord of Pheonexia, the Lord of the Righteous Land, accept this gift and punish him greatly!"

Ryan burst forward and punched the man across the face, sending him stumbling to the side. Rage grew in his eyes.

"BEAST!" he cried.

The insane woman ran towards Ryan and grabbed him by the shoulders as others tried hitting him with their hands. She was shaking as the rain pelted down on her, as if she was cold. She looked into his eyes with fright. "Why are you here?" she whispered, her breath rank. "He is not happy right now. Since the second you stepped into this place he has been speaking to me. Telling me. Purifying me with his words." Her mouth leaned in closer. "I know who you are."

Ryan turned away but the woman grabbed his face. "He is not happy with us. Look at the sky. Look at what you are doing. He says the end of days is nearing with you here. It will not stop until you are cleansed of your body." She squeezed his chin and lips with her hand the way an aunt would to her nephew that she hadn't seen in a long time. "Oh die. You must die, you must die," she whispered. "Die, die, die. Oh die, die, die."

Ryan pushed the woman away forcefully, but this only made everyone else angrier. He felt his tweed jacket being ripped off his body.

"He will pa—pay," stuttered the bearded man, covering his nosebleed and pointing at him. "Re—remove him from out world. KILL THE BOY! SACRIFICE HIM TO THE GREAT ONE! THE LORD IS GETTING ANGRIER AT US THE LONGER WE WAIT!"

"He is?" asked the woman in a scared voice. She looked up at the sky and shuddered. "Speak!" she cried. "Great one! Speak to us! Our Lord!"

Ryan tried with all his power to get away from the deranged people, but he could only feel the rain and the blows he was receiving to his face and body. He looked up and saw the last traces of the crimson sky and overlapping black clouds looking back down at him. Something was staring down at him from inside those clouds... they were eyes... two red eyes. The Lord was watching him... He was the monster, not him. Ryan closed his eyes as something started to speak to him.

"Die..." said a deep and vicious voice inside his head.

What did I do?

It cackled deeply but didn't respond.

Ryan was thrown to the ground as a man grabbed a rope and tied it around his neck. Everyone around him was laughing and pointing as the noose was tied tighter, making him gag and choke, coughing up saliva. He could feel the buildup of blood in his mouth and thick drops were falling from his head and onto people's shoes. He couldn't distinguish the raindrops from his own tears. There was lighting now, and thunder. *Boom, boom, BOOM!*

Just as they started hoisting Ryan up with the rope secured tightly around his neck, he looked down and saw something small and black roll across the ground towards him. He reached down to pick it up before he was hoisted up away from the ground. As he was pulled up onto a box and the end of the rope was thrown around a pole on a wall, he crushed the Orb between his palms. There were shocked gasps and screams from people as they saw the boy in front of them disappear. Ryan ripped the rope off and pushed everyone away as some fell back and others ran away in fright. He also took this opportunity to punch some of them—just returning the favor.

Ryan briskly ran for his life down the dirt wet road and darted through the black market. He looked behind and saw the mobs running about, either in fright or just pure anger. There were mothers with their crying children who were rushing them home as fast as possible. He tripped over a couple times and fell into the wet mud, but picked himself up as fast as possible and kept going.

He leaped into Brazz's shop and slammed himself onto one of the chairs in the corner. Brazz was behind the counter, staring at him and laughing quietly to himself. His cloak was wet from the rain and there was a customer skimming through at a box of candles. She heard the noises from outside then immediately dashed out.

"What are you laughing at?" asked Ryan irritably. "I find this hardly funny. They were hanging me!" He felt his neck and rubbed it, feeling the pain throbbing in his pulse.

"Sorry," said Brazz. "I was just thinking of a joke that someone told me the other day. You were almost hanged you say? How awful."

Ryan rolled his eyes and gave him the middle finger, knowing that Brazz couldn't see him do it. "Thank you so much for the Orb. I can't tell you how much I needed it." He closed his eyes and put his head back against the wall, almost about to cry with relief.

"I can see how much you needed it alright," said Brazz loudly. "Just think. You would have been dead right now if it weren't for me."

Ryan shuddered slightly. "Thanks," he said. He felt something wet dripping down his face—it was blood, and there was quite a lot of it. "What's wrong with those people? I was scared out of my mind."

"Like I said," said Brazz. "People here are different. It only takes one person to get worked up then the whole lot join in. Not everyone is like that though."

"Different as in complete psychopaths," spat Ryan as he grabbed a rag from off a shelve and started wiping the blood from his wounds, which lead him to swearing quietly from the sharp stinging. "I heard someone speaking in my head."

Brazz looked up at him; more serious than ever before.

"It was… I don't know… a man's voice. He wanted me to die. It didn't come from any of those people. I've heard it before."

Brazz appeared extremely interested. "Did you see anything… out of the ordinary?"

Ryan gave him a dumb look.

Brazz grunted. "You know what I mean."

"Anything more unusual than the unusual? Well, yes. I saw a pair of eyes looking down at me from the sky… it was like they were laughing while watching me die. But honestly, it could have just been nothing. I was probably just imagining it. A lot was happening."

Brazz moved a box to the side of the counter and folded his arms. "It was the Lord," he whispered. "If you lived here, I would have called your bluff for he cares for no one here. Many claim that the Lord has spoken to them but they are just delusional. You are invisible but I can see that you are telling the truth and it was not your imagination. The Lord has come to you. Just don't let Him get inside your mind. Look at what happened to our poor mayor. The Lord speaks to him all the time."

"The Lord of the Righteous Land one man said," said Ryan.

"It's an old name," said Brazz. "That's what they used to call Him. Centuries ago."

"What is Ethklemena?" asked Ryan meekly. "I heard a man talking about it. He said it is where my life will lead."

Unwillingly, Brazz answered. "It's the shadow realm. The land of the dead."

"Hell," said Ryan.

The screams and yells outside were growing, and they seemed to be getting closer.

"It would be best if you leave now," suggested Brazz. "You can't go back out there. The word is out and it will spread fast. How they suddenly found out about you, I don't know. But they will search everywhere for you. If the Lord wants something done, then they will do it for Him regardless. You are indeed safer in the city now. You must flee and never come back into Copper Town ever again."

"But then they will find the route," said Ryan. "They are looking everywhere."

"They will *not* find the route," said Brazz, reassuringly. "The route is cleverly hidden behind the rug. They're so stupid that they will only look in corners and small crevices. They would not think that a hole through Dunger Wall would lead into the city. The wall is just too thick for something like that."

"Well how did you make it then?" Ryan got up and continued to whip away the blood with the rag. It became so soaked that he had to reach for another one.

"A lot of time and effort. Nobody heard me though. I also invented an Orb that blocks out sound within a small radius so that no one from outside could have heard."

"That's smart," said Ryan, not really listening to Brazz but to the noises outside. He looked into a piece of glass inside a cabinet and saw his reflection, realizing that he wasn't invisible anymore. Brazz reached into a drawer and pulled out a pile of clean clothing. It was a type of uniform, almost resembling that of an army officer and looked similar to a Secret Service agent. It was black with a white dress shirt and black tie underneath. Attached to the jacket was a gold and circular badge that had an iridescent red shine to it with no engravings but an embossed border.

"This was very hard to get," said Brazz, flicking his finger against the badge pinned to the front of the jacket.

"How was I able to be invisible though?" asked Ryan. "I thought the Veil Orb could only be used at night."

"It was fooled," said Brazz. "Like humans, Orbs have minds of their own. Open to deceit. It never rains here, except for today. The Lord's doing no doubt. The sky was so consumed with those dark clouds that it appeared night to the knowledge of the Orb." Brazz shuffled some things around in a box hastily. "You better hurry. I believe the raid has begun."

Ryan quickly got up and ran over to the counter. He picked up the uniform and let it slip through his fingers. "What am I supposed to be?"

"You'll figure it out," mumbled Brazz.

More cryptic secrets, thought Ryan, hastily dressing into the uniform. He decided to put the uniform over his current outfit. He felt that maybe he would need his other clothes later on.

"Wait," said Ryan as he put on the black visor. "Why don't you just give me the Veil Orb instead?"

"You need to check into the hotel somehow. And this disguise will be perfect. You are staying in the city now, not just visiting. You don't want to walk around for the next few days having to rely on invisibility. Always worrying about when to use the next Orb or how much time you have left before it runs out. They can only be used during the evening, remember? You do not want to be stuck in hiding during the day. Nobody will notice you wearing this—believe me."

Ryan groaned. "I'm taking your word."

"And these," said Brazz, handing him a pair of shiny black shoes and white gloves.

"Shouldn't I wear sunglasses too?" asked Ryan curiously.

"No," said Brazz hurriedly. "Your uniform isn't Secret Service, even though I'm dressing you up similar. That badge though is very important.

You will be respected with the upmost courtesies from most when they see it. Enough talking though. Go, now!"

Ryan gave the store one last look and stepped into Hoarder's Tunnel.

"You still have the coins?" shouted Brazz.

"Yeah," yelled back Ryan, feeling his pocket under the uniform. He reached into his pants and took out the bag out of his other pants and put it into the uniform ones. "I'm glad that I did that thing for you. You still would have given me money anyways, right?"

Brazz laughed. "I wouldn't even be doing this."

It was easy enough to only imagine the commotion that was taking place on the other side of the wall, but Ryan couldn't hear it, neither could anybody else in the city—that was good. Once he made it onto the main road, his suit helped him camouflage into the city very well. There was no rain or black scary clouds on this side, which made Ryan all that much happier. It was the first time the red sky felt welcoming. He also liked the fact that he could walk around like a normal human being now instead of always hiding himself (technically he was still hiding himself though).

If anything, Ryan's attire was bringing more glances than he had hoped for, something that everyone else also recognized. Kind gestures and pleasant smiles met Ryan's eyes. Apparently news hadn't spread yet to the city about what had happened—the shouts from behind the wall didn't even make a whisper to the ear. Hopefully it would stay that way.

The city felt less intimidating in the afternoon than it did during the late hours when he last visited. But the black gothic skyscrapers and towers that surrounded him were still as menacing as ever. What a terrible sight it was. The hustle and bustle was as prominent as ever with people from all different walks of life. Like Copper Town, there were carriages pulled by horses and coachmen but they were more of an updated version of what he was used to seeing in the town. The carriages flashed like rubies in the light as they bumped along the uneven roads, brining people on and letting people off.

He decided that it would be best to find a hotel while it was still the afternoon, and not wait until darkness fell. He scouted around for a hotel complex, but found it difficult as none stood out as one. He had to examine signs carefully and even ask passersby who gladly helped him with directions. When half an hour had past, he finally came to a street where a hotel was located. He was so bad with directions that he was glad he didn't get lost.

The hotel was one long tower filled with brightly lit windows on each side and hundreds of balconies jutting out. There was a square metal banner above the entryway that read: *The Classer Hotel.*

A bellhop pleasantly greeted him as he entered. There weren't many people in the lobby as he walked in, and he didn't expect it to look as good as it did from the outside. The lobby was amazingly big and gold in color––this was obviously a five-star hotel. There were gold chandeliers hanging from the ceiling and he could see various staircases and old fashioned elevators along the walls. The rug was carefully detailed and exquisite with dark green couches and tables sprawled on its surface. There were a few people reading and gossiping at the tables and a bellhop clad in maroon attire was helping a struggling fashionable woman with her luggage into an elevator. Ryan reached the front counter just as a man left with a room key in his hand. The woman behind the counter reminded Ryan of someone that you would have seen in the fifties. A blue hat covered her short platinum hair and she wore bright red lipstick, her face slightly chubby. She was wearing light blue work attire with white gloves and her eyes were like looking into a cloudless afternoon sky.

"Hello," she said kindly. "Welcome to the Classer Hotel where... um... I forget what to say next."

"Hi," replied Ryan, looking at the metal plaque that had her name engraved on it. "It's okay. I would like a room to stay in for a couple of nights, Susan."

"Okay." She reached over for a pen and notepad. "What type of room are you looking for? I expect a gold one?

"Excuse me?" asked Ryan.

"Oh, the rooms are rated gold, silver or bronze based on quality and how expensive they are."

"How much is the most expensive room?"

"Ten dressels a night. The least expensive is eight comets. However, it looks like all the rooms are booked except for gold room number fifty-three."

"That's fine," said Ryan. He calculated the price and learned that Brazz gave him enough money for almost four nights. "I'll take that one then, the gold one. Number fifty-three."

"Alrighty," she said as she scribbled down information. The whole time she was looking at him, her eyelashes fluttering and not paying attention to what she was writing. She giggled. "I'm just going to need your name please."

Ryan stared at her for a couple of seconds. "Henry... Je... tar... bee."

"Okay Henry Jetarbee, and this is for how long? May I see some identification as well?"

Oh shit.

"I'll try four nights for now," he said. He pulled out his pouch and gave her the coins necessary. "And I, uh, haven't gotten my ID yet... because... I'm new... and they haven't given it to me yet." He smiled, his biggest smile ever. Damn fucking white strips better be paying off now.

Susan pursed her lips together and squinted her eyes at him, looking him up and down. Her suggestive stare then turned into splendor. She laughed and waved her hand at him. "Nahhh, I'm just twisting your arm. I trust you. What are you, an escaped murderer? Hahaha." She snorted slightly.

"Hahaha," laughed Ryan sarcastically. "No. Not today."

Susan got up and walked to the cubbies that held all the keys. She handed Ryan his. It was thick and clunky with dents and marks all over it. "This will be your key for room number fifty-three. I just know it will be to your liking, Mr. Jetarbee."

"I'm sure it will," said Ryan. "Thank you for your help." He turned around with his key, but then couldn't resist doing something that he had always wanted to do. He looked back at Susan and tipped his black visor to her in which she responded with kneeling slightly. Ryan gave her a small smile then went to the nearest elevator.

The operator pulled a type of crank and the door opened for him. Ryan stepped in with him and the door closed. At least there wasn't any terrible elevator music to irritate him.

Twenty seconds later there was a faint *ding* and the door opened. Ryan stepped out into a nicely furnished hallway. A mother was sitting on a purple couch, reading to her young child when Ryan passed. He tipped his hat to her and she smiled back.

"See," said the woman quietly to the little boy on her lap. "That man has a lot of money. Something that you will have someday if you work very hard."

Ryan's smiled faded and turned his mind to looking for room number fifty-three. His eyes caught site of a gold 53 sign hanging on a polished oak door. Ryan turned his eyes to the door across from him and saw that it had a bronze 54 nailed to it.

Ryan put the clunky key into the hole and turned it until he heard a quiet *click*. The door swung open and a magnificent elegance touched his eyes. The room was a grand penthouse. There were three windows on the north wall that had rose colored light seeping onto the white carpet like stained red wine. There was also a balcony that had silky white curtains floating over it through the breeze. The master bed was against the wall beside a smaller room that had a kitchen. He removed his shoes at the door and stepped further inside, the white carpet glimmering as his feet stepped onto it. Ryan noticed that there were small cut crystals etched into the carpet itself. Paintings were placed all along the walls as well as beautiful vases and sculptures. There were no plants, which Ryan assumed was because of the dry heat. But what did he know, really? He threw his visor and gloves to the ground as if he was coming home from a long day at work and jumped onto the fluffy cotton bed like it was the pool from his own backyard back home. He sank into it as he grabbed a large feathered pillow and put it between his arms. This was it. He was back in paradise.

The milky curtains over the balcony swayed gently as a breeze swirled into the room. It was soothing and comforting, but the smell wasn't the most pleasant thing in the world. It smelt like burnt... he didn't know. Ryan pulled the pillow closer to him and his eyes began to grow heavy as the softness of the bed was overtaking his senses. His eyes finally closed and he was about to drift off when he heard a soft crackling sound on the ground beside the bed. Ryan jumped up, his eyes darting around.

"Hello? I know you're there," came a voice from the floor.

Ryan looked down and was tempted to run out of the room as fast as possible. This room might have been bugged... or someone was under the bed!

Ryan sprang off the bed, grabbed his visor and gloves, and dashed for the front door. The noise was now coming from the bundle in his arms. He looked down at the visor and gloves and heard more crackling.

"I know you're there, boy. Don't get panicked. It's just me."

"Who?" asked Ryan as he dropped the visor and gloves to the ground.

"Brazz, you idiot. Sorry. I forgot to mention that I used a Communi-kay Orb on your visor. Oops."

"What?" said Ryan. "You bugged my hat?!"

"No, not bugged. We can both speak to each other. However, I'm the only one who can access you. You can't access me because I was the one who activated the Orb. I hope you feel special."

Ryan's heart rate lowered. "So what do you want?"

"Wait. Where are you?" asked Brazz. "Are you in a hotel?"

"Yes. And I almost fell asleep until you woke me up."

"Did anyone recognize you?"

Ryan looked around the room and could see his reflection in the bathroom mirror that was right across from him. "Nope. But I actually look really hot. Who's that stunner?"

Brazz made a sound that could have been him spitting repulsively. "Don't flatter yourself. I just called to inform you that my shop was raided a couple minutes ago. Don't worry though. They were too unintelligent to look for the route."

"That's good," said Ryan. He let out a low sigh. "That's very good. So they still think that I'm still over there?"

"Yes. But they may get suspicious if you aren't found soon. Never take off your uniform. You never know who could be watching."

Ryan breathed a sigh of relief. "I guess I got out just in time."

Brazz coughed like a chain smoker would. "I suggest you stay in your room for the rest of the day. Wait it out until tomorrow."

"Yeah, I think I'll do that," said Ryan.

"Good. I have to get back to work. Time is money. Don't get in too much trouble and I'll call you tomorrow to check up on you... if you aren't dead."

Ryan laughed sincerely. "Thanks for that. Talk to you later."

Once Brazz's voice was no longer coming from the visor, he slid down onto the floor in exhaustion.

"How do I get out of here?"

His body was sore and broken, he felt. He forgot what time it was. He forgot what year it was. But the thought of venturing out into the city tomorrow made him nervous and excited at the same time. He could go anywhere now. No hiding and no having to worry about an Orb's T.U.D. He was free. Yet, he thought back to a couple hours ago when he was brutally beaten by those savage people. People that Ryan thought were nice when he first came here. *I almost died,* he would think to himself constantly. What had he started? What was happening there now? Would news spread? Would they find out about his disguise? Ryan didn't want to think about the *what ifs* any more. There was plotting happening somewhere out there, and he needed to start doing some of his own. He had to understand the portal and how it worked. Now. Not in a couple days. Not next week. Now. He couldn't go around asking people about it for fear of his identity being broken. He couldn't go read it in a book with fear of someone seeing him. But who was the one person who knew about it enough who could help him?

Ryan nodded his head in assurance. Otis.

PART III

SETTING THE BLAZE

TEN.

THE FIRE'S DEPTH

WAS HE DREAMING? COULD IT POSSIBLY BE REAL? HE wasn't sure. It was one of those rare dreams you only get once in a lifetime, something so out of this world that you never forget it—ever. He was inside an incredibly large chamber with rows of thick stone pillars all around. He was sitting down with his back against one of the pillars, looking into the face of someone he could not see because of a strong white light illuminating from behind. It could have been an angel; an angel telling him something that he couldn't quite here and him responding to their voice. The voice was blurred as if he was underwater or wearing ear plugs, and he desperately needed to hear what was being said to him and what he himself was saying back. The figure slowly got up, turned around, and faded off into the light until the light itself disappeared, leaving him in darkness and shadow. The raging sound of water was all around him… then all went quiet.

Ryan's eyes didn't open for several more minutes afterwards. His mind was left in a blank and dark wasteland of thought. Once he did wake he soon realized that he wasn't sleeping in the bedroom that he had grown accustomed to for the last couple days in Renny's house.

He rose up and felt undoubtedly more refreshed than the day before. He couldn't remember the last time he slept that well. He even fell asleep in his uniform. The warm burgundy light from early morning came spilling in through the balcony's silky transparent curtains that were blowing in the breeze within the extravagantly furnished hotel penthouse.

As he washed up in the bathroom he felt like he was back in his own home for once, except here the fascists were made of pure gold and the water smelled of lavender. On the counter beside a stack of folded towels was a wicker basket filled with pink and blue Orbs. Ryan picked a few up and read the tags attached to them. *The Slumber Orb: to allow oneself to fall asleep almost instantly. The Rosie Sunrise Orb: engulf the whole room with a pleasant fragrance of red roses.*

A bright purple Orb named Sea Harmony would omit the soothing sounds of being near the ocean. Ryan broke it against the counter and could hear the loud splashes of waves against the sand with seagulls flapping their wings in the air. He even picked up the faint aroma of salt water. It was just like home. What he wouldn't give to be able to go swimming right now.

After eating a large breakfast of omelets, bacon, fruits and champagne provided by kind room service, he put his visor and white gloves on then jogged out to the balcony to see a full view of Blazing City. It was a city bathed in rich red light, the light that usually came during sunset, but deeper. It wasn't a harsh light like what he was used to back home. This one had a type of brilliance yet hellish aura to it. You didn't even notice the sometimes ugliness of the city because you were so far up. If anything, the height accentuated the city's gothic beauty. There were thousands of people below walking on the streets and being carried around in carriages pulled by horses and coachmen. The city spanned out in all directions, much vaster than he initially thought. He saw Dunger Wall that separated Copper Town from the city. Just the other day he was on the other side of it and now here he was, hiding from the world.

There was another thick wall that circled the entire city itself, encasing the land so nobody from the outside could enter or leave. Against the northern part of the perimeter wall was a magnificent formation of large boulders and stone that almost resembled the side of a mountain and went all the way up to the top of the wall. Ryan bent over the side of the railing slightly to see better and made out tiny little openings in the rock. There were hundreds of them. It looked like some old Mayan creation that was built long ago.

Ryan turned his attention back to the buildings and tall skyscrapers, hotels and penthouses that glistened against each other, reflecting the sun's rays and dazzling the millions of windows. In the middle of the city was the biggest tower of them all, the tower that Ryan had seen a couple days before... and he never forgot it since. The sleek black architecture and flat top was more modern and lavish than the rest. The sides could have been constructed out of ice because they were so slick. Could Otis be in there? It seemed like a good place to start. Maybe he would ask around...

Once he looked beyond the city and its brilliance, he saw something else that intrigued him even more. Beyond the perimeter wall was an open landscape of green meadows and rivers. Because the city looked so murky, the grass and streams were bursts of color that made the city itself look drab in comparison. Further past these meadows were forests and farmlands. More noticeably, the sky over this landscape wasn't red like over the city, but bright blue. Blazing City wasn't *the* world. Blazing City was only *part* of the world, and more of it was out there. It had to be one of the most pleasant sceneries he had ever witnessed in his whole life. In his world, places like this just didn't exist, at least, not where he lived. An earthly and lively landscape that looked so peaceful and spanned out further into the distance with small rolling hills and hundreds of thousands of dark green trees was something that Ryan had never seen, only in pictures and movies. You could even see the faint outline of snowy mountaintops in the distance as well as a desert. Was that an ocean too? Unbelievable.

In the other direction, there was another environment much different from the rest. The red sky morphed into grey and beneath it was another wall that was ten times the height of the one circling the city. Just like there was a wall surrounding the border of the Blazing City, the wall around the perimeter of Frostbite Village made it impossible to see the actual village except for a few tree with white foliage poking out from the top. *Those must be some really tall trees*, thought Ryan. *They must be as tall as skyscrapers.* He remembered back to when he first walked down the path outside of the gate to the courtyard. He came across the gate that was too cold to approach.

Ryan backed off and tore his eyes away from the scenery in front of him. There was a whole world out there to explore and he wanted to see it. No, he couldn't. There was no way. Focus, Ryan. Focus. You need to go home. Screw home.

He left his room and walked down the hallway towards the elevator. Once he reached the lobby floor, he got out and went across the exquisite carpeting, making his way towards the front double doors. The lobby was bustling with activity with dozens of guests checking in and out. Everyone was seemingly dressed like the 1920's with their handsome suits and captivating attire.

"Have a nice day, Mr. Jetarbee!"

Ryan turned around and saw Susan behind the counter waving at him with her white gloved hand. He waved back and returned her gesture with a smile. Odds are she didn't hear him because it was so loud and she was too busy tending to guests.

It was absolutely dry and warm outside. It seemed like the temperature had risen another ten degrees since yesterday and Ryan's forehead was already beginning to sweat. The uniform he was wearing wasn't appropriate for this kind of weather. He walked along the sidewalk and looked at all the citizens passing by. There were people in a variety of uniforms in an array of different clothing styles. It was nothing like Copper Town. Most must have been outside for hours and none of them were sweating profusely like he was, in fact, the heat didn't seem to bother them at all. Perhaps they had grown accustomed to the warm climate. But once you put on a suit that covers every inch of your body it would become over heated no matter how used to the heat you were.

Twenty minutes into his exploration, Ryan was the furthest he had ever been inside the city, and from his point of view, the city only seemed to become more pleasant even though the buildings themselves were still menacing as ever. They were still very different from the ones in Sortonia City. There were shops down every block such as *Ruth's Readings, Orbs Emporium, Fine Dining Done Right* and *Lucy's Lights and Wardrobes.* Ryan really wanted to know what all the different kinds of Orbs were and what each one did. From what Brazz had told him, there were thousands of different kinds. The whole concept of them was intriguing enough. *Magic in an Orb*, he thought.

He walked up to the front of *Orbs Emporium* and looked through the display window. There indeed were thousands if not millions of Orbs placed all along shelves and inside bins. There were glass boxes filled to the brim and some were scattered about on the floor. As he walked inside there were two iron poles on each side of the entrance. As he passed them they would glow lime green. Ryan came to the conclusion that it was probably a security device and that if you walked past them with a stolen Orb it would go off. The image of Brazz came into mind.

The customers in the store were all holding a wicker basket where they placed the Orbs they wanted to purchase (it reminded Ryan of Easter egg hunting). He looked at the shelves that held a wide range of colors, picking up a few and reading the tiny tags.

The Star Light Orb: omits a small burst of light in your hand wherever you are to help guide you in darkened areas. The Soapy Water Orb: great for cleaning your dishes at a moment's notice. The Instant Cooler Orb: creates a small chilled breeze in any room on warm days.

Ryan could probably have spent a full day looking at every variety of Orb possible. There were posters and guides on the wall to help customers locate a particular kind of Orb, as well as books and diagrams, pamphlets and even associates who walked around to aid in customer's questions or concerns. With the money that Brazz gave him, he ended up buying various different kinds including a couple of The Star Light Orbs, the Instant Cooler and a quite expensive one called The Age Increaser that he thought was pretty cool. It increased your age by ten years for just one hour. On the tag Ryan read that it was age restricted to those twenty-one and older. But he was hoping he would be able to get around that somehow. All in all, he still wasn't impressed with the selection. More so because he couldn't find what he was looking for. All of these seemed pretty basic. Where were all the cool ones? He caught the attention of a passing associate.

"Hey, I have a question."

"Fire away," said the young man with his pearly white smile. He seemed just a little too happy for Ryan's taste. "What can I do for you, sir?"

"Well, I'm just curious. I was looking for an Orb that… well… could make you fly."

The man gave him a dumb look. "That Orb has been banned for decades and decades. It does not exist."

Ryan swallowed. "How about… an Orb where you can make someone who was attacking you fall over or an Orb that can make a small explosion or something along those lines."

"Sir," said the salesman politely, putting his hands out. "I will have you know that we only sell Class C Orbs in this store. If you want Class B or, dare I say, Class A, I suggest you find the other *Orb Emporium* stores if the ones here aren't fitting your needs. Good day." The man appeared nervous and abruptly walked away without another word.

As Ryan stood in line behind a talkative woman who was blabbing about her homemade strawberry bread to her girlfriends, Ryan looked over at several bins next to the checkout that held Orbs called Sweat Preventers. Ryan reached over and picked one out and read on its tiny tag that they prevented one from sweating for twenty-four hours in warm environments. This was the answer. He decided to take a handful of them and stepped up to the cashier as he was next in line.

"Why, hello," said the cashier in a sweet voice. She glanced down at the basket of Orbs that he had placed in front of her. She looked at him up and down, pushing her glasses up slightly.

Ryan's mouth fell slightly open. "What?"

She took the basket and calculated out the cost of each Orb by tapping them one at a time onto a round piece of glass that glowed green each time an Orb touched it. A number would then appear on the surface of the glass, like digital.

"Let us see here. An Age Increaser? Didn't know we even sold these. Martha! Where is Martha? I need to ask her about this one. Ugh, she better not be out on lunch." She examined the Orb closer. "I believe this is a Class B Orb." She tapped the Orb onto the glass. For a second, the surface glowed red but then quickly faded back to green. The woman stared at the glass then back up at Ryan, suspicion in her eyes. She kept tapping the Age Increaser onto the glass and each time she did the glass would keep glowing green. It was as if she was determined to make it red again. "Martha! Someone please go find that woman. Barr, where's Barr? Ugh, can someone please help me?"

"Excuse me," said Ryan. "I'm in a bit of a hurry."

The woman sighed. "That will be three dressels and five comets please, sir. I'm sure this is all fine. Don't really care though. Not my problem if something happens to you and you blow up or something."

Ryan pulled out the black pouch and dug inside for the coins and handed them to her. "I'm sure I won't blow up," he said. "Thank you."

He grabbed the bag of his Orbs and went towards the exit. He stopped in the doorway as the iron poles on each side glowed green. He looked back at the woman who was busy tending to another customer. Once he stepped outside, the man he spoke to earlier grabbed his arm.

"Where did you get that?" he asked urgently.

"What?" asked Ryan, caught off guard. "I paid for these. Ask that woman in there if you need confirmation."

The man grabbed the bag and pulled out the age restricted Orb. "We do not sell these Age Increasers. Those are Class B and they do not belong in this shop."

"I just found it on the shelf," explained Ryan as he started to get warm from the uncomfortable situation.

The man sighed and shook his head. "A few manage to get mixed up through the manufacturing process. This is not good."

Ryan wasn't getting it. "What's the big deal?"

"Are you new here, sir? Or have your parents sheltered you so much that you have no idea? Or you just got a new job?" At this, he looked him up and down, just like the cashier. It was the uniform Ryan was wearing. It was the stupid gold and red iridescent badge. He was reluctant, but nodded his head.

"Orbs are just a means for helping one's life," explained the man. "They make one's life easier and more convenient. Those are the kinds of Orbs we do sell. But there are Orbs that are not made for that. There are Orbs in this world made and used for bad purposes. Used to harm. Used to kill. Used by bad people, sir."

Ryan nodded his head again. "Ok, but I'm not bad."

The man smiled slightly. He dropped the Orb back into the bag then handed it back to Ryan. "Let's hope not, sir. Have a good day. Please shop with us again. You are always welcome." He looked at the plastic bag one last time, put a great big smile on his face, then returned back into the shop.

Ryan turned on his heel and merged in with the bustling crowd. Before he started his venture further into the city, Ryan grabbed one of the Sweat Preventers and crushed it into his hand. Almost immediately he felt the sweat strands on his forehead and neck disappear and replaced with soothing cool air. What a relief. It was like his suit had a built in air conditioner.

During the next hour, he felt a cramp develop in his legs and decided to sit down for a couple of minutes. He found a bench beside a group of people waiting for a carriage to pick them up. Through his observations, he put together that this city had elements of the new and old, the modern and mid-century. How people still rode carriages, but used digital devices like in *Orbs Emporium*. How there were futuristic towers but vintage clothing. It didn't make sense. It was like it wanted to be two different things at once.

He thought maybe he should come up with a job for himself. What if someone asked him what he did here? He didn't really know what people dressed like himself did around here. From the vibes he was getting from everyone, and the way they looked at him or smiled at him, or how they always seemed to attend to him, Ryan believed that many thought that he was a person of high importance. Brazz certainly wanted him to look the part for one of the most accomplished jobs that one could get in Blazing City. He just wasn't quite sure what that was yet. Ryan tipped his visor to an older woman passing by then got up and continued on with his journey.

He came to the decision by mid afternoon that he would have lunch in an actual restaurant this time. No more pears and peaches from the marketplace. Denise's cooking would be missed though, excluding the burned trout. The thought of Denise saddened him. He felt bad about taking her pendant and selling it out of desperation. What a shitty thing to do. For all he knew it used to be her grandmothers. He wouldn't even be able to apologize to her now.

He stopped into a rather fancy looking restaurant named *Duke's*. Inside, the décor was old-fashioned glamour with subtly dimmed lights and small square tables and red leather booths. Since it was lunch time, all of the seating spots were packed completely. Ryan power walked towards a booth that a couple were getting up from before anyone else could take it. He looked around and noticed a variety of different looking diners, all with one thing in common; their style was impeccable. Some of the men wore various types of uniforms that ranged in different colors from brown to green to purple. And when they weren't wearing black visors, their hair was put together neatly. The woman wore clothing that was similar to the men's, except theirs were knee length skirts with button up jackets. Most of them were talking and laughing, smoking cigars and drinking from crystal glasses. At random tables sat men dressed sharply in a tuxedo or women wearing a pristine dress with a large peacock hat. To Ryan, they resembled wealthy millionaires or celebrities from the older years.

At one of these tables sat a group that was especially talkative and loud while eating their meals. There were eight men and two women sitting side by side, all seeming to not care about being too loud (Ryan assumed that some of them were on their way to being drunk). On the table in front of each of them was a pair of aviator sunglasses, and this in particular sparked something in Ryan. Secret Service. Those were the only ones who wore these types of shades from his knowledge. They wore the belts with Orbs lining the sides and the dark navy suits that he remembered seeing in Mainbreak Hall. It had to be them. They stuck out like a sore thumb.

Amongst the group was the strangest looking woman. Her face was like a porcelain doll; white, shiny and frozen. Her eyes were hidden behind a veil that went down to her nose and was attached to the rim of her oversized purple hat. Her blonde hair was styled in a bob and was pressed against the sides of her face and down to her neck. Her lips were ruby red and they didn't move except for when a long cigarette slipped in and out of her mouth. From the way she was seated, with her legs crossed below her purple dress, it would seem she was looking straight at him. He, in turn, turned away.

"Can I take your order, sir?"

Ryan looked up at a dark skinned waitress with a rebellious sort of look to her. He grabbed the menu and quickly browsed through it.

"Yeah, um... I'll have the cheese pasta." Ryan looked up for a second. "Do I really want that though? I've been eating so healthy lately and this will just ruin everything I worked for. It will encourage me to eat even more pasta and that will lead to the doom and gloom garlic bread and..."

The waitress was looking at him with a bored expression. "You *are* fat," she said.

"What?" said Ryan, smiling at her and knowing that she was just playing along. "No, but really. I'm not fat." He wanted to lift up his jacket and shirt to prove her wrong but that was just his ego rearing its ugly head again. Oh hello there douchebaggery, haven't seen you in a while.

"Tomato soup or crab salad to go with your pasta, fat boy?"

"Crap salad. I mean, crab salad please."

"Oh, that is very good," she said in a soft voice. "Do you enjoy it?"

He looked at her. "I've never really tried it before. I bet... it's... healthy..."

"I mean," she said, even softer this time, as she leaned in closer to him. "Do you really like it?"

Ryan gulped hard as he looked into her brown eyes. "Yes, I do." He smiled. "So, do you like me?"

"I don't date fat boys," she said with a grin, fixing his collar. She leaned back and bit her lip as she continued to stare at him. "It should be ready in fifteen minutes. Don't disappear on me or else..."

Once she walked away, there was a burst of laughter from the Secret Service table as they told drunken jokes to one other. Drunk at lunch was very uncommon for Ryan (but not so uncommon for his Aunt Marie), and he couldn't help but laugh a bit, but stopped when he saw the porcelain-faced woman again. She was sipping red wine out of a glass but was turned away from him this time. He hated when people smoked during his meal, as he himself wasn't a smoker. He was coughing and at times had to squint through smoke that started to become unbearable. It was like a mist throughout the restaurant.

"You filled up, fat boy?" asked the waitress half an hour later, just as he put the last piece of pasta into his mouth.

"Yeah, it was really good. Thank you." He patted his stomach and smiled at her. *Wow, Ryan. Really?*

She picked up the plate and handed him a receipt. "It will be two comets and two flaks. But because you are cute, it will only be one comet. How about that? Do you like it?"

Ryan looked down and laughed. "No, you don't have to do that. Really."

"Okay," she said, shrugging her shoulders. "Four comets and eight flaks, plus tip, fat boy." She put her hand out, her red nails sharp and her fingers snapping. He handed her the appropriate amount of change.

"Welcome to the city," she said as she walked back between the tables and towards the kitchen.

Ryan got up from his table. "Thanks?"

"No problem," she said, giving him a wink. She went back up to him and whispered into his ear: "Don't worry, I won't tell anyone. It will be our little secret."

"How could you tell?" he asked, thinking that his uniform didn't really camouflage him after all.

The waitress smiled once more and dusted dirt off from his shoulder. "You're just... different," she whispered again, then walked away and went back into the kitchen. Ryan got up and quickly left the restaurant before anyone else noticed just how different he really was, something that a uniform couldn't cover up. How hard was it to become someone else?

Once he left *Duke's,* he was sure those guys didn't know who he was. They didn't even look at him, except for that woman. But what the hell did she know? They were all drunk anyway. For the first time in forever he thought about the orange cloaked woman who saved him twice. He hadn't seen her since that night she threw him down into the trapdoor below the bathroom. She wasn't there when he was about to be hanged so it wasn't like she was his guardian angel. He hoped he would see her again so that he could thank her.

Later on, and a few stops along the way, he had finally reached the center of the city. It was a beautiful, wide open courtyard. He was sure that the further into the center of the city he went, the more modern and well kept it was, the complete opposite from the area bordering the city. Here, there was no ash floating in the air. There was no graffiti or broken windows to create an uneasy environment. This courtyard was completely different than Copper Courtyard. This one had benches and water fountains that had actual water coming out of them. In the middle of it all was a magnificent black tower. It was the exact same one that he had seen twice before from afar. The sleek black sides and glistening windows were something to marvel at, and it was obviously a building of great importance. All the other buildings were rough textured or had spikes and spires at the top, whereas this one was just flat. It almost seemed out of place from the rest, as if all the other buildings were centuries old and this one was just recently built.

People were walking in and out of the tower and there were others reading books or chatting it up with one another on benches. Some of the men were wearing tuxedos and top hats and some of the women wore beautiful gowns with large feathered hats like some of the guests he saw in *Duke's*. Mostly though, the rest were just wearing uniforms.

"Hello, sir."

Ryan turned and faced a large mature looking man wearing a tuxedo and top hat. "Oh, hi."

"I'm sorry for being rude, but are you new here?" asked the man through his bushy white beard. He had age lines along his face and small glasses fitted over his beady eyes. "You don't look very familiar. Sorry for prying."

"I'm pretty new here," replied Ryan casually. He was becoming uncomfortable with the beginning of this conversation already. The man had better not ask him the question that he had been dreading to be asked this whole time.

"What is your job title then? I'm very curious in meeting new workers. You do look young, however."

Damn it. "My job title? Well, I'm…" He looked up at the tower and pointed. "I work in there."

The man turned around and shielded his eyes as he looked up. "Well I'm sure you do. Only ones who wear that specific badge work in Triumph Tower. You work for the city my lad. And from what I see, you are a part of the city's council."

Holy fuck

"I can also see that you are new to this position, because your badge has yet to be engraved with your name and title. You also appear lost, naive and quite dumbfounded."

Ryan sighed annoyingly. "Really?" he asked. "I mean, yes, you are correct sir. That is my job—new job. I'm quite nervous though. I love this city to death, so why not have a hand in running it? It truly is great."

"It *was* great," said the man with a disgusted face. "Until Zephyrus Jenkins died. Then it all went downhill from there. Don't even get me started on that debacle."

"Who was Zephyrus Jenkins?"

"Don't be silly. You know who he is, my lad. Zephyrus Jenkins was the great man who was the previous mayor of this city. He had the greatest work ethic and was loved by everyone. But a few years ago, he disappeared. It was the worst thing to befall this city. You should really get caught up on your history. I thought it was a job requirement. But who knows what's happening around here anymore. Inexperience is running amok nowadays. No offense to you, sir."

Ryan tried to steer the conversation away from him. "Yeah, but I hear the current mayor is quite the heartache."

The man looked at Ryan and laughed. "That's saying it politely. That man is a joke. Apparently he was Zephyrus's son, the heir to the city. At least, that's what he has told everyone. But I think otherwise. The brute is only twenty-one. Mr. Jenkins doesn't give a darn about anything or anyone and he probably doesn't want to be mayor of this city. He acts like a twelve-year-old. Me, me, me, I, I, I."

"Well, can't you just… get rid of him or something?" asked Ryan. "How much longer is his service term?"

"I like your thinking. But the way things work around here is when the mayor dies his son or daughter becomes the new mayor. Sometimes a family will hold the 'mayor' title for generations. If there is no offspring, then there is a re-election and a new family takes over—which is very rare. It has only happened once in my lifetime. So his term is forever, or until he dies. I cannot tell you how many people have tried assassinating him. All who try just get burned alive or thrown down into the dungeons—or worse. They get thrown down into Catadorga beneath the Fire's Depth." The man shuddered.

Ryan had a terrible gut-wrenching feeling in his stomach. This whole thing was just getting worse.

The man noticed Ryan's anxious face. "Don't worry. You should do well. Nobody really even sees him. The council does most of the city's planning and takes cares of most of its affairs. The mayor doesn't seem to do anything around here anymore so you have your work cut out for you my young lad." The man fixed his top hat and waved to a woman sitting on a bench. "Where did you say you were from?"

"I didn't. I'm from the… mountains."

"Really?!" said the man in surprise, his eyes widening. "I know a few people from the Auroraborry Peaks. I myself live in the Great Imperial City now. I'm an ambassador. But I go up there once in a while for the tour of the mountains. I've been on that tour twenty times at least. The mountains are always changing. Have you been on the tour? Of course you have, what am I saying…"

"I actually haven't," said Ryan, following along. "It's really cold. Not really my thing. That's why I left to come here."

"Yes, I suppose. But the cold is nothing compared to Frostbite Village, right? You know, they should really let the tours go further into the mountains. They stop right when it's getting to the good part. I would love to see the Salter's Bridge across the Louise Canyon and the Ancients' Temple again—those were probably the most interesting parts of the tour. But nobody really knows about them though because they're so secretive and forbidden. Oh, I just saw your ears perk up a bit. Are you interested in them too?"

Ryan was trying to sort out this information that he knew nothing of. "Not really," he said.

The man waved to another person walking by. "Anyway, I'm afraid I have to be off. I'll be having a late lunch from the looks of things. You have a good afternoon yourself. My goodness, I didn't even ask for your name! My apologies sir."

"That's okay. It's Henry Jetarbee."

"Well, hello and goodbye Mr. Jetarbee. Yes, that sounds like an Auroraborry name. My name is Damien Durks the Third. And might I add, just from speaking with you I can tell that you'll be a great asset to this city. Good day, sir."

"Good day to you too, sir." Ryan reached over and shook his hand.

"If you ever find yourself in the Great Imperial City Mr. Jetarbee, just ask for me and give them your name. I shall remember who you are no doubt. You will have somewhere to stay."

"Thank you," said Ryan sincerely.

The man walked off and left Ryan standing alone. Everyone else seemed to be leaving for lunch or back to their work. He looked up at the monstrous black tower as the red light shone onto its surface. He walked up to the front entrance and went inside. Might as well see where he worked.

The inside looked like a mall of sorts with countless rooms upon rooms on each floor. There were hundreds of floors with dozens of elevators moving up and down in constant rotation. Thick, marble cylinders were holding up each floor and the railings were sterling silver. On the grand lobby floor were long red granite counters with dozens of receptionists answering to a constant ringing. Ryan looked at one receptionist and saw that she was speaking into a pen. Ryan couldn't help but wonder if they were using the Communi-kay Orb, the same kind that Brazz bugged his visor with. It was obviously the same thing as a headset or telephone used to speak with one another from all places. And how stupid he felt, thinking that it was some kind of device used only by spies, when in fact everybody in the tower used it to communicate with different floors and probably the outside world.

He walked around in awe with his head up and looked all the way up to the top where the ceiling wasn't even visible anymore. The whole tower was lit brightly with dozens of chandeliers. It was all posh and extravagant, like the Classer Hotel, but grander in scale and wonder. This was where he fit in.

"Excuse me?"

Ryan spun around and saw a young man. His hair was waxed and slicked back, with light stubble around his chin and checks. His skin was also very tanned. He was wearing a sharp black suit and dress shoes and numerous rings on his fingers. His eyes however were red and puffy, as if he had been crying or had been up for days. Regardless, he still looked extensively handsome and rich, standing out from everyone else in the tower. *How familiar he looked,* thought Ryan.

"Hi," said Ryan. "Can I help you?"

"Yes. I couldn't help but notice that you're fairly new here."

Ryan tried to not to show his nervousness. "Yes, you're right... but I'm just kind of lost."

The man smiled kindly. "Everyone who works here wears a special badge that says their name and occupation." He pointed to Ryan's chest. "I see that you're part of the city's council. I must have forgotten to engrave your badge for you. A member of the city council should never be neglected as one such as yourself."

"It's honestly okay," said Ryan. "I've been meaning to get it done." His eyes darted around. "I just have to leave for a second though. I'll be right back. I forgot my.... bag outside."

"It's okay. This will only take a moment," insisted the man, placing a ringed hand on his shoulder. The light danced off an emerald encased in gold. "You can't be in here without your proper credentials. No engraving, no job. You had better get it now. I'm in charge of the badge registration of all employees so if you would just follow me up to my office, I'll let you fill out some documents with your current information and we'll get you set up. You'll be on your way. My name is Mr. Powell, in case you forgot from our previous meeting." His grip on Ryan's shoulder seemed to tighten. "Just this way. Your backpack will be fine."

Ryan looked down at his hand on his shoulder.

The man smiled. "Follow me."

He could just run. Run out of here and never come back ever again. But reluctantly, he followed the man into an elevator. He waited inside as a few others got on. It closed and took them up to the floors above. Nobody talked, so Ryan didn't say anything. Strange glances met his eyes and it felt uncomfortable. It was like he was caught stealing and was being carried away by the police. He looked up at the numbers above the door to distract himself and noticed that there were almost two hundred levels to this tower. As more people got in, the whisperings amongst them started. It was like high school again.

When they arrived at the right floor, him and the man got out. The man led him across the ninety-eighth floor towards another elevator. Ryan caught a quick glance over the railing and looked down to the very bottom. Everyone looked like ants, and Ryan wasn't a real fan of heights either so he quickly turned away.

They entered a black elevator that held just the two of them. The man pushed a single brown button and the elevator shot up at a faster pace than the other, not even making a sound.

"My office is on the tallest floor," said the man.

The door opened and they stepped out onto a small lobby with a wide stone balcony lined with pillars that looked down over all the floors in the tower. Strange abstract statues were placed all along the floor and there was a wooden double door across from the balcony. The noises from the people down below didn't even carry over to this height—it was like being on the top of a mountain. They walked over to the door and the man opened it, ushering Ryan to step inside.

The room was a superior space for an office. The desk at the far end looked so small and insignificant compared to the size of the room and the height of the ceiling. The long red walls were filled with shelves that held countless books and other miscellaneous objects. Behind the heavy oak desk was a fairly large window that took up the entire wall itself and had a red velvet curtain draped over one side of it. In the middle of the window was an opening to a small balcony that looked to be made of glass. The red light from outside made everything look maroon, as if a sunset was receding inside and the shadows from the furniture stretched out along the carpet.

"Well, this is it," said Mr. Powell. "Just have a seat at my desk and I'll be right with you." The man went over to a tall wooden bookcase as Ryan sat down at his desk as instructed.

When he sat down, he reached over and organized some book ends that were sitting at a weird angle as well as some picture frames that were not equally spaced out. As he continued moving things, it was making him more uneasy. The desk was messy. He grabbed some pens that were on a stack of papers and lined them up almost perfectly along the table's surface.

"What are you doing?"

Ryan turned in his seat and saw the man standing over him with a red folder in his hand.

"Oh, sorry. I sometimes do stuff like this, like when I'm nervous. It's just a bad habit."

Mr. Powell looked at the desk suspiciously. "Why are you nervous?

You're not in trouble." He raised his chin. "Some people call what you're doing O.C.D."

"I guess," said Ryan. He didn't like it when people used that word. "It only happens sometimes though."

Mr. Powell put his hand up and chuckled lightly. "I didn't mean any offense." He went around to his chair and threw the folder onto the desk, making the pens scatter. "I have A.D.D. A few think it's something far worse than that. They call it anger. I call it passion." He scoffed. "I don't really pay attention to what others have to say though. Most of them just lie anyway. They tell you what you want to hear while keeping their true own thoughts and true insecurities to themselves. They lie to you so you don't become afraid." He looked at Ryan as if expecting him to say something.

Ryan didn't, but instead looked at the red folder that he threw on the desk then at a pen that rolled over the edge and onto the carpet with a *thud*. He looked over his shoulder to the closed door.

Run.

"Is the door shut?"

"Yes," said Mr. Powell, sliding a ring off his thumb. "Can't you see that it is?"

Ryan licked his lips and shook his head slightly, noticing a large portrait hanging over the door. It was the exact same one he remembered seeing in Mainbreak Hall, except this one was five times the size. He suddenly put two and two together and his heart skipped a beat. How did he not notice before? He whipped his gloves across his pants as if they were dirty then looked at the folder that was slightly bent at the corner.

Mr. Powell followed his gaze. "So, anyway, this is awkward." He turned around and stood in front to his window, looking out with his arms folded. The red light filled his face and he shielded his eyes with his hand. "I haven't been very happy lately."

Ryan kept looking down at the folder on the desk. He slid the folder towards him and read the label on the front that said *HOME*. He pushed it back to its original position.

"There are many reasons why," continued Mr. Powell. "It's because of one thing on my mind right now. I'm going to ask your opinion on it."

"What is it?" asked Ryan.

Mr. Powell turned around and faced him. He grabbed a pen and started clicking it slowly. "For the longest time, I didn't really understand why people here acted a certain way. You and I both know that where we come from, it's not like this. Here, one person thinks something bad will happen, then they convince someone else, then everyone loses their minds. But, thinking about it now actually, it isn't much different from where you and I come from. People are insane wherever you go, but it's the ones you least suspect who are the ones you have to watch out for. Because they can crack at any second and go ballistic. Just. Like. That." He snapped the pen in half. "You can make anyone go crazy from the most simplistic thing. All you have to do is keep making them fail. All you have to do is light a match. The rest naturally takes care of itself."

Ryan felt his heart racing more and more as if it was about to burst out of his chest. "*Just run. Run out of this room, run out of this building and run out of this city,*" said a voice inside his head. Even the window looked tempting.

"Have you heard of an island, Ryan?" asked Mr. Powell. "This specific one that I'm thinking of has a beautiful white bridge with a most beautiful city next to it... I'm sure you have seen it. For I have seen it as well."

Ryan shook his head. "I honestly don't know what you're talking about. And I never said my name was Ryan."

"Think hard," he urged, his eyes narrowing.

Ryan gave him a black stare. The sweat on his skin felt like rain rolling down his body. The Sweat Preventer was pure useless it seemed. "I don't know what you're talking about. Sorry."

Carson slammed his fist onto the table. "Stop playing games! I know where you come from, damn it! You happened to come across a dark room inside your high school. Right? You went into that room out of curiosity and ended up here?! Speak the truth!"

Ryan's mouth opened. "No," was all he said.

Carson walked around the desk and looked him in the face. "No? Are you intellectually stupid by nature or do you just have a hard time using that non-existent brain of yours?"

Ryan gave him a nasty look. "Hey, man—"

Carson grabbed his chin. "As mayor of this city, I know everything that happens. Nothing gets passed my Secret Service." He let go of his chin roughly. "You will not lie to me again."

Apparently Secret Service haven't been doing their job very good then, thought Ryan. He fidgeted a bit. This was him? This was the mayor who wanted him captured? Not threatening at all—Ryan could defiantly take him if he needed to.

"So, here you are. Face to face with me from your own doing. How pathetic is that? I had to rely on your own stupidity."

"Wait a minute," said Ryan finally. A light bulb went off in his head. "Were you one of the students that went missing from OceanView a few years ago?"

Carson was caught off guard. "No comment," he said.

"I remember now," said Ryan. "It was all over the news. Is your last name Powell?"

Carson signed loudly as if annoyed. "Yes! I've already told you that that was my name. Don't you listen? Apparently not. Too busy with your mental illness."

Ryan ignored him. "I should have known. Why didn't your last name ring a bell when I heard it? But there were two others that went missing as well. Two girls named Carmen and Cassidy. Where are they?"

Carson stepped forward. "You don't need to know that, Jack."

Ryan got up from his chair and turned towards the door. "I'm not Jack. But I guess we're buddies now, so I'll just leave."

"Sit your bitch ass down!"

Ryan didn't sit, except just look into Carson's savage sleep deprived eyes. "Make me, bitch."

Carson's eyes widened and looked as though he was about to lunge at him, but then his demeanor changed and softened. "I'm sorry," he said sadly, looking down at his desk. "I didn't mean to yell like that. I'm just impatient."

"Too busy with your mental illness I guess," remarked Ryan.

Carson shot him a dark glance but held his composure. He reached for the folder labeled *HOME* on the desk and grabbed it. "The sheets in this folder are the key to getting me home. I've been researching the portals of Pheonexia for just over a year now. Tell me what you know of them."

"I have no idea," said Ryan, pulling his visor down over his eyes. *Wait... portals? There was more than one?*

"Well, firstly," said Carson. "I must say you are incredibly stupid. I mean, I can be too, but you're in another league of your own. Can I ask you something? Why on God's red earth would you walk around this city like a stupid idiot, walk into random buildings like a stupid idiot and talk to people you don't even know? Why would you take things from people who you don't even know? Do you not think that maybe they would have alternate intentions? Why would anyone want to help *you?* Are you really *that* stupid? I don't even know how many times I've used the word *stupid* in the last thirty seconds."

"Actually you—"

"I'm not done!" he shouted. He grabbed a metal candlestick from off the desk and threw it past Ryan's shoulder, barely missing his head.

"Everything was functioning properly here until you came along!" He went up to Ryan and shoved the folder in his face. "Do you know what this is all about, Jack?" He opened the folder and Ryan saw dozens of maps and writings on old and wrinkled pieces of parchment. "You must think this is all funny. Some sick game you enjoy relishing in. You see me as some desperate fool perhaps? I'm reduced to scrambling around trying to figure out a way to get out of this hell hole all on my own. I live in constant fear everyday that I am here. The Lord watches me always. He sees you and gets angry at me that you aren't dead. I can't even step outside anymore without people attempting to kill me. But you. *You.* You can just walk around like a dumbass for days and days and not one person have the slightest clue. Unbelievable."

Ryan continued looking at the documents from beneath his visor, so Carson grabbed it off and threw it to the side.

"I don't have a portal to go back through like you do. I ran out of time and missed the one opportunity I had to do so." He looked away as if ashamed. "Do you know anything about the two hidden portals? Has anyone told you about them?" He leaned into his face. "Tell me about the Peril Escape. Tell me its secrets. Tell me the locations of the Ancients' Temples. You must know something!" He grabbed Ryan's collar. "TELL ME!"

Ryan stared at him. "I don't know anything Carson. Nothing about what you're talking about man. How am I supposed to know?"

"Because I know you've talked with Otis and I know he knows things that he isn't telling me. HAS HE TOLD YOU?!"

"No!" yelled Ryan who was getting a sense of major paranoia from Carson.

"Because if you tell me, I won't kill you. I will let you flee." Carson was gripping the folder harder now, his knuckles turning white. He finally threw the folder at Ryan. "Read it," he ordered.

Ryan opened the folder and looked down at it. It was obvious that many of the pages were ripped out form several other books. There were also writings from Carson and others on scraps of paper.

"Where is Otis?" he asked as he tried reading the papers. As he thought about it more, he was getting the impression that Carson would never actually kill him—he didn't seem like that type of guy to do something like that. In fact, he appeared to be a weak, just big talk. He was just threatening him. It seemed like Ryan needed Carson, and Carson needed Ryan. *We could help each other,* he thought.

"Otis is none of your concern right now." Carson started laughing in an inappropriate way as if he was watching a comedy. "That scum cow can't do anything right." He glared at Ryan. "Continue reading child!"

If I'm a child, then you're a toddler.

Ryan grinned and asked another question that he was curious about. "So how did you convince everyone here that you were their new mayor? Someone must have helped you."

A stream of black flames started forming along Carson's arm and up to his hand. A sudden burst of fire erupted from his palm and sailed up to the ceiling, burning the top. "READ OR I WILL KILL YOU!" His eyes faded from brown to black then back to brown again in the matter of a few seconds. He was shaking and looking around the room as if he heard a gunshot, his eyes nervous. "He is here with us," he muttered quietly. "He is watching and listening to what we say."

Ryan's eyes were wide with fear. "How the hell did you do that?" he asked. It got eerily quiet and the room seemed to have darkened. But now he couldn't possibly concentrate on the papers, and Carson spotted this.

Carson grabbed the folder out of his hand and shoved it into a drawer. "You don't need to know any of this after all. I know a better place for you." He walked around his desk and reached under it to push a button. "You're going to do something for me instead."

Ryan looked around the room frantically as the doors to the office opened, a creaking sound spreading across the room. His two bodyguards, Durt and Koi, marched in as if they were summoned for an extremely important duty. They stood next to Carson's side with their arms folded, smiling at Ryan.

"Since you don't have any choice in the matter, I want you to follow me." Carson straightened his suit out and walked ahead as the bald one with dark skin named Durt picked Ryan up with a single hand, turned him around, then pushed him towards the door. Koi trailed behind, his mouth smiling under his red mustache.

Ryan uneasily went ahead and walked out of the office. He couldn't imagine where Carson was taking him. All four got into the black elevator and waited as it declined down several floors. This elevator was not built for four people, especially two as big as Durt and Koi.

They got out and went towards the second elevator that would take them down to the grand lobby. Countless people were standing around and looking up curiously at what was happening in front of them. Ryan felt embarrassed.

Once they got off the elevator and went across the grand lobby to the exiting doors, even more people stopped and stared at the stranger that was being taken away by the mayor and his two men.

"Is that *him?*" asked a woman in shock. "Is that the monster that you and the Lord have warned us about? Have you finally caught him, Mr. Jenkins?"

"Bad boy Mr. Jenkins," said Ryan. Carson slapped him across the head and continued walking.

"That is him! He has been caught!" she shouted. When she said this, there were cheers and applause from the lobby and the floors above. Some even started throwing things at him.

"Destroy him!" shouted a man.

"Let us move faster here," said Carson nervously to Durt and Koi, quickening his pace as Koi grabbed Ryan out of the building. There weren't many people in the courtyard, in fact, there was nobody in sight.

"Unusual," Carson said quietly.

They walked for a while. The city seemed to remain silent as they got further away from the tower and to new areas that Ryan hadn't explored yet. The air wasn't pleasant anymore, and the buildings weren't beautiful with their gothic charm. He was now entering an area where there were chain-linked gates around countless factories. Machinery and heavy trucks would pass in out of these factories along dirt-filled paths. Carson was taking him away from the center of the city and towards the far perimeter via side streets and alleyways.

Almost an hour and a half had passed when they finally reached their destination. Spreading up in front of Ryan was a gigantic mass of stone and boulders that were piled up high towards the top of the city's perimeter wall. The pile was so extensive that it could have been the side of a mountain itself. The rocks and stone were jagged and treacherous. Just one misstep would result in a broken back or neck. There were small openings along the rocks, hundreds of them, that lead into the unknown. There were abandoned karts and trucks and heavy steam was rising and spurting up like ghosts. He remembered this place from when he saw it from his hotel balcony. It looked a lot worse up close.

"The Fire's Depth," said Carson.

Durt and Koi pushed Ryan forward, and all four of them walked up a terribly jagged path through the rock. Carson went ahead of him, clumsy in his walking. Ryan could just feel the dirt flying into his face.

They reached a cave that was about half way up. Carson stepped aside so that Ryan could walk in first.

"Go," he said, pushing him forward.

Ryan stepped in and had to bend over a bit because the ceiling was so low. It was pitch dark and it had to have been one of the stuffiest and most claustrophobic places he had ever been in. As he kept walking, he knocked his foot into a hard metal something that was embedded into the ground.

Carson yelled out to stop. He couldn't see what Carson was doing, but he could hear the sound of metal being thrust open and then a burst of orange light illuminating the dark and secluded cave. Carson had opened up a metal hatch. What was under the hatch made Ryan want to fight his way out of the cave, because he knew that he was being forced to go down beneath it.

Below the hatch was an opening big enough for someone to step down through. There was a slanted walkway that spiraled its way against a stone wall, down hundreds of feet. It was like a wide, circular shaft that went hundreds of feet down below the surface of the ground. Along the swirling stairwell were dozens of openings. Down at the very bottom, hundreds of feet, was a pool of lava. Every few minutes the lava would shoot up like a geyser through the middle of the spiraling walkway and hit the hatch door above. Ryan looked at the underside of the metal hatch door and saw that it was severally burnt.

Carson blinked his eyes a few times, his eyes watering from the striking light. "I would like you to go down there for me to fix a problem. A few days ago there was a small earthquake. It didn't really shake up anything above ground, but below it shut off an electricity panel that is used to power some of the factories. It's just a simple switch that needs to be adjusted."

Ryan looked at Carson, confused. "That's it?"

"I won't kill you if you do this for me," he said. "I'm letting you do a favor for me. If you don't do it though, then I will have to do the unpleasant right here and now. Do you value your life, Mr. Davidson?"

"And you'll let me go if I do this?"

"Yes," he said, maintaining a steady voice. "As I was talking to you... I felt angry with myself. Angry for what I felt like I had to do to you. There's no point to it anymore. I want you to go back home and not stay here for the rest of your life like I am. This will be my excuse if anyone should ask about what happened here today. I'll say that I threw you down into the Fire's Depth. You died from dehydration." Carson put out his hand. "All you have to do is this little job for me. Please."

Ryan looked at his outstretched hand and hesitantly shook it. "Okay."

"Thank you," said Carson. He withdrew a folded piece of parchment and slipped it into Ryan's front jacket pocket "Here is a map. It's easy to follow and read. The panel is a gigantic thing that you can't miss. Good luck."

Ryan tilted his head. "Gigantic thing?"

"Yes. You'll see it. It's labeled on the map I just gave to you."

Behind them, Durt and Koi were standing still as statues. He couldn't help but wonder if they were the same two that invaded Renny and Otis' home his first night here. They didn't dress like Secret Service, and according to Demi and Jacob, that's who invaded the house.

Ryan stepped forward and looked down before going down the hatch and onto the slanted path, which almost looked like it could have been a slide swirling downwards into the pool of lava.

"Goodbye," said Carson. He shut the hatch and fastened it tightly. He looked at Durt and Koi and snapped his fingers to them. "Durt, Koi, hurry up. One of you stays here though. I refuse to be alone."

Durt and Koi looked at each other and nodded their heads, agreeing in silence that Koi would go and do Carson's bidding.

Once Koi left, Carson leaned up against the cave wall. *I hate this,* he thought. *This shouldn't have happened. I was doing just fine.* He looked down at the hatch. "Damn you Ryan. Damn. You."

Less than an hour later, a scuffling sound came from outside the cave. Koi and his bushy red moustache returned, and this time he brought someone with them.

Carson grinned. "Hello, rat."

Otis didn't say anything except spit at his shoes.

"Oh, don't do that. I have a job for you."

Otis sighed angrily. "What now?"

Carson grabbed the handle to the hatch. "I need you to meet an old friend down in Catadorga. I'm sure you remember him."

"Ryan," whispered Otis

"Yes. I need you to kill him immediately."

Otis shook his head as he struggled in the bodyguard's grasp. "I will not do it. I don't kill people."

Carson laughed a dark humor. "But you do betray people like the snake that you are."

"I'm not a snake either," said Otis through clenched teeth.

"Oh you are. A weak and pathetic snake that can't do his job so is helplessly imprisoned for the rest of his days."

Otis continued struggling and Carson was getting annoyed. "Stop it," he said.

"You do it then!" shouted Otis. "You killed one of your other guards, burned him to a crisp. You also pushed your personal assistant out the window. What about Zephyrus? He was doing a good job running this city. What did you do with him? What's a mere seventeen-year-old to you? Easy target I would think. Is it because you would feel guilty for murdering someone who came from your own world? He is like your brother, is he not? You can't kill him."

Carson clenched his hands angrily as flames slithered around his fists. He grabbed Otis by the collar. "You do not speak about where I come from, unless it's about me being Zephyrus' son? Got that?" He glanced at Durt and Koi, who looked clueless about what was being discussed. "And are you telling me how to do my job, rat?" He raised one of his flaming hands into the air and slapped Otis hard across the face, twice, burning his face and making him yell in pain. Carson laughed in amusement. "Shut up, little wimp. SHUT UP! NOW!"

Otis looked up and laughed while holding his face. "Little wimp? You are the wimp. Look at you. Why do you always have these two guys with you? Scared someone is going to beat you up? You have the power of fire and you're too scared to use it."

The flames from Carson's hands disappeared and he flopped to his knees. "Can you please kill him for me? I'll kill your family."

"No you won't. You're just too scared. You're just a weak little boy."

"Alright, enough of this! I'll get those two to do it then!" He motioned his head to Durt and Koi. "Now get down there and kill that bastard!" He picked Otis up and threw him onto the hatch. "Don't patronize me! You are not only betraying me but the Lord as well! He is watching us, aren't you aware?!" His eyes dilated to black and his skin began to splinter and crack with red. He put his hands to his head again and muttered in a sympathetic voice: "Please. I don't want to die... He enters my mind and dreams and yells at me. His eyes glare at me. He tells me... Kill the boy. Kill the boy. KILL THE BOY!" His fists were clenched again and vapors of black flame swirled up his arm like a snake as he shook uncontrollably. He reached into his pocket and pulled out a large orange rock that was as bright as the sun and had tiny red spots all over it. It looked as though it would explode, making Durt and Koi slowly edge towards the cave opening, backing away from it.

Otis nervously reached for the hatch handle and opened it wide enough for him to get through. "Okay, I will go," he said quietly.

Carson's black eyes faded back to brown. He shook his head slightly as if he just woke up from a long sleep. "Thank you," he said gently.

Otis looked at Carson one last time then shut the hatch door behind him as he descended down. Carson turned around and saw Durt and Koi standing by the entrance with the red light from outside falling onto their faces. They looked petrified.

"What?" he said with a laugh. "You two aren't scared of the dark, are you?" He looked down at the rock he was holding. "Oh, I see. Scared to use fire am I? I highly doubt that."

ELEVEN.

CATADORGA

THE MERE HUMIDITY OF THE FIRE'S DEPTH WAS AN ELEMENT
that Ryan could not comprehend once he entered below. It was the
warmest he had ever felt. Once the hatch closed shut, he was left to look
down through the slanted walkway that spiraled around the vertical shaft
to the very bottom that was dozens of feet below. There was no railing to
hang on to, so he was forced to slide his back against the wall and grip his
shoes vigorously onto the walkway so he would not slip and fall through
the middle and plummet downwards. Everything was lit luminously; the
lava pool at the very bottom radiating a blinding surge of orange and red
light that looked neon against the stone of the wall.

Without any indication, a rapid gurgling sound emerged below and
lava burst up through the twisted walkway like a geyser and hit the hatch
above him. Copious amounts of spurts and sprays reflected off the metal
and landed onto the walkway beside Ryan. Dodging them quickly, he
almost slipped just as he desperately tried to cling on to the nonexistent

wedges and holes in the smooth stone. Along the curling path there were countless wide openings that lead further underground. Ryan knew about the dark and dangerous tunnels underneath some cities. He looked into the dark veils of the openings, not knowing for certain what was down in the unknown, adding to his disturbing anxiety.

He slid his body against the wall and continued to look down at what could be his pit of death if he wasn't careful. He didn't even want to move. If he moved, he would slip. He would die. This wasn't Carson's fault though. It was his own. He got himself here. Maybe he deserved this. Maybe he was being punished.

The nearest opening to him was a couple feet away, and he managed to reach over and grab the side of it and pull himself forward. He stumbled through and fell onto rough ground. The long tunnel that extended on was silent except for faint echoes of things being clanged together in the distance. There were other noises as well that were too small to fully make out, but not small enough to miss.

He pulled out the map that Carson gave him and edged himself forward on his elbows until enough light from the lava down below would brighten up the piece of parchment. It was impossible to read the map because there were so many lines pointing in different directions on every inch of it. He couldn't even find where he was. Then closing his eyes in embarrassment, he realized that it was purposely drawn that way. Carson purposely made it confusing. It wasn't even a map, but a bunch of lines and random words and phrases such as *dumb birdbrain, why are you so unintelligent?* and *monkey, haha.* In the corner there was a drawing of a smiley face with its tongue sticking out.

Ryan crunched up the paper, feeling more embarrassed and wanting ever so much to punch Carson's face several times. He looked at the crumpled map in his fist then dropped it down into the lava pit. He slid his body towards the wall and leaned up against it, angry and frustrated. He had never been so angry in his life.

Realizing the hopeless situation he was in, he cupped his face into his hands and yelled at the top of his lungs just as there was a prominent creak from the hatch. He heard shoes touch the walkway just as another geyser blocked out the sound.

Ryan budged his way across the ground and peered over the side of the opening. He glanced up and saw Otis standing in total frustration, cracking his knuckles and walking perfectly down the steep and twisting walkway as if he had done it many times before. Ryan darted up and had a quick debate in his head that lasted less than five seconds. Take his anger out on Otis or get away before Otis killed him, which is why he was down here in the first place. The whole point of coming into the city was to find Otis, to ask him questions. But now there was no time for that. He had to find his own way home now.

He ran through the darkness of the tunnel, daring to venture deeper without knowing what he would encounter. It was survival of the fittest now, and right now he was the prey that was being hunted. He reached into the pocket of his uniform jacket and pulled out the small bag of Orbs that he bought earlier that day. He grabbed the Star Light Orb and slammed it into his gloved hand. He didn't bother looking at the tag to read its T.U.D. His hand sprouted a strong streak of white light, but once he closed his fist the light would vanish until he opened it up again. He reopened his fist and put his hand out in front of him. He heard the echo of footsteps from Otis entering the tunnel, so Ryan picked up the pace. Where he was going, he didn't know. He was an athlete. He could run. Carson didn't want to kill him, so he sent Otis to do it. Otis was being forced to do it, as death would most likely be the penalty for him if he didn't. What was Ryan to him anyway?

"I hear you!" yelled Otis, a small sense of amusement in his voice. "You cannot hide from me! I know these tunnels better than you! You will get lost and die down in Catadorga like the thousands before you! Just look at the walls if you need proof!"

A *swishing* sound emerged behind Ryan that made him trip and fall flat on the ground. Something prickly was tightening around both his ankles. He shone the light onto what it was; a type of gold and fuzzy cord that was tied around both his ankles and tightening itself more with each passing second. Ryan reached down and attempted to remove it, but when he touched it would send out a sharp pulse of electricity through his body.

"I wouldn't touch that if I were you," said Otis as his face came into view. "It's called the Wire Clutch Orb. Nasty little guy. It will get very bad if you leave it on for too long."

Ryan looked up at him as moisture began swelling up in his eyes from the pain that increased with each passing second. It felt like hundreds of little pins were stabbing him all over his legs, like something was crawling around beneath his flesh and pinching his insides.

Otis squatted down to talk to him. "Let us try and get through this quickly so I can remove this thing before it leaves any permanent damage. I think you would miss your feet."

Ryan couldn't remain still as he moved his body around in several different directions as if possessed. Even breathing made it hurt.

"Killing isn't for me. It's a very nasty business… especially when you know the person. Makes it all that much harder."

"I don't know you," said Ryan through clenched teeth. "But I do know you're a traitor."

"That is correct," said Otis calmly, appearing ashamed from the look on his face. "But everyone has to betray one another at one point or another. It's human nature."

"So don't do it. Don't do Carson's bidding. He's not worth it."

"Carson's life will be at risk if you are not gotten rid of, Ryan. People are already suspicious of him, questioning who he really is—who he isn't. The Lord commands that you are destroyed, for whatever reason that still remains to be seen." Otis revealed a red Orb to him. "This is called The Implosion Explosion Orb. It blows up whatever it touches. It's quite rare and dangerous. You see, the moment I throw it at something, there will be just five seconds before it explodes."

Ryan laughed, which even that hurt. "So you want to blow us up? Great idea."

Otis smiled and chuckled in response. "No, this is different. It only blows up what it touches. So say I throw this at an orange. The orange will burst into juicy chunks of goodness while the environment around it is unharmed. Now, if I throw it at you… well, the only thing flying around down here will be little chunks of darling Ryan."

Ryan's face went from angry to disturbed, unable to respond.

"I wouldn't personally want to do something like this," muttered Otis.

"Carson sadly would though, since it was his idea. I would have just knocked your head in with a rock and left you to bleed to death or as you are now, since there is no T.U.D to the Wire Clutch. It will just sink into your skin, melt the bone away, and eventually tear your feet off."

Ryan was moving furiously around on the ground and whimpered like a child as the wire dug deeper through his pants and into his flesh.

"But..." Otis reached down to the wire and ripped it off. He threw it into the air, making it vanish from sight. "I'm not like that. I no longer do what Carson orders, for I no longer work for him. Apparently he forgot about that, as he was the one who fired me." He tucked the Implosion Explosion Orb away into his pocket and got up. "Okay then. We had better get going. You need to leave your hand open at all times for we need the light. Good thinking using it."

Ryan stumbled back up and looked at Otis with an exasperated face— he was in complete shock.

"What?" said Otis with a hearty laugh. "Did you honestly think I would do it? I hope you don't need to go into therapy after this. I was just acting you know."

"Well you deserve an award for best supporting actor then you little..." Ryan trailed off as his heart beat a million beats per second. He limped forward with his legs trembling, the force from each step sending sharp pains up each leg, making him swear loudly a couple times. "Damn! As if you did that man."

"Sorry. I didn't want you to run off. If you get lost down here, you are done for."

Ryan stopped and bent down, trying to get breath back into his lungs.

He lifted his pant legs up a bit and saw a bloody swore wound around both ankles. Hopefully it wouldn't get infected.

"Can we get back through the hatch?"

"No," said Otis. "Keep the light straight, Ryan. The hatch doesn't open from the inside. Only from the outside."

"So how do we get out? Wait a minute… if we get out, and you haven't killed me, then Carson will know."

"He will not," said Otis in a loud voice. "I won't say that Carson is a stupid twenty-one-year-old because he isn't. But I like to think that I am a fairly intelligent thirty-seven-year-old who can outfox him. He doesn't pay attention to the little things. I know quite a bit about him, thus the way his mind works."

"Can you tell me?"

"No, not right now. Once we rest and set up camp for the night I will tell you more. You deserve to know some things."

"How can I trust you?"

Otis didn't look at him when he responded. "Because trust is all you have right now. And if you want to go back home, there is some information you really should hear." This time he looked at him, face to face. "I'm the only one you have right now, Ryan. You have to trust me."

The ongoing gloominess of Catadorga was something that would make anyone depressed and unhappy, maybe even contemplate suicide. As they got further into the underground tunnels, the walls started twisting and turning off into several directions. The ground was uneven and full of holes that had to be stepped over. The walls were stained with black dirt with broken bones and skulls attached to them and sprawled on the ground. Ryan refused to look at them, for it made him queasy inside. At times there were areas where the skulls were bunched together over an archway or pieced together on a wall. They belonged to people just like him who were lost and confused, and he hoped that he wouldn't end up as just another decoration next to them. It sometimes felt like they were staring at him from behind, watching him.

It could have been at least two hours before Otis mentioned that they should stop for a break. Ryan preferred the trapdoor under Otis' bathroom to this. At least in there he couldn't get lost. They stopped beside a thin stream of water that was sliding its way through the chiseled rock.

"Where is the water coming from?" asked Ryan. He reached for the top of his head and was going to remove his visor but remembered that Carson took it off when he was in his office.

"Oh, no."

"What is it?"

"It's nothing." Ryan wasn't sure if not being able to talk to Brazz was a good or bad thing. Brazz might get suspicious about his whereabouts. But did he really care about him that much? Was he just like Carson?

"This water comes from the underground lake. It is far down beneath us. As you can see, the water travels upstream."

Ryan thought he misheard Otis. "A lake? Underground the underground?"

Otis reached into his suit pocket and withdrew a small pouch. "Yes. I haven't seen it though. It's nearly impossible to find unless you know where to look. I do know that its entrance is beneath a well. I've talked to others and read documents and books from all over the city and have recently discovered its whereabouts. Since I'm down here often, I decided to try and look for it myself. I found it a few months back. Right now seems like the right time to take advantage of it, or at least you will." He took out an orange Orb and dropped it on the ground. A small fire appeared and started flickering while providing heat to the chilly air.

"I didn't expect it to be so cold down here," said Ryan.

"Well, we are underground. The only reason Blazing City is so warm is because of the sky." Otis leaned his back against the wall and closed his eyes as if he was ready to go to sleep. He was just thinking though.

Ryan stared into the fire and tried to decide on what to ask next. He got the feeling that this was the best time to do it, as if Otis was waiting for him.

"You said you knew things."

Otis examined Ryan as if judging him. "Carson has confided in me to not tell anyone about his past and secrets. But that was before he fired me and before you came here. I am always around him and know things that no one else here does. The little brute has some serious anger. He is the only one who the Lord communicates with regularly. The previous mayor, Zephyrus, wasn't the most faithful to the Lord and never listened to Him. I don't even think the Lord ever talked to Zephyrus at all. He never mentioned it to me and I was very close with him, like a brother. We grew up together when we were kids. He was the one who hired me and trained me to be the best I could, promoting me to Number Two. He wasn't a push over like Carson is. But sadly, three years ago, Zephyrus just disappeared.

One of the most terrible things to befall this city in a long time. It crushed me."

"Did Carson have something to do with it?" asked Ryan.

Otis shrugged. "How? Carson comes out of the portal just like you, and not just by himself, but with two others, and is mayor within weeks. How could that be? How could he do something like that?"

"The Lord helped him," guessed Ryan. He paused. "Who is this Lord anyway? Is He... bad?"

Otis raised an eyebrow and looked to be debating as to whether he was going to answer him or not. "He is not human. He is nothing but a spirit, or what I like to call Him, a shadow. Different people give Him different names. Usually He's just simply known as the Lord. You may hear some call him the Lord of the Righteous Land which is a very old name. He is not someone to take lightly though. But there is so little that you know about all of this—thousands and thousands of years of history."

"I need to know though," pleaded Ryan. "I am apart of this mess now. I need to know what I'm up against. If it will help me get home, then I need to know."

Otis shook his head. "It will drive you crazy. As it drives even me crazy. You either believe that He has always been the creator of Pheonexia, or you believe that there was another who created the world that you are in right now. What I am about to tell you Ryan is the biggest debate and divide that has corrupted our world for thousands of years amongst our people."

"Who created this world if not the Lord?" asked Ryan.

Otis smiled. "A goddess created Pheonexia a very long time ago. Not the Lord as everyone here believes. She was somehow dethroned and sealed away when an evil entity invaded Pheonexia and took over by force—the Lord. It's what people call the Great Battle of the Invasion; an incident that many people deny ever happened. In particular, those who support the Lord and claim he has always been here since the dawn of time. But this Lord, Ryan, who everyone in this city worships is actually a demon spirit from the Shadow Realm. Or Ethklemena, as it's rightfully called. People in this city unknowingly worship a demon from the realm of the dead, the Lord, who they believe was the real creator of Pheonexia. He tricks them. Brainwashes them. History was rewritten thousands of years back by supporters of his to make it appear that the Lord has always been here, erasing traces of the goddess. And so, generations grew up not knowing the goddess. Her stories and history were never passed down and now more than half of Pheonexia are believers of the Lord. I have done readings from all over. I have gone on journeys years ago to find the answers to questions that did not seem right."

Ryan shook his head in bewilderment, not wanting Otis to stop as if he was telling a great suspenseful story. "And?" he asked. "What did you find?"

"I have found," began Otis, "things that people here refuse to believe. There are secrets hidden all around us. The Lord is worried about something. Not until Carson, Carmen and Cassidy came through the portal from your world did I even know that there was a portal. Nobody did. Until Carson came along and told me personally, as he trusted me. And ever since you set foot in here, not them, it has become chaos. Now that's interesting. Why does the Lord want you dead and not the other three?

What is it about you? He wasn't so intrigued on getting rid of the other three, but there is something about you he fears. So much so that he's now trying to get the guy that came from your own world to kill you. Now that is strange. Can you answer this Ryan?"

"No I can't," said Ryan somewhat angrily. "What did I do to Him?"

"That," said Otis with a smile that didn't seem appropriate "is the one and only question that you yourself need to find out. Does Carson know? Nah. This is something the Lord wants to keep to himself. And why is there a portal to begin with? Do you know, Ryan?"

"I don't know anything," he responded.

"Are you sure? Think hard. Think really hard."

"I am Otis! I don't know!" Ryan fell onto his back and stared up at the ceiling, the light from the fire flickering against the stone and skulls. "But this Carmen and Cassidy. Yeah, I know who they are. Where are they now? Do you know?"

"I know that Carmen stays in Triumph Tower where Carson resides. She is his advisor. I see her a few times. Nice looking girl but very sly. Where Cassidy is, I don't know."

"But how did Carson go from lost like I am to mayor of the city? He's not the son of Zephyrus or heir to the city."

"No," said Otis. "I don't know how or why, but Carson and those other two are different from you and me."

"No shit," said Ryan. "Our brains are actually functioning and there's aren't."

Otis smiled. "No, no. They have these… weird qualities about them. I'm also wondering if you have one yourself."

Ryan fidgeted a bit. He didn't like it when people said he had "weird qualities" to him. He would become sensitive and reject them socially if they did.

"I believe that when Carson came through the portal, he was given a kind of strange element infused into his body. Maybe the Lord cursed the portal when He created it, or whoever created it. Carson has the power to use fire whenever he wants. But he can also channel the dark forces of that element, called the Moral, against his own will, almost killing himself when he does so. When I saw those eyes for the first time, those black soulless eyes, I felt terrified. I have never seen him channel it fully. There would be great destruction if he ever did. But I've seen stages of it. Especially when he gets very stressed and mad or when the Lord is actually communicating with him one on one, not just whispering into his ear."

For a second, Ryan felt jealous of Carson. "Are you kidding? So why can't I shoot fire?" He raised his hand into the air and nothing came out of it.

"Maybe you don't have one, or maybe you have to access it differently. I have not seen what Cassidy can do, but Carmen's I've seen traces of. But believe me Ryan. It's nothing to be jealous of. Be thankful you don't have it."

"Unbelievable." Ryan sighed. "And they went to my school."

"If you say they did. They missed their portals when they opened and were unable to get back once they closed. Zephyrus then disappeared and everyone was told that Carson was Zephyrus' heir, which was convincing because he does look like me in a way. I on the other hand knew it was a lie instantly. Zephyrus never mentioned to me that he had a son and we were quite close. So Carson's story about coming out of the portal didn't leak out to the city. The Lord obviously had some part to play in this. He is now demanding that Carson gets rid of you somehow. Whether it be him doing it himself, or someone else like me. The Lord is using him as a puppet. If Carson lets you live, then he fears his own life will be at risk, fearing the Lord will try and get him killed."

"So why doesn't Carson just kill me? He had the chance a couple hours ago. I was sitting right in front of him."

Otis grinned. "It's because he can't do it. I don't think he wants you to die Ryan. Carson isn't a cold blooded murderer; he's a kid who is scared—like you. He sees you as his kin. Perhaps he has feelings for you. A bond. That is why he threw you down here. He may not show it, but he actually does care for you to an extent. You may need see it... but I do."

Ryan grabbed some rocks and tossed them into the fire. Compared to now, he felt so stupid a couple of hours ago.

"When can I go home then? Renny said you knew all about that."

"Did she now?" he said, smiling. "You will know when it's time for you to go home. I know this because I saw it happen to Carson. If what I remember is accurate, then the same thing that happened to him will happen to you. Once you start to glow red. That is when your portal is open, and will remain open for only one hour so you must be quick."

"When will I glow? And why red? Doesn't sound cheerful."

Otis sighed. "That is the difficult part. I don't know when it will happen. Maybe when you are in extreme danger, or when it feels like you are ready. Those numbers above the portal indicate how much time is left until it opens."

"No way," said Ryan as if all hope was suddenly lost. "The numbers read something like sixty-four million the last time I checked."

"Sixty-four million years is right," said Otis. "But that was very early on. The number must be significantly lower by now."

"I hope so," mumbled Ryan. That seemed to have ended it.

"Well, that's enough. More for another day, which may never come if you do go back home. I have only scratched the surface of what I can tell you. But now you know the important parts. I've told you what I believe and and what I've tried for years to understand, not what is confirmed as true. Everything about Carson is accurate. But the rest... I will leave it to your judgement as to what you will believe."

Ryan wanted to know more, but didn't push it, knowing that Otis was stubborn that way.

"Otis?" he asked. "What's this world called again?"

"Pheonexia," he said, the mere word making him smile. "Some parts are terrible, like this city, but others are just beautiful. The Auroraborry Peaks along the east coast and the GloryRise Palace in the Delezary Desert—oh, what beauty. Maybe you will see them one day."

"Yeah," said Ryan, looking into the fire. "Maybe. I don't even know what beauty looks like anymore."

"I assume you really want to go back home, almost desperately. I can see it now. I didn't before."

"That's because I know how serious this is. I mean, look where I am. I'd do anything to be home right now. I wish I could just click my heels together and it would all be okay again. However stupid that may sound."

"It's not stupid," said Otis. "I remember when I would see my wife and children everyday. A smile and hug was all worth it at the end of the day, just knowing there were people there who cared about you. Now, when I see myself gambling their lives away like I am right now..." He turned his face away and lowered it, trying to hide the guilt. "What has this world come to where we are forced to do things that are just not humane? Where does it get you? Waking up every morning worried and scared. The sad part is that I feel sorry for Carson. I think his days are numbered. He just wanted to go home too. What a nice kid he was when I first met him. He was your age, about three years ago when he came here. A little of a wiseass I must admit, but always had a smile on his face. But now, whenever I have to stay the night in that tower to work overtime or am being interrogated, I hear him screaming and yelling. Not in anger or pain, but in sadness. He just doesn't care anymore. He must want to die."

Ryan picked up another rock and started fumbling with it. "How could anybody want to die?"

Otis looked at Ryan for several moments. "Out of curiosity, what would happen if you missed your portal?"

Ryan shrugged. "I... I... don't know. I have a life back home. It may not be much, but it's all I got. I have nothing here. I'll be the first to admit that I'm not the greatest guy or nicest guy... or smartest guy in the world. But I try really hard to be somebody that represents me, and I don't think I've found him yet. I can't stay here. Even though the place where I'm going is all full of things that are just... I don't know... pointless and stupid. Worrying about parties and whether you're going to make an ass of yourself. Or stupid sunless tanners and what they fucking smell like. Oh, mine smells like cherry pomegranate and orange and it's from that place you visit all the time. Who gives a fuck!" He slammed the rock against the wall, his face fuming. He looked at Otis, embarrassed. "Sorry… it's just stupid."

"They are not pointless or stupid, Ryan. They are just the bits and pieces that make up your life. I know stupid—my life has been filled with stupid decisions, as will yours. I was your age. I know the things you go through and are still going through. They may not be exactly the same in your world as they are here, but trust me, I've experienced them. I believe we don't harness our true powers within ourselves until we show our true feelings deep inside, and are willing to let go of any past conflicts and just fight for what is right. Sometimes Ryan, that is all it takes." He rolled over onto his side and closed his eyes, seemingly ending the conversation with his back towards him. "Oh, and sorry about trying to kill you."

Ryan smiled. "Don't worry about it, man."

"It will be dangerous, Ryan. Be prepared."

Ryan scratched his head and stretched out his legs, pondering. "I just feel like you aren't telling me something. It's like you know something or are hiding something from me. Like some kind of messed up irony."

Otis didn't respond.

"I know you know more things, Otis."

There was more silence.

"There is a time and place for answers, Ryan. Knowledge can be a precious and a dangerous weapon. I just have to be sure that some of the answers that I believe to be true are actually right."

Ryan furiously sighed then let out a long yawn that was telling him that it was time for some much needed sleep. He didn't know what was in store for him. But he did feel safe… for the moment… inside the deep dark world of Catadorga.

For hours, Carson hadn't been able to stop pacing and thinking. Inside his office, he walked back and forth in front of his desk, muttering to himself non-stop. Carmen was sitting on his chair and staring at him for the past three minutes out of pure amusement. She tried to make him laugh various times, but it didn't work. She twirled her shoulder length blonde hair through her fingers. Her eyes were hidden behind the short veil that dangled down from her oversized hat and covered half her face. Her liquid purple dress spilled over her legs and onto the carpet like a waterfall.

"Am I bothering you yet?" she asked playfully.

Carson didn't respond.

Carmen's smile faded. "Hello? Paranoid much are we? Carson, God damn it!"

"Hey!" he said suddenly, looking at her fiercely "I'm not paranoid. I'm thinking. Do not interrupt."

"Right," she said, rolling her eyes. "You look like an angry ape right now."

Carson turned back around and nodded, as if coming to a conclusion inside his head. "I will have to kill him first. Wait! Ryan first, then Otis. Perfect."

"Oh God, Carson."

"Oh God what? I'm sorry, but this doesn't involve you. Those miserable peasants didn't hang Ryan like I told them to. Pathetic Secret

Service didn't find him in that house during that first go around. Nobody is trying to kill him. I'm doing it all myself. My options are growing thin! I will blow up the city if I have too! I will kill them all before the Lord has a reason to kill me!" He looked around nervously as if he was just caught stealing precious jewels. "He is listening and watching me right now."

"Settle down," said Carmen. She got up out of the chair and sighed. She walked around him and put her hands on his shoulders, letting her hands slide down his chest and unbutton the front of his white collar shirt. "You know, you don't have to kill either of them, or blow up the city. You will be safe. We both will be safe."

"What are you implying?" he asked quietly.

"People will do whatever you tell them to if they are scared," she said smoothly, gliding her hands over his arms. She paused for a second and bit her lip. "But instead of one person being fooled, the whole city will be. I mean, there are ways of getting out of Catadorga alive... Coal Lake, perhaps."

"Nobody knows where it is," he spat. "How will that little prick find it? And how do you know about it? Eavesdropping on my conversations?"

"You mean the conversations you have with yourself?" she insisted. "Otis will find it."

"Otis," he repeated. He went around his desk and placed his hands firmly over the edge. "Otis, Otis... OTIS!"

"Did you actually think that he would kill Ryan? You sent the wrong person down there. Otis knows everything, stuff we don't, and he can use that knowledge to help him."

"Well maybe you should have been here and mentioned something to me instead of always leaving to whore yourself around town or whatever it is the fuck you do."

"That wasn't appropriate," said Carmen with a half laugh, looking down at her finely manicured fingernails. "How sweet of you. Always the gentleman."

Carson sighed. "I'm sorry. I'm just pissed and upset. You are my advisor. You know I need your help with this. I can't do this on my own." He put his hand out for her to take it. "Please."

Carmen hesitated for a moment then took his hand, feeling one of his rings digging into her finger. He leaned in to kiss her on the lips, putting his arms tightly around her. "And yes, I did think he would kill him. I said I would kill his family if he didn't do it. But…"

"But you wouldn't have done that either," she concluded. "Dear, Otis saw right through you." She slid her fingers through his dark gelled hair. "You were fooled."

Carson's hands started trembling and Carmen prepared herself for what he was about to do. "FUCK!" He slammed his fist onto the desk and knocked everything off, kicking the desk over with his shoe. "No, they can't get out! Fuck, fuck, fuck my fucking life!"

The door opened and Durt poked his head in. "Everything alright in here, Mr. Jenkins?"

"GET THE FUCK OUT!" Carson shot a blast of fire towards the door, in which time Durt quickly shut it, the fire burning the door upon contact. Unexpectedly, there was a sudden crackling sound coming from down on the floor.

"What the hell is it now?" He reached down and picked up Ryan's visor.

"Hello," said a voice from the other end. "Ryan, are you there?"

"What is this?!" asked Carson in outrage, his voice cracking.

"Hello? Ryan?" whispered Brazz. "Your voice has changed. You sound like a rather annoying vulture now. Are you at the pub?"

Carson looked at Carmen, horrified. "I AM NOT HIM YOU IDIOT! WHO IS THIS?! I WILL KILL YOU IF YOU DON'T TELL ME SCUM!"

"Must you?" moaned Carmen. "Soft, gentle voices. Like me. Soft and gentle."

"I'll soft and gentle this hat up his ass, how about that?" said Carson irritably.

Carmen flung her hands up in the air and turned away in annoyance. The voice from the visor was no longer speaking.

"DAMN IT! GO DIE!" He threw the visor across the room like a frisbee and set it on fire.

"He used a Communi-kay Orb?" said Carmen. "How did he get one? You can only get them from our storage vault."

"Just like how did he get that badge he was wearing? I should have known! It was those conniving thieves! Brazz! No one could mistake that nasty ass voice! They stole everything and gave it to Ryan so he could get into the city somehow! They were in my tower! Who was it? Where are they? They will all die!"

"Carson, calm down."

"I WILL NOT CALM DOWN!" He fell to the floor and held his head and started swaying from side to side. His suit was throbbing with sharp bursts of black and dark flames began growing up his arms.

"Maybe," said Carmen as she tried not to sound incredibly nervous and scared as she was that very second looking at him. "But, if it helps, I have an idea."

The flames disappeared and he lifted up his head to look at her with solid black eyes that faded back to brown. "Will it accomplish what we need done?" he asked sullenly.

"Yes," she said carefully. She knelt down next to him and took his face into her hands. "We sometimes have to do things that we aren't proud of. Even if it means hurting ourselves."

"I've been doing things I haven't been proud of for the past three years," he said. "I just want to stop now." He took her in his arms. "I just want to go home."

Carmen kissed him on the cheek. "Me too."

TWELVE.

THE ASH CHAMBER

SOUNDS MOST FOWL WERE MURMURING ALL AROUND, their echoes sliding into the stone walls and out into the unknown tunnels. For the entire time that he was sleeping, Ryan believed that he was imagining them; rolling over onto his side to escape them... but they continued. They wouldn't go away. They kept pestering him. *Just leave me alone,* he thought. He was only trying to sleep, to try and regain much of the energy he had already lost. When he finally came to the conclusion that he wouldn't be able to fall back asleep he stopped trying to. He realized he and Otis weren't the only ones down in the dark and quiet world of Catadorga.

His body started sliding across the ground. His ankles were grasped tightly as he was being pulled slowly forward; his shirt and jacket sliding upwards by the ground rubbing against them, making his flesh bleed and sore. There was quiet snickering ahead of him... there was definitely something there. Ryan felt like he was in a dream-like trance. So much so that he couldn't acknowledge the person who was pulling him away from Otis and their camp. But was Otis the one doing this? Maybe he wanted to get going early so they could have a head start without waking Ryan up. But this wasn't something Otis would do. He wouldn't drag Ryan across the skeletal filled dirt like a rag doll. He would wake him up. Tell him they needed to get going and to get on his feet. Otis wasn't the type of man to drag someone along when they were fully capable of walking themselves. But was Otis still sleeping? Ryan couldn't tell.

Further ahead, a flicker of light from a flame was visible right past the threshold of an archway that curved around the corner. There was a long shadow stretched out on the wall to indicate that something was standing just around the bend. The light was now fully ignited; the fire that was held by the person unknown was waiting for him. He was meant to follow it.

Ryan rolled over and sat upright on the floor, frozen, as if he was stuck and couldn't move. He didn't want to move though. He didn't know what was happening. Was this Otis? If it was him he would have said something by now. Ryan glanced behind him towards the camp but he was too far off now to see it. The fire's light from around the corner bathed his face faintly and the walls around. Human skulls were staring back at him and their bones were pointing in the direction of the illuminated archway.

As if responding, foreign words were muttered followed by hissing from the entity around the bend. The shadow moved onward, as did the light, fading away until the tunnel was dark once more. It sounded like a command to follow, but Ryan wasn't eager to do so. He was alone now. Alone in the catacombs of a vile and disgusting city. It was dark and cold.

He didn't know where Otis was. For all he knew, he was still sleeping back at camp, oblivious to everything that was happening. But Ryan didn't know where camp was now because he was pulled so far away. If he tried going back, he would just get more lost than he already was. He would just just stay put and hopefully wait for Otis to find him. But what if this someone wanted to help him and found a way out for him? His skill in finding the right people to trust hasn't really done him any good so far.

As if making up his mind for him, the flame from around the corner returned. This time it was being visibly held in plain sight of Ryan on a torch. This someone was still unknown to Ryan because whoever was holding it was standing right behind the wall of the bend, with just the torch outstretched and visible.

Ryan thrust himself up and walked cautiously towards the torch, having to feel the rough and bumpy walls for proper direction, but pulling away once his fingers got caught in an eye socket of a rotting skull. He gagged and almost threw up.

Once he got close to the archway, the torch disappeared and continued on down the tunnel. Ryan passed the bend and saw that whomever was holding the torch, they were already down at the other end. One second they were right around the bend and the next they were already at the far end of the tunnel.

"I'm going to die," muttered Ryan to himself, taking in a deep breath and walking onward. "Yup, I'm going to die."

To catch up with the torch, Ryan started jogging carefully down the tunnel. After only a few feet, he suddenly tripped over a type of knot in the ground and fell forward, slamming onto steps that declined downward.

He caught his fall, but not fast enough. He crashed down, hitting his body against the stone and having to cover his face with one hand and trying to his catch his fall with the other. He managed to stop his decline after a few seconds, the light now further away inside the new tunnel he just fell down into. This was just weird. How was this person already down on the other end of this tunnel, already so far off, when they were just up in the one above a second ago? With no time to answer his own questions, he saw the flame disappear again around another bend. He couldn't lose it. He was for sure lost now. If things turned bad, he always had the bag of Orbs he bought earlier at *Orbs Emporium*. Hopefully they would come to some kind of use.

The air was colder as he descended further below the ground, feeling disturbingly frigid like the waters of a deep ocean. Once he made it around the bend, the flame suddenly greeted him like an old friend, the flame being the biggest and brightest it had been so far. However, the fire was no longer inside a torch, but cupped inside a hand. The one who was holding the source of light had stopped, and Ryan was terrified beyond words at what greeted him.

The creature was standing completely still with its large, sphere-shaped eyes fixed on him. The flame was cupped in an outstretched hand that had long and curved nails reaching out from each finger. Ryan almost ran away out of instinct once he saw the hideous creature, but it was the flame that made him stay, his gaze always going back to it like a magnet. The creature itself was horrible to look upon. The eyes were the first thing Ryan noticed, as they were very large and white, almost like glass, and seeming to illuminate like light bulbs. The head was wrinkled and dark, very shriveled and old with a nose and mouth not clearly visible and a few long hairs on the top of its head that draped over its shoulders. It was wearing a ragged black robe over its short and small frame that was half the size of Ryan, almost the size of a dwarf. The robe dragged behind it as if it was a burden for the creature to carry.

Ryan looked briefly around and noticed that he was in a small room, not a tunnel anymore. A thick layer of ash had formed on the ground, but it wasn't this that bothered him. It was the hundreds of full skeletal bodies that were lined up on every inch of the wall and ceiling from top to bottom. To his left was a stone chamber. You couldn't see what was inside because there was just one lone door made of metal, leading into the chamber itself. Ryan couldn't take his eyes off it even though he wanted to run away. The creature was the first to talk.

"The chamber is the gateway into the flames of the beyond. It is where one goes to look upon thy Lord." It spoke in a scratchy, old voice that suggested death. "You must go and settle your claim with thy fallen, thy majesty. It is what He wishes." The creature walked smoothly up to the chamber as if walking on ice and dragged open the door. Once open, it threw the flame inside, leaving the door wide open and pointing inside for him to enter.

Ryan stood still and fixated. It sounded like someone was singing somewhere close by... inside the chamber itself.

"May I ask what you are?"

The creature's eyes glowed a bit brighter, still lit in a solid white glow. "We are the remains of what used to be thy world long ago. We have evolved to withstand the deep dark world of Catadorga."

Ryan was still transfixed by the doorway, not even listening as if hypnotized.

"We cannot see, but we can sense. We cannot breathe, but we can smell." It was still pointing into the chamber. "To see thy Lord thy majesty... enter."

Ryan shook his head, but his body was telling him otherwise. He walked forward slowly until he stood in front of the threshold to the chamber, the flame inside barely visible now, as it seemed to glow more dim the closer he got to it. He entered without hesitance.

"Enter thy chamber to look upon thy Lord. Look into His eyes and take thy destiny. Enter thy chamber... and never return."

"I will not return," said Ryan quietly, shutting the door behind him.

He had stepped into darkness, except for dozens of luminous white orbs all around him, swaying and floating slightly from side to side. There were whispers all around, coming from these orbs.

The flame that was practically extinguished started growing in the middle of the chamber. Lines like a spider web formed along the walls. The flame lifted upwards like a ghost until it was just a couple of feet off the ground, its size growing until it was the size of a boulder. The whispers grew louder in anticipation. There were others in the room with him. They were singing some terrible song... or was it a spell?

"The Lord has come..." said the voices.

Ryan looked into the flame with his dead-black eyes.

"No boy, leave this place..."

Ryan turned to the sound that came from his left, then back towards the flame as if his eyes wouldn't let him look away.

"Get out of here boy. Or you will die."

"Go where?" asked Ryan. "He wants to speak with me." He heard someone get up onto their feet.

"He wants to kill you. Don't let Him." The person that spoke ran forward and latched himself onto Ryan and pulled him to the side. He was spun forcefully around and was face to face with a terrified man who looked like he hadn't eaten or slept for weeks, his grey hair damaged and wild with tattered and dirty clothes over his skeletal body. The glowing white eyes from the dozens of creatures had fixed themselves onto the man. Angry whines were released that were merged with threatening hisses.

The man stared at Ryan as if he couldn't believe who he was seeing. "No... it can't be you... is it really you?"

Ryan showed no emotion in his face. "Who?" he asked simply. "Who am I?

As if the question was a terrible curse, the flame became darker and burst. Two red eyes appeared in the middle. All went quiet.

Ryan looked back into the flame, into the eyes of the Lord. The man grabbed hold of Ryan as if it was his own life.

"Do not look into His eyes," whispered the man in a terribly shaky voice. "The way He communicates with us is through eye contact in which He gets into your mind and talks to you."

"I have to," said Ryan, his eyes drained of light. "He wants me to come towards Him and into the fire. He wishes for me to die. I can't say no to that."

"Yes you can. You cannot die. All will be lost. You must understand this plight."

"I am meant to die," said Ryan, his black eyes not blinking.

The man was forcefully pulled back as small hands grabbed onto him and pulled him away. "Not him! Let me go! Take me instead!"

"Never," shrieked voices within the chamber. "The boy must go forward to meet his destiny." The other voices repeated the words in high pitched moans.

"Meet his destiny."

"Meet his destiny."

Ryan stepped forward, and as he did so, his skin began to splinter and age as if it was hardened sand.

"My destiny," he said.

The flame flickered wildly as he neared.

"I have to die." Ryan put out his hand and into the flame. "It is the only way."

"No!" yelled the man as he reached forward. He lurched towards him, away from the creature's grasps, and pushed Ryan to the side and onto the ground. Ryan got back up and attempted running back towards the flame, but the man pulled him back down.

"I want to die!" screamed Ryan.

"You don't want to die!" said the man. "I am Zephyrus! Listen to me!"

Ryan stopped struggling. "That name... it sounds familiar."

"My boy, I see what He is trying to do. He is a monster not of this world. Do not listen to His words. You must remember who you are! Please remember! Come back to us! Help us! We need you back!"

Ryan's face tightened in anger. "I will not listen to your words, Zephyrus. Why should anyone care for you? You seem to only speak lies and deceit. Nonsense as well. Such terrible nonsense indeed." His eyes closed and he looked down. "Your life is meaningless and I hate it. Oh, what is that you say my Lord? He is also a danger and threat to me? He must be destroyed? I need to kill him? Kill this man. Kill this man."

"Kill this man."

"Kill this man."

Zephyrus looked up at Ryan in pure horror, shaking his head. "Please," he begged.

Ryan smiled. "You will die. Then I myself will fall into shadow, for that is my real home."

Zephyrus' eyes widened. "No!"

"YES!" shouted Ryan. "I WANT TO DIE! FUCKING KILL ME NOW!"

"Die! Die! Die!" chanted the voices in the chamber. The creatures gathered around and their eyes shone brighter as if the anticipation was unbearable.

The large flame suddenly burst and spread itself around the chamber and towards Ryan at full force, illuminating the whole chamber and shining its aura on all the sphere-eyed creatures that were running towards the walls for defense, terrified with the Lord's sudden wrath. Zephyrus pulled Ryan to the back wall where the red lines in the stone were growing thinker and pulsing like veins. Ryan tackled Zephyrus to the ground and pinned him. He grinned. It was no longer his voice coming out of his mouth.

"Oh dear Zephyrus, it is now time for you to leave. This boy shall kill you and a most painful death he'll receive. Down through ash and right through flame, letting me begin my redemption rein!"

Zephyrus breathed heavily as he tried pushing Ryan off, but Ryan slammed his fist into his face repeatedly for almost a full minute, each blow becoming less powerful as time went on. Zephyrus no longer moved after that minute was done. He was dead.

There was a deep chuckle and out from the flame a head stretched itself outwards. It was a face out of death and horror. The coal black skin with a lashing red tongue and sharp teeth looked down at Ryan, the two horns on its head sprouting up to the ceiling. Its red eyes were burning into Ryan's mind and making him fall backwards and cringe until he was crying with his hands placed over his ears. The flame burst once more and spread itself completely around the rest of the chamber. The creatures were unforgivably set on fire and fell to the ground as they burned to death, vanishing behind the fire with the chamber walls, swallowed in a cyclone of fire. A harsh wind was blowing as the face drew itself closer to Ryan... and then it was like he had gone deaf.

Ryan opened his eyes and looked into the red slits staring at him, the murderous fire all around him that felt like his was in a twister made of flame. The mouth was wide open with fangs lined all around, about to destroy.

"RYAN!"

What felt like his last breath before the plunge, a bright beam of light illuminated the background and shone its rays across the chamber. There was one last demonic roar before a loud splash of sound ripped through the air and sent the walls around him collapsing to the ground. As the walls crumpled around him, someone grabbed his hand and his body was pulled towards the doorway.

Rubble was falling on top of Ryan, gashes opening up all over his skin. He was dragged out from the chamber as it crumbled into a heap of brick and stone, dust cluttering up the air and making it difficult to breathe. A sudden flash of light burst beside him, the source from Otis' outstretched hand.

"LET'S MOVE!" he shouted, running down the tunnel. Ryan quickly got up to his feet and followed him in the sprint of his life. He and Otis ran up the stairs and down another tunnel when a terrible roar erupted behind them.

"What just happened?" asked Ryan. He looked behind him. "What the hell happened?"

"Nothing," said Otis. "You're fine. That's all that matters."

Ryan looked down and noticed cuts all over his body. His clothes were singed and burn marks took shape on his arms and hands.

"You will never remember what happened in there. You were in a dark trance called the Moral. It's a state in which you were being instructed and spoken to by the Lord himself, but much more controlling and powerful than what Carson is usually under."

"What did He make me do?" asked Ryan in a frightened tone. "Otis, what did He make me do?"

Otis took a second to swallow his words. "Nothing. I came just in time."

Ryan breathed a sigh of relief. "What are those things?"

"Those Catadorga dwellers are called Halzers and they are the most conniving creatures you can come by. They dragged you away from me and planned to sacrifice you to the Lord like so many before you."

They flew past another bend and dashed endlessly up and down several stairways and passages like a maze.

"We are getting close," said Otis, looking down at a piece of paper that was a self-drawn map. "You feel that? It's getting colder. We are close."

From further behind them came the sounds of fast paced movements as though a group of giant children were running. Ryan stopped and looked behind him. He already knew what it was. "Those little pricks," he said.

Otis grabbed Ryan's arm and made him start running again. "It doesn't matter who or what is chasing us anymore. We are dead if we don't move. Please don't stop running again."

It felt like the further they ran, the more intense the whines became. The Halzers could be heard hissing in shrikes and moans as they banged things against the walls, making bits of rock fall from the ceiling. Otis was pulling Ryan in several different routes and passages that it boggled his mind. The beam of light coming from Otis' hand was now flickering, signaling the end of its use.

"It's running out," said Ryan, stating the obvious.

"I have more," replied Otis. "Don't panic."

The loud thumps from the Halzers running were so close now. "Catadorga is ours! You cannot escape! All must die in the hands of thy Lord thy majesty!"

"They will catch up to us soon," said Otis. "But you will be gone. As will I."

"Why won't you come with me?"

"I can't. I need to be the diversion so that you can escape."

"Why are you doing this for me?"

"Because I need to do this for me Ryan. There have been many times where I've betrayed young men like you to their deaths. I don't want to die knowing that my life was meant for that."

"It wasn't," said Ryan.

Otis stopped and examined a wall that was in front of them, tucking the map away into his pocket. Before the light in his palm went out, Ryan noticed a small opening in the bottom of the wall big enough for one person to squeeze through.

"Excellent. It's right here. I will continue on, but you will go through this hole towards the well. Once at the well, use the ladder or rope or whatever there is to help you get down to Coal Lake. Hopefully there will be a boat or something for you to use. Once on the other side of the lake, go up the stairs until you reach the exit. Where it will take you, I don't know."

Ryan was extremely nervous. He was terrible at remembering directions and he always wanted someone with him so that in case he did forget, the other person would remember.

The rumbling was right behind them now and the white lights from the Halzer's eyes could be seen reflected against the walls.

"GO!" yelled Otis, pushing him down towards the hole. "If this is the last time I see you, then I wish you nothing but the best of luck. It will be dangerous. Carson will try everything in his power to keep you from returning home. Find a way to avoid him or make a diversion of some kind—blow something up if you must."

"Thanks man," said Ryan, about to shake his hand but Otis went in for a hug instead.

"Nothing but the best for you," said Otis, smiling. "You had to grow up a lot these last few days Ryan. You aren't a boy anymore."

Otis dropped a couple Star Light Orbs into his pocket, patted him on the back, and continued down the tunnel into darkness and out of sight. Ryan wasted no time. He got down onto the ground and wedged his way through the hole. It was no easy task and Ryan struggled to push his body through. He could hear the quick and nimble footsteps of the Halzers running past the opening. Even so, his pulse was still beating quicker than ever before.

When Ryan feared that he would be stuck in the hole forever, there was a burst of cold air once he reached the other end. He crawled out and looked around at the black nothingness around him. He used one of the Star Light Orbs that Otis put in his pocket and carefully felt the ground around him with his shoe in case the well was a just hole in the ground. There were skulls and bones on the ground as well as small scurrying creatures rubbing against his pant legs. A part of him just wanted to stay here. Nobody knew where he was. No one could hurt him. But he knew this wasn't a realistic option to take seriously.

His shoe finally hit against the brick wall of the well. Ryan felt the sides of the circular formation and touched the opening in the center.

He picked up a tiny lose rock from off the ground and dropped it down the hole. A couple seconds later there was a slight *clunk* at the bottom; no water. He bent over the edge and tried to find a type of rope or ladder or something to crawl down with. He was not about to drop down on his own.

Sure enough, there was a thick and tattered rope hanging against the side. Ryan was praying that it would hold him and not snap and send him plummeting to his death. *So many happy thoughts.*

He grabbed hold of the rope and began making his way down the moist and damp descent below the catacombs. He put his feet against the wall and leaned back as he stepped down slowly, inch by inch. The climb down was full of nerves and horridness. He didn't know where he was going for sure, and just the fact that he had his gloves on to prevent possible rope burn was one less thing to worry about. He remembered long ago when he took rock climbing lessons at a birthday party years ago, and those skills were coming in handy now.

After a few slip ups, he could now see a dark maroon light at the bottom. Once the rope was at its end, he let go and fell a couple feet down onto a wooden surface.

He was inside a dimly lit cave the size of Blazing City itself. It was lit not with fire, but from the lake. Coal Lake gave off a red glowing aura that shined off the expansive walls like mirrors. As Ryan peered over the side and into the clear water he could see down to the bottom where trillions of coals lay. The cave was probably the biggest place that he had ever stepped into. He couldn't see what was on the other side of the lake, but he knew that it would be a vast and long journey to the other side—it was an ocean he had to cross. There had to be way to get across. He wasn't going to swim. It was impossible.

Further down the rusted wooden dock were a couple boats. They were made of wood and were quite small, but big enough for just one person to use. Each had two little paddles for moving and turning. Who knew how long they were down here. Possibly centuries. They appeared quite old, but the wood wasn't that decayed and still looked sturdy.

Before he got into one, he took his heavy uniform jacket off as well as his gloves and threw them to the side. His shirt was practically black now and was torn badly, but it was lighter in material and wouldn't help overpower the boat and sink it like his jacket would. He stepped into the boat and grabbed the paddles that were placed at the bottom. Once he sat down, he felt like his weight would make the boat sink, but luckily it remained calm. He took a deep breath and started paddling across the red tinged water.

Everything was silent, but this was a different kind of silence. It wasn't the type of silence that you experienced at night when you are asleep, or the kind of silence that one would feel in the woods. This was a dead silence, an empty silence, a silence that didn't have anything living around it. Even the noise that the water made as the paddles pushed through it was almost mute. He could hear his breathing and even the sensations that he got in his eardrums that were trying to pick up any sounds. This must have been what the earth sounded like when nothing lived on it. Like sound had never existed.

As time passed, Ryan was given the opportunity to think uninterrupted. He went through everything that had happened and thought about what was to come. In the days that he had been here, only once had he thought about the people he knew back home. He would have given anything for one of them to be here right now. To be able to talk to them.

To see them. To feel them. To try and help him understand this mess. For Tommy to make him laugh. To tell him jokes. He thought about Mickey and when he told him that he would be back to talk to him. He thought about how much of an ass he was to Ashlee, and how she didn't deserve such hate from him. How he might never see his parents ever again…

He started crying. Everything was coming out. Nobody knew where he was. Where would they think he had gone? Would they think he had run away? Did they think he was dead? Not only was he in another world, but he was thousands of feet below the surface of that world, and alone. He wiped away the tears from his eyes.

I'm going home. And no one is going to stop me.

As one hour turned to two, and two turned to four, Ryan couldn't stop letting things flow through his mind. What if he wrote a book about what happened here, and passed it off as fiction? Would anyone believe him except his dog? Man, he missed him the most. Charlie. Overtime, a dream-like trance was coming over him as the light from the bright coals beneath the water danced against the boat. He shook his head to keep himself awake, even slapping himself on the head.

Out to his right, he saw something out of the corner of his eye that made him stop. Across the lake was a speck of bright red light amongst the black shadows. It was so far away—at least a day's worth of paddling. The boat continued drifting onward and the red speck started to disappear. The light reminded him of the two balls of light he saw in the room behind the cafeteria. Ryan knew better now. Whenever there was a light, mostly red, or a fire that tried to pull him away from whatever he was doing, it was a sign that meant something bad would happen. God knows it happened too many times already. *Red lights and fires equal bad,* he told himself. *Bad, bad, bad. Got that Ryan? Bad.*

Time continued to drag onward like a lazy work week. All awhile, the trip across the lake seemed unfathomably long. He looked ahead and he could now see the dock another two hours away or so. He put all of his attention into focusing on his paddling. He was getting a bad ache in his back from bending over and his arms and legs where terribly numb. He wasn't cold since the lake seemed like it was heated and gave off spurts of warm air.

For the last few hours, the boat started to fill with small amounts of water, and the water that formed around his shoes was bitterly cold. He didn't understand the elements that were down here. One minute it was warm, the next it was cold. Then it was very humid, then back to cold again—almost like it couldn't make up its mind or was bipolar. Was he inside of Ashlee's head? The thought made him smirk. He could only imagine the bickering and complaining he'd have to endure if she was with him at this moment. He wouldn't have minded though. At least he would have had someone...

Truth be told though, if it was her instead of him that took those frozen hamburger patties to the cafeteria and ended up here, she wouldn't have made it to Renny and Otis' house. She probably would have got herself caught and killed instantly. Ryan laughed. Oh those hamburger patties. Seemed like a lifetime ago...

Once two hours past and turned into three, he started convincing himself that there wasn't actually a dock, and that he just imagined it. Maybe the dock actually was there, but the closer he got to it the further away it was—like some sick spell or illusion. And when he finally collapsed and died from starvation his body would fall into the lake and the boat would return to dock and wait for its next victim years from now.

But after at least ten hours of trudging his way across the lake, he finally got to the dock which seemed to have magically appeared in front of him. As he attempted to step out, his body wobbled and cracked and fell back down into the boat. Some of his joints were pulled from having to sit down for such a long time. He slowly got back up and stumbled onto the wooden dock. He lay down on his back and just looked up into the shadows of the sky (he couldn't even call it a ceiling). For the first time in days, he was looking up at what could have been a night sky instead of red.

It took him a while to get back up. Once he did, he looked around for some kind of stairs or opening. He wasn't ready to take a break, even though he knew he was safer down here than up there. He glanced back at the boat and saw it starting to sink as the pressure he gave to it when he got out made the wood tear and break even more. Otis said there would be stairs somewhere once he crossed the lake.

Almost accidentally, his eye caught sight of a dark opening in the stone that he could have easily missed. He stumbled forward and entered the doorway clumsily as if he were drunk. His heart was beating fast and so was his breathing. He had no clue where these stairs led, but all he knew was that he didn't want to be seen by anyone who would harm him. His best hope was that this would lead to a different part of Pheonexia, and far away from Blazing City. But not too far. His portal was still his only means of getting back home and to safety. He didn't want to leave it behind.

He couldn't see anything, blind as a bat. But he was used to it. He had experienced enough darkness to last a lifetime. He almost felt like he was turning into a bat himself or like one of the Halzers. Ryan couldn't help but think when the last person to use these stairs was. Had anybody even used these stairs before him? Was there ever anybody like him who was running for their lives and towards freedom... or death?

After almost an hour of walking up the stairs, Ryan bumped his head into a hard surface. He reached up and felt a smooth and warm piece of stone above him, wondering if it was a dead end. No, it wasn't a dead end. This had to be the exit. He pushed and pulled with all his might. Surprisingly, the stone budged to the side and Ryan continued pushing as his face turned red.

Light flooded onto his face and he was welcomed with soot and ash that trickled down through the opening. He grabbed the sides and pulled his head out just enough so that he could peek out for a couple of seconds. The problem though was that something was blocking his view. There was stone circling around him that made it feel like he was in a type of large bowl. He cautiously pulled himself out and stood up in what was a basin, a basin for a fountain. Except there was no water in it, just ash and vines. Ryan finally realized that he was in Copper Courtyard outside of Blazing City. And there, a few feet away from him, was Mainbreak Hall. Almost unnoticeable against the red of night atmosphere. There was no one around and the lights from the security station in front of the city's entrance gate weren't on. No one was monitoring it.

He jumped out of the basin and looked behind him. He saw the gate that lead out of the courtyard and down the enclosed pathway towards his portal. He didn't even need to think twice about what he wanted to do. He closed his eyes, took a deep breath, then ran as quietly as he could towards the gate. He went through and jogged down the path. The wall to his left was the wall that bordered the courtyard, and the one to his right went hundreds of feet high—the wall that bordered Frostbite Village.

Once Ryan got closer to the portal, he made himself as quiet as possible. Then, in all its glory and wonder, he saw the portal that began his decent into madness. He walked up the steps and looked up at the black and vile creation. The red numbers above now read:

18,699,001.

Ryan sighed angrily. It was much lower than last time, but not low enough. He wasn't in enough danger... it hasn't deemed him worthy enough to go back home yet. What did he have to do? He just wanted to stay in front of it and not leave for the eighteen and a half million years as indicated. The whole thing was ridiculous. There had to be a trick to getting it open somehow.

Even though he didn't like it, he turned back around and down the path. That portal was his only way out, and he was leaving it behind. Something needed to happen. And fast.

Before he went back into the courtyard, he peered through the frozen gate that lead into Frostbite Village. Too cold to approach, he kept his distance a few feet away from it. How could he get in there? He knew there had to be an Orb that could make you immune to the cold, so he wondered if it were possible to use this as his escape route if he had to. He needed to find a way to get into the village—if all else failed.

He turned away and grudgingly went forth into the courtyard. Everything looked exactly the same as he had left it. The sky in the courtyard was the bloodiest looking out of the entire city. He trudged half-heartedly across the enclosure and felt the sensation of sleep growing into his mind and body like last time. He wouldn't sleep ever again. Not until he got home.

He walked past the fountain and looked up at Mainbreak Hall. He now had three options. Go back into Cooper Town, use the unmanned gate into Blazing City, or climb back up to Mainbreak Hall. It was unsettling that there were no Secret Service patrolling the gate, but maybe that was a lure of some kind. Maybe they were waiting for him.

He thought about the books that were in the hall. What if he took some of them then ran back to the fountain and hid under it for however long he needed to? Do some research. That sounded like a good idea... until he realized he had no food and was starving. Screw the books. He would just go back to the fountain and wait until he came up with something. It was better than staying out here in the open. He didn't trust Copper Town. It was suicide. Everyone was still probably on the lookout for him. He thought about running to Renny and Otis' house but that was too risky. If only he had some Veil Orbs... where was Brazz when you needed him? Brazz's shop would be the ideal place to hide but he wasn't sure if Brazz would help him this time. With Brazz, you had to give in order to receive and Ryan was running out of patience for playing his little games. Where was someone to help him when he needed them? His dad would know what to do. His eyes teared up at the thought.

The thought maybe Renny was inside Mainbreak Hall. There were only a few lights on inside so there had to be someone in there… maybe he would peek in for a second.

He stepped up onto one of the steps with both feet, but then took one off. What if it was a trap? What if they were waiting for him? Impossible. They still believed he was down in Catadorga. How could he have gotten out without being detected? Through the lake? No, they didn't know about its whereabouts.

Ryan stepped up again onto the stair, but just as he did he felt a surging blast of light and heat that he had never experienced in his life. The sound was that of several trains crashing into one another. Before he knew it, he was flung backwards with such force and strength that it felt like he was catapulted. Pieces of debris went flying past his body and smacked into him, creating gashes and cuts anywhere and everywhere. He was flung to the ground in front of the fountain, just as two giant black gates went zipping over his head. There was fire and smoke everywhere with screams and yells beginning to unfold in the distance. A terrible ringing erupted in his ears and he had to place his hands over them, his hearing dropping to almost nothing. His biggest fear at the moment was that the blast made him deaf. So he kept rubbing his ears, hoping it would help. Ryan pulled himself up onto his knees and witnessed the catastrophe before him.

In front of him, in a massive pile of rubble and flame, were the destroyed remains of Mainbreak Hall. This was it. The storm he had been waiting for. He knew what just happened, and he needed to get away. He looked over the basin and thought about going back inside. He was too weak to pull the slab back into position once entering. He couldn't go across the lake again. Instead he just ran. He ran into the city, dodging the people who were running towards the commotion. He ran like he never ran before and tried to stick to the shadows and away from the light that the flames brought with them.

The large platform that held up the hall was now crumbling and falling apart as it crashed to the ground in piles of dirt and stone. There were people from Copper Town and Blazing City running through the gaps where the two gates used to be, with horrified looks and expressions on their faces, their hands on their heads.

"What is this?!" one yelled. "Who has done this?! There were people in there!"

A woman looked at the ruins and flopped to the ground, yelling her head off. "My husband was in there! NO! What have you done?! WHAT HAVE YOU DONE?!"

More citizens were gathering around by the dozens. Most were crying and screaming. The bearded man from the marketplace approached with murder in his eyes. He flung his hands up in anger. "We are being punished! Our Lord is furious! We let that boy get away, and as punishment this angry wrath has occurred! Do you not see people?!"

"He did it!" yelled another. "The boy! He must die! Mr. Jenkins did nothing!"

"Yes!" yelled the bearded man. "He must die! He is planning more attacks like this! Mr. Jenkins knew about this! Kill him too, they are both responsible! We will destroy the boy and Mr. Jenkins for the Lord!"

"That is it then!" shouted a woman. "No one sleeps until both are good and dead!"

Through the smoke emerged Carmen. She stepped through the rubble and smoke, covering her mouth with her hand. Her face was completely visible for the first time, full of horror.

"Look everyone!" she screamed. "The mayor! HE IS DEAD!" She pointed behind her at Carson's burned and bloody body, lying amongst the burning rubble, motionless.

"THE BOY KILLED THE MAYOR!" she shouted. "The evil boy murdered the mayor and will so to the rest of you! He killed all those good people who were in the hall out of pure enjoyment! This is what the Lord was trying to tell you! The boy is a dangerous threat to us all!"

"My son!" yelled a man. "My son is dead! I know it! He has been missing for hours and I cannot find him! He killed my son! I know it!"

Carmen nodded her head. "Then the boy is responsible! Destroy the boy of evil! It is now time for you to prove yourselves to the Lord and to act on his behave for something that Mr. Jenkins was unable to accomplish, resulting in his death!"

Everybody who was in the courtyard, which must have been hundreds by now, all agreed with cheers.

"She is right! It is time!" declared the bearded man. "It is time to eliminate all who have done wrong—starting with the boy!"

"And search everywhere," bellowed Carmen as if she was speaking though a megaphone. "Search every nook and cranny! Some go into Frostbite Village if you must! Spread the news like he himself has spread the disease that infuriates your Lord!" She paced around for a couple of seconds, tripping over some of the black stone clumsily. "Tonight is history," she said. "Tonight will be remembered and relived in the stories of old. Decades from now, the young will ask with wonder about this burning night. Tonight will be deemed history and you are all a part of it. It is the night where all evil beings were finally destroyed and the biggest threat to ever befall our world was finally eliminated. The boy will die in the flames of this city."

Everyone cheered one last time and scattered in all directions. Carmen turned around and frowned at Carson's body, her face reflecting sorrow for what was just done.

Carson opened his eyes and gave her a quick wink. "I love you," he said.

THIRTEEN.

SMOKE AND MIRRORS

THE NEWS SPREAD LIKE WILDFIRE. THE FEROCIOUS SHOUTS from hundreds of tormented people echoed out through the thick air and the thousands more within the city that heard began to find out about the recent travesty.

"What is going on out there? Excuse me, sir. Do you know what all the fuss is about?" one civilian would ask to another.

"Did you not hear it? That big explosion that destroyed the hall was done by that bandit boy and it killed a heck load of people. We had better be on the lookout for him in case he decides to blow up the city as well."

"It is all unspeakable. The wrath of the Lord is upon us. I heard from my neighbor that it's the sign of the end. We had better be taking care of ourselves by getting out of here instead of looking for some murderous child."

"I hear he has claws for hands! He'll scratch your eyes out before he carves out your heart and eats it! That's what my sister said she heard from her friend! I swear I saw it happen once myself, I know it!"

"He is indeed a dangerous boy. Mr. Jenkins was right about him all along."

As Ryan eagerly poked his head out around the shadows of the cityscape, he could feel the tension from everyone that he saw or walked by; dwelling on the horrific images that they conjured in their heads of what this murderous boy would do if he wasn't found soon. His hearing was approving just after a short while, and he could still recognize Carmen's loud and demanding voice in the background, barking out orders and setting fear into the sanest of minds. He wanted to slap duct tape across her mouth and toss her into a lake. For him, the safest place that he knew was nowhere in sight. What he would do once he found a temporary hiding spot, he didn't know. Since it was the evening, the only light that helped guide his way was what the moon gave off as well as the street lamps. There were a few citizens who already started searching in buildings and beneath benches for the murderous boy.

Ryan kept on running. He finally slid his way in between two buildings and stood against an ally wall, alert and tense, trying to come up with his next move. He looked up towards the sky and stared at the tops of buildings and towers, watching as lights were turned on and windows were opened to scream below to passing searchers, demanding silence because their children were sleeping. Shouting also started spurring inside of apartments and… hotels! Ryan's eyes lit up. His room inside Classer Hotel was still in his name. Before Ryan could translate his idea into a strategic plan, he was forcefully grabbed from behind and pulled forward by a man who was much bigger than himself.

"There you are," he whispered. "I am a lucky man to be the one to kill you. I shall be rewarded handsomely for your death." The man reached into his belt and pulled out a long carving knife as he held Ryan against the wall with his other hand. "In the name of the Lord… your blood is now His."

Ryan looked to the side and instinctively reached for a lid on top of a garbage can. "Not today buddy." He raised the lid into the air and whacked it against the man's head three times, sending him sprawling onto the ground. Ryan threw the lid at the man's unconscious body and bent down to pick up the knife. He looked above him and saw a fire escape zig zagging up the wall. He jumped up as high as he could and grabbed hold of the ladder, latching on with both hands and swiftly climbing up.

Before he was halfway to the top, he felt a rattling of the ladder and he started swaying back and forth. The man, who Ryan thought was unconscious, was furiously shaking the ladder with anger and started ripping the metal from off its hinges.

"YOU ARE DEAD! YOU ARE DEAD!"

Finally, the ladder tumbled down, hitting the man in the head. Ryan fell a couple feet to the ground, but was fast enough to get back up and dash away just as the man tried to trip him.

He departed from the ally and into a street that was almost deserted; clearly no one got word about what was happening over here yet. A few anxious people looked out their apartment windows, sleepy eyed then shaking their heads and pulling the curtains over the window. The man came out of the ally seconds later, rage in his eyes as Ryan jogged further away. All those years of track where finally paying off for something, and

Mr. Eby, his gym teacher, was right when he joked about how it was going to pay off when they were being chased by a serial killer someday.

Lost in confusion and direction, he tried to remember the direction of the hotel. When the man had finally given up on chasing him, Ryan started remembering the familiar roads that he took a few days back. As he turned a corner, a cathedral suddenly appeared in front of him. It was so magnificent that he had to stop and stare at it in awe. It was not a house of God, but as a house for something else... a house for the Lord of Pheonexia. It was black, rough and crudely built as if it was built out of coals. It must have been centuries old. The most noticeable attribute of it was its two spires built on each side of its roof, almost like horns. In the center space above the door was a circular pane of stain glass. It flickered red, indicating the inside was lit. He would stop here first. Looking both ways again, he slid into the shadows of the nearby buildings then jogged up the stairs to the front entrance. He pulled open the door and entered.

Hundreds of pews were lined in many separate rows, facing the altar at the other end. The altar's platform was raised higher than usual and the steps leading up to it were long and draped with a maroon carpet. Above him was a dome unlike anything; so beautiful and detailed with traces of past history of Pheonexia. Stained glass windows lined both walls on either side and candles shone above each one. There was a wide balcony above the entrance to fit hundreds more guests.

A few people were sitting in different pews, knelling down with their heads up and looking towards the altar. Ryan snuck around the side and sat down on the furthest pew to the back. There was an older man sitting there already, but he didn't bother looking at Ryan. He spoke anyway.

"Are you scared?" asked the elder.

Ryan looked at him. "Yes."

The man turned to look at him. "The candles are going out," he said nodding his head a few times to the candles above the windows. "The second you entered, they all began to go out one by one."

"Not because of me," said Ryan, trying to decipher the man's cryptic speech. He looked at the candles fading out slowly, darkening the cathedral.

"Oh yes," replied the man. "I know what is happening right now; out there in the world. I see you, sitting beside me and not knowing what to do as you are hunted. Hunted. Oh yes, you most defiantly are." The man's eyes widened as if he was suddenly frightened of Ryan. "I see it in your eyes," he whispered. "I see it inside of you. For it is also inside of me." The man turned away and continued praying, kenneling down this time. "There is no sanctuary for you inside this building. Inside a building where the Lord sees you this very moment. He is here."

Ryan looked up towards the altar and saw a tall white statue against the back wall behind the altar's table. It was carved in the likeness of a man dressed in a robe, holding out one of his hands and the other clenching a sphere close to his chest. His stone hair was covering his eyes and nose, with just his mouth smirking to one side.

"He will watch you until the moment you take your last breath," said the man.

"Are you scared of Him?" asked Ryan. "No one should ever be scared of their Lord."

The man looked at him, the whites around his eyes showing. "The reason I pray, like this very moment, is so He will not harm me." He suddenly lunged at Ryan and grabbed him, his breath rank. "Get out. Run. He is watching you. He is *always* watching."

The man let go him. Heeding his advice, Ryan got up and raced for the exit. Before he left, he saw a black jacket and top hat hanging on a peg across from the door. He quickly snatched them and threw them on himself before leaving the cathedral.

As Ryan got closer to Classer Hotel, everywhere he turned there were groups of people forming. Ryan hunched behind a stone stairway that lead up into a store that was locked. He pressed his back against the stone and closed his eyes for several seconds, trying to plan out a route to the hotel that was just across the street from him. He peered around the stairs and saw Dunger Wall in the distance. It would only get harder as each minute passed, so he couldn't wait. He reached into one of his pockets and pulled out the plastic bag that had the Orbs he purchased earlier. He spilled them into his hand and looked through the few he still had left. There were a few Sweat Preventers left and the last one was the Age Increaser.

"Thank you," he breathed, grateful and hopeful that something finally went his way. He looked at the tag for the Age Increaser and read that it would increase his age by ten years, but the T.U.D was in one hour. He peered one more time over the stairs then scrunched the Orb into his fist, hoping the age restriction would not affect him.

He felt a strange feeling go through his body for only seconds, like his body was rubber and it was being stretched. He sat for a few more seconds then looked down; nothing appeared to have changed down there.

"Bummer."

He got up and stared at himself in a smoky glass window.

"Dear God," he said, smiling and seeing his twenty-seven-year-old self staring back. It worked.

"Hey, who are you?!"

Ryan spun around and saw a group of three citizens run up to him with torches in their hands, their faces like murder.

"I—I—"

"I—I," mocked one of the men. "What are you doing? Are you searching for the boy or not? You look incredibly suspicious here all by yourself."

A woman walked behind Ryan and closely examined him. "What are you hiding here?" she said, kicking a few pieces of paper into the air and catching them in her hand to read intently as if they were clues to the fountain of youth.

"I am so looking," said Ryan, deepening his voice. "And what are you three doing? Huh?" He stepped around them with his hands behind his back, examining them as well. "I am looking by myself, thanks. I am not a child and will not be spoken to like that! Get back to work!" He grabbed a torch from one of the mob members and sped off across the street.

He emerged in front of Classer Hotel and stepped inside. To his surprise no one was around. He casually walked up to the service counter where Susan was reading a newspaper called *The Blazing City Archives* while sipping on a glass of what could have been red wine. What a relief. Hopefully she wasn't completely sober.

She glanced up as he reached the counter and her eyes widened in splendor. "My, my. Who do we have here? Looking to spend the night in

Classer Hotel where our services are keen on…" She gave him a blank look then laughed, snorting slightly. "I forget the rest. Please don't tell my boss. This is my first week here. Um, we are keen on and… and devoted to making sure that your stay here is… what do you want?"

"Listen," said Ryan quickly as he noticed a person entering the lobby, looking around. "I checked in a few days ago into a gold room. The name is Henry Jetarbee. I misplaced the key to my room and I was wondering if you could give me a new one. This is urgent."

Susan smiled and flashed her bright white teeth as if she was on a first date, flipping her blonde hair back and sliding her glass to the side. She put her elbow on the counter and her hand under her chubby jaw as if she was deeply interested in what he was saying "Jetarbee? Oh, I think I remember you! You were that handsome boy who looked lost and was pathetic in his speech. My, you age very fast. You will be eighty before next week I fear. It also appears that you just rolled out of a chimney. How dirty you are." She scrunched up her nose as if he was suddenly unpleasant. "But I suppose men get dirty for a reason." She puckered her pink lips slightly. "So they can be washed clean again." She giggled and snorted, lowering her head then raising it back up again, causing her hat to fall off. "But you know, I—"

"Yes," said Henry as nicely as he could. "Baths are so fun! But, could you do another favor for me? Could you lock the doors to this hotel for a couple of hours? You see, there is an escaped murderer on the loose—"

"Escaped murderer!" she yelped. "Are you sure? Yes, I know about that. That's all my coworkers have been talking about for the last hour. They are quite silly on the matter. Probably in the kitchens right now gossiping with our new cook Kenny." She got up and reached under the counter for a ring that held one solid black key. She quickly ran around the counter in her light blue attire, grabbed his hand and they both jogged towards the entrance. "I am sure there is some protocol for something like this. Safety for our guests is our number one priority! Or is it our second priority? Who knows! Want some wine?"

"No," said Henry. "Well, maybe later."

Susan put her gloved hand on the knob and turned the key into the lock. She pulled down the blinds and squatted to look through a tiny slit. "No murderer is coming in here today," she said, watching the people going by. "I will turn the lights off as well. Everyone in here is sleeping so they will not mind."

"That won't be necessary," he said but she was already running back to the counter.

Henry looked through the blinds at the people that were converging around the hotel and all down the street, searching in stores and apartments. Was coming in here really the smartest decision? He was starting to second guess himself—again. He turned to Susan as she ran back to the door. The lobby was now in darkness except for a few lit candles on the walls.

"And the key?" he asked.

"Oh," she said, laughing loudly. She held it up. "You can have this one. It opens all the doors in the hotel. I was just a tad lazy and grabbed this one since it's easier. I'm sure the boss will not mind one bit! Don't lose it though. It's the only one."

Henry grabbed the key as people started pounding on the door to come in.

"Who is it?" asked Susan.

Henry rolled his eyes. "Thank you so much! You were a lot of help!" He turned and ran towards the elevator just as a man with a black mustache came out of a room from behind the counter, looking aggravated.

"Susan! What is this nonsense? I have been getting complaints through the windows that the front door is locked! Why are the lights off?"

As Henry entered the elevator, Susan unexpectedly slid her way in with him as the panels shut. She laughed and Henry looked at her, amused.

"I'm in so much trouble," she said, laughing as she covered her mouth and held onto Henry Jetarbee's hand. "Mr. Classer is so funny when he's mad."

"Thank you again," he said, feeling her sweaty hand entangled with his.

"You are so welcome Henry! I'm quitting tonight, so this is very appropriate given the circumstance." She cleared her throat then looked to her side for the rest of the ride up.

The elevator opened and they both got out. Henry kept eyeing for his room number fifty-three as Susan tip-toed towards a window and looked out.

"My goodness, there are people everywhere. You would think with an escaped murderer on the loose that they would be in their homes keeping safe." She looked at Henry down the hall for his response but suddenly froze. Her eyes narrowed then she looked out of the window again. "I don't suppose…" she whispered quietly.

Henry found the right room and unlocked the door. He stepped inside then went back out to see if Susan was coming. He couldn't see her in the hall anymore, which was just lit by candle light. He shrugged his shoulders and was about to close the door when a sudden thump against the door made him jump back as if the door just gave him a shock of electricity. Susan gave hurtling into the room with a candlestick in her hand, thrashing it wildly at him and screaming like a mad woman.

"You lied to me! You are the murderer! I know it! I knew it all along but was too blinded by your lying eyes and lips!"

Henry stumbled backwards in surprise, shielding himself with his arms and batting the candle stick out of the way. "No, Susan! I'm not a killer! Listen to me!" He quickly dodged one of her blows as he was forced back across the room. She reached over to him and yanked the key out of his hand sharply, scratching his hand in the act with her long red nails.

"Do not lie to me! I thought you were nice and dumb but you just turn out to be a big ol' psycho! Were you playing on killing me next? Look at you! You have blood all over you! Murderer!" The candlestick was pelting hot wax everywhere as the enlarged flame was still lit on the wick.

"Watch it!" he yelled, defending himself with his hands as if there was a raging lion in front of him. "Okay, I will be honest. Those people outside do want me dead. But it is all false information you have!"

"Like what?" she said sarcastically. "News travels fast. I know it was you, I know it!" She seemed to have stopped her candlestick acrobats, but then a new realization seemed to spark in her mind and she was going all out again.

Henry tried to run back to the door but she was blocking him, the candlestick like a sword in her hand. She stepped backward and slammed the door shut.

"You will stay here until they come," she said fiercely. "An Age Increaser? Very smart, Mr. Jetarbee. If that is your real name! I'm not stupid!"

"How will anybody know I'm up here?" he said. "It could take a long time for them to even consider coming up here, in which time I would have already murdered you with my crazy psycho murdering skills!" He made a deranged face and opened his mouth, sticking out his tongue. "GARRRRRRRR!"

Susan gave him a dark smile then tossed the candlestick onto the feathered bed, igniting the blankets into instant flames. "They will now. Our romance has OFFICALLY ended!"

"Oh please," said Henry. "What romance? You are not my type."

Susan's mouth fell open in terror. She ran around him towards the balcony and tossed the key over the edge as well as a small gold one that she had in her pocket. It was the spare key to his room that she was hiding all along.

"You little liar," said Henry with a surprised smile.

She laughed. "Hehehe what a naughty and smart girl I am. Quite intelligent I must say and that is not the wine speaking. Just outwitted a crazy psycho murderer! Once the door to one of our rooms is closed, it will not open without a key!" She laughed again as if it was the most brilliant thing she ever came up with. "You are locked in here until they come for you!"

"What the hell did you do that for?!" yelled Henry. "How will anyone get in here and how will we get out without any keys?! This room is on fire now!"

Susan's smiled faded and her jaw dropped. Tears started to fill her eyes as the fire spread to the ground and up the walls. "I do not know what I just did! Oh no! What did I do?! I didn't mean to!"

Henry started backing away towards the balcony as the fire blocked the door. He shook his head and refused to look at her as he stepped out onto the cement.

Susan couldn't help but scream as she looked down below over the edge. "I'm sorry! Please forgive me! I was only trying to do something good. I thought that maybe if I caught you then I would get a reward or a promotion."

"You lied to me about quitting," said Henry, trying not to tear up from the terrible situation that was taking place as he looked over the balcony. "Stupid!" he shouted, making Susan flinch. "I trust another person and I get screwed in the end! Enough of this!" He turned to Susan. "Big mistake," he muttered quietly. "You are stupid!"

"I'm sorry," she mouthed, not being able to form words. The fire caught onto the curtains over the balcony and dark, heavy smoke was pushing into the air like a chimney. Henry looked back down over the sides of the balcony and saw people pointing up to the smoke and others rushing into the hotel, the entrance busting open. He looked out at the city in front of him, the blood-red sky and spires all around him being clouded with mist and smoke from all directions.

Suddenly, he could hear someone yelling to him from right beside him. He turned to the balcony next to his and there was a man and woman waving their hands for them to jump over into the room next to his. Both balconies were very close, but the jump would be risky. He was confident that he could make it. He turned to Susan.

"We need to jump," he said.

The smoke was making them both cough deeply and constantly. It was almost impossible to see anything now, but he could feel the heat getting intense.

Susan looked mortified at him. "I am not going to jump down. What do you think will happen once we hit the bottom?"

Henry rolled his eyes and dragged her towards the side. "Not jumping down. Jumping across to the balcony beside us. We have to do it now. I'm doing it first. Come if you want." Without thinking or hearing a response from her, he got up onto the ledge and with a minor resistance threw his body into the air. There was a second of blank space then he landed perfectly onto the cement of the other balcony. The woman quickly helped him off the ground and lead him into the room. Henry pushed away from her and rushed towards the door. He tried to rip it open but remembered it needed a key.

"I need you to open this!" he demanded.

"But what about your friend?" asked the woman as she grabbed the key from out of a drawer and unlocked the door for him. "You can't just leave. Your room is on fire and is spreading!"

"I don't care," he said, dashing out down the hall. "Thanks for your help!"

He tried not to look around as he merged with guests who were running down the hall and away from their rooms, smoke billowing through the halls. There were people who came from outside that managed to already make it up to this floor and were running down the hall towards his room, wanting to see if he was still there, and alive. He got into a crowded elevator and tried to hide himself under his hat and beneath his jacket, the smell of smoke poignant on him. He was in fast forward mode now. He just wanted to run, and there was only one last safe place that he could run to.

Before the panels of the elevator even opened, they were pushed apart by several people who wanted to escape the hotel. He was swarmed by dozens in the lobby as he made his escape in disguise. It was all a terrible messy blur, but he set his mind on only one thing, and that is what he needed to focus on. "Don't get distracted," he said to himself.

It was a non-stop search for the alley that hid Hoarder's Tunnel and connected it into Brazz's shop. He blended into the city again, trying to convince others further by occasionally looking into a house for a few seconds or under a carriage then immediately dashing on in haste. Random horses would gallop down the street in fear, free from their carriages and finding ways to flee the madness around them.

Once Dunger Wall was close enough that it loomed over him, he jogged up and down dozens of side streets and alleys before he finally found the specific one he needed, which was still abandoned and deserted and extremely dark. He ran towards the wall and felt his way with his hand until he felt the opening. Behind him, there were shouts echoing down the alley and thunderous footsteps of groups running back and forth. This route was clever, easily hidden in the darkness as well as the alley itself. He thrust himself into the tunnel and ran furiously at top speed until he reached the other end. Hopefully there would be no one there except

Brazz.

As he neared the end he saw light coming out from under the purple rug. Ryan tip toed his way towards it and lifted up the side carefully. There was no one around, except for someone standing behind the counter and tossing countless diamonds into a cardboard box. Ryan went towards the front entrance and poked his head out.

"There you are," said a surprised Brazz. "What are you doing here, boy? Or I should say, man? Hm… very clever indeed."

Ryan was peering outside and was trying to find anything suspicious but there was no one around. "This is the last place I could think of," he said. "I'm not safe anywhere. I've been through hell and back again."

"Shouldn't this have been your first choice though?" asked Brazz from beneath his black hood, using his raspy voice as always. "And were you ever really safe?" It sounded like he was quite amused by something. Not by Ryan himself, but something that Ryan wasn't understanding. "What happened to you anyway? You looked so pretty and nice the last I saw you. Ready to take on the big city. Now… you look like death itself. But I admit, less dumb."

Ryan shrugged off Brazz's comments. He started moving nervously back and forth inside the shop with his face in his hands. "It has been a hard couple of days for me."

"Do explain. And don't worry. The raid from a few days ago only lasted a little bit then the fools gave up. Of course, I couldn't tell you this because I lost communication with you."

"It wasn't my fault," said Ryan.

"I'm sure it never is," replied Brazz.

"Didn't you hear that explosion though? The one that I supposedly did?" Ryan tried being as quiet as he could without yelling. "You have to be deaf to not have heard it. And now people are going crazy because of that stupid bitch."

"No," said Brazz. "I mean; I did hear the explosion. But I just thought it came from inside the city somewhere. Things are always going... boom, boom, boom in the night."

Ryan fell into a wooden chair, wanting to punch someone out of anger. He removed the coat and hat that he took from the cathedral. "I just want this to stop. This is scary Brazz. What can I do? Please help me. You are all I have left. What are my options?"

Brazz took a beautiful silver goblet from out of the box. It was lined with emeralds along the rim. "Would you look at this. Do you want it? It's worth a fortune. You'd get so much gold and silver for it."

"It don't care," said Ryan softly. "Blow something up if I have to. That's what he told me to do. Someone already did it for me, and now Carson is dead."

"Whose advice? What? Carson is dead?"

Ryan looked at him. "Can you help me please?"

"With what?" asked Brazz, tilting his head. "Is something wrong? You don't look good."

Ryan sprang up then went around the counter and pushed Brazz up against the wall, slamming his fist against the counter.

"I DON'T THINK THIS IS FUNNY! BE SERIOUS ABOUT THIS!"

Brazz chuckled at Ryan, his white teeth smiling. "I'm sorry my dear boy. I'm a little behind the times." He rattled a bag of coins in front of his face. "Will you accept a bag of gold coins in exchange for not killing me like you so desperately want to right now?"

Ryan didn't let go of him. "I need you to help me right now," he said calmly. "You *will* do this for me."

"I will," said Brazz quietly. His smile faded. "Only if you help me."

"What? No. Are you brain dead? This is not the time! I've helped you enough already!"

Brazz grabbed Ryan's shoulders and pushed him off forcefully. "Now you see here boy. My help comes with a price. Everything does. And this is no different. This is your entire fault, so be quiet and listen." He grabbed Ryan by the collar of his shirt. "DID YOU LIKE BEING DOWN THERE?! IN THE FIRE?!"

Ryan cringed a bit, not because of Brazz's shouting, but because he feared someone might hear him and come inside. "I thought you said you didn't know where I was."

"It's called a lie," said Brazz. "I tried communicating with you over your visor but Carson picked it up somehow. I knew then you were most likely finished. There goes another valuable ally to do my bidding."

"Bidding?" said Ryan. "So that's all you see me as?"

"Well, let me see. You lie, you steal... you murder. You're going to Ethklemena now. But, don't worry. We're all going there anyway."

"I haven't murdered."

"Of course you have. All those people in the hall would still be alive if you were never here. And this abomination would not be happening right now."

Ryan shook his head. "That's different. I didn't do that—I didn't purposely decide to come here."

"You did so," said Brazz in a childish voice. "If you didn't decide to step through that pretty little portal... but, enough of this nonsense. You need help, and I will give it to you if you help me. Agreed?"

"Yes, whatever" said Ryan. "And what is this deal?"

"Never mind that now. Just steal something again once this all blows over—no pun intended. Do we have a deal?"

"Yes. Deal," said Ryan, annoyed and flustered, wanting to kick Brazz in his annoying little face. He shook hands with him. He might as well have been the devil himself.

"Good. Now, considering the sever danger that you're in, your portal may open now. Any hour, you should start to glow red. This will be the sign." He reached over into a drawer and pulled out a black Orb. "You will use the Veil Orb when we finally leave. No one will see you. These are freshly made, you know."

"That's it?" asked Ryan.

"No. We need to figure out how to get your portal open. What does dear Ryan need to do..."

Ryan looked at the store's entrance and sighed. "I'll have to go back out there, won't I?"

"Perhaps not," said Brazz. "Perhaps we just need to talk."

Ryan gave him a weird look. "Talk? Talk about what? The weather? Oh yeah, it's so nice out there. Hopefully it doesn't rain. I really want to start my gardening today. Do you want some tea?"

"You aren't very funny," said Brazz.

"Funnier than you," he said.

There was a sharp bang from outside as shouts suggested large numbers of people were walking around outside.

Brazz peeked out the entrance. "Not good. Quick, you need to hide. And not with a Veil Orb. You need to recover and gather your wits. You're in no state to make this final push to your portal being as weak as you are."

"I am *not* weak," said Ryan.

The voices were now directly outside the shop.

"Check everywhere!" shouted someone. "Before he tries to escape, he will die!"

Ryan gave an exasperated look and rolled his eyes. "Okay, I get it. You want me to die."

Brazz walked over to his counter and started throwing objects into a box.

Ryan looked at him. "Um, are we leaving?"

"No. This will have to do." He reached over to the middle section of the counter and pushed it back. Ryan noticed a type of trapdoor in the ground, cleverly hidden beneath the counter that was built in three different sections.

"A trapdoor? You have got to be kidding me."

"Stop whining," said Brazz, opening the door. "This is your life. So stop whimpering and get in if you want to keep that precious possession of yours."

Ryan didn't hesitate for a second (okay, maybe one second) and jumped into the pit of darkness. There was a thump then a creak as Brazz jumped down after him with a cardboard box under his arm. He shut the door then something started scrapping across the floor above.

"What is that sound?"

"It's the counter moving back into place. It automatically does so. Very special contraption. Unlike you."

Ryan couldn't see anything but he wanted to remain quiet. Only moments had passed before terrible yells entered the shop. There were countless screams and giggles and things being thrown around and smashed.

"What if they find it?" asked Ryan.

"They will not," whispered Brazz. "It's well hidden. They may find the route though. It's a pity they're destroying my shop."

"You said no one would be able to find the route because that was cleverly hidden too."

Brazz didn't say anything but look up into the darkness. Ryan thought he had better shut his mouth. When he sat down on the floor he felt a wooden chair beside him. He sat down on it and waited as the people above left and moved on.

Seconds later, he felt a weird sensation overpower him as a light puff of cool air fell onto his eyes. His eyes shut and he fell asleep.

It all happened so fast. She had no idea what she was doing. Denise ran down the stairs, across the kitchen and directly into the living room to glance out the window. When she saw the torches and angry mobs running through the streets, her heart stopped. She was scared, above all else. But she couldn't just run. She had two others to take care of now.

Jacob and Demi were busy building pillow forts with the glow of a

Star Light Orb shining from Demi's hand, meant to be a lighthouse. Denise threw a pile of blankets on top of Demi, cutting out the light.

"Why did you do that?" asked Jacob, laughing. "She is a lighthouse. My ships will sink without it." As he reached over to pull the blankets off his sister, Denise grabbed him and pulled him up like a rag doll.

"Come quickly," she said, grabbing Demi's hand and pulling her up. "You need to go to your rooms now. It's very important that you understand this."

"I'm not tired!" yelled Jacob. "This is stupid. Just like your boring food. Stupid."

"Stupid Denise," echoed Demi, trying to escape from her grasp.

They passed through the kitchen and started up the stairs. Jacob and Demi glanced through the window and saw the shadows of people holding their torches and running back and forth in the streets, cackling and shouting through the night air.

"What is that?" asked Demi, her eyes widening.

When they reached the second floor, the front door burst open and all who entered began throwing things about and shouting obscenities.

"ANYONE HOME?!" one screamed. "Come out boy! We have presents! A nice bloody knife in your stomach!"

Denise gasped out in terror. Once all three reached Demi and Jacobs's bedroom, she shut the door quietly and ran towards the two beds where she placed the two children.

"Appear you are sleeping," said Denise as she tucked them under the sheets. "If anyone should venture in here, do not scream or become frightened by them. They will not hurt you because you are not what they are seeking."

"Where is mother?" asked Jacob through small coughs. "And father? Should they not be here right now?"

"Do not worry; they are safe inside Mainbreak Hall. You don't need to worry about them right now."

The corruptive sounds from downstairs started to intensify once the mob made their way up the stairs and down through the hall.

"The Lord requires your sacrifice! Die for your Lord!"

"Where is Ryan?" asked Demi. "Did he go back home?"

Denise held Jacob's hand and didn't respond to her. "It will all be over soon. Just a little longer."

The door to the bedroom was flung open and one by one people poked their heads in and looked around. Some entered the room, ignoring Denise, Jacob and Demi as they searched through all the toys and furniture and under the beds and in the closet. Each one carried flame lit torches, and Denise feared that they would ignite a fire. After their search of the room, they left and went on to the next.

Denise got up from the bed and grabbed the doorknob to close it, but the door was pushed back and a man stepped in. Denise stepped back and stared at all the smeared soot and dried blood all over his face and suit.

"My dear," said Carson. "How do you do?" He glanced at Demi and Jacob for a quick second then directly back to Denise. "Sorry," he continued. "I must look like death. I was just looking for you by the way."

"You were?" she asked. She looked behind her towards Jacob and Demi who were staring at her through the covers.

"It's nice being able to... connect with old friends," he said. "We haven't seen each other in such a long time that I thought I'd offer you an important job."

"I believe I'm busy at the moment," said Denise more confidently. "Possibly some other time, surely. There are more important things to be worrying about other than giving people jobs, Mr. Jenkins. Isn't that right?" People continued running back and forth down the hallway, ignoring Carson and not taking into account that he wasn't dead.

"Unfortunately, you don't have any say in the matter," Carson said. He opened his fist and a fireball of flames flickered and lit up the room. "I'm sorry to say that if you do refuse, then I will have to burn this house to the ground. I mean, the house won't burn to the ground, as these homes are built with stone. But the inside is perfect for feeding and spreading fire." He grabbed her chin in his hand and held it close to his face, staring at her, eye to eye. "And I always get what I want."

"Is that how you talked to your mother?" said Denise, her lips pressed together in Carson's hand. "I would have slapped you long ago."

Carson let go and slapped her across the face, sending her hair brushing to the side. She refused to cry at the pain. Instead she stood straight, her chest out and her face emotionless.

"What?' said Carson. "You thought I was expecting you to cry?"

"No. I was expecting you to be a man. Not a child," she replied.

Carson's eyes widened, his hand twitching. "The job that I was speaking of before actually isn't a job. I'm forcing you to come with me. I need someone who has a heart of gold, of cherished happiness and of true good. You seem like one of those people." He looked down. "I remember how good you were to me and the others. How you were... just a really good person. I never had the chance to thank you for what you did for us."

Denise tried to fight off the urge to wipe her eyes. "I remember how good you were too," she said. "How scared you were, but how you smiled when you weren't. How bright it was. Your laugh. The jokes you would make. I can never forget him, even though that man is gone now. He is never coming back." Carson reached out to touch her, but she backed away. "But looking at you now, you might as well be dead." She ran to Demi and Jacob.

"Leave them," he said with a flick of his head. "They can't help you."

Denise knew she was being forced away. One way or another, he would make her come with him. She kissed Demi and Jacob on the cheek. "I have to leave now. You will be safe if you stay in this room. Stay under the covers. Tell stories to each other. This will all be over soon. I'll... I'll be back in time to make lunch tomorrow. Okay? Something special."

"Cherry pies," said Demi and Jacob together.

"Your favorites," she said happily, smiling. She hugged them both. "I will never forget either of you. No matter what happens." She got up and walked back over to Carson. He put his hand out for her to take it but she ignored it.

Once they left the room and were in the hallway, Carson reached for the door to close it. Before he did, he gave the two children a stare of complete and utter sadness. As he was about to leave, he felt a strange spasm go through his body and his head bent backwards a bit, his pupils dilating to black. He adjusted his head quickly and looked at Demi and Jacob, smiling.

"I believe your parents are long dead," he said. "I never really did like them." He smiled wickedly then shot three bursts of fire throughout the room. "And I never liked you two either."

"WHAT ARE YOU DOING?!" screamed Denise, running for the door. Carson grabbed her then placed his hand on the inside doorknob and made it wicked hot. He slammed the door then blasted a fireball on the outside doorknob for good measure.

Denise was screaming with tears as she was pulled away towards the stairs, clawing at him to let her free. She finally broke loose from him and plummeted down to the landing where she became unconscious. Carson stepped over her and set fire in every direction before picking her up again. Everyone who was in the house jumped out as smoke rose up into the blood night sky.

FOURTEEN.

RACE AGAINST TIME

AN EAGER MOUSE PUSHED AND SHRUGGED ITS WAY through a hole no bigger than a lemon and into the dimly lit reading room. It was brightened only by the fireplace inside a wide hearth and the flames from candles hanging from scones on the walls and candlesticks on tables. In such quiet stillness, the mouse's quick steps made soft rustling strides along the carpet. But even its presence would go unnoticed. Mainbreak Hall was unusually quiet tonight. There was something in the air that felt unsettled, and it unnerved her. If it was any other night she would have thought nothing of it, but this night, this week, had been anything but normal. Something was wrong.

Of course, the hall was always quiet at this time of night, but tonight in particular it was unexplainable. Just hours before closing time, Renny told all the workers to go home early because there was no need for them to stay tonight. The truth however was that she didn't feel safe. She knew that all the workers thought something was wrong by the unusual and questioning glances she got as they passed through the front door. To keep her mind off such troubling thoughts, Renny found herself dusting shelves, something she hadn't done in years as she never had much free time to do so. The cleaner often took care of it, but she was sent home along with the other staff.

She didn't know where Otis was. He had never been gone for this long without her knowing of his whereabouts, and the fact that Ryan suddenly up and left a couple days' back was also troubling. *No one ever tells me anything*, she thought to herself as she glided her duster in between bronze candle sticks, their flames flickering from the upward gusts it made. Otis was always stubborn like that. He took his work too serious. There was a time for work and a time for family. Often times she would think there was very little of the latter with him. She understood his position, the risks and devotion it would mean when he signed on years ago to be a part of Zephyrus' Secret Service. He wasn't a man meant for a desk or to plow a field. He needed to be in the front line, to guard and protect. It just felt like at times he did more protecting of the city than of his own family.

"We moved here to have a better life," she told herself out loud. She saw no point in it, but he did. Once Jacob and Demi were born, they simply weren't making enough while living in their small and meager cottage with its large attached windmill. Raising and selling beef and chickens and growing crops from their farm had its modest returns. But they just weren't well-known enough and didn't have all the buyers like the other farms did.

"What will this city and job provide you once we take up residence?" she asked him the day before their departure, their minimal belongings propped up on wagons and their remaining cattle and chickens bought sold.

"A purpose for me and a better life for you three," he would say each and every time. As if he didn't realize that he had a purpose already. To be a father.

"And how can I be a father if I can't support them?"

"Of course that's important," she said undeniably. "But this job you are taking. Are you sure it's safe? Are you even qualified?"

"More than enough," he snapped back, looking at her as if offended. Of all places, why did he have to find a job in the city, *that* city. No good was ever spoken of it. The land of the ones who worshipped and prayed to the false Lord of Pheonexia. Full of criminals and terribly deranged people who would slit your throat just because it was all good fun, and would later justify your death as being a sacrifice to their Lord. She had never been there herself and had to intention of ever doing so. Her father always forbid her, his only child, from ever going there when she was younger. Why couldn't Otis find a purpose in the Great Imperial City, the frozen village or anywhere else but there? Damn it, she'd even take the Peaks over that fiery rot of land. He didn't even try going to those other places, she knew. He stopped going to the Great Imperial City every month even though they were their biggest buyers. It was always off to Blazing City for business, assuming it was just to sell beef, chickens or crops but she quickly figured out the plan. They could have made it work here in the Hustel Lands. They could have kept trying, sought out more buyers. The competition from the dozens of other farms and towns was immense, but they did it over and over so they could keep doing it again and again. Yet here they were, years later. A better life finically, yes. A better family, no. He ruined it all. They even had to stay in hiding in their dingy house in Copper Town because the city's criminals never did like the Secret Service… or their spouses. Their safety always seemed to be in question. She knew after a while that it wasn't about the money and making their life more well off. It was about him. He wasn't fulfilled in life. He wasn't meant to do what he had been doing on the farm. Here in Blazing City, he found his place. And yes, what a terrible place it was.

A metallic *ding* suddenly struck the air and shook her out of her locked away memories, making Renny drop the duster in startlement. She turned toward the counter and noticed a tall someone standing in front of it, waiting for service. She didn't see or hear anyone come in. Was she so lost in thought that she didn't even hear the front door open and close? You would have to be a ghost to be so quiet. It was rare for someone to even come inside during this late hour. The last time that happened was a few days back when a lost and stupid boy stumbled up to her, asking for help. She learned her lesson.

When Renny stepped forward to attend to the woman, the woman herself turned her head in Renny's direction, staring at her from behind a black veil that covered her eyes and brushed just the tip of her white powdered nose.

"Hello there," said Carmen confidently as Renny made her way behind the counter, determined to remain professional. Carmen was wearing an oversized purple hat that was tilted slightly to one side so the brim was hiding half of the veil. Her lips were plump and dull red, an expressionless mouth against a pale face of makeup. Her purple outfit was tight fitting as ever, as if she squeezed herself into a dress two sizes too small, but oddly fitted her well in a contorted sort of way. A strong collar expanded from her neck and shoulders like two crow's wings and a plunging neckline pushed her breasts together. Very unnatural, thought Renny, her face grimacing at such exposed skin. She looked very doll-like, as if she was about to attend a funeral in a fashionable manner with purples to compliment the blacks. She carried and leaned against what looked like a cane, but a cane not meant to aid with walking. It was an accessory, a black metal stick with beautiful purple and gold embroidery that looked more like something you would use to knock someone's skull in.

Renny sucked her lips in, staring at this woman and her cane. Though oddly, she tugged a little on her own dusty purple blouse as if she was ashamed of her attire compared to Carmen's lavishness, and feeling oddly underdressed for no occasion at all. Her own purple hat was like the ugly stepchild to Carmen's beautiful monster. It was as if her outfit was making a mockery of hers, a super stylized version of her own.

"What are you doing here?" demanded Renny in a tone that shocked herself.

Carmen cleared her throat as if offended. Her lips pursed together like a prissy little bitch. "Well, that's quite rude of you to talk like that. I am a citizen of this city and have the right just like everyone else to venture inside this government building until closing. I have come here to offer you a tip that I would like to pass on to you and everyone here tonight."

"A tip?" asked Renny as if she wasn't impressed. *That's it? Why bother. Ha!* She forced a smile. "And what would that tip be darling?"

"It's actually a tip from someone else," replied Carmen coolly, "and

I am saying it on their behalf, is that okay? I hope so because I'm saying it anyway." She looked down at Renny's fingers that were drumming lightly on the wood of the counter. "Excuse me, don't give me attitude. Take your hands off the counter. Please and thank you my love. I see professionalism isn't your strong suit."

Renny smiled and stared straight at her without doing what she asked. *Who did she think she was? You had better hold that cane close or I ought to grab it and whack your about-to-burst tits with it and send you falling to the floor blubbering*, she thought happily.

Carmen put a black gloved hand on the counter and picked up a pen from a holder and started fiddling with it. "Anyway, the tip is actually a suggestion. I would just like to inform you that this hall will be blown up in less than ten minutes from now." She said this statement as if she just ordered a sandwich. Renny's eyes widened, wanting to take drastic action immediately.

"So I suggest everyone be evacuated, if you take this tip seriously. It could just be a joke however. The person who told me to tell you about it could have been lying to me, thus me lying to you, for their own amusement. I fear, though, that this is not a joke. What an unfortunate event in such an untimely manner." She giggled and put her hand over her mouth.

"What is wrong with you?!" shouted Renny, pointing her finger at her. "How dare you come in here and threaten me and this hall with such an accusation! Legal action will be taken!"

Carmen abruptly stopped laughing; her face resembling no emotion. It was just blank and porcelain, as if it was a wicked dolls face mixed with beauty and poison. She swatted Renny's hand out of the way forcefully. "Don't you dare point your dirty finger at me! You stupid ugly cow!" She started clicking the pen rapidly, causing the pen to slowly freeze and incase itself in dark ice. "I wish to speak to your boss about your nasty customer service skills. Oh, I am? How wonderful. Please tell your employee, that horrible bitch at the front counter, to not talk back to customers, because customers are always right! No matter how wrong they are, they are always right and nothing, absolutely nothing, is wrong with them!"

"I will not leave," said Renny sternly. "You can tell *your* boss that." With the threat that was just issued, she found herself smiling at her. "Have a nice day my sweet lady."

Carmen sighed and shook her head slightly. "Then sit here and get blown up for all I care. I do find this amusing, I must say. Have a nice day, Mrs. Kendall." She flicked Renny's nameplate with the frozen pen then threw it over her shoulder. She turned around and walked towards the front door, her black cane making *thudding* noises against the thick carpet. The pen started spreading its icy substance where it had landed next to a circular reading table, as if it broke and its ink was now spilling across the carpet.

"What a pity he has become."

Carmen abruptly stopped and turned around to look at Renny from behind her veil. "Pardon?"

"Carson does not need to do this, and neither do you. You are treading down the wrong path of destruction. You will regret it in the end."

Carmen put her gloved hand up to silence her. "I'm sorry, but the next time I need advice from someone, I'll ask myself. Thank you." She looked away. "And the end has already come I'm afraid... for you and your husband. It's only a matter of time now."

"Get out!" shouted Renny. "Get out!" She reached for a drawer beneath the top of the counter where specific defensive Orbs were hidden for situations like these.

"Yelling won't be necessary," said Carmen quietly. Within seconds, she withdrew an Orb from what seemed like out of nowhere and threw it directly across the room and towards Renny. It slammed into the side of her head and sent her tumbling onto the floor, leaving her unconscious. Her hat slid off and slumped down next to her shoulder.

Carmen barely grinned. "And what an ugly little corpse you will be."

She reached for the doorknob and pulled the door open, but not before looking over at the bookshelves to her right. She let go of the knob and stepped over to the shelves to grab a couple books then exited the building quietly, closing the door behind her.

Ryan awoke, dazed and confused. He looked groggily around to see that he was in a small and beautifully furnished cellar beneath the trapdoor. It was no bigger than your average bedroom. The walls were plain stone with all of them covered with hanging crystals, banners, swords and gems and other expensive trinkets, shining and reflecting the light from a warm fireplace that was built into the wall across from him. Ragged boxes were filled with hundreds of gold and silver rings and pieces of armor, small swords and daggers with gorgeous hilts. Glass figurines and pearls were placed in glass cabinets with goblets perched on top. What seemed like they didn't belong in the room, a bed, hammock, chamber pot, stove and wooden table with a couple chairs were also present. More boxes were piled up against the walls and a few were open on the floor as Brazz rummaged through while seated. The smell of cooked salmon wafted in the air, making Ryan sit upwards in his chair with his mouth slightly watering. He hadn't eaten in days it felt, which might as well have been.

"How long was I asleep for?"

"A few hours," mumbled Brazz, not looking up from his boxes.

"Did you do something? I don't usually fall asleep that fast."

Brazz snickered as if it was a stupid question. "You were making too much noise with your whining, so I decided to put you to sleep with an Orb. I kept thinking about how pesky you would be with your endless crying and blubbering, so I let you sleep, and sleep you did. Had sweet dreams did we? Not here, I can tell you that."

"I don't cry and blubber," said Ryan defensively. "And yes, I did have a few dreams…" His voice trailed.

"Of what?"

"Things I know a sane person would never dream of in their life."

"I don't dream," said Brazz, lifting a small tarnished shield from out of a nearby box and examining the tiny emeralds and sapphires engraved along the sides. "I also believe that dreams are gifts to people, something that keeps one's conscious mind interested while sleeping; a portal to a new world that is just our own for a few hours. I noticed that as I got older and the more, let us say, treachery I did wrong in my life, the more retched and violent my dreams would become. So much so that I could not sleep. I would not sleep. I then chose to eliminate them entirely from my memory—by choice. The dreams reflected who I was and what I was doing with my life at the time, and once I knew that there was no turning back from it I decided to erase them permanently."

"How did you do that?" asked Ryan. "Please don't say you had a part of your brain ripped out through your nose or something."

Brazz looked directly at him for the first time in what felt like forever. "I had my imagination evaporated. It is best to not think about the things that bring you bad ideas."

Ryan gulped and looked in the other direction. *But how?* He chose not to ask.

"Here, have something to eat," said Brazz, putting some cooked salmon onto a plate and sliding it towards Ryan who gratefully reached over and took it. "You need only ask. I have more than enough to share."

Ryan grabbed the salmon and ate it like he would if he were alone and no one was watching. *How embarrassing*, he kept thinking. But he didn't care anymore.

"Nice place you got here." It wasn't a lie. He was genuinely impressed with all that he had collected.

Brazz laughed. "This is where I live. I like it very much. It's quiet. Up there are where the real problems are."

"And this is where you keep all the good stuff," said Ryan in awe. "All for yourself." He abandoned his empty plate and got up, looking into the surfaces of several small statues that were lined on crowded shelves behind glass panes. There was an angel with a sword clutched in its fist and next to it what looked like a stone gargoyle. "What do you do?" he asked.

Brazz put down the shield he was polishing. "What?"

"What do you do? I mean, whenever I've come here, all I see you do is stand behind a counter and do... nothing. You barely get any customers."

"Does that bother you?"

Ryan shook his head quickly, thinking Brazz was offended. "No, sorry. I was just curious..." He continued to look around with his back turned to Brazz.

Brazz squinted at him with his gold eyes beneath the rim of his hood. "What are you thinking?" he asked.

Ryan sighed. "Just... lots of things. Home."

Brazz picked up the shield again and continued polishing it with a tattered rag as Ryan turned back around. He took a dagger from off the wall and unsheathed it, the fire's light reflecting against the steel blade and the rubies along the hilt. He had never held anything like it before. He bet it was sharp. He bet it was used to kill many men. Maybe kings or pirates. Maybe it was owned by a pirate at one point. He liked it.

Brazz saw him smiling down at the dagger as if it was a bar of fudge. His mouth curled downward. "This shield I have here. Look boy, this shield right here. It's very unique. It was forged thousands of years ago. Used by warriors and princes in long battles with blood from their enemies still etched within the fine lines and preserved within the gold forever. It was even said to have been used during the Great Battle of the Invasion... for those who believe in such tales. All of these jewels and wonders you see around you have been stolen. They are for me and no one else. I try to get rid of them, but at the same time I don't. Lord knows I have enough.

All the things I have done and seen. But now that I'm nearing fifty… I guess it's just another brick in the wall of my life."

"That's so interesting and so… troubling to hear at the same time," replied Ryan, smiling unnaturally. "So why do you do it? Why do you steal?"

"What else am I supposed to do? I am a criminal. I barely cease to exist. This's what I do and what I have become. The question after all is not why I do it. The question is why I did it. The Thefty Thieves of Thirty was a great asset to me, back when we were at the top of our game. Back when we escaped and made off with anything we wanted. No one ever caught us. We were anywhere and everywhere in Pheonexia year after year, taking and taking and selling and selling. But somewhere along the lines, it just began to fall apart… with… differences amongst us. Of those original thirty there's only one left that still commits to the group which is myself. I don't know where any of the others are, whether they are dead or alive. I don't even remember most of their names." He parted some of his hood and Ryan could now see his gold eyes and tanned face in full sight, revealing more of this man called Brazz, who all in all started looking more normal to him. "What did you think of Blazing City when you first entered it, Ryan? Was it all you hoped it would be?"

Ryan sat down and took a deep breath, still holding the dagger close to his chest as if it was a newborn child he didn't want to drop. "No it wasn't." He looked into the fire inside the stone hearth and deep into the flames within. "I hate this place and I will never come back."

"Are you sure about that?"

"Of course I'm sure. Who would want to come back here? The things

I have seen and… being down there… fire. Fire everywhere."

"Oh, you don't want to come back now. But curiosity is a tricky thing. You tell yourself one thing, but your brain and gut tell you the other. It's like a virus that consumes your body. You become intoxicated with desire and want."

Ryan shook his head. "Well, I'm done. I'm not that stupid that I would come back to this place." He glanced back at Brazz with slight hostility. "Believe me."

"I'm not talking about Blazing City," said Brazz in his raspy voice. "Of course, it would be stupid for you to come back *here*. But the rest… the rest of the world of Pheonexia. It's just one step outside your backyard, and you want to see the rest of it. I know you have seen bits of the hills and the mountains beyond the wall. The farms and towns of the Hustel Lands as well. Wait until you see the cities and palaces, the desert and the forests… the ocean… and the depth of the ocean."

Ryan's eyes glazed over as he thought about it. "Of course I want to see that. You know I do. But I'm done being here—there ain't no second tries for me. I'm not coming back Brazz." *Fuck this place,* he thought. *But no, love this place. Love it Ryan. Make it your new home. Forever.*

Brazz sighed and smiled as though he didn't believe him. "You know. When I first met you, you reminded me of Carson."

Ryan wasn't overly shocked from that statement. He stood the dagger up on his thigh with the hilt down against it, placing his index finger and thumb around the blade and moving it back and forth. "Oh yeah?" he said.

Brazz nodded and looked above Ryan where a few swords were hanging clumsily upside down, their blades pointing down above Ryan's head. He lifted his chin up at him as if he was trying to observe something. "Yes, back when he first came here with the other two brats. They were walking around one day, just like you. Hopeless teenagers. However, they did not stop by my shop. I was out walking about myself, trying to check out the competition of other sellers. When I brushed past them, I knew they were different. Even with the ridiculous clothes that they tried to disguise themselves with. Nobody else knew, but I did." Brazz got up from his chair and walked towards the fire and stroked it with a pair of bronze tongs that were laying against the wall beside the hearth, his back hunched over in front Ryan. "I just said a quick hi to them, but they didn't say anything back—they might not have heard me. That was the last time I really saw him. What a story it turned out for him. Mayor just like that. Just Wow. The Lord works in mysterious ways."

Ryan looked down and nodded, slightly upset, his index finger now jabbing itself into the tip of the blade. It felt good to hurt and feel blood, to mix his blood with the ancient blood of the kings and princes before him whose internal organs had hopefully touched this blade. He looked up at Brazz, who still had his back to him. Ryan smiled.

"Did you feel sorry for him?" asked Brazz quietly, still stroking the fire. He reached down slowly for a dagger that was pushed behind a box that was against the wall. "Did you feel sorry for his life and the man he had become?"

"Yes," muttered Ryan, his body sweating.

"Do you like blood, Ryan?" asked a voice.

No, thought Ryan. *But yes.*

Brazz's eyes closed. "If you could have saved and helped Carson, even if it meant putting your own life in danger, would you? Would you have saved this man?"

"The blade is sharp. The blade has bite."

The dagger's hilt was now in Ryan's shaking hand. He closed his eyes. He wanted to give an honest answer, but something wouldn't let him.

"Come and die, come and die," rallied the sinister voice.

"Come and die, come and die," repeated Ryan.

Brazz turned around suddenly, dagger in hand and looking up at Ryan who was standing over him, dagger in hand as well. They both stared at each other, not moving. The first one to strike would get the kill.

Ryan finally sighed. He dropped the dagger to the ground and it rattled to a stop once it spun a couple times on the stone. "I really would," he said quietly. "Even if he wouldn't have done the same for me… yeah I would have saved him. I feel like I've known him my whole life somehow. Like he's always been a part of me. I feel like he'd have been my brother. Maybe in another life. I genuinely cared about him." He could feel his eyes becoming moist. "He deserved a better life than this."

Suddenly, a bright white light illuminated the room like a dim fog. Ryan had to cover his eyes from the severe strength of the light.

Brazz looked at him and smiled, putting the dagger into a pocket inside his cloak. "Congratulations. The OroAurum has just opened."

When Ryan was able to open his eyes again, he looked down at his body and saw the white aura shining through his flesh. "I can go home now," he breathed with a sense of finality, not able to believe it. "What the hell did I say?!"

"From your heart," said Brazz with a small grin. "Sometimes, that's all it takes. Sometimes, love is the key… especially for an enemy."

"Excuse me?" muttered Ryan, dead faced. "I don't love him. I hardly cared about him, really."

"You said so yourself," replied Brazz. "You saw him as a brother."

"But… that's twisting what I meant," said Ryan defensively.

Brazz made a face at him. "Alright then."

Ryan's heart started beating fast. The thought of getting out of here was a very possible idea now. He couldn't help but feel rejuvenated. Whatever he said or did or felt, it worked. That's all he cared about.

Brazz got up and put his hands together. "Now then, we need to act immediately. Just let me tell you a few things first. We are about to venture out into a battlefield, so we need to protect ourselves. Things have changed within the last few hours, and you have only one hour to get to your portal before it closes forever." He grabbed a box from off the ground and pulled out a dark purple pouch from inside.

As Ryan stepped up to the trapdoor opening, Brazz took out a handful of Orbs. "Remember," he said. "You can't use more than one Orb on yourself at one time. When you break an Orb while you're already using one, the power of the previous one vanishes and the power from the one you just broke takes its place. You must use them wisely. One can get ignorant or even nervous when using them. It's a trickery and an art to use them skillfully; one after the other, planning ahead which ones you will use next. Your opponent may be faster than you so you must be quick. Each Orb has a T.U.D, which as you remember is stated on the tags. So if you plan on using one for its entire use without switching, you must be weary."

"I think I'll really only use one," said Ryan. "I only need to be invisible, don't I?"

Brazz shut the box and extinguished the fire. "Out there is unpredictable and we need to be prepared for what may happen. Being invisible can only get you so far. Remember this; there are Orbs that can be used against the ones that you yourself are using, making them powerless. But enough said. If you are ready, then it's time for us to get out of here." Brazz gave Ryan two Veil Orbs. "These ones last just fifteen minutes each."

"What about you?" asked Ryan, sliding them into his pant's pocket.

"I will use them as well. I can only imagine what they would think of me if they saw me with you. I steal for a living, and doing something like that will eventually get you caught, or put to death. He reached towards a chair and lifted up a black hooded cloak. "You may want to use this," he said, handing it to Ryan. "That damn glow is not going away anytime soon, so perhaps this may cover it once you become visible. Thankfully the glow only comes out of your exposed skin, and not through your clothes."

Ryan grabbed hold of the material and felt its silk against his fingers, not even debating in his head if he should put it on or not. He threw it over himself and tied the front up, pulling the hood over his head so that it covered just his eyes. When they both broke a Veil Orb, Brazz climbed up the short ladder and tapped on it three times with his knuckles. Ryan could hear the counter above moving to the side as the door opened. Brazz slowly poked his head out to investigate as flickering red lights streamed into the underground room.

"I believe it is clear," he said, "let us go."

It was the heat of the night, and everywhere was pandemonium—a jungle of madness and destruction. In every direction of the marketplace there were people pulverizing booths and terrorizing anything and anyone they came across. Countless people were setting store booths ablaze as others ran crazily around and attacked other civilians. Ryan tried to move as fast as he could to keep up with Brazz's pace. All he could see was a blurred mix of red, black and smoke. He was bumping into people and others were running into him, not even noticing or trying to figure out what the invisible mass that knocked into them was. He had things thrown at him and had to dodge people who were getting pushed to the ground and getting beaten, people who were being mistaken for him.

"I found him!" one person yelled.

"No, please, I am not him!" screamed a young boy in fear who was exactly the same age as Ryan. Ryan stared at him, with the boy looking back at him as well, right into the eyes, as if he could see him. It was as if he was asking for help.

"I do not believe you!" yelled the peasant as he started hitting him across the face. "You will die! In the name of the Lord!" He pulled out a knife and stabbed him several times in the chest. It was all Ryan could bear to watch, absolutely terrified as the boy yelled in agony.

He turned away and continued running behind Brazz so that he wouldn't lose him. They reached the middle of Copper Town where each of the homes were being broken into and set ablaze as people came jumping out, laughing hysterically with their torches flashing everywhere. Every second there was glass being blown out and shattered into his face from the breaking of windows. Many of the carriages were pushed over and were being burned slowly as more objects were getting tossed onto the flaming piles such as books and furniture. The shadows of everyone were long and pointed, as if gremlins were running around. There was a woman pleasantly rolling around in a pile of ashes, picking a handful up and letting it trickle down through her fingers like water. She smiled disturbingly as if it was liquid gold. She started rubbing it all over her face with pure joy. "Oh what a pleasure it is to feel you my Lord," she said orgasmically. "Thank you for these gifts."

Ryan saw a glimpse of Renny and Otis' house ahead. He ran past the entrance and could see that the door was ripped off. The inside was a fire pit of flames, with smoke escaping through the windows. All the lights in each house were now extinguished and people abandoned their torches, for the fires themselves provided enough light for the whole world to see. Because the homes were made of stone you couldn't torch them down, but the insides were brightly blazing from furniture and fabrics, causing the stone to crack and crumble. In a frantic rush, families escaped out from their houses with few pieces of belongings. One girl was being ripped away from her mother by a man who demanded her stay and take part in the Lord's demands so she could learn and grow.

Brazz was ahead of Ryan, but he stopped abruptly, causing Ryan to stop too.

"I forgot something my dear boy," he said. "I have a gut feeling my shop may not exist once I return, so I have to retrieve them. I will be right back." He turned around to leave but Ryan stopped him.

"No, forget it. You have to help me. You are all I have left." His eyes started watering as he looked around him. "I can't do this on my own

Brazz. I'm not going to make it."

Brazz put his hand on his shoulder. "We will still make it on time. Or at least you will if you choose not to wait for me. You started this journey alone. Suppose you were meant to finish it that way." He slid his hand down into the pocket of Ryan's pants, dropping something inside. "You are the good one out of the rest of us villains. I should hope you will remember that." He pushed past Ryan and ventured back towards his shop, sliding in between people who were running in the opposite direction from him.

Ryan looked on until Brazz was out of sight, worry in his eyes. He moved out of the way and towards the side of a house, his eyes darting every which way. He was prepared to leave Brazz behind; there was no time to wait for him. He was right. This was how it was meant to be.

Then it decided to get even worse.

Further back towards the black market, the row houses began to collapse one by one as heavy amounts of smoke and dust started billowing down the road towards him; like a river dam had just opened and water was now rushing down towards him. Dunger Wall moaned and cracked and started falling down and pulverizing the homes as the dust alone was a force more powerful. Everyone was hysterical as they ran in the opposite direction in a frenzy as more homes crumpled down, adding to the dust and smoke that started sweeping towards him, extinguishing the fires.

"It's the end of days! The end of days!" shouted a man. He jumped in front of the wall of dust and stone and held his hands out as if it was a welcoming friend. "I'm ready to be sacrificed to the Lord almighty! I'm ready to make my return to the Dawn Kingdom! To gaze upon your glory!

To encompass your spirit! To revel—"

The man was silenced as the dust took him. People screamed and yelled in panic, seeing the horror emerging behind them. Many were trampled over and crushed to death as rubble fell from the sky like meteors, dozens perishing every second. A large stone managed to whack Ryan across the side of his face, blood opening up across his check. He stumbled down and fell onto a plate of glass that could have been a window, cracking it beneath his weight. People ran over him, his fingers getting crushed against the glass and the points of shoes hitting his head. He jumped up and accidently slid and lost his balance on the glass, falling back down and bringing several people down with him. He was elbowed in the face and chest as small rocks hurtled at his face and into his mouth.

Ryan kicked his way up and merged with the mobs as the dust from the collapsing wall swamped everything around. The row homes started falling down, one by one, and creating an ocean of debris. His hair was covered in dust and the cloak that Brazz gave him was shredded and falling off, bursts of light from his body shining all around as the invisibility had worn off.

He approached the opening into Copper Courtyard where the black gate used to be and dashed out with hundreds of others. The remains of Mainbreak Hall were still hot as small flames licked the now black stone. The dust was chasing everyone like a monstrous animal into the courtyard. Everyone ran past the rubble of Mainbreak Hall and into Blazing City, where some of the dust seemed to spread into there as well. Ryan did not follow any of them. Not a single person stayed in the courtyard for more than a minute, and no one tried to flee into Frostbite Village.

He knew that he wasn't invisible anymore, but it did not matter as the dust engulfed him and the rest of the courtyard. He held his breath and covered his face with the cloak, trying to memorize the direction from memory and not get suffocated from the grit and debris. He reached the gate that lead out of the courtyard. The dust, thankfully, did not reach this far as the air was finally clear again.

Ryan stuck his head out from behind the gate and looked down both directions of the path to see if anyone was around. Directly across from him was the gate into Frostbite Village. The two monstrous gates that used to be on either side of Mainbreak Hall were now two masses of iron on the ground, flung across the courtyard during the explosion. Ryan had come to the conclusion that an Implosion Explosion Orb was not used on the hall. Carson, or however did, just simply blew it up.

Ever so slowly, step by step, Ryan tip toed his way in silence. It was like he went deaf all of a sudden. The sky above was a crimson death red, and the moon looked so dazzlingly white and bright that it could have been a gateway to heaven. He lifted up his cloak and saw that he was still shining, though it was growing fainter.

Then finally, right ahead, was the portal that Ryan had been hoping to get back to for so long now, but it might be impossible now. Standing in front of the portal, with their backs turned to him, were three people. They were all dressed in white robes and waiting quietly. The entrance of the portal was shining boldly, waiting for him.

Ryan took a deep breath and stepped forward. He was not going to let them get in his way. As he took a step forward, a shock of electricity went through his body and it jolted him to the core. He fell down and began yelling while dragging himself across the ground as the static made him shake uncontrollably.

The three robed individuals turned around and gasped.

"That is him," one person said quietly.

"Yes," said another. "He is disguised, but it is him."

Ryan looked up at the OroAurum as Carson stepped into view with a frown on his face as if he was disappointed. Ryan couldn't speak and had to put his head back down.

"I'm so sorry about that," said Carson as he knelt down, removing the hood off Ryan's head. "That was just a Shock Wave Orb. Anyone who walks through the barrier will be shocked cruelly and released of any power they may have on them."

Ryan sluggishly got up as his energy started coming back to him again. In that second, the swirling white entryway of the portal started to darken. He stared at it as tears built up in his eyes. He ran forward, but Carson pushed him back to the ground.

"I'm sorry, Ryan," said Carson in a soft voice. "But you can't go back home. You must stay here."

The three robed people were silent, nervous expressions on their faces. None of them looked angry like the people raiding the city. They just looked sad.

"Don't do this," said Ryan as he tried to get up again. "Carson, please let me go." He looked at the three and pointed at Carson. "See, he wasn't really dead after all. He was the one that blew up the hall! Can't you see he was lying!"

"They know. I told them you did it," said Carson. He turned to them.

"I am sorry. This boy is just very disturbed in the head. Pay no attention to the lies that pour out of his mouth like vomit. Blowing up buildings and killing innocent people is frowned upon by the Lord. Is that right?"

Two of three nodded their heads.

Ryan appeared as though he was going to pummel Carson. "You little—"

"Compliment," interrupted Carson, putting his dirty shoe onto Ryan's chest and pushing him back down.

The robed individuals looked at each other as if they were exchanging words. As Ryan examined them more closely, he saw Denise standing amongst them, her head down low and tears rolling down her face. Ryan kept glancing back to the fading light of the portal, then down at his ash and blood stained hands that were barely shining anymore. He couldn't help from tearing up as the pain he felt inside was turning into hopelessness. He swiftly jumped up, pushed Carson to the ground, and made a dash for the portal. But Carson immediately threw an Orb at him, making him fall back to the ground as electricity shocked through his body once more.

"These people are here to send you away, Ryan," said Carson in a sympathetic tone, getting up and dusting off his suit. At mentioning this, Carson blinked his eyes a couple of times and furrowed his eyebrows. "I decided that this would be the better way to do it... and for the greater good. They have gathered here to do bidding worthwhile for you—to free your soul."

"The greater good would to let me go you asshole!" yelled Ryan. "Why are you doing this? WHAT IS WRONG WITH YOU?!" He made another attempt, but Carson grabbed him and pulled him back sharply, holding him in place as he continued to thrash.

"What did I ever do to you?!"

"I'm sorry, Ryan." Carson shook his head and Ryan could see that his eyes were moist.

With one last slice of light, the OroAurum finally stopped glowing, as did he, and no numbers appeared above. The entrance became rock solid like hardened lava. The portal had closed.

Ryan shut his eyes and his heart felt like it stopped. He couldn't hold anything back anymore as Carson let him go, letting him fall to the ground and sob. Carson stared down at him, and on his face was an emotion that reflected sorrow, even regret.

"Okay then," said Ryan with his face still looking down. He took off his tattered cloak and threw it to the side.

"Try me," said Carson quietly.

Ryan lunged forward, forcing Carson to punch him right in the chin, sending him spinning to the ground.

Ryan wiped away the blood from his mouth, not getting up just yet. "There were at least three different instances where you let other people try and kill me, yet you could never do it yourself. It's because you can't! You come from my world, and you can't do it!"

Carson's mouth opened as he looked around at the three robed figures. They lifted their heads and stared back at him with confused faces.

"What does he mean by that?" asked the man. He looked at Ryan then back at Carson. "You came from his world? That can't be. It is... it is..."

"I did not!" barked Carson. "I never *came* here. I have always *been* here." He glanced at Ryan and bent down beside him, looking into his face. "I suggest you don't make up lies about me."

Ryan looked at him as if he was highly amused. "Fuck you. You know I'm not."

Carson went in closer to his face and grabbed his neck. "I will murder you right now you little shit," he whispered through clenched teeth, his grasp around Ryan's neck tightening.

The man and woman studied Carson, and it was almost like their eyes were piercing into his brain.

"No," said the man. "He is Zephyrus' son, the heir to the city. He looks like him, his father. The child is making up lies. He is trying to turn us against our mayor." The woman nodded her head in agreement. Denise did nothing.

"No," said Carson angrily to the man. "I do not look like my father."

Ryan saw his chance and abruptly grabbed the hair on Carson's head and pushed his head downwards toward the ground, smashing it against the stone. He then got up and started kicking him in the stomach and face as hard as he could, over and over again. Ryan, however, was already weakened, and he could not do this for much longer.

Carson got up and pushed Ryan backwards, raising his fist into the air and slamming it against the side of the head, almost knocking him out. He reached down angrily and pulled Ryan up and held on to him in case he tried getting away. Carson was breathing heavily, blood oozing from his head and mouth and spreading into his eyes. He snapped his fingers, signaling the man, woman and Denise to step forward. Each pulled out a single silver stone that seemed to glow just like the moon above.

"I can see the real you somewhere in there. I kind of always have," said Ryan quietly in a deadened voice. "If we hung out back home, and none of this ever happened, I would have thought of you as my brother. I think we would have been good friends you know."

Carson's expression changed from dark to light in less than a second. "You mean that Ryan?"

"Every damn word," he replied.

Carson smiled slightly. "I think so too."

She emerged in front of her almost ironically.

The black elevator that lead up to Carson's office on the top floor opened, but Carmen was not yet ready to enter past the threshold. Her eyes were glued to the person who was already inside, standing in the corner with their hand on the railing. This figure was wearing an orange silk cloak over their entire body, their eyes hidden beneath the hood.

Carmen's mouth twitched as she entered before the panels closed shut and stood on the opposite side of the cloaked figure. Carmen was a complete standout herself with her own purple outfit and black veil and large purple hat. It was as if both were trying to conceal something from one another—an identity—and one spoken word from either would break that mystery anonymity. So they remained silent... but not for long.

"What floor?" asked the figure.

That one single question sparked an instant name to the person beside Carmen. She was utterly baffled and started to fidget, not knowing if to answer back to her. The bulb lights above the door that indicated what floor they were passing kept climbing.

"The top," said Carmen simply.

The figure stood frozen for the entire ride up, a slow ten seconds. The doors opened and Carmen walked out as gracefully as possible, not looking back as the figure spoke one last time.

"I'm actually going down. My mistake... bye." That one last word was pronounced rather spooky and threateningly, as if the person was smiling as they said it. It sent a shudder down Carmen's spine.

The panels closed and the elevator declined down. Carmen walked across the glossy floor to Carson's office but stopped and turned around. What the hell was *she* doing here? What was *she* doing...?

Carmen turned away from the office doors and made her way down the long stairwell that would take her down to the bottom lobby, deciding not to take the elevator. She looked over the railing as she walked down and saw the figure emerge from out of the elevator and into the grand lobby.

What is the little rat up to? she thought curiously. Cassidy's parlor tricks seemed to be in full effect once again.

FIFTEEN.

THE ALTAR VOW

RYAN WAS STRUGGLING TO GET HIS ARMS FROM OUT OF Carson's grasp. He managed to elbow him in the stomach, finally punching in the face with a forceful blow. When someone is struggling to remain alive against all negative odds, violence, unfortunately, is the key. And in this circumstance it felt liberating.

Carson gasped then shouted boldly in surprise, deciding not to wipe the blood away that was now running freely down from his nose. He still held on to Ryan as if he was his secret shield, refusing to let him go and squeezing him even tighter. He looked at the carriers to acknowledge them. "Please, excuse me for a quick second," he said sternly. He dragged Ryan towards the brick wall and slammed his back against, grabbing his face and staring at him in pure resentment. His eyes became solid black as the Moral began to crawl back into his soul. Dark flames curled up his legs and around his chest, singeing Ryan's clothes.

"You will not hit me ever again," said Carson, pulling Ryan away from the wall a couple feet then slamming him back against it with more force. He did this several times in a row, again and again, with the back of Ryan's head and spine smashing into it. He did it faster and faster and harder and harder, his eyes wide and mad, his teeth barred and his grip digging into Ryan's flesh. His mouth was open and he omitted a deep growl like an angry beast. A new and familiar voice was now emerging from Carson's mouth as his lips curled into a smile.

"You may not know me Ryan Davidson but I know all about you. Watch as your blood spills and whimper as your body shakes. Vision the light drain from your eyes and into mine. I shall watch you die with admiration. With your death comes a new age. An age where my shadow touches all land, sky and sea. I have waited a long time for this. You took it away from me once. This will not happen again."

Ryan looked into Carson's dead eyes. "I'm sorry. But I'll have to watch you die first." With nothing more than an instinct, he grabbed Carson's arms and pushed them away so forcefully that Carson spun to the side and fell to the ground. The dark flames were put out and grey smoke rose up from his body. Ryan slid down against the wall and collapsed onto the dirt with an aching body. He was out of breath and exhausted, feeling half unconscious from the beating his skull and back received. He felt warm blood spill down the back of his head and neck like water.

Carson pulled himself up and seemed to have gained normality again, looking confused for the slightest second, staring at Ryan in the strangest way. He stumbled towards him and picked him up by his torso, setting him upright like an infant. The three carriers were so silent that you would have thought they were not there at all, except for Denise. She was crying, not bearing to look up or even open her eyes at the terror that was just demonstrated.

"I don't know what I'm doing Ryan," said Carson, confused and perplexed. He stood up behind Ryan with one hand on his shoulder for support, breathing as if he had just ran a marathon. The energy that the silver stones were omitting was intense. They were seemingly not only draining the energy out of Ryan, but Carson as well.

"The Silence of Death," he said quietly over Ryan's shoulder, "is a ritual for the lost and tortured spirit within. The stones that each person holds before you contain sprites from the Deep Reach of Pheonexia; the freest and purest place that ever existed. Once they are summoned and break from their shell, the sprites form a bond with each other. As they come towards you, you feel a sense of relief. It's like you are going somewhere special. Somewhere of pure peace and beauty. A place you will remain forever."

Ryan stared into the stones, the light shining off his eyes. "That does sound nice," he said.

Carson nodded his head, staring into the stones too. He dragged Ryan towards the wall again. "A sprite can only be released by someone with a noble and good heart. Unheard of if you really think about it. Someone who has never done anything despicable or vile upon themselves or others. I searched high and low for three lucky people who fit that description. You can imagine my frustration. Where do I actually look for people like that? Even in a city as horrid as this one, there still had to be a ray of light somewhere. Three bright souls. Bringing a soul into the Dawn Kingdom is such a beautiful process that it must be done by only the brightest."

"But I won't be going there, will I?" asked Ryan, his eyes still fixed on the stones. "The Dawn Kingdom."

"Oh no," said one of the carriers, the man. "Ethklemena."

The woman next to him nodded her head. "The Lord of the Righteous Land speaks of one land of light and one land of shadow. The land of shadow is where the darkest of souls go. The ones who did great wrong with the lives they were given, and never deserved to live in the first place. They never belonged."

Denise continued sobbing, rubbing her puffy eyes with her wet fingers. Ryan looked away from the stones and made eye contact with her instead. Her eyes told a whole story that didn't need pictures or words. Looking into them for a long enough time, he knew that she cared for him from the tears she was shedding. Something made her feel proud about what she was doing, as if what she was doing was right. Who was he to say that it wasn't anymore?

"Run away," said Ryan quietly. "You are more than this Denise. Just go."

"I'm sorry," she said meekly. "This seems to be for the best."

He stared at her in frustration. "For the best? You know I wouldn't do anything to hurt anyone unless they deserved it. I'm sorry for anything I may have done to make you feel the way you're feeling right now." He tried not to show the weakness of tears, but he couldn't resist. "You have a good heart."

Denise closed her eyes. "I don't have a good heart. If only you knew..." Her eyes reopened and her glance met Ryan's for a quick moment then she looked at Carson. "This will not work Carson. This won't work with me here. I fear that if we try to go through with this sacrifice, and if one or all of us are not worthy enough to hold these sprites, then it may... go wrong."

"Go wrong?" he said distastefully. "Like that childish and girlish brain of yours? Who cares what you think." He looked at Ryan. "You, Ryan, are a beast. Isn't he people?"

"Yes, she has feelings for a beast," said the woman coldly, looking at Ryan as if he was poison. Denise signed loudly and looked at the woman with annoyance, appearing to have the urge to say something back. The woman looked at her with a displeased look. "I fail to see any brightness in you, my sweet girl. Darkness easily influences you. Just look at these tears you shed. The Lord warns us of the manipulations from the wicked. He has manipulated you." She turned her attention to Carson. "This girl is not worthy of one of these stones. Please cast her away." The woman grabbed Denise's hand and tried grabbing the stone out. "Give it to me girl. Come now. Listen to my words."

"Stop it!" yelled Carson. "The girl stays. I don't have time to run around a burning city for a special little pixie soul. Ugh, so annoying. Just want to..." his fists tightened. "Burn you all."

The woman let go of Denise and remained quiet beside the man. Within the silence, they were able to hear the screaming coming from inside the city. Twisting metal and crumbling stone echoed through the land like groaning monsters. It made Ryan smile.

"I think... your city... is burning... to the ground," he said through fits of breathing. He could feel his oxygen being cut short little by little as the light from the stone grew. He started laughing. "I burned your city to the ground people! Take me away! That's right, you use those sprites. You damn well use them on me. Because I'm going to kill you all if you don't. I'm a crazy psycho ready to snap at any moment. Not only will I kill you, but I'll blow up your homes as well. I'll watch your children burn… that is, if they haven't already."

The woman put one hand over her mouth in horror and the other on the man's shoulder, squeezing it tightly. The man grunted angrily, then chuckled in amusement. "You condemn yourself. The shadows are ready to take you. But don't think it will be over once you die. You *will* be punished, that is for sure. Over and over again. For all time."

Carson looked up towards the top of the wall where ash was floating in the red sky and down towards them like pieces of confetti. "Not much of a loss anyway this city," he said. The man and woman looked at him in surprise. Carson stepped to the side and hid his face behind Ryan's head as if using him as a shield to hide from their piercing stares.

"Excuse me?" asked the man as if he thought Carson misspoke. "You are the mayor of this city. What makes you think you can throw around a comment like that?" He exchanged looks with the woman, as if they had their own nonverbal conversation going on. "We seem to be the only noble ones here m'lady."

"The only noble ones left in the city."

"Maybe even the whole world," he finished. They held each other's hands and looked at Carson.

Carson laughed behind Ryan. "I didn't mean any of that," he jested. "And neither did this guy. Little rascal he is. Say you're sorry, Ryan. Say you're sorry for saying such fowl things." His voice deepened. "Go on boy."

Ryan sighed angrily, his mouth twitching. "I'm sorry I said your city is burning to the ground."

"You see," said Carson happily. "All is well."

The man shook his head and scrunched up his face. "Our Lord," he spoke cautiously. "The Lord of Pheonexia does not tolerate these games. Or any games for that matter. He expects the truth."

"Then why does he lie to you?" asked Ryan. "The Lord of Pheonexia is a demon from the shadow realm, from Ethklemena. Or do you not know the story?"

The man's eyes widened. "You dare mock Him?"

"Do you not know the story?!" yelled Ryan in anger. "He has tricked you! The Goddess was the real creator of your world! He imprisoned her! Your people rewrote history thousands of years ago to make—"

"LIES!" yelled the man. "Another hardened mind. Take him away! I can barely look at him any longer!"

"You ignore it because you don't want to face it," said Ryan. "You don't want to accept it!"

"Listen to me!" shrieked the woman, as if a sensitive nerve was hit. "You think He is evil, do you? Look around you. Look above you. He is everywhere. He is in the stone and in the earth. He's right about your head child. *You* bring nothing but evil and *you* are what must be exterminated for the safety of everyone. You speak in games and lies and choose to ignore the one and only truth. You choose to believe fables and lies. Look around, child! LOOK!"

"I AM LOOKING! What do you want me to look at?! What am I

going to do to you?! Tell me! What am I going to do to you?!" Ryan lunged forward on purpose, causing the man and woman to flinch and shield themselves with their arms in fright. Ryan chuckled.

"Murderer!" shrieked the woman. "You are nothing more than a plague, a cloud of poison to be inhaled. Look at what you have done to our great city. It's being ruined and tarnished because of you! Oh Lord, our Lord! Listen to him speak with malice and lies! Look at your city! All because of this unsavory!"

"Your Lord imprisoned the Goddess," demanded Ryan.

The woman and man looked at each other in bewilderment and laughed. "There was never such a thing. No Goddess ever existed," growled the man. "Take your nonsense to the Great Imperial City where they believe in such rubbish."

"But he won't have a chance," said the woman. "Evil is about to be removed from our home." She pointed at Ryan. "That evil."

"If there is anything evil here, it is the Lord," said Ryan. "That is a fact. I see Him in my head sometimes. He has talked to me. Has he talked to you? I doubt it. I see Him burned into my eyes. He brought me here. I have seen and heard Him. He is nothing like what He has told you to believe. He is not a good Lord—ghost—spirit—or whatever he is. He is a monster!"

"You lie!" she screamed again, more upset than ever, her hand over her mouth. "YOU ARE LYING!" She ran up to him and slapped him, sending the blood from his face spurting to the side. "Don't you ever say that again!"

"Go to hell!" snapped Ryan, pushing her back.

"Enough!" said Carson suddenly. "That is enough!"

The woman stepped back and looked down as if ashamed. Denise was frightened, her eyes wide and terrified. There was a silence unlike anything. You could actually hear the city being torn apart in the background, the cries and yells.

"No one will speak unless spoken to," snapped Carson. "And you, prepare to die." He gave Ryan a small slap on the cheek. "It's now time."

"NO! LET GO OF ME! LET GO!" Ryan thrashed in Carson's grasp, but Carson was stronger than him at the moment. He felt like he had no energy left. "Please... I didn't... do anything!"

"You brought it upon yourself," said the man. "For you are the evil one that you are describing. Your words scorch any morals one would have and you bring the plague that signals the end for us all."

Ryan rolled his eyes, tears filling them once more. All of the sorrow and anger he felt, he couldn't express it through trying to run away. He turned his head to the side and looked up at Carson's face from over his shoulder. He gave him a face that didn't reflect anger, but the simple damn question of *why?*

"I didn't do anything," he said simply, in a defeated voice. "Why won't you help me?"

Carson stared down into Ryan's eyes and ever so slightly shook his head, as if realizing his mistake. "Because," he replied quietly so no one but Ryan could hear. "*I'm* the monster. I wish I could save you... I'm sorry."

The man and woman gathered in a straight line. The woman yanked Denise next to her unwillingly so that all three were facing Ryan.

"You do as we do, pretty girl. Or you may not come out of this as fortunate as you had thought."

Denise looked shocked in her facial expressions, as if she didn't know what she was doing anymore. They held each stone an arm's length in front of them. The stones glowed white light, the same light the moon above omitted. The man began speaking the chant and Ryan took a deep breath and closed his eyes... and waited for the end.

"Your soul will leave; your body will die."

"Your soul will leave; your body will die," repeated the others.

"Up through the clouds and into the sky."

"Up through the clouds and into the sky."

At this, all three raised their stones into the air. Ryan felt a sudden cold force go through his body, something that made him buckle and fall down out of Carson's arms. His energy was being drained. His soul was leaving his body. Ryan lay on the ground, practically lifeless. The world around him was spinning and slowly vanishing as his eyes started closing. Blossoming towards him were three fluttering sprites that merged together to form one great winged ball of light. The light itself, however, seemed to be faltering, dying before it was even born like it didn't have enough energy to power it.

The last thing Ryan saw before he closed his eyes was the stained red sky above. It looked like an ocean filled with blood, his blood. He could almost see a pair of large black eyes staring down at him. Both eyes turned into small slits, the way they would had the mouth been laughing or smiling. But he didn't see a mouth. It was evil that was staring down at him, and whatever the evil was, it had conquered.

The fluttering ball of light lifted itself towards Ryan's almost lifeless body, seconds from death.

"And now it is time, please let him be free."

"And now it is time, please—"

BOOM!

Before they could finish the incantation a portion of the wall exploded with a haze of dust and stone, sending bricks hurtling on top of the carriers. It was impossible to tell if they were still alive or dead afterward. Denise screaming was the last thing Ryan heard as he was picked up with a forceful grip into a pair of strong yet weak arms. The ball of light split back into the three sprites then flew off into the sky and out of sight.

Ryan couldn't even open his eyes because he didn't have any energy left to do so. He was being carried along in someone's arms at a fast pace. The smoke from the explosion was now escaping into Copper Courtyard and it was a perfect camouflage.

"Who is it?" asked Ryan groggily, not even sure if he was forming words.

"I'm here to help you," replied the voice.

Ryan barely opened his eyes before he shut them again, but was able to catch glimpse of the person carrying him. "I…know… you," he said between breaths.

"It's me, Otis. But don't talk. You need to conserve your strength. I'm taking you somewhere very special. Away from here."

"Where," asked Ryan, ignoring Otis' advice on not talking. "What… just… happened? I don't really…"

"You don't need to make sense of this right now," said Otis urgently.

"I am taking you back home."

As Otis kept running, he managed to jump over some of the remains of Mainbreak Hall and a couple dead bodies, darting through the gap where the gate used to be and into the city. Inside, it was like the whole of a civilization was burning right there in front of you.

From behind came a swift *swooshing* sound. Out of nowhere, three large rings of fire came swirling at them, burning anything they touched. They were spinning rapidly like a pair of bike wheels slicing through the air.

"Great," groaned Otis. He reached into his pocket and pulled out an Orb. He threw it to the ground and out from inside its shell emerged a wall of water roaring upwards. The rings of fire were spinning their way towards Otis and Ryan, slicing off a piece of stone from a building like a knife through butter. The rings hit the water and extinguished the flames, falling to the ground with a *clang*. Afterward, the rings melted into a type of silver goo that spread across the ground. As people trampled over the substance, their shoes would stick to it and the goo would latch itself onto them. It swiftly climbed up their legs and body like a living organism. The goo itself was still boiling hot though, so you can probably guess what happened next… imagine a lot of screaming and flailing, okay?

"I think I'm… dying," said Ryan slowly as horrific screams erupted from behind (there we go). Mobs started forming around them and they would run towards Ryan and Otis, zigzagging around dilapidated towers and through stores as well as across the tops of buildings like apes. Every once in a while a body would fall from the sky and smack down onto the ground in Otis' path, blood splattering upward and bones crunching. It was all just part of the nightmare now. It was all part of Ryan's hell.

Civilians in the streets stopped whatever it was they were doing and stared at Otis and what he was carrying in his arms.

"Look!" one shouted. "Can *that* be him?!"

"That man has him! After them!" yelled another. "KILL THEM!"

Dozens by the second joined in and ran towards them at full speed with stakes and torches and knifes. One man got so close that he slashed his knife into Ryan's arm. But Ryan couldn't feel the cut. He was quite numb, on the verge of death. The slit oozed large amounts of blood and it spilled onto his shirt and stained the ground, mixing his blood with the blood of other innocence that had fallen before him.

A vicious looking woman through an Orb at Otis and it landed a couple feet from him. It unleashed a surge of ice that crawled across the ground towards him. However, before it could get far, the ice melted from the heat of the environment before it could get to him. The water sprayed and splashed as the ice turned into a cold stream, pulling dozens down along the road towards their unfortunate demise.

Otis yelled in surprise as a black Orb hit him in the back. Four black globs weighing ten pounds each clung to him like parasites, slowing him down drastically. As he slowed, dozens more people bogged him down and took advantage of his lack of acceleration. They tried doing anything they could do kill Otis and Ryan. Someone jumped from behind and stabbed Otis in the back with a small dagger, withdrawing it immediately but then falling to the ground when Otis shoved him back, snatching the weapon from out of his hand. The man was then crushed beneath the trampling mobs, his body nothing more than a sad and flattened squash.

The faces all around Ryan weren't right. They were black and pointed with red demeaning eyes, getting worse by the minute. He was scared. He was losing grip on what was real and what wasn't.

In a frustrated yell, Otis withdrew a large orange rock from his jacket. It was glowing radically as if it had a pulse and small red spots ran along its exterior like freckles. Many stared in terror at what Otis just revealed, dropping whatever weapon they had and retreating immediately, howling with fear.

"I should never have had to use this," he said regrettably. "May this be worth it." Otis took out an Orb and shoved it into Ryan's hand, forcing him to break the shell with his fist. A thin white layer spread around Ryan like a shield, incasing him in a bubble. Ryan was now smelling the freshest oxygen he had smelt in days. It was as if he was in the middle of a forest meadow and a brush of cold air was hitting his face and body like a vent of air conditioning.

Otis tossed the orange rock behind him a far distance then jumped to the ground with Ryan. Ryan couldn't see anything properly, but he could hear everything. The rock smashed against the ground as if a star had just burst and out from it came a flash of gold light that resembled a powerful firework. It unleased a melodic sound as a flaming phoenix rose up and flew up into the night sky. Small at first, then bigger and bigger it grew as its fiery wings expanded over the city and lit up the whole land as if the sun itself was just seconds from the ground. Each and every person had to turn their eyes away or else get blinded from the brightness. The sky was washed out with white light that slowly warped into waves of red and orange and gold. It was as if the sun itself had just hatched. The scene was beautiful. Terrifying, but beautiful.

With one sharp shriek, the phoenix's wings expanded even more and its beak opened up to produce a golden red flamethrower that spiraled downward onto the city. There was no time for anyone to retaliate, and all anyone could do was run away, or be burned alive.

The flamethrower spread across the ground in a gold blaze, burning everything in its path. Towers erupted and toppled over and people were scorched alive as the flamethrower took advantage of newly blinded people who were cowering on the ground, succumbing to the fire's scalding embrace. The flamethrower flew back up into the sky then disappeared into the phoenix's fiery wings. With one last shriek, the phoenix flew towards the center of the city and floated above for a couple of seconds as the last remaining traces of fire within the city were sucked up into its raging wings like a vacuum. Once all traces of fire had been drawn into its core, the phoenix slammed down sharply into Triumph Tower and burst into a haze of ash. All the lights throughout the city suddenly went out and the ground beneath Triumph Tower started to shake more gradually with each passing second. A large crater began to spread out and grew wider as Triumph Tower crumbled towards the ground, level by level with a puffs of heavy clouds following in its wake. Other buildings around it were ripped down and sank below the surface of the ground and into the deep massive crater that was forming in the middle of the city. It was like a black hole was sucking everything around it into its devastating core. The crater dug thousands of feet down through Catadorga and into Coal Lake below, bringing down the remains of towers with it. The blood-red sky had disappeared and they were now left in a world of blackness with next to no light anywhere.

Otis was curled up on the ground with Ryan beneath him. When he opened his eyes, all he could see was darkness and all he could smell were the suffocating clouds of dust and smoke. It was a perilous task, but he had to get up and keep moving. He was coughing and aching and bleeding. He wanted ever so much to collapse and die with everyone else, but he couldn't. He noticed sparks from fires that were being lit up again by people who were gathering their torches once more for light. Otis quickly ran towards someone and knocked them to the ground, stealing their flame-lit torch from out of their hand.

"I can't carry you anymore," said Otis. "Can you manage on your own?"

Ryan got up and nodded, still protected inside the Life Protection Shield that was surrounding his body. "Is this the end of the world?" he asked.

Otis coughed. "Not yet," he said. "That part all depends on what happens to you." He grabbed his arm. "Let's get out of here."

Far back, Carson was standing on top of the mostly dilapidated hedge that circled Copper Courtyard, looking out at the destruction that had just occurred to his city. He began swinging his arms in the air, murder in his eyes from the Moral that was consuming his soul. Two flamethrowers erupted out of each of his arms and went bursting towards the city at full speed, bashing through walls and hitting several people, burning them to a crisp. His whole body erupted into flames and turned into a cosmic fireball that gathered speed then followed the direction of the two flamethrowers like a shark towards its prey. The flamethrowers blasted forward and finally merged together when Otis and Ryan were within sight.

Ryan was trying to keep up with Otis as they ran through the city of dust and stone. Ahead of them were the great rock formations of the Fire's Depth. He did not want to go back down there again.

"I don't want to go back in there," said Ryan, very scared. "I need to go home."

"You are going home," said Otis.

"How?

"I'm taking you to the secret portal in this city."

"Secret portal?" asked Ryan. "What do you mean?"

From Otis' left side came a swirling red and orange ball of flame. It pulled Ryan and dragged him along a couple feet away from Otis. The fireball extinguished and revealed Carson holding his arm around Ryan's neck, staring at Otis with a satisfied look.

"No one can protect him now," said Carson in a deep voice, his eyes black and empty. "Not even you. Looks like I have to kill him myself after all."

"Carson, don't." said Otis urgently, reaching for an Orb. But Carson was faster. Carson dropped Ryan to the ground then shot his hand up as if signaling the flamethrower. He grabbed hold of the end like a string to a kite then dragged it around Otis so that he was incased in a wheel of fire. He let go of it and let the flamethrower surround Otis.

Carson picked Ryan back up into his arms and ran off, terminating the shield that was protecting him with a knife he found on the ground. Ryan saw the wheel of fire that trapped Otis and felt a tear fall from his eye as the wheel grew bigger and spread to buildings nearby, setting them ablaze and making dozens flee in every which way. The smoke was getting to be unbearable, and the heat punishable. His insides were so clogged with dust and smoke that it felt like someone dumped clouds of chalk into his lungs and blood. He was too weak to do anything anymore. He couldn't escape from Carson this time. He couldn't escape from anything.

"Soon, Ryan. You will be dead, and as will I. This is a night that will be remembered for all. The night where everything changed forever."

Ryan looked up at Carson. "I'm already dead," he said. "The only exception to that is I'm still breathing."

Wherever Carson was taking him, it was much further away. There was less smoke, fire and yelling to blur the senses. Carson wasn't running anymore either. He was panting for being out of breath and had to walk the rest of the way... for what felt like an eternity.

Ryan reopened his eyes and was looking up at two black spires that jutted out from the top of a cathedral. They were walking up the stairs... a large metal door... it opened... they entered.

He stirred then suddenly gasped out as if was just holding his breath underwater for hours. Carson was sitting beside him on the flat surface of the altar, his hands folded together on his knees and his thumbs pressed against his forehead as if he was deep thought. Ryan was laying on his back on the top of the altar, looking around at his surroundings. There were wooden pews lined up in front of him as well as stained glass windows along the sides of each wall. A balcony loomed over the entrance and a great big dome occupied the majority of the ceiling. It was Orpises Cathedral.

"The boy must die, He says to me," muttered Carson in a drugged-like voice. "He gets into my head. He doesn't let me sleep. He gets into my dreams... you know what that is like." He sobbed quietly. "I feel Him in my body trying to control me. He laughs at me. He makes fun of me. If only you knew how angry He is right now. He wants to kill me now. But I will save Him the trouble." He turned to face Ryan. "I just want to go home. But the one thing He always told me is that I am never meant to go home. I was never meant to be happy. No one ever truly cared about me in the end. Only He did. But now He doesn't because I didn't do what He had asked of me—to destroy you. I became selfish and kept you alive because I could never just *kill* you. I mean, when I was in grade three, I remember my class had to read to you and the other kindergarteners... and I was paired up as your reading buddy.

"I remember... that," said Ryan quietly, his soul tired and weak.

"I read you this barnyard story," continued Carson. "I forget what it was called. I just remember I got in trouble for reading it to you. It was a little morbid... for a five-year-olds perspective I suppose. It was about an old farmer who raised chickens. He did this for many, many years. One day, the farmer took in a stray dog that he found hiding in his woodshed. It was starved, just skin and bones. So he took it in, and he fed it and loved it. He gave it a warm place to sleep beside his bed at night. But every day, the farmer would wake up and find one of his chickens were killed in the night. It couldn't have been the dog though. Of course it couldn't. This dog was not a killer. But one by one, the chickens were all killed. But still, it couldn't have been the dog. His dog was not a killer. This sweet and loveable beast was not like that. So the famer raised a new flock of chickens, but once again, they kept dying. This went on for years and years until the man finally died of old age." Carson finished then looked at Ryan.

Ryan's eyes were half closed, his breathing short. "I'm ready then," he said. "I'm ready to die. There's no use fighting it anymore. Everyone who trusted me is dead. Whenever I tried doing something to help myself, it only made things worse. I'm responsible for… for everything that has happened. I can't live knowing all the wrong that I have done."

Carson shook his head. "No. It was me. You did nothing. I made you do things that forced you to keep yourself alive." He looked right into Ryan's eyes. "I never wanted you dead, Ryan. You know that don't you? What you have to understand right now, while I am still me, is that there are times where it isn't me speaking, but someone else through me. It's Him. He makes me feel angry all the damn time. But do I look like a bad person to you?"

Ryan paused before answering. "You did. But I won't lie. You still do now."

"Take that fucking back!" snapped Carson, pounding his fist onto the altar. "Take that back! My whole life I was told what an awesome guy I was. Way to go Carson. Good job Carson. Take one for the God damn fucking team Carson!"

"Sorry," said Ryan quietly. "I'm sure you were a good person at one point."

Carson looked as tough he was going to say something, then his face became suddenly scared. He shut his eyes really hard. "He's speaking to me again. Not again. Go away…" He started hitting his head. "Go away… go away." He looked up at the tall white statue of the robed man that was against the wall behind the altar's table. "I'm so scared of what He'll do to me. I see Him watch me all the time. If I'm dead, then I don't have to endure the pain that He makes me feel every moment. He will make it a living nightmare for me if your blood is not on this altar as He wishes right now."

The door to the cathedral opened quietly and neither Carson nor Ryan noticed.

Carson gulped as he stared at the figure, his eyes hypnotized. "He's watching me now. He's telling me that I'm too weak to kill you. That I could never have done it in the first place. It is why I tried getting others to do it for me, when it was my responsibility all along." He got up and walked towards the altar's table and picked up a rustic blade that was lying in the center, as if planned, for this moment. He picked it up then knelt down beside Ryan, raising the blade above his chest.

"I can no longer live with this pain."

"Just because you can't do something, doesn't mean you are weak," said Otis, standing behind the back pews.

Carson still looked down at Ryan as he responded to Otis, as if hearing his voice wasn't a surprise.

"You know nothing of what I've been through," he said roughly, his words bringing back unwanted memories. "Before all of this. When everything went bad. Were you there when my dad left? He just decides, oh well. Screw my sons. I'll just leave and let them be raised in hell everyday as orphans. Without real parents. Do you know how bad that felt? To get beaten by people you don't know? To cry every night until it becomes normal?" He turned his head to the side and buried his face into his shoulder. "To live and die alone."

"Of course I don't know how that felt," lied Otis. "And what you are about to do right now… it must feel good… right?"

Carson's tears hit the maroon carpet, his hand that clenched the knife trembling over Ryan. "So… good," he said through clenched teeth. "Every time I see myself in the mirror, I see him looking back at me. Then I remember what he told me when I was really young. He said the world can be a cruel place. Even though I was only seven at the time, he told me that if I ever go looking for answers to not look further than my own backyard. The backyard is where it's safe, familiar, and nothing can hurt me. I know the trees, the flowers… the bugs. And if I ever decide to go beyond those trees, then that is when I have to be careful, because an unfamiliar world is dangerous."

"He was right, Carson," said Otis, walking slowly towards the altar. "Your father loved you. I'm not condoning what he did to you. But everything he told you was told to you because he loved you with everything he was and stood for. Being a father myself, I know this for sure. What do you think he would tell you right now if he saw you?"

Carson closed his eyes. "He would be… disappointed."

"What about your brother then?"

Carson screwed up his face at the mention of his brother. "I miss him so much. I left him all alone. By himself. Three years ago... I should never have done that. But I couldn't have known what would happen."

Suddenly, a small noise interrupted them. It was soft crying followed by murmuring. Carson turned around to look at Otis, and he responded with a head shake indicating that the noise wasn't coming from him. He examined the pews in front and almost swore out loud at what appeared from behind one of them.

A girl, not more than five, crawled from behind a pew and stood up, looking up at him. Behind her, a woman poked her head out from the side of the pew, very nervous.

"Violet, come back here."

The girl walked up the steps and knelt down beside Carson.

Carson looked at her, his eyes barely open, as if he had been awake for days. He smiled slightly. "What are you doing here?"

She looked up at him. "Stop, please. Why are you doing this mister? Stop."

Carson's mouth opened slightly and his eyes showed his weakness, displaying the tears of his anguish. "Because I have to. Because I'm a bad person... but I don't want to be anymore." He looked into her silver eyes as a bright aura shone around her tiny frame. "Can you help me?" he asked.

The little girl placed her hand on the side of his face and stared right into his eyes for several seconds. It felt like time stopped all together as Carson looked back into hers. The aura faded and she reached up and put her small hand around Carson's that was still fastened around the handle of the knife, inches from Ryan's heart.

"Don't be mean," she whispered.

Carson couldn't take it anymore. His eyes rolled back and he dropped the knife, falling backwards down the steps of the altar in a death faint. He lay at the bottom, motionless.

The girl gasped and crawled back down the steps to help him, but her mother quickly came up from behind the pew and grabbed her briskly. Without another word they both ran out of the cathedral.

Otis didn't move, nor did Ryan who was still lying on his back and staring up at the dome above him with his eyes wide open, as if he was dead. He was in shock.

Carson slowly moved and regained his composure. "If this is fate," he said. "So be it." He stood completely straight and limped up the steps to grab the knife from off the floor. In one swift movement he slit his arm then threw the knife at the statue behind the altar, splattering a faint smudge of blood against the white marbled face from the blade. He bent down and grabbed Ryan by the collar and tossed him down the steps, blood from Carson's arm smeared across his shirt and dripping onto the altar's steps.

"Go," he said. "Get out of here." He got up and Ryan was frozen, just staring at him. "Do you hear me?! I'm not going to do it!" He picked up the knife and threw it at the statue again. This time the knife deflected off the marble and flew back towards Ryan. Ryan quickly dodged it before it became lodged in his chest.

"I know you see me, and I see you!" yelled out Carson, speaking to the entity that was with them inside the cathedral. "I'm not listening to you anymore! Our deal is finished! You will not control me and I will not die!

I choose my own destiny!"

Ryan slowly got up and stumbled towards a pew and held onto it for support.

Carson flashed back around and pointed at him with the most frightening face Ryan had ever seen him give. "You will ever come back here, you hear me! Don't even think about it. No matter how much it crosses your mind. You stay away. You go use that hidden portal. I don't deserve it. But once you go back home, do not take it for granted because I have no home to go to. I don't even exist anymore!" His eyes were glistening as he dried his eyes with his sleeve.

Otis grabbed Ryan's arm urgently so that they could leave. "Let's go, Ryan," he said. Ryan ripped his arm away from him.

"Come with me!" he yelled. "Carson, come with me! We can leave this place. Both you and me. We can go back home!"

Carson looked down and shook his head. "The hidden portals can only be used by one person and one person only. If I was smart enough to have found it myself, I would have used it. Go Ryan. Get out of here. Leave me."

"Then I'm not going," said Ryan. "I can't do this to you. You don't deserve this. I don't deserve to go back any more than you."

Carson walked down the altar's steps and stood right in front of Ryan, almost chest to chest. He was a couple inches taller than Ryan. His suit was torn and burnt. His face had dried blood on it and there were long bags under the eyes. It was almost like looking into a mirror. He placed both hands on his shoulders.

"I need you to leave here Ryan. Not just for you. Not just for me. But for everyone who can't leave here tonight. Do it for the people who now have to live in this broken world. In a world divided. Do it for all the good people who just died tonight and never had their chance to escape. Just..." he looked down, "just please make sure my brother is still okay. When I left him he was not doing so good."

Just as Carson turned to walk away, Ryan grabbed him from behind and and went in for a strong hug. "I'm sorry," he said. "I'm so sorry Carson. It should never have been like this. I want you to know that when you are alone out there, and you feel like there is no one in this place who loves you... just know that I love you man. You'll see home again, one day. You'll see your brother. You'll see everyone. You'll get out of here and see our big beautiful city across the bridge. With its lights shining in the water. I make that vow to you. You will not die before me. Never."

Carson closed his eyes and held onto Ryan as if by letting go of him would mean letting go of the closest friend he had ever known. "Don't you ever speak of this place. Not to anyone. Not to my brother. You understand?"

"I promise," said Ryan. They let go of each other and Carson held out his hand so that Ryan could shake it, and he did.

"Good luck," said Carson.

Ryan smiled meekly. "And you too. God bless." He stumbled towards the front door and ran out with Otis, who looked back at Carson one last time.

"I don't want to see you ever again," said Carson. "Stay in the dust and ruin that is Blazing City all you want. For I longer will be part of it."

Otis shook his head. "No, I shall have no part of it either... Goodbye

Carson."

Carson looked up at the statue of the Lord. "You just saw what I did. I let him go. And if you want me dead, you will have to find me. I agree with them. I do not see you as everyone else does, or as this statue before me. But as the demon that you truly are. I'm choosing my own destiny. I'm getting out of here."

Every window instantly shattered and Carson was flung backwards down the aisle. He got up and ran out of Orpises Cathedral in terror. The statue was no longer smirking as a harsh growl hissed through the darkness of the world.

When Ryan and Otis left the cathedral, the sight before them was a war zone. Ash was falling through the sky and drifting in the smoky breeze that was accompanied with droplets of rain. The smoke was transparent and constant, almost like fog. It was all a grey haze with random noises everywhere echoing from side to side. A few people were running here and there, covered in dust and grit and trying to seek whatever shelter they could.

"Come on," said Otis quietly, coughing. He took Ryan's arm and walked with him through the deserted graveyard streets of the debris city. There was hardly anyone in sight as Ryan trudged alongside Otis, trying to remain vertical. He could barely keep his eyes open, which was good since he had to intention of witnessing the destruction that he had caused. He stumbled over rubble and wires and lost his balance more than he could count. He managed to find an abandoned torch that was lit. They used it as their only guiding light.

After a long and treacherous walk, they turned a corner and up ahead were the monstrous rock formations of the Fire's Depth. Otis led him up the boulders with difficulty, for Ryan had little to no energy to walk.

"I don't want to go back down there," said Ryan. "Are you sure this is the way?"

"Have you had any reason before not to trust me?" asked Otis quizzically. "We just need to retrace our steps a bit. That is all. Come on."

After what felt like an hour, Otis led him into the opening where Carson brought him a couple days back. They entered and examined the metal hatch in the ground. Otis opened it and felt the blinding surge of light from the lava pool at the bottom.

"If only Carson knew about where the hidden portal was before," said Otis.

Ryan looked down then turned away. "I'm not going."

"Please, Ryan. Carson gave you your life back."

"NO!" he yelled in a deep voice, slapping Otis hard across the face. He fell to the ground and his body began to tense up. He placed his hands against his ears and shut his eyes tight.

"Something is burning," he gasped. "He doesn't want me to go. He says I need to stay here, that I don't need to die. I can be powerful one day, a mighty leader. He says I can join him and together we can be one."

Otis bent down beside him. "Do not listen to Him, Ryan. He speaks nothing but lies. Tell Him no… Ryan… don't let Him into you…"

Ryan's hearing faded… then it was only *His* voice that he could hear.

"Why don't you stay? We have much to talk about…"

"No…"

"Stay for me…"

"Get out..."

"You will die and burn. You were born to die. If you leave, your world will walk on top of burned ash and beneath a sunless sky for all eternity. For all eternity. I will be resurrected soon. I will find you. I will kill everyone. Your friends. Your family. Your whole world. You will watch them die, then I will watch you die. Why have only one world, when I can have two?"

"Fight it..." said a voice inside his head. *"Ryan, you are stronger now. Don't let him win."*

There was an angry roar and Ryan was flung against the wall.

"Come on!" said the voice. *"Come on Ryan! Go home!"*

"I won't die!" yelled Ryan. "I WON'T DIE!"

He bolted up with renewed strength and pushed his way down the hatch, running down the swirling pathway around the shaft.

"Ryan! Be careful!" shouted Otis. He went down after him and caught up just as he reached the lava pool at the bottom, grabbing his arm and pushing him against the wall so he wouldn't fall over.

"You must wait for the geyser," he said. "Every time it shoots up, the wall at the bottom opens a small bit then closes once the geyser falls back down again."

"I don't see it," said Ryan desperately.

"It's barely noticeable," said Otis, "Look harder."

Ryan turned to face him. "Wait, you knew about this all along? Why didn't you tell me? When were you planning on telling me? I could have gone home all along?!"

"I didn't—"

"Do you know everything I went through? Everything I could have avoided! Look at what fucking happened! LOOK!"

"I know!" yelled Otis angrily. "I KNOW! If I only knew… if I only knew what would happen… I made a mistake. And I'm sorry. This portal can only be used once, Ryan. I had to be sure. I was waiting for the right moment to tell Carson, but then you came along… and it all changed."

Ryan tiled his head. "Sure of what?"

Otis looked down and smiled slightly. "I've left you with many unanswered questions already. What's one more?"

Ryan's face softened and he put his hand on Otis' shoulder. "Hey, you know what? It doesn't matter anymore. What's done is done. We can't go back in time and fix things. If I could, I would. But I can't… and I want to thank you. There are very few people in my life who I can actually call a true friend. I know that now. I didn't know what a real friend was until I met you. If I learned anything, it was just that. And I'm sorry for everything. It shouldn't have happened like this. I know that this was all my fault." Ryan could feel himself wanting to cry, looking right into Otis' eyes. "I am sorry."

"It's scary to think that I'm someone you would consider a friend. I never thought you would say that."

"Me neither," said Ryan. "I've surprised myself a lot actually. The people here are the realist people I have ever met. Good or bad."

"Just be careful who you say your friend is," said Otis. He patted him on the back. "I'm not your friend Ryan. Please understand that. Don't go back home thinking this was your fault either. Because it wasn't. Don't live everyday in regret for the rest of your life. Forget what happened here and move on. Do you promise?"

Ryan nodded. "I promise. Are you going to be okay? Where are you going to go?"

Otis smirked. "Don't worry about me. Worry about your own life. Love the people in your life. Be good."

Ryan put his hand out as if that was what he wanted to hear. "Thank you. There aren't many people that I know who would have done what you just did for me."

Otis smiled. "May I never see you again. If I do, you would have made the stupidest mistake of your life."

"Hey, I almost died three hundred times. You think I would come back here?"

Otis laughed and pointed onward. "Well, off you go then. And remember Ryan. Try not to remember."

The geyser rose up, and Ryan went around the pool of lava and pushed his body through the wedge in the wall. Once on the other side, the wall crumbled into the lava, resulting in the lava rising and spilling over onto the path inside the tunnel.

"Go!" yelled Otis. "RUN!"

His mind was a blur and he couldn't think; he just ran for his life. He was going to die right there; unable to go on if he stopped. There were rocks crumbling from the ceiling and the walls were shaking. If he didn't get out soon, then he would be crushed or melted to death as lava poured into the descending tunnel.

But to his relief, he saw something familiar. It was a portal ahead. But the entrance was omitting a solid black light and didn't have numbers flashing above like his did. But this was it. His way home.

The lava was sliding down behind him as if it was following a trail of oil, moving faster than Ryan himself was. He didn't hesitate as he ran up the steps and pushed his way through the opening. The next thing he saw was the moon in a starlit black sky.

He was floating.

SIXTEEN.

ONLY ONE WAY

IT WAS SOLEMNLY MORBID AND FORBIDDEN INSIDE THE expectedly humid dungeons beneath Triumph Tower. With no windows to look through and no one to inform him of the events that were occurring outside, he was alone. He let thoughts slip in and out of his mind as if he was going through various events of a story in random order. Was Renny alright? What about the children? Was Denise with them and making sure they weren't afraid? Where was Ryan? Dead? Otis would have given his left eye to know the answers to these dire questions. He would have given anything to ease his mind.

He paced the dungeon floor; concentrating, debating, back and forth, what ifs, hows...

Creeeeeak.

A shaft of red flickering light illuminated the stairs as the door to the dungeon was opened. Concealed under an orange cloak, a tall and lean figure appeared on the threshold.

Otis looked through the bars of his cell, pressing his scarred face against the cold steel as he stared up at the lit doorframe.

The woman shut the door and glided down the stairs slowly like water washing over rocks. Her figure was just a black movement of shadow now; merged with the darkness around and from within. The *click* from her heels hitting the stone was haunting, and each time he heard the *click* it would send a stab of fear into his heart. He pulled away from the bars, but not too far. When she came closer to him, some strange energy would pull him curiously forward again like a magnet.

She stopped in front of his cell in silence, not speaking or moving. It was frightening. He could almost hear her smiling and her eyes widening. Her arms moved forward, her hands outstretched and cold. He heard her grasp one of the bars firmly and start pulling on it as if she wanted to rip it off, her nails scratching against the steel. Then a quiet *buzzing* sound emerged somewhere close by. It was as though a bee's nest was hanging beside him, right next to his ear.

Otis couldn't say anything because his tongue wouldn't let him do so. He didn't know what to say. He felt darkness enter this dungeon like a gust of wind, and it wasn't the darkness that was already present. It was something more. It might be possible that they were not the only two inside this dungeon. Something you couldn't see was also with them; an entity of unimaginable evil. The Lord was a cunning villain. He most certainly was. The horrid false Lord of Pheonexia was coming to damn him. Otis believed that the Lord could only be at one place at any given time. Hopefully He was with Carson right now and not with him.

Then another sound made its entrance. Otis could now hear a *ticking* that grew louder with each passing second. It grew higher... then faster... then... *BOOOOOM!*

The cell imploded and a part of the ceiling collapsed down around him. Otis ducked for cover and jumped into the corner, throwing himself to the ground and covering his head for protection. His face was already scarred and sore from the wrath of Carson and Catadorga, but his head needed the upmost protection. He could feel the smoke and haze around his body. He could smell the melted steel and could almost outline the dust clouds forming. Then the *buzzing* returned once more. It was agitating— like an inch that you couldn't reach or an obnoxious person you couldn't slap.

"It's time to leave, sir," said the woman gracefully, yet bitterly at the same time.

Otis wasn't able to respond. Partially from the sudden entanglement of unexpected incidents within the last couple moments but more so because he had no idea with whom he was communicating with. He had to play this game, and quick. The woman continued when no answer was given.

"Blazing City is burning to the ground. As we are down here, safe from the harm that is occurring out there, we are oblivious to what is truly taking place all around. Things are occurring and changing every second. Well beyond our means of healing and stopping. Any type of help will be useless... except for one instance." She stopped and stepped a foot closer. "This city has been condemned. No one in their right mind would stay here. However, there is one person in particular who will need your help before you leave this city. Forever."

Otis tried to catch a glimpse of her through the dark somehow. He knew who she was through voice alone. That was true. But these words she was speaking were not hers. They were given to her by someone else. *Which puppeteer gave his new puppet a new mouth*, he thought. *Which puppeteer has been feeding her?*

"Who is this person you are speaking of?" he asked. But he already knew the answer.

"You know who. It is now time for Ryan to go back home through the OroAurum. It has opened for him. Carson will try to prevent this from happening. You need to stop him."

Otis sighed angrily. "I tried helping him already but it didn't work. I can't do much more. Whatever is to happen to him will happen. It isn't up to me to save him anymore. We can only save ourselves now."

The woman snickered as if she saw him as some pathetic weakling. "You give up so easily. Yet twisting one's fate isn't that unusual of an idea. I could kill you right now and that alone would be twisting fate. I'd be changing the course of not only Ryan's existence but of everyone else's as well."

"I could kill you too if these bars weren't blocking me," replied Otis. "Would that be twisting fate as well?"

"Killing anyone would be changing fate for someone," replied the woman. "Killing me would not accomplish anything in your regard however. Killing you though. Now that would destroy everything that we see around us. To death. To destruction. Forget the lives of the ones in this city tonight. For they do not matter anymore. Your role in this is more important than any of them would even dare to agree to. You have to save this boy Otis. That is your fate. Only you can do this within these limited minutes we have left for no one else will. You know how important this boy is. You know he can't die. If he does…"

Otis pulled himself up and steadied his balance around the rubble by grabbing hold of the wall for support. "I couldn't help him anyway given the current situation. What could I do? The boy is stubborn and stupid and listens to no one but himself."

"We are all stupid until we find reason," she said with a slight chuckle. She opened her fist and a brilliant orange glow lit up the dungeon. The large rock in her hand produced energy and power beyond anything imaginable it seemed. It was orange with hundreds of sprinkled dots of red all over its surface like freckles. Otis' eyes widened in astonishment and surprise. It was quickly adding up.

"Oh that is the…" he looked up at her for a second then back down at the rock. "…that is a Fire Bomb. You carry a most dangerous weapon." Behind the glow he saw a fraction of the woman's face. It was blooding her pale face and the straight black hair that hung over her shoulders and down to her hips. Her bangs hung perfectly over one eye and the other was exposed and looking right back at him, sizing him up. A sorcerer's look, he imagined. But still a plain young woman with a sharp nose and thin lips. It was how he remembered her the last time he saw her those few short years ago. Yet she changed in so many ways as well. What made her turn her back on her own kind? On her own two allies?

"It could blast this city into the earth," she said. "A bonus side to this task is that you and I can make Carson look like a fool. When you rescue Ryan from a most torturous fate, Carson will look nothing more than a failed slave to the Lord. And this will not sit well with the Almighty. Because we all know an angry Lord is a violent Lord." She handed him the rock through the bars and he took it hesitantly, as if it was about to explode at any moment.

He looked at the rock as though he was holding the sun in his hand, into the illuminating power pulsing from its core. "What do you expect me to do with this?" The fear set into his body like a flood at the mere thought.

"To destroy Blazing City forever," she said. "And to destroy Carson."

"I do not wish anything bad upon him," said Otis quietly.

The woman unleashed a high-pitched laugh. "He has fooled you with the sympathy that he tries to show you, which he has none of. He locks you in the dungeons, terminates you from the Secret Service, and you still respect him? In case you've forgotten, he has been doing some planning of his own. Planning that hasn't gone unnoticed to those willing to see. You know what he seeks and you know what he will try to do."

Otis looked at her and nodded his head, running his fingers through his greasy hair and confirming the suspicion he had all along. "He will try to open the Peril Escape."

"Of course," she said softly through a bright and wicked smile. "We both know the truth that the idiots in this city refuse to believe in. Too consumed with their own smoke and mirrors of delusions to fully understand what really is. But when Carson's options become thin and he realizes he will never go back home, he will self-destruct and die in self-pity and mourn his life and any failed attempt at salvation."

"Where did you get such a thing?" he asked, curling his fingers around the orange rock.

There was no response from her. The door at the top of the stairs opened and the red flickering light flashed across the dungeon once more as Cassidy left dungeon.

"Everything is about to change," he said quietly.

Otis shoved the rock into his jacket's pocket that resulted in it ripping from its mere size. He escaped the dungeon and followed the many passages through various cells that occupied the rooms beneath the tower that made it feel like he was back inside Catadorga. He had to save Ryan one last time. Hopefully he wasn't too late. Cassidy was no one he could trust. He knew who she aligned herself with now. But by setting him free, he was able to do what he always intended. To save humanity.

He emerged from out of a small crater that was carved within the ground of a large empty room of concrete. He ran up the steep side of the crater and onto stable ground, passing through a metal archway and into a long dark hallway of gold and red that directed him towards the main grand lobby of Triumph Tower. He slid through a large metal door that was left open just enough for him to get around and appeared inside the grand lobby that was in complete silence from the hush of night. Through the walls, there were yells and screams coming from outside. It seemed everyone had fled the tower—except for two. In the center of the lobby were two people standing face to face. Otis quietly jumped behind a nearby column and pushed his back up against it. He poked his head out and peered in the direction of the two speaking.

"These games need to stop," said Carmen forcefully. "There is enough happening already that we don't need you lurking around."

Cassidy smiled and took Carmen's hand into hers. "This is just the beginning. I'm just here to stroke the flames."

"You're here to add gasoline to the flames," said Carmen.

"So what are you here for?" asked Cassidy. "We both know you could never have blown up Mainbreak Hall. Carson didn't do it. There's only so few options left…"

Carmen looked at her as though something finally dawned upon her. "You've been helping *him* this whole time haven't you?" she said.

Cassidy seemed pretty pleased with herself up until this moment. Her smile faded and turned into a scowl. "How do you know about *him*?" she asked.

Carmen tore her hand away. "Because I've been helping him too. He's been playing us both for a fool. What did he promise you? That you'd be able to go back home?"

Cassidy looked down and shook her head. "No. You see; I don't want to go back home… alone. You know what he promised me? That I would be able to go back home… with him… and an army."

"Why?" she demanded.

Cassidy turned her back on Carmen and walked the other way towards the main door. "You won't be alive to find out."

Otis quietly moved towards another column that was closer to the exit. But not quiet enough. Carmen's eyes flashed in Otis' direction and a sudden shock hit her face. Instead of going after Cassidy, Carmen turned her attention to Otis instead. She raised her bare pale arms into the air and spun around several times. Ice pellets suddenly appeared out of thin air and began thrashing all around her. She slammed her hands out in front of her and sent the pellets slicing towards Otis.

He sprinted from column to column with his arm shielding his face as the grand lobby started to become encased in ice that was spreading from beneath Carmen's feet. The ice pellets stabbed at his arm, causing him to slip and slid onto the ground face first. He lay motionless with blood running down his face.

Cassidy took off her her orange cloak and threw it to the side to reveal her dress as black as night. She grabbed hold of the locked main door and tried pulling it open with force. It wouldn't budge as she tried yanking it open. She started kicking at the glass panes, resulting in a long crack along the center. She glanced behind her as dark ice spread up the walls and across the floor like an organism.

Carmen spun around and faced Cassidy. She put out her hands and blasted harsh waves of ice in her direction. Cassidy snapped to the side and slid against the ice floor. She curled up into a ball then spread out and unleashing a hydro force of water that contradicted the ice coming towards her. The ice froze the water upon contact and made it plummet to the ground like iron, splitting the marble floor and sending both sprawling to the ground in a heap.

One of the red elevator doors opened and Durt and Koi stepped out. Both were holding a savage metal rod that blazed with heat as though they were just removed from a cauldron of lava moments before.

Cassidy grabbed a chunk of the broken ice and scampered up. She smashed it into the glass pane of the door and made the crack widen and finally shatter. She stepped through the broken glass and ran out of the tower in haste.

Otis got back up and ran towards the door, hoping to take advantage of Cassidy's planned exit. He passed Carmen who was still motionless on the floor.

Durt and Koi turned to him and abruptly hit their rods against the ground, sending a shock wave of energy towards him like some powerful creature that was digging beneath the floor at a vicious pace.

Thinking on his feet, Otis stopped where he was and remained still as the burrowing force got closer. At exactly the right moment, he jumped up as the force below him dug passed and hit a nearby wall. It slammed against it with the might of three boars and caused the wall to vibrate and weaken and let loose large chunks that fell to the ground.

Otis nodded his head confidently and continued on running towards the door. Durt chased after him, his black bald head sweating profusely from anger. Koi remained guarded on the spot with his beady little eyes moving about so try and see if Otis was going to devise a new plan. His red moustache and hair looked as though they were on fire from the aura of the rod his hands.

Seconds later, Carmen's eyes snapped open and she rose upwards as if she was a puppet attached to strings. She appeared to be tightening her body in every way possible. Her eyes turned black and a dark glow formed around her body as she rose a couple feet off the ground. The Moral was making its vicious appearance.

All the lights inside the tower suddenly cut out from the intense cold. Otis was only seconds from the door, his bones growing cold from the ice around him.

Durt finally reached Otis and grabbed him from behind, but Otis was ready. He shot his foot backwards into Durt's knee with tremendous force, making his knee crack. Durt yelled in pain and dropped the rod onto the ground. Otis reached down and grabbed for it before Durt could and slammed it against his leg, making Durt scream and tumble through the door and onto the ground outside. He grabbed Otis with a strong gloved hand and pulled him halfway through the broken glass pane, his sides being pressed against the sharp glass that was still sticking out from the frame.

"Die now," whispered Durt with murder in his voice, gripping Otis' neck.

From within the tower, Carmen released a high pitched scream of pain as she arched her body backward like she would if she were hit from behind, sending a shock wave of energy throughout the tower. All of the glass from the windows, doors and railings shattered from the extreme cold that had been suddenly omitted, a surge of frostbite swallowing the tower.

Otis flung himself through the frame and out from Durt's grasp as the whole tower shook and tilted. Rubble fell down and crashed downwards upon everything and everyone. Koi's blood and body instantly froze, causing him to fall backwards and break in half like a statue.

For a mere moment, Otis caught frostbite on the side of his face. It burned so severally that he put his face against the ground and screamed in agony as the pain swiftly disappeared, the humidity from the ground erasing it. He looked around the courtyard of Triumph Tower and into the crowds of citizens who were either still searching for Ryan or running away in fear, their flame lit torches setting shadows over the several injured and dead innocence. He wasted no time in deciding where he needed to go. He just went.

"HELP ME!" yelled Durt in agony as bits of glass shattered down on him like rain from above.

Otis didn't respond. He just ran. Portions of Triumph Tower began its decent down towards the ground, mirroring the other towers that already had and would soon follow in its wake.

The aura shining above him was a heavenly glow. It was a full moon.

Ryan pried open his eyes and could feel water all around him. Tiny ripples of waves were gently lapsing against his body as he lay on its surface, floating. He blinked and turned his head to the side, a task requiring a great deal of strength as his neck felt strained. What he saw was the ocean. Above him were wooden planks of a dock with thin spaces in between where he could see the night sky and tiny specs of stars. Smoothly cut into the planks directly above him was a circular opening in the wood. It was as if someone took a chainsaw and cut it with great precision and care, showing the fluorescent moon clearly through it.

Ryan lifted his back and stood up in the shoulder length shore water beneath Pileer's Pier. He felt the wet clammy sand beneath him, and the sensation in his body and mind was equivalent to someone who had just woken up from surgery and the effects of the anesthesia was still lingering, making him lopsided and groggy. He grabbed hold of the sides to the circular opening above and pulled himself up from under the pier with weakened strength. Once his shoes were up on the planks along with the rest of his body, he looked to see that the hole had vanished and was replaced with solid wood again. Had this been a week ago, it would have made him question his sanity as to how something like that could have happened.

Rain was falling in small dribbles onto his face as the fresh salty breeze from the ocean swept against his soggy clothes. The softness of the water hitting the wood was almost harmonic. He looked up at the blackened sky where there were quick splits of lightning in the distance. An occasional boom of thunder would shake the water as it ripped through the sky. It was all so vile and welcoming at the same time.

He sat down on the dock and looked at the vast black ocean that spread out in front of him, almost blending in with the night sky where the two met on the horizon. *The Avaritia* was docked further down along the newer side of the pier. She looked so serene while floating there peacefully, waiting for her next voyage.

He didn't want to get up. He was safe now. He was free. He was home. Ryan got up and turned around to see the full range of lit houses in the distance, safe within Sortonia Crest. Every house was glowing from indoor light and they all looked just how he remembered them. It was as if he had been gone for several years and this was the first time he was gazing upon them again.

Unfortunately, before he could even appreciate what he was looking at, his ears perked up and zoned in on a variety of irregular noises. He could hear people yelling and screaming in the distance, sirens going off and loud snaps with fireworks being flashed across the sky. He didn't want to hear another scream or yell for the rest of his life. There were people running down the roads, and others were stepping out of their houses to see what was happening. Ryan promptly bolted down the pier, past the field and down the sidewalks as fast as his tired legs could take him. He seemed to be regaining his strength back again as he carried himself past houses and across moist lawns, skipping over sprinklers and abandoned sport's equipment.

He jogged past the carnival in front of OceanView High and saw dozens of people standing around outside, huddled in groups with umbrellas and jackets above their heads. Most looked confused and some were on their cell phones while others drunkenly tried setting off firecrackers. Lights were flashing from the fire trucks, police cars and ambulances with the unmistakable sharp buzzing sounds of walkie talkies and radios. The *Carni-Val* sign had fallen to the ground and people were eagerly stomping on it to help extinguish the flaming border that had seemingly burned grass and other greenery around the entrance. Firemen were inside the carnival putting out fires that broke out and were now unleashing smoke into the night. It felt like déjà vu all over again. He turned his attention away immediately. *What happened here?* He wanted to check it out, but he couldn't right now. He needed to get home. Nobody could see him looking like this. At present, he looked like a type of runaway criminal. Whatever was going on in there, it would have to wait.

He ran all the way home as the evening air slid against his face and the soft rain washed away any bad memories. His pants were so weighed down with water that they began to fall down. He had to constantly keep pulling them up and reach inside the pockets to pull out sand and clumps of seaweed, tossing them to the side.

Then, finally, the sight of his house was visible in front of him. The pool in the backyard was waiting for him to plunge his worries into. He didn't even want to think about what just happened. It still seemed like a blur, something not even possible. Cars were speeding down the roads to see what was occurring at the high school and, in the act, were splashing puddles of water onto him. He loved it. He loved it all.

As he walked up to the front door he had to stop for a second to look at the brilliance of the city across the water. Sortonia City was a gem of man's creation. The lights, the sounds, the ocean that reflected the city lights and the white bridge where cars were driving back and forth on was something he didn't know he would see ever again. But here he was, safe and sound. *This* was a city. The greatest city in the world.

He lifted up a rock from the middle of the flower garden and removed the key to the house. As he turned the door knob, he had a sudden realization. Charlie.

Letting go of the knob, he went into the backyard to where he saw Charlie's leash, torn and in a heap on the grass. He obviously escaped once Ryan didn't return. He grabbed the leash and went back into the house, thinking about what to do about him. Surely he was found by someone by now. He shut the door and pushed his back against it, breathing a sigh of relief. He wouldn't worry about Charlie right now. Tomorrow, he would.

He didn't know for how long, but when he slid down onto the hard wood floor all he could do was look around him, amazed and out of breath even though his lungs were completely full. He was going through everything, every damn detail and memory, blocking out the pain. What was supposed be the impossible in his world, was very possible in the world he just came out of. It would give him images he could not get out of his mind, almost like they were burned into his memory.

"How could that all have been real?" he said, as if what he was thinking was completely unrealistic. It was all a dream. Yes, a dream. An evil yet beautiful dream. The beauty of it all, and the red scorching hatred. But it didn't matter anymore. He was home. This was his house, and he was never going to leave it ever again.

The air conditioning turned on and the house filled with cool beautiful air. So beautiful. Everything was beautiful. His couch was beautiful. His carpet was beautiful. His big ass television was the gorgeous of the lot. His fridge... hell fucking yes his fridge. With his food. He was going to wreck that. His bed. His sheets. His shower. His computer. The anticipation of being able to release himself over and over again, something he hadn't done in a week. The surge of ecstasy that would go through his body. It was like he won the lottery.

But in the back of his mind he still knew. The city was still there, planted inside like a stamp. A world was still haunting his mind. He still had questions digging away at his brain. There were questions that sill needed answering. What did the rest of that world really look like beyond the city and its brick walls? Ryan smiled for the first time since he got back.

Only one way to find out.

The Journey Continues...

A World Divided: Frostbite Village

Fall 2016

Also from Jesse Roman

She saved the only man she ever loved.

Now she has to pay.

FALLEN
GUARDIN

AVAILABLE NOW

Made in the USA
Charleston, SC
28 July 2016